One Horn To Rule Them All

One Horn To Rule Them All

Edited by Lisa Mangum

WordFire Press
Colorado Springs, Colorado

One Horn to Rule Them All

Additional copyright information on page 301

ISBN: 978-1-61475-192-2

Cover painting by James A. Owen

Cover design by James A. Owen
and
Art Director Kevin J. Anderson

Book Design by RuneWright, LLC
www.RuneWright.com

Published by
WordFire Press, an imprint of
WordFire, Inc.
PO Box 1840
Monument CO 80132

Kevin J. Anderson & Rebecca Moesta, Publishers

WordFire Press Trade Paperback Edition August 2014
Printed in the USA
wordfirepress.com

Contents

INTRODUCTION

Purple Unicorns? Really?

Bookstores are filled with theme anthologies, some of them with terrific concepts, while others fall under the "What were they thinking?" category.

Purple unicorns? Really?

What were they thinking?

For almost twenty years now, my wife, Rebecca Moesta, and I have given classes and lectures on professionalism and building a writing career. We tell both established and aspiring writers that they must always deliver their best work, no matter what the project is. Whether it's an obscure story, an article, an interview, that piece will be *some reader's* introduction to your work, and you don't get a second chance to make a first impression. Don't phone it in—put 100% into the story, and if you can't do that, don't accept the job in the first place.

For instance, if you agree to contribute a story to an anthology about purple unicorns, don't just roll your eyes and whip off something mediocre because, well, who cares about purple unicorns? Maybe the theme of the anthology makes you roll your eyes, but don't think that gives you an excuse to deliver a bad story. The people who *buy* an anthology about purple unicorns really want to *read* about purple unicorns, and if you accept the assignment then you are obligated to deliver your best possible story about a purple unicorn. And if you do write a terrific purple unicorn story, the readers of that anthology may well remember your name and seek out your other work.

It's one of our most important lessons. But it's become more than that, too.

Over the years, various writers have come up to me after we give that lecture. "You know, Kevin, I'm going to write a purple unicorn story for you. I accept the challenge." It was always a joke, but then it got more and more serious.

In 2010, Rebecca and I launched our intensive business-related Superstars Writing Seminars with fellow writers Brandon Sanderson, David Farland, and Eric Flint. Every year, Rebecca would give our professionalism talk, using the purple unicorn example. And more and more students would offer to write stories for the now-legendary Purple Unicorn Anthology.

At the 2014 Superstars Writing Seminar, one of our guest lecturers was Lisa Mangum, an editor for Shadow Mountain Publishing, and she heard our professionalism talk. A few weeks after the seminar, she wrote me to say she couldn't get the idea out of her head—and she proposed that we do the anthology. For real. Something that would be open to submissions from all the past Superstars attendees. She offered her services as editor if WordFire Press would be interested in publishing the book.

Hmmm.

We continued discussions and realized that we could do the volume as a benefit for Superstars, with all profits going toward a new scholarship fund that would allow a disadvantaged person to attend the writing seminar. Bestselling YA author and artist James Artimus Owen, one of our Superstar instructors, offered to do an original cover for the anthology. The WordFire team would publish it—and our Superstars tribe would get behind it.

Lisa developed the guidelines, opened herself to a flood of submissions, and our students got to work. But word leaked out, too.

Todd J. McCaffrey, well known for the Dragonriders of Pern novels coauthored with Anne McCaffrey, sent me a story out of the blue, which we were delighted to include. Delighted that we were so delighted, Todd sent us a second story, with which we could bracket the anthology.

I told him, "You know we're not paying anything for this, right?"

"Yes, but it's for a good cause."

Then *New York Times* bestselling author Jody Lynn Nye offered to write us a new story.

Then the legendary Peter S. Beagle, author of the classic *The Last Unicorn*, gave us a story. Free. For the scholarship.

Cool.

None of these big names took slots away from the students; with well-known authors in the table of contents, I just added extra pages to the book. (As WordFire Press publisher, I can do that!)

The submissions came in, and Lisa received about four times as many stories as she could use, and the Superstars students cheered each other on, knowing that most of them wouldn't make the cut.

And now you have in your hands *One Horn to Rule Them All: A Purple Unicorn Anthology*, and I venture to say that these are the very best purple unicorn stories ever written.

Until the next volume.

Kevin J. Anderson, publisher
WordFire Press

Rhubarb and Beets

Todd J. McCaffrey

The elvish girl walked spritely up the path.

"Gran!" she called, stopping for a moment to peer ahead and then starting forward with a skip in her step. "Gran, where are you?"

There was no sign of him in the front of the stone cottage.

"Eilin?" an old voice called in surprise. The doddering old man, steps quick but wobbly, rounded the corner from the back of the cottage. He had a guarded look on his face and then smiled as he spotted the girl. "Eilin, what brings you here?"

"My lady was worried," Eilin replied, peering up at the silver-haired man. "She didn't see you in the garden."

"Oh, I was around back, just pottering."

"Pottering?" Eilin repeated. It was a strange word, like so many of the other words he used.

"Aye, nothing more," Gran replied, gesturing toward the front door. "Come in and I'll put on some tea for ye."

Eilin nodded, not trusting her face. Gran was forever going on about "tea," but it was always hot water poured over strange roots and never quite the amazing brew he made it seem. She glanced back over her shoulder down the path she'd taken. Finding no respite—no signs of her lady mother beckoning her back imperiously—Eilin knew she had no choice but to accept her Gran's offer.

"And what brings you here on such a fair day?" Gran asked as he opened the door to his cottage and bowed her in.

"My lady mother—"

"Ach, lass, that's what ye *said*," Gran interrupted. "I meant the real reason."

The silver-haired man followed her into the cottage, waved her to her favorite seat, bustled about near the stove and came back, beckoning for her to stand again, while he settled in the one plush chair and settled her on his lap.

"Was it the spiders?" Gran asked softly as she lay her head on his warm shoulder.

"No," Eilin said in a half-drowsy voice. Her lady mother said that they kept Gran because he was so good with children. Perhaps it was true: Eilin could never listen to his singsong voice for long before falling asleep on his lap. "Not spiders."

"The prince, then," Gran decided.

"The baby, actually," Eilin allowed. Her brother, the prince, was no longer a pest after she'd discovered that he was more afraid of spiders than she—one night harvesting the worst of them and laying them over him as he slept cured the Prince of any desire to annoy her—which was as it should be.

A whistle from the kettle on the stove disturbed them, and Eilin allowed herself to be manhandled as Gran stood, deposited her gently back on the warm chair, sauntered over to the stove and poured steaming water into a clay pot.

Eilin's nose crinkled as the strange smell came to her. *Another of Gran's terrible brews,* she thought.

How long had it been now? Twenty years? Forty? More? Once his hair had been red, his eyes keen, his face fresh like a new apple. Now it was lined, his eyes were dimming, his hair all white and lanky. Even his body seemed smaller than once it had been, as though time had forced it to curl in obeisance.

Changelings never lasted very long. She'd only just gotten him properly broken in and now he was all worn out and creaky.

The smell shifted and Eilin sniffed again, her eyes open and senses curious. This time Gran's brew did not smell so bad.

Gran came back with two mugs on a tray and set them near the sofa. He scooped Eilin back up, settled himself, and pulled a mug over in one hand.

"If you'd care to try …" Gran offered.

"Of course," Eilin said, never one to refuse a graciousness. She sniffed, took a quick, thin sip and—amazed—her eyebrows rose in pleasant surprise. She took another sip, a bit deeper but only just; the liquid was piping hot.

Gran chuckled at her evident pleasure.

"Rhubarb and beet," Gran said. He took the second mug for himself.

"What's it for?"

"It's for the unicorns," Gran said.

Eilin took another sip. It was always unicorns with Gran. Always the same joke.

"Do you think they'll like it?" Eilin asked, deciding this time to play along.

"We'll see," Gran said, taking another sip. "We'll see."

"Tell me about the unicorns," Eilin said as she'd said most every day she came to the cottage. She sipped her tea and wondered why in the Elvenworld Gran could ever come to the notion that unicorns might drink such brew.

"What's to tell?" Gran teased her.

"No one can see them," Eilin said, repeating his old story. Days and years he'd told her, put her to sleep with his singsong, sad, sorry voice telling her about the unicorns.

"No one can see them," Gran agreed. "Their horns take them from Elvenworld to our world and back."

"They brought you here."

"When I was just a lad," Gran said in agreement.

"And now you're here and you'll never leave," Eilin finished. She leaned back, resting her head on his warm shoulder companionably. "You belong here, with us."

"Forever in Faerie."

"With the Elves and the unicorns, my lady mother, lord father, and the prince, my brother," Eilin concluded. "This is your home and we love you."

"I had a home," Gran reminded her, his voice going soft and a bit hoarse, "and those who loved me."

"Long gone, time slips differently here," Eilin reminded him.

"Drink your tea," Gran said, raising his mug to his lips and draining it impatiently.

For once, Eilin did as he said.

"No one can ever see a unicorn," Gran said to her as she drifted off into pleasant slumber.

It was weeks later when Eilin came again. The prince, her brother, had discovered the thorny roses and had tormented her by presenting them to her as a gift, then hiding them in her bed as she slept.

The pricks and pains of the thorns had sent her, crying, to the comfort of Gran's cottage in the distance.

"Gran!" she cried. He had the greatest cures and poultices, perhaps he could pull the sting out of her. "Gran!"

No answer, no movement from the cottage. Alarmed, Eilin picked up her pace.

No sign.

She ran around the cottage to the back, crying, "Gran!"

"Shh!" Gran called from the far end of the garden. "I'm here, no need to shout!"

"What are you doing?" Eilin asked, eyeing the green growth and dirty ground in surprise.

"Just tending my garden, princess," Gran told her, rising from his knees to stand and then bow in front of her.

"My brother, the prince, used thorns!" Eilin cried, raising her pricked palms toward him and then pointed to the gash in her neck and the others on her arms. "He put roses in my bed."

"I can help you," Gran said, nodding toward his cottage. "A bit of brew, some cold water, and you'll be right as rain."

"And how is rain right?"

"It's right when there's a rainbow and the air is clear of dirt and full of freshness."

Eilin nodded. Rainbows were expensive outside of Faerie; her father had the drudges work until they expired to find the treasure required for each rainbow. Gran had once called him too vain for his own good, but Eilin could only think of the pride of the kingdom and the bounty of the Elvenworld. The drudges were only human, lured by the same gold they died to provide, and of no matter to her father, the king, nor even to Eilin herself.

Gracefully, Gran followed her to the cottage and bowed her inside, gesturing toward his comfortable chair. She sat, waiting in pain while he pottered over the stove and set potions to brew.

Presently he was back and had her in his lap again, gently applying his hot brew and holding pressure on her pale white skin until the thorn-punctures closed and the pain went once more.

"Do have you more tea, Gran?" Eilin asked as the last of the pain faded into dim memory.

"Tea?" Gran asked as he put his potions and cloths to one side.

"The purple tea you made," Eilin said.

"Unicorn tea," Gran said in a questioning tone.

"Yes."

"No one can see unicorns," Gran said, half-teasing her.

"The tea was good," Eilin said, feeling her eyelids drooping as the rise and fall of his chest and the warmth of him calmed her.

"The tea will make your stings come back," Gran said. He took a breath, then continued, "Let me tell you about the rainbows."

"There were three that day," Eilin said, recalling his words from so many times before. It was a marvelous story, Gran told it so well, and Eilin always filled with pride at the brilliant trick her father had played.

"Three rainbows and only one with gold," Gran said by way of agreement.

"Fool's gold," Eilin remembered, a smile playing on her lips.

"Fool's gold," Gran agreed. "And the fool was me, parted from friend and family by the faint hope that I could find enough gold to save them—"

"—from the famine," Eilin finished, her eyes now closing. "The unicorn ripped through that day, ripped from our world to yours three times."

"Ripped indeed," Gran agreed, his tone tightly neutral. "But no one saw them."

"Unicorns are invisible," Eilin agreed, closing her mouth at last and snoring gently on the old man's chest.

"Clear as the water they drink," Gran said softly to himself while the little elvish girl slept on.

☙ ✧ ❧

"Gran!" Eilin shouted as she traipsed up the path to the cottage. Drat the man, where was he? "Gran!"

He usually replied by now, doddering out from his cottage or around from the silly garden on which he so doted. He was being slow, and she'd make him bow so long in penance that his back would hurt.

Well … maybe not *that* long.

"Gran!"

No sign of him in the cottage. He was old, Eilin remembered and picked up her pace. Disposing of bodies was something she never liked, and then there'd be the bother of having to find a new human. She sprinted around the corner, looking for him kneeling over some of his silly rhubarb or his beets, but he wasn't there.

His garden opened up on the fields of cloudgrass—the favorite food of unicorns. Gran had insisted on it as inspiration and best location for the sun his plants required.

Every now and then over the years, she'd find him looking at the fields of cloudgrass, waving white and brilliant, watching as clumps were eaten by invisible grazing unicorns.

"What do unicorns eat?" Gran had asked early on when he still dreamed of escape from the Elvenworld.

"They eat cloudgrass and drink clear water," Eilin had told him expansively. "That's why they're invisible."

"And how they can cut between the worlds," Gran guessed.

Eilin didn't know and, as it was inappropriate for a princess to be ignorant, she said nothing, pretending that he was correct.

Eilin gazed from Gran's garden to the field, and her jaw dropped as she spotted the path. She followed it with her eyes, even as she willed her feet into action.

"Gran!" she cried, racing into the cloudgrass fields. She couldn't see him, the grass was nearly taller than she was. She'd forgotten that most days when they'd gone into the fields she'd been riding on his shoulders—Gran being her very own special two-legged beast of burden.

"Gran!"

In the distance, she heard thunder. Unicorns were racing. She saw lightning where their hooves struck hard ground.

They were stampeding. Soon enough they'd bolt and tear holes between the Elvenworld and the slow world of humans.

Was Gran hoping to catch one? How could he—they were invisible!

"Get on!" a thin reedy voice came to her over the winds and the thunders. "Ride on, go on!"

"Gran!" Eilin cried. "No, Gran, you'll never catch one!" He'd be trampled for certain, unable to see the unicorns, unable to dodge their panicked flight.

"On with you! Thunder and lightning!" Gran's voice, exultant came over the noises and the cloudgrass.

Eilin remembered a knoll nearby and raced toward it. It was only a few quick strides for Gran but for the little elvish girl it was nearly a hill.

At the top she could see over the cloudgrass, across the fields and—there!

"Gran!" Eilin cried. Oh, the fool, the fool!

He was riding a unicorn, his weak old arms tightly clasped around its neck, his bony legs gripping its withers tightly, and in one hand he held a long-stemmed rose, waving it wildly, striking the unicorn's hindquarters—the unicorn's *purple* hindquarters.

Rhubarb and beets, Eilin thought to herself with sudden clarity. All those years he hadn't given up hope, he'd merely been planning. Oh, clever human!

He'd raised the beets and the rhubarb for the unicorns. Fed enough, the usually invisible hide took on a faint, purple hue. Coaxed with a gentle voice and the sweet and the sour of the rhubarb, it was no trouble to bring one of the unicorns to within hand's reach.

"Gran!" Eilin cried, her thin voice dying in the winds. "Oh, Gran, take me with you!"

The old man didn't hear her.

"Gran!" Eilin cried at the top of her lungs, realizing at last how much she loved the old human. How he'd been the only one to hug her to him, the only one to ever care the slightest about *her* as a person. "Gran!"

Thunder. Lightning tore through the sky and, suddenly, the wicked electric-blue glow of lightning burst from the purple-veined horn of the unicorn Gran rode.

In an instant, the Void was torn and the far human world sprang into view. The unicorn, goaded unerringly by Gran, leaped through and the tear closed.

A final burst of lightning and thunder rolled through the skies—unicorn and rider were only a dimming memory in the elvish girl's eyes.

Purple is the New Black

Jody Lynn Nye

"We need something new this year, darlings," the court wizardess Windesa said to her four apprentices, tapping her quill upon her polished ebonwood worktable. She frowned at the curling sheet of ecru parchment, which instantly smoothed itself out. She sat back upon the narrow stool, straightening her narrow back into a ramrod perpendicular to the seat. "Our patroness, Princess Amy, is getting bored of the same old thing. I had hoped that our last offering of hens that lay candy-filled eggs would last, but she has taken to throwing them at the courtiers. We need to change direction and come up with a completely new concept that she will love."

"What about curly horned deer?" piped up Negara, the youngest and newest of the quartet, all of fifteen, whose waves of shining black hair always peeked out from under her white lawn veil. "She has curly hair. She might enjoy seeing wild animals that resemble her."

Windesa smiled. Negara might not have been the brightest candle on the mantelpiece, but she was always the first to volunteer an idea, even if it had to be shut down immediately.

"King Foghorr will see it as a new kind of prey, dear," the enchantress replied, her tone gentle but firm. "I am afraid that the princess will freak, and you know how much trouble *that* will cause in the court."

She gave the youngsters a moment to ponder upon the last time, when Princess Amy, who had been under a curse since her first birthday, poor thing, long before Windesa came upon the scene, had overreacted to a negative stimulus. Under stress, the heiress to the throne of Biggleswade deformed into bizarre shapes one after another, each possessed of terrifying magical powers. She could only resume her adorable, very feminine shape when coaxed to calm down. And, considering her not inconsiderable temper, it was not easy.

Even King Foghorr, not shy about declaring war upon whichever of his neighbors had displeased him that season, tiptoed around his volatile daughter. It was for that reason that he and Queen Melba had sought out a witch or wizard who could beguile Princess Amy into a good mood on a regular basis.

Windesa had not been the first of her guild to assume the job, nor might she be the last. Princess Amy had been known to take against the witches and wizards hired to entertain her. If they were lucky, she only terminated their employment. The churchyard had a corner set aside for the burial of the unlucky. The king paid top wages because he had to add hazard pay to the usual stipend enjoyed by court magicians. Windesa shared the bonuses showered upon her by the senior royals with her staff, knowing full well that she stood or fell depending on their loyalty and competence.

The biggest problem that she and her assistants faced was no matter how marvelous the marvels they created, no matter how fantastic the fantasies, no matter how unreal the unrealities they presented, Amy was just like any other girl of adolescent years. She became bored with things that had fascinated or delighted her before. Hence, Windesa had to convene these idea sessions frequently. She tried not to rely upon brainstorming, usually because of the adverse effect it had upon the kingdom weather. The Cloud Wizard, who occupied the other tower opposite hers, was jealous of his purview.

"I won't seek to amuse the princess, if you don't interfere with the rain over croplands," he warned her when she had arrived six months before. He had nodded significantly at a lightning scar on the lintel above the door to her tower, leaving no doubt that he was responsible for its presence.

Windesa had taken the warning. Her responsibilities were all she could handle as it was. Princess Amy's whims could be aroused by the arrival of a new troubadour, or a reading from a history scroll by her tutor, or news of a curious foreign custom brought to the court by a lady sent by King Foghorr's fellow rulers to join the princess's bevy of nobly born companions.

Windesa sighed. She looked at the sheet of parchment, still lamentably empty.

"I want sixty ideas by nightfall, children," she warned them. "Or I will inform her highness that it was you who deprived her of her next amusement!"

One couldn't waste an exit line like that. Windesa swept up her arms and vanished in a blaze of light.

She had only made herself invisible, of course. She always found it instructive to see how her apprentices coped with having the impossible dumped into their variably capable laps. They had to be capable; one day they, too, would be employed as senior witches and wizardesses in castles and mansions across the continent.

Tall, blonde, pale Ingvie immediately took the silver ring she kept on a chain in her belt pouch and dangled it above her other palm, seeking to divine ideas from the symbols the pendulum sketched in the air. Plump, ruddy-haired Corema put her fingers in her ears and screwed her eyes shut. She always thought better without distractions from her other senses. Golden-skinned Saisun went to the bookcase and began to peruse the codices that leaned against one another in their individual protective boxes. But Negara just looked at the stool where Windesa had been sitting.

"I will go and ask her highness what would amuse her," she said.

"That's foolish," Ingvie said, with a firm shake of her head. "Her ideas are always madly far-fetched."

"Outlandish," Saisun agreed.

"I don't have to take her suggestions," Negara said. "But at least I'll know what she doesn't want."

Hovering invisibly in the middle of the room, Windesa smiled.

"Well, your highness, I hope you will be pleased by our small offering," Windesa said, curtseying deeply before the heiress to the throne.

Princess Amy, her taffy-colored hair hidden beneath a black veil and her weekday crown (the one with the single large emerald in the band), lounged in the salmon-pink seat, with one tiny, ladylike fingertip pressed to her apple-like cheek. It added to her air of thoughtfulness, though Windesa knew that there was very little going on in her mind. Although she saw herself as a leader and a trendsetter, the girl was young and very easily led. The same went for her retinue. Each of them also bore her own curse or ill-blessing, like Marquise Adamine of Coquet, who turned into a wolf at the full moon. Princess Amy was comforted to be among those who were like her in affliction, but she allowed them to have more sway over her than Windesa thought wise.

They were all dressed in the height of extreme fashion. Gone were the comfortable gowns that allowed one to breathe during exertions such as dancing or riding out to the hunt. The current trend, brought to Biggleswade by a peddler who drove a cart full of luxury silk fabric from Clementine to the south, demanded that ladies cinch in their waists until their ribs met their backbones, yet the décolleté was draped over by embroidered shawl on top of fichu on top of chemise until the wasp-waistedness below was nearly completely concealed.

All of the garments were black, so that the girls, young as they were, seemed to be in deep mourning. (Fashion-conscious Saisun had sighed for such a costume. Windesa had allowed her to wear a borrowed gown for one day until the girl collapsed on the long spiral staircase from oxygen deprivation.) In no time at all, those ridiculous outfits would be back in the seamstresses' quarters, awaiting deconstruction and reincarnation in future garments.

Princess Amy glanced at her friends, as if awaiting permission. A majority of the girls inclined their heads a finger's breadth, so she nodded to Windesa.

"All right, enchantress, show me your marvels."

Windesa clapped her hands together. The room darkened to stygian blackness. Low, thrilling, otherworldly music began to play. Near the ceiling, a pearl of light glowed. From it emerged a quartet of pastel-colored spirits who represented the four elements. Windesa had learned long ago that simply presenting her gifts to the princess was tantamount to having them handed back to her at once with a bored yawn. Coming up with an exciting presentation was tedious, but necessary. Fortunately, Saisun was a genius at such things. She had a knack for obscure symbolism. Anything that was hard to understand was irresistible to the royal lady.

A shrill shriek arose.

"Is that you?" Windesa whispered in the darkness to her apprentice.

"No, mistress," Saisun replied. "I believe it is Countess Primrose Akanamawe."

"Good," Windesa said, with a nod. "At least we have their attention. Proceed."

She had great hopes for this marvel. As predicted, Negara had returned with a blot on her nose and a list of things the girls found boring. Ingvie had come up with the creature at the heart of the wonders to come. Windesa held her breath as the tableau unfolded.

The spirits spiraled down to the floor and began to draw out tendrils of light between their narrow hands. Where they touched one another, riotous rainbows leaped and bounded. Windesa heard delighted giggles from the noblewomen. She was pleased. All of their careful research was paying off.

At last, the pearl began to descend. Its luminescent glow lit the upturned faces of the entire court. All looked awestruck. The globe of light dipped slowly—but not too slowly—until the anticipation made even Windesa's nerves tingle.

When the orb touched the ground, it exploded in a burst of flames and an ear-shattering *crack*. At its heart stood a tiny blue dragon. The ladies of the court emitted a collective, high-pitched "Ooooooh."

The music turned from a grand crescendo to the questing trill of a single flute. The little dragon looked around. With a loud coo, it recognized Princess Amy, whose image had been placed by Windesa into its gestating mind. Its jeweled eyes widened, and it began to make its tottering way toward her.

The girl straightened up, an expression of delight dawning on her face. She held out her hands. The little dragon gurgled and toddled faster.

"Look at him!" squealed Amy. "Isn't he darling? I've never seen anything like him!"

"We've *had* dragons," Lady Anatolia said, leaning back and gathering her swathes of black silk around her. "Four seasons ago. Don't you remember? They smelled like brimstone!"

"Yes," said Countess Primrose, her snub nose in the air. The others all nodded. "It was so tedious. It was always trying to eat our songbirds."

"What?" Princess Amy demanded. She turned away from the approaching dragonet and glared at Windesa. "It's been done before? How dare you bring me old fashions!"

"This was your idea," Windesa said, turning to Ingvie. "Didn't you research all her past gifts for dragons?"

The blonde girl turned scarlet.

"I … I thought it was long enough ago, Mistress Windesa! And this one has blue crystal scales. The last one had green velvet skin."

"This one doesn't smell," Negara said to the princess. "He's very sweet. And he smells of cloves and ginger. That was *my* part of the spell."

"I don't care!" Amy declared.

Gathering her dignity, Windesa approached the throne.

"But he is such a fashionable dragon, your highness." She scooped up the little creature, who seemed stricken that the object of his affections wouldn't even meet his eyes. "Look how well he fits into your arms. We beg you to accept him. He was made for your pleasure." She held him out to Amy. The girl hesitated. Windesa let her stern countenance relax into an encouraging smile, and proffered the dragonet again. "Go ahead. Take him."

Reluctantly, Amy put out her hands. The little dragon almost leaped from Windesa's grasp into them. It snuggled into her arms, cooing and burbling. Amy stroked him, and smiled.

He was irresistible. In spite of Ingvie's error, this was a perfect pet. Amy could not help but be enchanted by him.

But so were the others.

"Let me see him," Lady Penela said, reaching for him.

Amy, not wanting yet to relinquish her new pet, turned away. Then she was facing Countess Primrose, who petted it, but tried to use the gesture as an opportunity to lift it out of Amy's arms.

"Oh, come, my sister. I want to hold him."

"No!" Amy said, batting her hand away. "Wait! Not yet!"

"But he is so cute," said Lady Anatolia.

The girls began to fight over who got to hold the dragonet. Amy turned this way and that to avoid their grasp.

"He's mine!" Amy protested. Her round face flushed red. The other girls were relentless, circling her like alligators in a pond.

"But we share everything!"

"Let me hold him."

"See? He wants to come to me!"

Battered and bumped in their midst, the baby dragon's crooning turned to whimpers, then screeches of fear.

"No," Corema said, hands raised in warning. "He's still a dragon! Look out!"

Too late. In terror for its life, the little dragon belched out a tongue of flame. Silk dresses ignited. Windesa was prepared with an extinguisher spell, since they were dealing in dragons. She put out the flames, but it was too late. Princess Amy's dress was ruined. The girl glared at the dragonet, at her friends, and at the wizardesses. She began breathing hard. Her pink face turned scarlet, and she squeezed her eyes tight shut. To Windesa's horror, the girl began to grow. And grow. And grow. The blush turned to brick red as she increased in size, towering over the rest of the courtiers. The lacings of her fashionably tight corset broke with the sound of sprung harp strings.

"You ruined it!" Princess Amy shrieked, her face now over a yard across. "My special new gown! It was the latest style! A dragon is not new! How dare you give me something old!"

Lady Penela turned into a puff of green smoke, abandoning her scorched garments. The others scattered in haste, getting out of the way of their playmate's now gigantic feet.

Windesa feared the dragon might go off again. She hurried to retrieve the infant creature, now forgotten and sitting alone on the floor amidst the shrieking girls, looking panic-stricken. Windesa grabbed him up and held his snout closed.

As she straightened, an enormous shadow fell over her. Fingers as thick as her leg closed around her narrow ribcage, squeezing her so tightly she squeaked. The huge hand lifted her off the ground, and brought her close to two glaring red eyes and an open maw filled with long, sharp, white teeth.

"I don't like it!"

Windesa had seen Princess Amy freak, but not with so many different stimuli. Her heart pounded with fear, and dismay. They could all die. Hoping to touch the core of the girl that was still human, she held out the small dragon. Bravely, it blinked its large blue eyes at Amy and flapped its tiny crystalline wings.

"Now, princess, he wanted to show you how much he loves you!"

"Take him away!" the ogre that was Amy screamed. Her shrill voice, magnified a dozen times by the increased size of her windpipe, filled the room. The rest of the courtiers turned and fled, leaving the king and queen and the guards trembling. "You bring me a dragon that is four seasons old! I want something new! Right away!"

The small dragon whimpered. It scrambled up Windesa's arms and hid behind her neck.

Windesa ignored the bleeding scratches and the rents in her best court gown. She smiled calmly at the girl, even while Amy shook her like a terrier with a rat.

"Calm … yourself … high … ness," she stammered. Amy held her high in the air and opened her mouth wide, dangling her over a two-yard-long red tongue. She was going to eat Windesa! "Now … highness … think of … your diet! Too … much … protein gives … you *nightmares!*"

Amy deflated suddenly. She dropped the wizardess and dragonet.

"Cushion!" Windesa barked. The air gathered itself into an enormous, translucent pillow that caught her before she hit the floor. The dragonet let out a startled "Peep!"

The apprentices hurried to help Windesa to her feet, but she waved them away and went to comfort the princess. Once again, Amy had become just a teenaged girl in a torn dress. She climbed into her throne and rocked back and forth on the down-filled cushions, her arms around her knees.

"I don't want to have bad dreams!" she cried.

"Now, now, princess," Windesa soothed her, stroking the girl's hair with a gentle hand. "You know I won't let that happen. I must go. My apprentices will see to your wardrobe." She shot a poisonous glance at Ingvie, who hurried up, readying a repair spell. "We will seek to amuse you better another time."

With a courtly dip of her head but keeping her spine stick-straight, Windesa marched out of the throne room. The presentation had been a failure. All the buildup had been for nothing, because of bad research.

❧ ✧ ❧

The little dragon ate from the cats' bowl in the corner while the wizardesses conferred until late in the evening. Ingvie didn't say a word all afternoon. She was ashamed, and Windesa was not letting her off lightly for her failure. The apprentice's mistake reflected poorly upon her. Windesa was lucky not to have been eaten; the girl would have paid dearly for that. As it was, she felt as if her efforts had been set back months.

"What *has* been done?" she asked, at last.

"Better to ask what hasn't," Corema said, opening a thick codex, the style book that dated back to the day of Princess Amy's birth. "Our predecessors have tried everything, it looks like."

Windesa skimmed a few turns of the heavy white pages, then pushed it away. She frowned, trying to come up with the most obscure creature she knew.

"Minotaurs?" she asked.

Corema ran a finger down the illuminated index. "Six years ago, for her tenth birthday."

"Giants?"

"Twice, when she was two and three. She liked them. It says so in the comments."

"Talking flowers?"

"Yes."

"*Singing* flowers?"

"Yes."

Windesa was beginning to feel desperate.

"Dancing rosebushes?"

"Yes. And lilacs and lilies and oak trees. All of them were part of spring festivals, during," Corema peered down the list, "Princess Amy's third, seventh, and ninth years."

The wizardess wrung her long hands together.

"Very well. Let us cross-reference the mythic bestiary, the royal treasury, and the kingdom herbal together with the record. There must be something that none of our predecessors have offered as a royal gift. Something no one else has tried in history! We must do what is new and different! You cannot tell me there are no new ideas. We must find one!"

The princess still demanded marvels on a weekly basis. She threw increasingly unsubtle hints about the approach of her upcoming birthday, when she would turn sixteen. A marriageable age, though Windesa felt sorry for any husband who might be chosen for her. A suitable wonder was called for, and she hoped that they could discover something that would do the trick.

While their research went forward, they were forced to produce minor amusements of varied kinds for the princess and her court. With varying degrees of success, they presented new fashions, magical gowns that changed color or texture, mirrors that flattered one with tailored compliments, sweetmeats that shifted from flavor to flavor in sequence from subtle to outrageous, even a luxurious pillow that carried one into the air like a bird. Each time, they offered only one gift, because too many choices bewildered the princess.

Two factions erupted in the bevy of noblewomen. One, led by Countess Primrose, rejected every new gift as being tedious and stupid. The other, under the sway of Lady Anatolia, was willing to like the magical treats and toys, but only if Windesa pleaded with them to accept them with as much unctuousness and humility as she could muster. If the object was acceptable, but the pleading was insufficient, they would reject it. Those girls! They may have been born on the right side of the noble coverlet, but they were as common gossips as any village maiden who ever sat on a ducking stool. They made snippy comments upon Windesa's wonders, spoiling Amy's pleasure in them. Windesa knew it was sheer jealousy. Their parents had not hired wonderworkers for *their* daughters.

"These pillows, wizardess," said Marquise Adamine, fingering the broad silken cushion on which she had just taken what by all evidence had been a ride she enjoyed enormously. "They are … somewhat interesting. But …"

"But what, your ladyship?" Windesa asked, curtsying low. The pillows were a work of art. Everyone in the court had admired them enormously.

"But they are purple." Adamine patted a yawn daintily with her fingers. "That is so … ordinary."

"Ordinary, madame?" Windesa asked, as if she could not believe her ears. She could not voice her outrage. Ordinary? It was incredibly difficult to make royal purple. It required fairy dust from the Stone King's realm and three kinds of precious gems, all mixed together in a cauldron in the dark of the moon.

"Yes," Princess Amy said, hastily echoing her friend. "Ordinary. And boring. We hate boring. They should be black."

The other girls smiled smugly, knowing they had had their way again.

Windesa swallowed all the bilious words that came boiling up in her throat. She could only say, "Very well, your highness. I only wish to please you."

The amethyst hue had been so difficult to achieve, and so lovingly applied to the precious silk. But with a fierce wave of her hand, Windesa blotted it out. The pillows became unadorned black, which was the way she probably should have made them in the first place.

"My birthday is next week," Princess Amy reminded the wizardesses as they curtseyed and prepared to depart. "You had better come up with something really wonderful. You have to make something for my ladies, too. But mine must be the most special one of all."

Windesa retreated, chivvying her apprentices before her. She worried that she would not have a job one week from then. Amy didn't want to stand out too much, but she wanted to be first among equals. It was a difficult balancing act, for all of them.

❧ ✧ ❧

"It is so trying that they cannot see how wonderful these things are," Saisun said, when they returned to the workroom in the tall tower.

"They can see it," Corema said. "But it is too easy for them. We beg them to accept our work, giving them the chance to reject it."

"All that tells me is that they really don't know what they want," Ingvie mused, "except it is whatever they do not have now. And it must be black. There are so many colors in the world!"

"It's not the color," Windesa said. "It is the rigidity of peer pressure. They feel safe not having to make a decision beyond that one point, no matter what they give up by making it."

"Alas for that beautiful purple!" Ingvie said, her lovely face a mask of sorrow. "I stirred that cauldron for *hours*. And they made you blot it out in a twinkling. They don't appreciate anything we do."

"But what is the answer?" Negara asked, holding her hands out, palms up. "We can't not offer them the finest that we have at hand. We must not hold back our best. What example would it set if we did?"

Windesa was caught off guard. She turned to regard her youngest apprentice with astonishment. "Say that again, my child."

The young apprentice repeated her words, looking bemused.

Windesa favored her with a maternal smile. "You are absolutely wrong, dear. We *should* hold back our best. We must make them demand what they don't have. We must turn this state of things around, so that instead of us begging her to accept our gift, *she* will beg us to give it to her."

"And how do we do that?" Negara asked.

"By making our best idea an exclusive one. By not presenting it on a silver platter. They want to be the only ones with something. But we can do that, too. We shall make her demand that which is new and different."

"How will we figure out what that is?"

Windesa looked at the bookshelf ruefully.

"Research, my children. And this time we will make no mistakes."

After another weary night in a string of long and weary nights, Negara raised her head. Her pale green eyes were rimmed with red, but she looked triumphant.

"Unicorns," she said.

Windesa had been drowsing over the enormous book that contained the entire catalog of the treasures held by the kings and queens of Biggleswade over the nine centuries the kingdom had been united under that name. She blinked.

"Unicorns? Are you sure?"

"Yes, mistress," Negara said. "Winged horses, water horses, fairy horses, horse-headed nymphs and goat-hoofed satyrs, miniature ponies and giant war horses, but never a unicorn."

"Hmm," Windesa mused. "I wonder why?"

Over the course of the next few weeks, Windesa threw herself and her apprentices into research, unscrolling tome after dusty tome and gathering stories from gaffers and gammers, hedge witches and storytellers in the surrounding countryside. Of course unicorns roamed—or had roamed—Biggleswade at one time. Their present absence was undoubtedly due to the propensity of King Foghorr and his ancestors to ride out and slaughter anything that moved, whether they planned to eat it or not. The celebrated Blue Unicorn of Biggleswade was a symbol that had ceased to have any real meaning except as an oath of disbelief and the occasional sign hanging by the door of a country pub or two. Windesa shared a cup of wine or two with the local wise men and women as they speculated on whether unicorns were lucky. The general consensus seemed to be that it was, if for no other reason than one would be lucky to see a unicorn at all.

✧

"Unicorns?" Princess Amy asked, as Windesa stood before her. The noble ladies leaned forward, listening eagerly. "You will bring me a unicorn for my birthday?"

Windesa allowed her one wintry smile. She did not want to seem too eager.

"Yes, your highness. Like the unicorns of legend, these are biddable, beautiful creatures with a single horn of pearl."

"I like that idea," Amy said, sitting back in her throne with a pleased expression. "I want one."

"We do, too, dear princess," said Lady Anatolia, eagerly. "We must each have one."

"You know about unicorns, don't you?" Countess Primrose laughed, her dark cheeks creased with glee. "They are only attracted to … certain damsels. I didn't think you qualified!"

Lady Anatolia made a sour face. "If these are magic unicorns, they shouldn't care about things like that!"

A few girls tittered behind their hands, but Windesa knew that Princess Amy had never had relations with men, so the legend would not bother her. In any case, Lady Anatolia was correct.

"Make it so," Amy said. She waved her hand imperiously. "That will be a suitable birthday present for me."

The tower was a buzz of activity. Corema drew the correct invoking pentacle on the scrubbed stone floor of the workroom. Saisun hummed a sweet tune as she sifted the finely ground powdered gemstones that would go into the cauldron with the potion that Ingvie was very carefully concocting on the high worktable. Windesa, erect upon her tall stool, dictated the spell to Negara. The girl scribed the first fifteen verses in silver ink onto a sheet of virgin vellum with a pen made from a feather plucked from the right wing of the castle's most senior raven. Windesa stopped to refresh herself with a goblet of wine. The cup was enchanted to keep the pale vintage at the perfect temperature.

"These verses will form the magical eggs from which will hatch our unicorns," Windesa said.

"Do they all have to be black?" Negara asked, a little sadly. "Not even one pretty roan one? Or blue? Or green?"

"Not all," Windesa said, with a conspiratorial smile. "I have something much more interesting in mind. Now, listen carefully to the final clause of the spell."

As she unfolded the last three verses, the four girls' faces lit up. At the end, they were all beaming.

One week later, the girls all crowded around the enormous basket to watch the hatching of the unicorn eggs in the tower. Pieces of shell flew outward with explosive bangs and cracks as the tiny creatures kicked themselves free. The infant unicorns, the size of miniature greyhounds, that emerged from the eggs underneath the soft feathers of Windesa's pet phoenix were exquisite in every way. All the girls marveled over their slim, delicate legs and goatlike hooves. Their coats were glossy black, and their tiny single horns pure white and soft like a kitten's ears.

All but one egg. Windesa let Negara care for that one particularly. She had sprinkled it with special dust of a different color. It rocked more than the others. The shards of eggshell burst outward, and the last unicorn was born.

It was purple. Its coat was amethyst, and its eyes were the same hue as a stormy sky. It bounded out of the nest over the backs of its brothers and sisters and danced around the room like a tiny whirlwind. In fact, it was the most beautiful of the entire herd. The girls were concerned for Windesa's sanity.

"Are you certain about this, mistress?" Ingvie asked. "Princess Amy will have a terrible fit when she sees that!"

"She will not," Windesa assured her.

"Why not?"

"Because we are not giving it to her. She has no reason to fuss."

"Why create it, then?"

The enchantress smiled enigmatically.

"You'll see."

☙ ✧ ❧

One week later, Princess Amy's birthday dawned. The castle was in a tizzy of preparation. Guests streamed into the capital city from all over the known world. The aristocrats whose daughters were Amy's companions arrived with vast entourages, filling every available sleeping room, stable, storeroom, and side chamber for miles around.

The apprentices stayed out of the way in the tower. In any case, they had plenty to do caring for the unicorn herd. The heraldic beasts grew with remarkable speed. They required ten meals a day, and were so eager to explore their surroundings that Windesa had to erect a magical barrier across the stairwell and over every window lest they bound through them and spoil the surprise by falling into the courtyard. They weren't pegasi, after all.

Even so, it was difficult to conceal a squealing, bucking, energetic herd of juvenile unicorns as the girls guided it down the stairs. Windesa had thrown a cloaking spell over all, so they seemed to be escorting a gaggle of particularly tall black-feathered geese through the crowd of courtiers and aristocrats gathered for the birthday feast. To add to the parade atmosphere, she and the girls were dressed in new gowns of grape purple with veils to match.

The sound of musicians playing and singing threaded thinly through the loud hubbub of excitement in the huge, vaulted expanse of the great hall. The crowds of well-wishers and visitors filling the room all but leaped aside to make way for the wizardess and her procession.

Near the rear wall, upon which hung vividly colored arrases and tapestries depicting victories of her ancestors, Princess Amy sat in the place of honor at the long head table between her father and mother. Queen Melba, a warm and motherly woman from whom Amy had gotten her looks, could not have been more proud of her daughter. King Foghorr, already well into his cups, exchanged jests and guffaws with the Archduke of Onagawa, Countess Primrose's father, who sat at his right hand. All of Amy's friends sat at tables set at angles to the right and left of the center board. All of the girls, Amy included, had donned black garments and veils in spite of the happy occasion. Many of the courtiers had followed their example.

The second-to-last course had been served and cleared, making way for the parade of gifts given to the birthday girl. Heaps of jewelry and bowls of precious stones already filled the trestle tables. Works of art both ancient and new were stacked against the far wall with a pageboy to prevent them being trodden upon by revelers.

Windesa watched Amy's face as each gift was presented. She looked to the right and left to see what her friends thought of them. If they frowned, she frowned, offering only a curt thanks to the donor, leaving that person looking unhappy and disappointed. The girl needed to learn graciousness, but first she had to learn to make a decision on her own. That would come.

The steward kept a trumpeter by his side to blow a fanfare when he needed the crowd's attention to announce the next donor and read his or her birthday wishes. At last, the wizardess's name was called. Windesa stepped forward with her entourage at her back. The seeming flock of geese elicited derisive comments. The commenters stopped talking, horrified, when Windesa turned to glare at them. No matter. It was all illusion, anyhow. She stopped before the table, her apprentices flanking her two and two.

"Happy birthday, your highness," she said, inclining her head a mere inch.

"How kind of you," Amy said, graciously. "I am so excited to see your promised gift."

Windesa stepped to one side.

"And here it is."

The geese hurried forward, honking. Amy laughed in surprise, then gasped as the illusion was swept away. Freed of their disguise, the herd of young black unicorns, horns of polished pearl and tails of stranded silk, danced and cavorted in the square space before the head table. They rushed to nuzzle at Amy's hands, each crowding its head under others, even poking their companions out of the way with their ivory horns, to the laughter of the crowd. The princess couldn't pet all of the long, silky manes at once, though she tried. Once she had caressed them, they allowed the clamoring girls at the other tables to pet them, though they returned over and over again to Princess Amy.

"Which one is mine?" she asked, almost bewildered. Windesa inclined her head again.

"Whichever one you like, highness. Choose well, because it will be your companion for a lifetime. The others are our gifts to your noble friends."

Amy looked from one to another, trying to decide. Was one more special than another?

The last unicorn revealed, the purple one, did not hurry forward. It stayed at Windesa's side, nuzzling in her hand for treats.

It took Amy a moment to notice him. How could she not? His amethyst coat gleamed in the light of the myriad beeswax candles. His sunset-sky eyes were the most beautiful things in the room, more than the artwork, the embroideries, the flowers, and the jewels. His horn was creamy white with a line of pure gold spiraling up from the base to the tip.

"What about him?" Amy said, pointing, her eyes wide with enchantment.

"Oh, I'm sorry, your highness," Windesa said, evincing deep regret. "He is ours."

"But he's a unicorn! And this is my birthday. My sixteenth birthday."

"But he is purple, your highness. Unique, but most unfashionable. Purple is a wizard's color." Windesa smiled as she indicated her own costume. "We do not seek to be stylish or à la mode, we who deal with the eternal and the unknown."

Amy very nearly pouted.

"He's prettier than the others. I want him."

"Are you certain, highness? He is … different. If you accept him, *you* would be different from your companions."

The noblewomen were horrified, looking from the unicorn to Amy and back again.

"Oh, no, princess," Countess Primrose protested. "Doesn't he stand out … rather too much?"

"I like that," Amy said, then glanced at her friends. "I think."

"It would be a humble gift, since he is such an unfashionable hue, but it might be all right," Lady Anatolia said, with a haughty eye. "If the wizardess offered him to you properly."

"I'm afraid not, your ladyship," Windesa said, curtly. "He is rather too special to be rejected, so the offer will not be forthcoming. Please enjoy your gift, your highness. These unicorns are all very healthy and easily trained to do tricks. I wish you a very happy birthday."

She laid a hand on the purple beast's neck and turned away. The apprentices gathered around her. Negara's eyes were dancing. Windesa had all she could do not to answer with her own twinkle. She kept her face deliberately expressionless.

"Wait!" Princess Amy cried. "Don't go, wizardess!" Windesa took her time turning about. A sly smile had spread across the faces of the girl's parents. "Please don't take him. He is very beautiful. I have never seen a purple unicorn before. I would like to have him." She swallowed hard. "Please."

Windesa raised an eyebrow.

"Even though he is different?"

"Yes! Mostly because of that."

"You don't *mind* standing out?"

Princess Amy hesitated.

"I … I …" Amy swallowed, and her voice came out very small. "No."

"Well done, your highness!" Windesa said. Relief rushed through her. The girl had done it! She was capable of striking off the shackles of peer pressure. "Then he is yours."

The purple unicorn let out a shrill neigh of joy and reared, pawing the air with its tiny jeweled hooves. It galloped from Windesa's side. It leaped over the table as if it was knee-high and snuggled into the space between the queen's chair and Princess Amy's. The girl threw her arm over its silky mane and stroked its violet ears and ivory horn. The other noblewomen looked envious, but only to an extent. It was hard to be jealous when one had one's very own unicorn, even if it was not the same color as the princess's.

"Our work here is done, girls," Windesa said, gathering her apprentices together with a gesture and making for the door past the startled steward. "We have started a new fashion."

A Single Spark

Mary Pletsch

The foreigners wanted her to help them kill a unicorn.

Sharareh knelt on a rug inside her father's tent, by all appearances the dutiful daughter, but her keen hearing picked up the murmured words of the men outside. Fear acted as a flint, striking a single spark off her soul—her hidden wrath, her secret rebellion.

It was definitely her the strange men were interested in; her money-hungry father, Abbas, was even now insisting that she was the purest, most obedient, and most devout of all the unwed women in the tribe. None other would entrance a unicorn as quickly and as readily as his Sharareh. His asking price was, in the end, a bargain.

Overhead, the desert sun blazed with its customary ferocity as it climbed towards high noon. The tribe's encampment in the oasis took shelter from the unforgiving heat in the dappled shadows cast by the long fronds of palm trees. Sharareh struggled not to sneeze as the white veil she wore across her face tickled her nose. She was not accustomed to the formal clothing her mother had dressed her in that morning in accordance with her father's wishes.

She wondered if her mother had known what she was doing when she named her youngest daughter *Sharareh*—a name that meant *a single spark*. Why had her mother bequeathed her such a destiny, only to spend the next twelve years teaching her to bury it?

A thin dagger of sunlight slit the flaps of the tent, tracing a line across the floor that stopped just before Sharareh's knees. She leaned forward until the strangers' horses came into view through that narrow gap. The northern leader, a man with the strange name of John—a name so blunt and harsh next to the lyrical names of her people—had ridden to the camp atop the biggest of the horses. Sharareh watched as the huge black horse nudged his way in between her father's camels for a chance to drink at the oasis spring.

The horse managed only a few sips before the camels squeezed together, crowding him out. His owner did not seem to care that his mount was struggling; he was too busy bartering with Abbas. Similarly, Sharareh was certain her own father gave no thought to how his daughter felt as she waited for him to decide her fate.

Sharareh's sisters had been married off for the highest prices their father could get, and now only Sharareh was left. She had known she would be sold eventually, but she'd hoped for a few more years before she'd needed to fear a husband. Yet here she knelt, barely twelve years of age, dressed in her older sisters' wedding clothes. The robes gaped open against her flat chest and snarled her ankles with excess fabric.

A listless breeze blew her father's words to her waiting ears. John expressed his approval, agreeing that Sharareh was the type of girl they sought, and then Abbas began to feign second thoughts. *Perhaps,* for a few more shekels or a goat, he might be willing to trust the men to safeguard his daughter's virtue during their hunt.

Sharareh pressed her lips together and gagged down impotent rage. It caught fire in her guts, leapt from her roiling belly and clawed its way up her throat, burning. Though she swallowed down cries of fury, she could not prevent the bitter flavour of anger from rising into her mouth and curling her tongue with its vile aftertaste.

Abbas had argued with the other men of the tribe that morning, even going so far as to call in unpaid debts to ensure that he would be the one to barter with the foreigners. None had stood against him: not the other men, not their wives, not Sharareh's own mother, and, in the end, not Sharareh. She raised her hand to rub the bruise that bloomed beneath her veil.

Sharareh forced herself to breathe slowly and deeply, but her blood roared in her ears like the flash floods of spring. These foreigners wanted bait, not a concubine, she told herself—until the fear in her belly demanded to know what would become of her once they'd caught their unicorn. She had no answer.

She could strip off her robes and run, risking the fate of disobedient maidens. She had seen what had happened to Rasheesh: stoned to death, her body left for the vultures. Abbas had taken Sharareh's arm tightly in his grip and hissed into her ear that she was looking at her own future should she not learn to mind. Sharareh knew that although she was a swift runner, she could never hope to outpace John's horse, or her father's camels. She would be caught if she tried to flee.

Desperately, Sharareh mouthed prayers to a god whose existence she'd long doubted—or maybe God, like unicorns, had no interest in willful girls. Outside, Abbas loudly protested John's bag of gold was still worth less than his daughter's bride-price … and there was no guarantee they would catch a unicorn and return his dear Sharareh. Sharareh snorted and gave up on her prayers when the strangers doubled their offer and Abbas finally agreed to the deal.

Through the flap of the tent, Sharareh watched John's horse sidling anxiously, shifting its head from side to side. It would have made a fine stallion, had the Northerners not gelded it. It lifted its head to the wind and gazed out into the desert. The look in its eyes became distant, as though it saw, somewhere near the far horizon, the life it might have led before it had been broken to saddle and bridle.

Yes, the great black gelding recalled freedom, however faintly and fleetingly. Sharareh could not mourn the loss of something she had never known, and she wondered if perhaps the horse's life was harder than hers, because it remembered what it had lost.

Sold, like a horse or a goat. As a child, Sharareh had gotten through each day under her father's thumb by living in the small pleasures of the moment. Now, riding on this stranger's gelding, she found herself forced to look upon her future. She beheld a horizon as forbidding as the desert around her, drawing nearer with every beat of the black horse's hooves.

The image of that rapidly approaching horizon gripped Sharareh's mind as she sat on the saddle in front of the man called John, riding through the wastelands of the desert under a pain-bright sky. She had not been permitted to change out of her bridal attire. John and his men had been in too much haste to leave; their greed for the unicorn's horn oozed out of every sweaty pore as they galloped through the heat of the desert like mad things, undeterred by the brutal heat of the noonday sun.

She did not understand the language of the foreigners, but she knew this area of the desert. She could guess where they were headed: the forbidden oasis, a quarter day's ride away. There was nothing else in this direction. She bit her lip and wondered if she could find within her soul any reserves of fear. Right now she felt nothing but numbness creeping through her heart. Legends told around smoking campfires hinted at the reason why none of the tribes would pass through this quarter. The abandoned oasis was the haunt of a desert demon.

Sharareh did not believe in demons any more than gods; they seemed to her to be two sides of the same coin. Mankind did not need the assistance of a supernatural entity to give their lives over to temptation. Sharareh asked only why some people, like her father, were permitted, even encouraged, to do so, while others, like herself, were forced to choke down their own wishes in the name of others' desires. God, as usual, did not bother to justify Himself.

A flash of light in the distance stirred some small ember in Sharareh's soul. She narrowed her eyes, squinting against the glare rising off the sands. Strange shapes sprawled midway up a sand dune a short ways off, as though the desert had vomited them up from its dark and secret gullet. Sharareh debated pointing them out to John, but while she weighed risk against potential reward, one of the other men spotted the anomalies and pointed, shouting.

The riders diverted to approach the mysterious objects. John drew the black gelding to a halt, and Sharareh stared down at the remnants of a caravan. The dune had only partially reswallowed the mummified corpses of camels and men, their remaining flesh dried to jerky, their visible bones bleached to ivory by the scouring sands. Ruined saddlebags spilled precious cargoes of coins and jewels like entrails from slit bellies. Food spoiled in the sun next to gutted water skins. The well of fear that Sharareh thought had run dry burst inside her, splashing her insides with panic.

The man who had pointed out the bodies turned to Sharareh and asked in her own tongue, "What has happened here?"

Bandits would be the easiest answer, and an explanation these men would readily accept. It would also be a lie. What bandit would leave precious stones and shekels strewn across the desert sands? What brigand would slash water vessels and leave bread to become infested with beetles?

"The oasis that lies near here is forbidden," Sharareh said, her voice quavering. "All the tribes of the desert avoid it." She did not believe in demons, but mortals could also be monstrous.

The other man looked to his leader. His comrades were too busy pillaging the bodies to pay Sharareh any mind. "The shaykh was very clear," the other Northerner said. "This is the oasis where the unicorn has been seen."

Sharareh drew a deep breath. Maybe these strangers would listen to reason. She was not one to spook at shadows, but the stench rising from the flyblown corpses was no myth. "If we trespass in the oasis, we can all expect the same."

John snorted and laid his hand on the pistol at his side. "I am not afraid of thieves."

Sharareh watched the other men loading their saddlebags with plunder and said nothing. She was afraid of thieves, but she feared her destiny more.

Sharareh had fought, and she had been defeated. She had held silent, and she had been ignored. She had spoken up, and she had been dismissed. The bruise under her veil throbbed as the Northerners' horses picked their way down a slope littered with loose stones, riding to the bottom of the valley that cradled the forbidden oasis. It seemed as though no matter what Sharareh did, all control of her life had been taken from her.

She regretted all those years she wasted praying to an ambivalent god to deliver her from an early marriage. Would a bridal tent have been so much worse than to be here, in this forsaken place, with these foreign strangers, on a fool's mission to kill a unicorn?

Why were all things meek and beautiful also endangered?

John drew his gelding to a stop on the bank of the pool. A rock wall rose on the other side of the oasis; a few shelf-like ledges were visible just below the water's surface, tapering away until the stone formed a cliff, higher than the black gelding's head, too steep to climb.

John signaled, and his men stopped admiring their salvaged riches long enough to swing out of their saddles and dip their water skins. He permitted Sharareh to dismount, but his hand on her shoulder stopped her from kneeling to take any water for her own.

"You understand what you must do?" John asked.

Sharareh nodded.

John regarded her expectantly, and Sharareh lowered her gaze and spoke. "I am to sit on the bank, a slight distance from the water. I am to be quiet and still. I am to wait until the unicorn comes to drink, and if it does not take notice of me, I may sing softly, to draw its attention. I am to allow it to come to me, and it will lay down before me and put its head in my lap, and I may stroke it to lull it to sleep. Once I am certain it is asleep, I am to raise my hand to summon you, and I am to continue soothing it until ..." Her voice broke. "Until you are in position to collar it or cut its throat, or until it bolts to its feet and threatens to trample me."

Assuming a unicorn did indeed appear, trampling was a likely outcome of the encounter. It depended on how close the unicorn got before it recognized the anger in her thoughts, or the utter lack of purity in her soul.

At a distance, a unicorn would simply run the other way, and if she were lucky, John and her father would blame the unicorn's flight on her loud breathing, or her sisters' perfume on her clothing, or if she were very fortunate indeed, on some ill omen wholly beyond her control.

If she were not lucky, John would call her a liar and a harlot, and she would not be able to convince her father otherwise. She thought again of Rasheesh, and how her father already had his profit from these men. It might be better if the unicorn failed to realize its error until she touched it. It might be faster, less painful, to die beneath its hooves.

John's upper lip curled into a hunter's smile. "Exactly," he said softly, and his approval was a cold and dismissive thing. He turned his back on Sharareh and filled his own water skin, then turned his gelding loose and led his men to cover in a clump of long grasses several paces downwind.

As instructed, Sharareh found a place a few paces from the water where the desert palms cast strong shadows and the ground appeared comfortably dry. She sat down on the short grass and crossed her legs, arranging her skirts around her. From the corner of her eye she could see John and his men settling into their hiding places. The shadow of a vulture passed between the sand and the sun. Sharareh shivered, despite the fierce heat of the midday desert.

It would be a long wait. Sharareh steeled herself for strength. These Northerners were impatient; mad, even. There would be no animals moving about now. Creatures waited in shady nooks for the setting sun to bring some relief to the desert. They went about the business of eating and avoiding being eaten during the cool of the evening. Sharareh tried not to think about the corpses of the caravan slowly cooking in the sun, or what might have been responsible for putting them there.

Sharareh did her best to stay still in both body and mind, but as the sun crawled across the heavens, her muscles cramped painfully and her thoughts chased themselves round and round in circles. If there were a God, should she pray for Him to bring a unicorn to her lap, or to chase them all far away from here? Sharareh's head nodded as fatigue led her into a near-trance. Her lips cracked, but rising to sip from the oasis pool would doubtlessly irritate John. She could hear her father now, cautioning her against "unnecessary motion."

She licked at her mouth with a tongue swollen with thirst, pretending she was drinking. She could almost taste sweet water. Sharareh could imagine how it would feel to plunge her hands into the cooling pool of the oasis, to raise her cupped palms to her mouth and suck water through her lips. She could hear the light splashing ...

She could hear.

Sharareh startled, as though emerging from a deep and dark sleep. Claws of thirst still scratched at her throat, threatening to gag her, but she forced herself to swallow down a passage that ached with dryness. She lifted her gaze to the spring and held her breath at the creature that stood there, knee-deep in the pool, its arching neck curved to the surface of the water, its long black tongue lapping up life-giving moisture.

Death was drinking there.

Sharareh had seen a unicorn once, a pale and spindly thing hardly bigger than a goat, standing on the crest of a faraway dune, the desert moon turning its heels and horn to silver. The Northerners had hunted them to the brink of extinction, driving them ever farther from their native habitat. Now only a handful remained, crouching on the verges of the Northerners' voracious civilization. Her tribe knew that the Northerners had been coming here to the desert to make war for generations, that these Crusaders had driven unicorns before them as they'd advanced, and that a few of the elusive beasts survived in hidden oases even now. These were the animals John and his men were hunting.

What drank from the oasis was not a Northern unicorn.

From fireside tales she knew the creature's name. Taller than the hunter's horses, taller even than John's great black gelding, the beast was easily the size of a camel. Like a camel, its hooves were split in two, the better to carry it across the shifting desert sands. Its tongue descended to the surface of the pool from between two razor-sharp fangs that protruded over its lower lip. Its horn was a serrated scimitar, caked with dried blood. Its thick hide, like leather armour, glistened in the sunlight, glittering the resplendent purple of kingship. Sharareh beheld it and understood why the storytellers called it the *lord of the desert.*

Sharareh looked closer at its groin, her eyes narrowing. This lord was, in fact, a lady; worse, then, for Sharareh, for the female of the species was said to be even more deadly than the male. Her eyes returned, unbidden, to those dagger fangs and the gory horn, and she remembered that while Northern unicorns fed on flower petals and dew, this one preferred to sate itself on brambles and freshly spilled viscera.

She looked back over her shoulder, seeking direction from her employers. Surely John would have mercy. Surely. Sharareh had been willing to bait a Northern unicorn; she had been prepared to grovel shamelessly if she failed.

She had not expected to face down a karkadann.

John's face was too far away for her to see clearly, but from his rough and vigorous gesturing—*turn around, turn around*—she could guess he was angry. Automatically, Sharareh obeyed, her head turning and bowing even as her mind caught up with her and screamed that she should be *running*, that the karkadann was a far more immediate danger than John's displeasure. Did John even understand that the purple beast with the crescent horn was as merciless as the desert heat, as relentless as the infinite dunes, and as vicious as a sandstorm that flayed flesh from bone?

From under lowered eyelids, Sharareh lifted her gaze to the creature and her breath shriveled in her throat. The karkadann had noticed movement, and it had left off drinking, regarding her with an eye that burned hot like the desert sun.

Sharareh watched the karkadann watching her and was aware, more than aware, that to pretend to be a dull-witted virgin was a death sentence. She was looking at the end of everything and now, face to face with the destroyer, she had only one choice to make: to meet it on her knees, or to meet it on her feet.

She remembered Rasheesh crying and kissing the shaykh's sandals, praying for a mercy that was not granted. She remembered kneeling in her father's tent when Abbas entered with his bag of gold and told her that she would go with John and do as he said. She felt the bruise on her cheek, recalled the greed in John's eyes, and within her soul a smoldering ember burst at last into flame.

She had done nothing to earn this fate. To the Inferno with her father, who had sold his daughters for lucre. To the outer wastes with the Northerners, who knew nothing of the desert and cared only for their own profits. She could bow her head and accept this final injustice, or she could practice how she would face her God when He condemned her for the sins of a disobedient heart and a wrathful spirit.

Sharareh rose.

The karkadann stepped towards her, and Sharareh saw its great cloven hoof press upon the moist earth where the soil met the oasis pool. The urge to turn and flee crashed over her with the fury of a flash flood, accompanied by a voice in her head that sounded like her father's demanding to know why she was not already moving. She spat back at him that she again had a choice to make: to die running or to face down the karkadann. The thought of Rasheesh's bloodied and broken body filled her with fury. It sickened her to imagine her father shaking his head, looking down on the corpse of his cowardly and useless daughter. No. Her father would know at the end of things that she had been irredeemable, defiant to the last.

The purple lady of the desert came to a halt barely a step away from her. Sharareh hardly dared to breathe. Her mother had taught her that when confronting a wild animal, she should pretend it was her father and never look it in the eye. It would only provoke the creature, she said, only incite it to wrath; but if Sharareh glanced away, she might as well be running.

Sharareh met the karkadann face to face, eye to eye. A sliver of lavender iris formed an endless ring around the karkadann's huge black pupil. The lady of the desert looked at her and *through* her in a manner that stripped her bare, tore off her veil, flung open her robes, pushed aside her flesh, and stabbed straight through to her soul. For a moment it seemed to Sharareh that she could see something in the karkadann's eye, not the reflection of a child bride, but a glimpse of a warrior-woman regarding Sharareh with her head lifted in challenge.

Distantly, Sharareh heard a sharp noise like two rocks banging together. The karkadann ignored the sound, so Sharareh did as well. Then a whistle, unlike the sound of any desert bird, pierced the air. Sharareh realized it must be John's men, attempting to get her attention without spooking the karkadann by using human language.

What did those fools want her to do? Sit, and pray the karkadann would kneel? The lady of the desert would not kneel. This purple shaykha would be no slave; she was no man's servant.

Did they want Sharareh to cast herself on the karkadann's horn, then? To sacrifice her life on the altar of their greed?

Sharareh felt a mantle of disdain settle on her shoulders. Let *them* come this close to a karkadann and see how well they fared.

The lady of the desert lowered her head and whuffled softly.

Disbelieving, Sharareh wound her hand into the thick bristles of the karkadann's mane. For a moment, she hesitated as a ribbon of fear coiled around her heart. Then she thought of that bridal tent, that future as bleak as a desert horizon, and she asked herself, *On my knees or on a karkadann?*

Sharareh clasped her other hand as far over the creature's back as she could and jumped, and the karkadann bent her knees and *dipped.* Sharareh could not determine the degree to which she threw herself onto the karkadann from the degree to which the karkadann maneuvered to catch her, but the next thing she knew, the purple shaykha had turned her back on the Northerners and was walking away from the oasis, with Sharareh clinging to her neck.

They had moved several paces before the Northerners understood that they had been dismissed. Then the men started shouting, swearing, John roaring out Sharareh's name. All the while the karkadann moved serenely forward, as though she were a vast ship sailing over a smooth and placid sea, undeterred by the obnoxious cries of birds.

John began to scream and curse, yelling all manner of hateful epithets, and Sharareh could not help but tremble. She had seen her father in such a state far too often, and she knew what would come next. The noisemaker rocks would be thrown at her, pulverizing her bones, like poor Rasheesh. Or the men would raise their long guns to their shoulders and fire, not caring if they shot Sharareh so long as they brought down the karkadann.

The karkadann raised its neck and tilted its head, rolling one eye to look back at her, and it whickered, as though amused.

Sharareh, filled with hope, smiled. Her fingers wound tighter into its mane.

Then they were galloping forward over the sands. Guns fired with a volley of pops and snaps, and Sharareh was certain she saw a bullet glance off the karkadann's thick purple hide, but surely she dreamed such a thing. Surely. The karkadann sped up, and time around them seemed to slow. Sharareh saw the surface of the water float gently past below them, and droplets rose up in twin plumes behind them, leaving a rainbow to mark their passage. The rock wall rose ahead in a sheer, smooth barrier, impossibly high, and Sharareh braced herself. If the karkadann did not balk, they would be dashed against the stone.

The lady of the desert reared up onto an outcropping. Then she tucked up her knees and soared. Her powerful hindquarters launched them skyward with a force no horse could match. They were airborne, flying over the canyon wall, the horizon a brilliant blue and countless leagues away.

For just an instant, Sharareh looked back. The last thing she saw was not John or his men or the last vestiges of her old life vanishing behind her, but John's nameless gelding, watching them with an expression Sharareh could only describe as envy. Sharareh's destiny stretched out into the far distance ahead, unseeable, unknowable, but the moment did grant her a revelation: whatever her future, it would not be the same as his.

☙ ✧ ❧

Sharareh did not know how long she rode. She was dazzled by thirst, overcome by fatigue, dizzied by the sheer power of the karkadann and the fierce, intoxicating taste of freedom. It might have been minutes or days before the purple shaykha slowed to a trot, and when Sharareh focused her eyes on the sight before her, she saw the fantastic mirage of a flaming sun setting behind the walls of a city whose name she did not know, and a still more impossible sight standing just outside its gates.

Sharareh let go of the karkadann's mane and rubbed at her eyes, convinced that she must be sunstruck. She scoured until her eyeballs ached, but when she moved her hands away and opened her eyelids, the vision remained.

There were four of them, each mounted on a unicorn, and they all stood as still as a carved relief against the limestone walls.

The rider to the left had pale skin like John's and hair the colour of ripe grain. She wore heavy metal armour on her chest, shoulders, and thighs. The biggest sword Sharareh had ever seen hung at her side, long and straight and broad; it would surely take two hands to lift it. Her mount, too, was massive: its back wide like a rhino's, and its feet the size of a water pail, fringed with wispy hair. Its nose was blunted, and its horn was thick at the base, tapering rapidly into a long, narrow lance.

Next to her rode a fine-boned woman with dark and perfectly straight hair worn loose over her shoulders. Sharareh at first thought the stranger squinted at the sky until she realized the other woman's eyes held that shape permanently. Her clothes were made of finely embroidered silk and featured a strange vertical collar embellished with ornate ties. She carried a rippled blade that appeared, to Sharareh, like water incarnate in a sword. She rode a creature with a horn that branched into two points, so that from a distance it might almost resemble a gazelle's antlers....but no gazelle had a long, thick tail like a serpent, or fine scales that Sharareh had almost mistaken for armour.

The third … Sharareh had no words for the third. It seemed, on first glance, to be a man: he had soft down on his face, the beginnings of a beard, and his shoulders were broad beneath his robes. Yet the person was shorter than Sharareh and wore long, braided hair and the traditional robes of a woman. She—or he, Sharareh could not guess which—sat astride a delicate white Northern unicorn, with its tiny beard and tasseled lion's tail. Sharareh smiled, wondering what John might have said had he seen the prey he sought with the strange company it kept.

And the fourth—the fourth sat mounted on a karkadann, a mare even larger than the purple desert princess that bore Sharareh. The other karkadann's hide gleamed golden yellow, and its back was striped with striking blue slashes the colour of sapphires. Its horn, a brass sabre, sat on its brow like a crown.

The karkadann rider was no less regal than her mount. Her skin was as dark as the fabled soil of Kumat, and on her head she wore a diadem in the shape of a cobra, dangerous and proud. Her hair had been woven into short, strong tails tipped with beads, like the tendrils of a whip. She wore the leathers of a warrior tailored to fit her feminine form, and she held a scimitar, the blade of the prophets.

Sharareh had heard tales of the people of Kumat and their rich black land faraway across the red desert. The leaders among them were called *pharaoh:* god-king. Sharareh had imagined a god-king to be much like her own tribe's shaykhas, but now, ah, now she understood the difference. No shaykha would dare sit astride a karkadann as though it were a camel; no shaykha would wear both the garb of a woman and the blade of a warrior, in defiance of all man's laws. Only God could judge this dark rider, and Sharareh was not convinced the pharaoh woman was not divine herself.

"Ho," she said in Sharareh's own tongue, her voice husky and low. "Azazel returns." Her head tilted with curiosity as her full lips formed a half-smile. "And what is this she has brought with her?"

"I think it is a desert rat," laughed the woman in silks. "Azazel, you should put it back."

The creature beneath Sharareh spoke, and the deep vibration of the karkadann's words traveled through her thighs and shook her bones, until her whole being trembled with the power in the purple unicorn's speech. "Would you go back home, little one?"

Sharareh's throat tightened with fear. She could hear her mother's soothing voice in her mind, calming her, telling her she needed only speak a few words. Just a few words, and the karkadann would return her to her father's tent, unharmed. Just a few words and she would be back where she belonged, back among the familiar, safe …

No. Not safe. *Never* safe, in a tent where her father would sell her to the highest bidder for a goat and a bag of shekels. *Never* in a family where a mother stood meekly aside while her own daughter became sacrifice. *Never* among a people who called such actions virtue.

Sharareh's hands tightened in Azazel's short mane until the wiry strands threatened to cut through her skin like garrotes. The word she had retched halfway up her throat and gulped back down to gag on for her entire life spewed forth at last.

"*Never,*" said Sharareh.

The he-woman and the Northern warrior exchanged glances.

The pharaoh's karkadann sidled up next to Azazel, and Sharareh found herself facing the woman's piercing gaze. Her head bowed of its own accord.

"Look at me," the woman said, as she pressed a water skin into Sharareh's hands.

Sharareh glanced upward. The weight of authority pressed her down, and she squirmed, uncomfortable, feeling the force of the queen's judgment like a physical burden. Sharareh fought years of teachings in her battle to hold the other woman's gaze. The accumulated wisdom of history shrieked in her ears, and her heart clenched, warning her she deserved whatever punishment this woman chose to give in exchange for her audacity in daring to deem herself worthy to look the pharaoh in the eye.

How could she stand up before a karkadann and still be so cowed by a fellow human being? Fury smoldered in her belly, raging that she should have to debase herself, and then Sharareh realized with some surprise that she did not feel denigrated in the slightest. She sat astride a karkadann of her own, and she faced this woman, if not quite as an equal, then at least as a fellow rider.

It was not her place to demand the other woman's name, but neither did she shy away from her. She lifted the skin and drank deeply of sweet, clear water; then she hooked it to the sash of her robes and waited.

"I am Anpu, *the jackal*, guardian of buried knowledge, and this is Samiel, *the poison wind*." The goddess-queen stroked the golden neck of the karkadann that bore her, for it seemed now to Sharareh's eyes that the woman did not master Samiel so much as Samiel suffered her human companion to ride upon her back.

Samiel spoke in a brassy voice like distant thunder. "With us are Huojin of the kirin, and her companion, Yi, bringer of justice; Citrine, from the lands to the northwest, and her partner, Anahita, healers both; and Liberata and Quiteria, warrior saints, who among their people are called the holy sister and her mount." Samiel whickered, as though laughing, in mockery of the fools who did not recognize the heavy-set unicorn as the equal of her rider.

Sharareh felt her ears burning, ashamed that she had been surprised when the karkadann had spoken in a human tongue.

She raised her arms in her tribe's traditional gesture of welcome, but all the while, she despaired. What did she have to offer these people? She was no lawgiver, like Yi; no doctor, like Anahita; no holy woman, like Quiteria. She was certainly not royalty, as Anpu must be. She did not dare imagine herself the equal of the unicorns. She wondered what her father and John would think, if they were to see this gathering, and she knew what their blindness would suggest to them: four mere women and a man who wished to be a woman, sitting atop five stupid beasts.

"How do you call yourself?" Anpu inquired.

It took a moment for Sharareh to understand the pharaoh's question. "I am Sharareh, *a single spark*."

"Ah," said Samiel, and Anpu echoed, "Ah." And it was only then that knowledge dawned upon Sharareh as well, like the first glimmerings of violet in the morning sky.

"A single spark," said Sharareh, slowly at first, "can, it is true, glow for a short time before it is extinguished and forgotten. But," she continued, her voice growing stronger, "a single spark can also be the flame that starts a wildfire, or the flash that ignites a candle to provide illumination in the darkness."

"I am Azazel," rumbled the purple karkadann, "*rugged in exile*. If you come with me, Sharareh-a-Single-Spark, you will be forever cast out from your people."

She lifted her eyes to the horizon, thinking of John's horse, who dreamed of the freedoms he had lost. She would not pass her days in her father's tent, looking, like the black gelding, into the distance and wishing.

"If you bury a spark beneath a bushel basket," Sharareh retorted, "you will smother it, and it will shine no more." Her lips curved, and she saw the other women nod and return her smile. "My destiny is mine to make, and I would go with you."

The unicorns lifted their heads and gave voice in recognition of her choice. Citrine's high clarion blended with Liberata's baritone and Huojin's melodic piping like the sound of wind through reeds. Samiel loosed a cry like a hawk's, Azazel replied, and then Sharareh was yelling, laughing as the group of unicorns and warrior-women moved forward, taking Azazel and Sharareh into their midst. The unicorns surged into a gallop, and Sharareh spread her arms like wings and sang, bride of freedom, warrior among warriors, partner of a karkadann, a single spark igniting.

Best of All Possible Worlds

John D. Payne

"Dammit!" Lem shouted, reaching the bus stop just after the CT2 to Kendall/MIT pulled away. He ran a few more steps and then gave up with a heavy sigh that he hoped would attract the attention of the girl who sat waiting inside the booth. She didn't look up.

Tresses of dark brown hair with magenta streaks spilled out from underneath her oversized Panama hat and fell on an olive drab coat that looked like it had seen combat. She had been wearing a different hat every time he had seen her—four or five times over the last couple of months. Although he'd tried to catch her eye, so far he hadn't even got her to acknowledge his presence.

It made sense. Even a nice bus stop wasn't a great place to meet people, and this one wasn't nice. Beat-up Plexiglas walls sported a discolored map, an ad for a cancelled TV show, and lots of graffiti—including the words "PURPLE UNICORN" in large, silver letters. The roof and sides were spattered with the poop of the ten thousand pigeons who made their home under the McGrath highway overpass. In short, the place lacked ambience. This wouldn't be easy.

Fixing a wry smile on his face, Lem stretched out a hand toward the bus, now well on its way down Washington. He pursed his lips and blew out another sigh of disgust, but the girl in the hat appeared to take no notice of him. Slender white cords ran from her earbuds to the tablet in her hands.

"Can you believe that?" Lem said, shaking his head. "They must have seen me, but they didn't even stop. I was right here."

"Not really."

He froze. She'd never spoken to him before. In fact, the wide brim of her hat hid her face so completely that he hadn't seen her lips move even now. But the only other person around was the homeless guy who always had one eye screwed shut, and his voice was raspier. And he pretty much only talked about (and to) things that no one else could see.

Both elated and terrified, Lem realized that first contact was within his grasp. He also realized that he hadn't responded, hadn't said anything in … too long. Awkwardness had filled the vacuum left by his complete inability to hold a normal conversation with a cute girl.

"Uh …" he said.

"You weren't here. You were late. Maybe you should get that app." Her fingers flicked idly across the screen of her tablet, presumably turning digital pages.

Lem closed his mouth and then opened it again. "Funny story. I actually have that app."

"Funny," she said, flicking her finger across the screen, "but not ha-ha funny."

"Oh, I love that episode," Lem gushed.

She looked up. "What?"

It was his first good look at her face. She wore big black glasses like from NASA mission control. Most people's glasses made their eyes look smaller, but if anything, hers were magnified. They had to be. They were huge, like ridiculously Japanese-cartoon huge. And beautiful with thick, dark lashes like Elizabeth Taylor's. If only he were Richard Burton. Hell, he would even settle for being a regular guy who didn't know anything about NASA or Japanese cartoons or Elizabeth Taylor.

Sports. He should know about sports.

"Uh …" he said. "That line. It's from a *Simpsons* episode."

She raised an eyebrow.

"The one where they go to Camp Krusty." He felt his face growing warm. He'd wanted to talk to this girl since the first time he saw her, and this was the best he could come up with? He searched his brain for some smooth line. "It's a really old one. You've probably never seen it." Better yet, why didn't he just shut up?

She looked away, following the passage of a helicopter as it whupped across the sky. Damn, her eyelashes were like butterflies. How did they not knock her glasses off?

In desperate need of something else to talk about, his eyes lit upon the graffiti scrawled on the bus stop wall in what looked like silver marker.

"'Purple unicorn,'" he read, pointing at the tag. "What's that? Like, Somerville's gayest street gang?"

Her eyes narrowed a bit, and she cocked her head to one side.

"Not that there's anything wrong with that," he amended, spreading his hands and making an awkward shrug.

Both her eyebrows went up, and she gave him that kind of tight-lipped smile that let him know she was feeling embarrassed for him just in case he wasn't feeling embarrassed enough for himself. "Okay then," she said, returning to her tablet.

That was good-bye. And who could blame her? This was just like the time he'd been in an elevator with Summer Glau and had geeked so hard he hadn't even been able to get his own name out. It was understandable. What red-blooded nerd wouldn't have been just as nervous? The real question was why he found the girl in the hat nearly as intimidating.

She certainly had an exotic look: olive skin, unbelievably big eyes, striking nose, strong jaw. Persian, maybe. Or Arab. Was there a polite way to ask? No. It was a micro-aggression, an otherization. Instead of staring at her and trying to figure her out, why not just get to know her as a person?

He took a deep breath and stuck out his hand. "Hi. I'm Lem."

"You're … lame?"

"Lem. Short for Lemuel." He shrugged. "I know, it's an old man's name. Blame my parents."

She took his hand and shook it, looking amused—of course.

What is this, the forties? Who shakes hands? Gah!

"I'm Pris," she said. "So I know what you mean."

"No, that's nice. Pris. Like—" He stopped abruptly and tried to cover it with a fake cough that would fool absolutely no one. Still, better than telling her how cool it was that she shared a name with one of the androids in *Blade Runner*. "So, what do you think that is?"

She glanced at the graffiti tag. "What, that?"

"Yeah. I mean, who would write that? If I were a teenage hoodlum, I'd try to come up with a name that sounded a little more threatening. Or at least … cool." *Not that I would know anything about sounding cool. Hoodlum? Who says that? What is wrong with me?*

"Oh, I don't know." She switched off her tablet. "Purple unicorn could be a very cool name for something. Not a gang, though. More like a LARPing group."

"LARPing?"

She blushed. "Live-action role-playing. It's—"

"Oh," he interrupted, "I know what LARPing is. I go to MIT. There are people who cosplay not just on campus but in class."

"You study engineering?"

"Linguistics. My thesis is about how lexical ambiguity is resolved through the pragmatics of …" He shrugged. "It's super boring. I got into it because of Tolkein, to tell you the truth. All the languages he created."

She gave him a sly smile. "So you were one of those nerds who dug into the appendices."

"Damn straight." He leaned back against the wall of the bus stop with arms folded, trying to look confident.

"Me, too. Nerd power." She raised a fist and stuck her lips out in a defiant pout.

"Represent." He bumped a fist against his chest. This was going even better than he could have imagined. He pointed once more to the graffiti. "Purple unicorn's a little on the nose for a LARPing group, I think. Plus, it's not plural. Maybe a band."

After a moment's reflection, Pris closed her eyes and grabbed an invisible microphone. "Hello, Boston! We're Purple Unicorn and we're here to rock!" Opening her eyes, she shook her head. "Fails the arena test."

"I was thinking nerdcore. Or filk."

She made a face like she had taken a swig of milk that was three days past its sell-by date. "No, it's no good."

"All right," Lem said. "What do you think it is?"

"Sounds like one of those cupcake places." She leaned forward and rested her chin in one hand. "Employee-owned, a co-op. And only women. The name is playful to let you know they have a sense of humor, but they're serious about being socially responsible with their product."

"Vegan soymilk cream cheese frosting. All-natural fair-trade hot pink food coloring. Organic, locally grown sprinkles."

"You see it." She shared a knowing little smile with him, a facial expression that didn't come his way often. He liked it a lot.

"I do," said Lem. "Although the cupcake market is getting pretty crowded. I hate to say it, but I think our all-femme worker's cooperative might have trouble drumming up business."

Pris gestured at the graffiti. "Thus, their unconventional advertising strategy."

Lem nodded and tapped the side of his nose. He hoped it made him look intriguing and cosmopolitan, rather than like a guy who watched too much *Masterpiece Theatre.* Or reruns of *Doctor Who,* which is where he had actually picked up the gesture.

"How about a bar?" Pris asked.

"What? It's like ..." Lem glanced at his phone. "Nine eighteen. I don't even know what would be open."

Pris rolled her eyes.

"Oh. You mean—"

"Yes."

"For the purple unicorn. For the bar. For the name. The name of the bar would be Purple Unicorn. That's what they would call it." At that point, his brain mercifully shut his mouth down so he could devote himself fully to thoughts of suicide.

She nodded slowly, her eyebrows raised. "Uh-huh."

"Kind of a froufrou name for a bar," Lem said. "Unless it's a gay bar."

"Back on that again, are we?"

Lem felt a hot blush hit his face. "Hey, tell me 'purple unicorn' doesn't sound just a little bit gay to you. I mean, think about it. That could be like the whole theme of the bar. No." He held up a finger. "A dance club. Oiled-up muscular dudes in fluffy purple chaps and unicorn masks."

Pris blinked a couple of times, which was hard to ignore given her immense lashes. "That's an oddly specific image, which you came up with rather quickly."

"Tell me that place doesn't already exist in P-town."

She laughed. "Yeah, but the only ones who go there are tourists. Locals find it ridiculous."

"Except for one thing. Everyone loves the club's signature drink, also called the Purple Unicorn." He spread his hands out before him like a magician finishing a trick.

"Ooh!" said Pris. "I like that. Obviously the color would be purple."

"Grape schnapps."

"Blackberry vodka. And for a stirrer, they use a lollipop or a sucker."

"Poking out of the top of the drink like a unicorn horn."

"Precisely."

Lem smiled. Finally, he was digging himself out of the hole. Of course, this was also usually the place where he completely torpedoed the conversation by getting too excited and pushing too hard. Better to play it cool. Stick to small talk. The basics.

"So, um," he began, throwing a hand in her direction, "what do you do?"

"What do I do?" She looked amused.

"Sure. I mean, like I study linguistics. What about you? Are you in school or do you have a job, or…?"

"I knew someone who said the problem with Americans is that we think our identities reduce to our occupations. 'What do you do?' As if our answer to that question could really capture who we are." She sighed and looked back down at her tablet.

Was she foreign after all? She didn't have an accent, but you never knew. "Okay. I can see that. The triumph of materialism, corporations, all that stuff." Lem pushed his glasses back up his nose. "But on the other hand, America also gave the world *Office Space* and *Dilbert*. So we got that going for us."

She gave him a grunt that was not quite a pity laugh and flicked a finger across the screen of her tablet. Once again, the brim of her hat completely hid her face. Three feet away from her, and he might as well be in another state. Damn it, how had he blown this? She was so cool!

He sighed quietly and stepped out from under the cover of the bus stop. Another CT2 was coming down the street. He glanced at his phone. Maybe he should just go.

"I have a research job," Pris said.

Lem turned around, letting the bus pass by behind him. She was looking up at him with those gorgeous Elizabeth Taylor eyes of hers. He smiled.

"Really? What do you research?"

She shrugged. "Had to sign an NDA. Sorry. I just … I get tired of explaining to everyone that I can't really talk about my work."

"No, it's no problem. I get it. One of my buddies works at Lincoln Labs." Actually, less of a buddy and more of a guy who occasionally dropped in to ruin the weekly Pathfinder game by being a ridiculous rules lawyer. But close enough.

Stay on target, he admonished himself. *Don't get lost in your own thoughts. Pay attention. Keep the conversation alive.* The problem was, all he could think of at the moment was her mystery job. He had all kinds of questions he wanted to ask about that, but she had just said she was sick of people bugging her about that stuff.

He glanced back at the silver graffiti tag on the wall. That had been working.

"What if purple unicorn doesn't mean anything?" He stroked his chin.

She followed his gaze and smiled. "It probably doesn't—our imaginary Provincetown dance club notwithstanding."

"No, no, no." He narrowed his eyes. "What if it's a code phrase? 'Elvis has left the building.'"

"'Climb Mount Niitaka.'"

"Right. So then the question is, who do we say this to, and what happens next?"

Pris considered this carefully. "You say it at the Dunkin' Donuts down the street and they give you a free squirt of jelly filling into any pastry you want. It's like asking for your fries 'animal style' at In-N-Out."

Lem jerked a thumb behind him. "The Dunkin' down by Union Square? Or the one over on Cobble Hill?"

"Forgot about those. I was thinking of the one on Broadway. But obviously the correct answer is all of the above."

"Nice," said Lem. "I was thinking of something with a bit more intrigue and danger, but your idea sounds pretty delicious. Mmm … In fact, all I can think about now are jelly-filled bagels."

He closed his eyes and rubbed his stomach sensuously, which earned him a laugh from her. It was a great big snorty braying laugh, like a drunk donkey being tickled to death. She blushed ferociously and pulled her scarf over her mouth, trying to keep it in. But it was absolute music to his ears.

Then he got an idea.

"Hey," he said, as she got a grip on her laughter, "we should go there some time and try it."

Her forehead wrinkled with an unspoken question.

"Dunkin'," he said. "Ask for the purple unicorn. See if it works." He shrugged, striving with desperate intensity to look nonchalant. "And if not, maybe … we … have coffee."

She pulled her scarf back down and lowered her hands, staring at him with those impossibly big anime eyes of hers. He very much wanted her to say something. Even no. But she said nothing.

Lem adjusted his glasses. "Or not. You know, whatever."

She nodded. "Hey, you said you had a more dangerous idea."

"Yeah, no. It was stupid."

"Come on," Pris said, leaning forward. "Spill. Dangerous like international espionage, or like underground cockfighting?"

Lem took a deep breath. "Okay. So, there's something weird I've noticed in this town. Every time they're doing work under the street, like any time you see a manhole cover off, there's always a cop there. You noticed this?"

Pris narrowed her eyes. "Not really."

"Trust me. Now that you know about this, you'll see it every time. And why do you think they always have a cop there?"

"Union regulations, city ordinance, I don't know." Pris shrugged. "Either way, it's cushy duty for the police. Nothing for them to do but stand around drinking coffee."

"So it would seem," Lem said.

"But things are not as they seem," Pris said, in a conspiratorial stage whisper.

"Indeed. A secret menace lurks under the streets of Boston. What was it that delayed the completion of the Big Dig? Simple corruption?

No. Hideous mutants, the products of radiological experiments, with a taste for human flesh."

"And this radiation," Pris said, "has it left their skin discolored? The ugly purple of an old bruise, perhaps?"

Lem nodded. "And they get calcium spurs growing out of their frontal lobes. Very distinctive. Hard to mistake for anything else. Which is why this all has to be kept so hush-hush. Even at the police station, only specially cleared personnel are cleared to know about the purple unicorns."

"I love it," said Pris.

Lem blushed. "Thanks."

"Except," Pris said, "that you've gone back to the plural, which led to my poor LARP group being disqualified."

"Right."

"Fun while it lasted, though." She stood up. "All of this, I mean. Thanks for helping me pass the time. That's my bus at the stoplight over there."

"Oh, okay," said Lem. He moved out of the way so she could slip past him. "It was nice talking to you." It had been. Despite crashing and burning once or twice, he couldn't remember the last time he'd enjoyed a conversation so much. "Guess I'll see you around. Maybe someday we'll even get to the bottom of this mystery." He inclined his head to the graffiti.

Pris tucked away her tablet. "Maybe."

Lem nodded blankly. His mind raced. Optimism and pessimism held a brief but passionate debate on the topic of whether or not this meant he had chased her away forever by boring her with a bunch of nerd talk. She hadn't said yes to coffee, but she hadn't said no, either. And now that they had been introduced, the next time they saw each other it would be easier to talk. Once they got to know each other a little better, he could try again—if she ever came back.

"Huh," he said.

The light changed, and her bus pulled through the intersection and stopped at the curb where Pris stood. With a hiss and a groan, the doors opened, and Pris reached up to take hold of the handles on either side.

Abruptly, she turned to him. "So what do you think it is, really?" Her immense, violet eyes were surprisingly intent. "Distant nebula, Wi-

Fi password, mysterious vigilante? Cryptic line from a Nostradamus prophecy?"

Lem nodded. "Pirate ship, designer drug, Internet meme, the world's largest uncut amethyst." He shrugged. "Why limit ourselves? In the best of all possible worlds, they're all true."

Pris tilted her head and parted her lips slightly, before being interrupted by a blast from the bus's horn.

"Hey!" cried the driver, a heavyset African-American woman. "You getting on?"

Pris whipped her head around and shouted, "Give me a second, all right?" Then she turned back to Lem. "Listen, I'm going out of town for a while. But next Friday you want to meet me at the Dunkin' on Broadway about quarter to nine?"

"Yeah!"

The bus driver honked again. "On or off!"

"Fine!" Pris pulled herself up and into the bus, throwing Lem one last smile over her shoulder as the doors closed.

With a conscious effort, he succeeded in keeping himself from running after the bus or even waving, and instead merely watched it drive down Washington with a huge, goofy grin plastered all over his face.

☙ ✧ ❧

"Sorry, Jules," Pris said, standing directly behind the white line painted on the floor of the bus.

"I been young," said the bus driver, her eyes remaining on the road ahead. "And they ain't nobody else on the bus anyway."

"Slow day, I guess."

"Mm-hm."

The bus stopped in Union Square, but Jules didn't open the doors. A South Asian man in a long coat called for her to open up, but Jules merely pointed to the marquee on the front of the bus: Out of Service. The man pointed at Pris and demanded that the doors open, but both women studiously ignored him.

"You like him?" Jules asked, as the light changed.

Pris shrugged. "He's kind of sweet." She wasn't sure she had the patience for him to develop a little self-awareness, gain a little confidence. But he was cute, and bright, and almost charming—in an awkward, earnest sort of way. "Might be worth a coffee."

"Well, he sure likes you," Jules said. She turned her head slightly and raised one eyebrow. "Any potential there?"

Pris sighed. "I don't know. I hope so. I'm tired of always having to wonder if a guy will be cool with it."

Jules reached a hand over to give Pris a little squeeze. "Well, try not to break his heart."

"Oh, that's your job."

The older woman cackled with laughter. "You got that right."

They crossed Beacon and continued past Harvard without picking up any other passengers. As they turned down Cambridge Street and approached the underpass, the bus began to vibrate.

"Here we go," said Jules. She shifted the gearstick into the final position, and the lines of the buildings around them began to blur. With a flash of red light, the bus grew translucent. Outside the bus was formless blackness, lit only by the aura of the bus itself, now glowing orange.

As the light shifted to yellow, the bus appeared to Pris to balloon outward. Its roof and sides swelled and rose upwards, becoming the vast envelope of a dirigible. The floor of the bus became the wooden deck of the airship's gondola.

Pris reached down for the deck with arms that were growing longer, fingers that were fusing together into hooves. She tossed her mane as the green light shifted to blue, feeling her horn stretch out to its full and glorious length. No longer chained to human form, she exulted in once again being a purple unicorn.

"End of the line," said Jules, now an enormous robotic beetle, steering the wheel of the airship with two of her six gleaming limbs. Her iridescent metal carapace reflected the light of the warp bubble as it passed from indigo to violet. "We are arriving at the Best of All Possible Worlds. Please watch your step as you disembark."

Korgak's Daily Schedule

Jeanette Gonzalez

Korgak the Orc, Head Guard for the Tower Gaols, second only to Grugrak the Fierce, kicked the rusty bucket with his boot. Putrid contents slopped into the gutter. Korgak spat a lugie at the stone wall, where it dribbled a shiny trail through moss and lichen. He fished a rough-hewn pencil from his pocket, meticulously added a check mark to *Empty dungeon toilets.*

On his way to the kitchens, he missed almost every rat with his carefully aimed boot. He'd already gathered the prisoners' food and water bowls that morning and checked that task from his list. Now he rinsed the bowls under scalding water, winced with each burn, and dumped them on the table. He filled the bowls, then rifled for his list and checked off *Fill bowls with fresh food and water.*

"Stupid prisoners," he grumbled at the bowls. "Stupid Grugrak the Fierce."

He cringed and looked over his shoulder. Complaining got orcs beheaded.

Feeling particularly rebellious, he withdrew his list, hunched over the table and very carefully wrote in his very best handwriting, face screwed up and biting the tip of his tongue, *Piss in food bowls.*

Korgak chuckled to himself as he slid the bowls into the prisoners' dank cells. He liked the way they eyed their bowls and made retching noises.

Back in the kitchens, Korgak cleaned the big orange bowl—the favored bowl of Grugrak the Fierce. Korgak filled it to the brim with gruel, glanced over his shoulder to make sure he was alone, then added a new line to his list and did his deed with another chuckle. He checked off *Spit in Grugrak's gruel.*

His next task was the highlight of his day. He completed *Torture the prisoners* with smiles and out-of-tune whistling. But when he returned the prisoners to their cells, he was met with a surprise—a skinny knight with long blond hair. Puny Lokolok held the end of the prisoner's chain.

"Found this outside skulking." Lokolok jangled the chain and flashed his rotten teeth. "Stupid human. Too small and slow."

"Get back outside," Korgak spat.

Lokolok grumbled and turned away.

Korgak yanked the prisoner's chain and did a double take. Prisoners never smiled. He gave the scrawny knight a suspicious glare as he stomped down to the end of the line, past all the broken knights who barely lifted their heads at the sight of him.

"Why you so scrawny?" Korgak asked as he shoved the newcomer into an empty cell and pulled the door shut with a clang. Knights never came pathetic. Months in the tower made them that way.

The newcomer raised a brow and cocked his head, hands on hips. "Are you really that daft? I heard orcs were stupid, but really."

Korgak made a blustery noise. Knights usually struggled and fought, never insulted. He leaned closer to the bars, furrowing his brows and looking quite menacing. He was proud of this practiced glower. Broken knights squirmed beneath it. "You not be smiling when I torture you tomorrow."

"You would torture a woman? A *princess*?"

Korgak snorted and stepped back. He'd never seen a human female. Frankly, they all looked the same to him. But now it made sense why he'd never seen one before. Females were small and weak. Why else would the village send only males in gleaming armor? The tower walls were slick as sewer slop, the rock hard as diamonds. Guards captured every knight who came in search of the secret entrance.

Korgak shrugged. "Make no difference to me. Sure you scream just the same."

But the female would not be cowed. She stepped from the gloom. Torchlight sparkled in her soft hair and long lashes—ugly as a swan. The corner of her mouth turned up. "I seek vengeance on your purple unicorn."

Korgak frowned, then burst into laughter. "You fight Krezul?" He doubled over with a painful belly laugh, then straightened and wiped his eyes. Tormenting weaker orcs had never been so funny.

"Your fire-breathing unicorn burned my kingdom. You filthy people are nothing without your beast to do your dirty work. Cowards, the lot of you."

Korgak clenched his fists. In that moment he didn't know which one he hated more: Grugrak the Fierce or this puny human female. He almost pulled out his list and added *Prisoner has accident with gruel processor* but managed to keep his fury in check. For now. Grugrak the Fierce liked to hear the prisoners scream. He'd not be happy to hear Korgak had killed one accidentally on purpose.

"Well, today's your lucky day, then," Korgak said with his most unpleasant smile. "You get your wish at four o'clock. Too bad you so slow." He laughed all the way to the can.

After relieving himself, Korgak had to make his mandatory appearance in the great hall. All orcs were required to demonstrate their fealty to Grugrak the Fierce with lots of song and dancing at three o'clock every day.

"Stupid Grugrak," Korgak muttered on the way out of the raucous hall. His thighs and throat burned. He checked off *Dance and sing like fool for Grugrak.*

Korgak dreamed of replacing Grugrak. Then he'd be able to play cards and drink all day. Have orcs dance and sing for him. Torture whenever the fancy struck him. He'd be the king's favorite, instead of Grugrak the Fierce. But that would only happen if Grugrak displeased the king.

Well, at least Korgak could nurse his wounded pride with a little fun. His next task was almost as thrilling as torturing prisoners, and the final count was always a mystery, which really was the best part.

Korgak released the prisoners, one at a time, chained them together in a line, and marched them to the great wooden door at the end of a maze of tunnels. They begged for mercy. Korgak liked that. Only the scrawny female was quiet. Korgak hoped she'd be among those who failed to report at the end of their run.

Korgak gripped the thick metal ring, gave it a hard twist, and heaved the heavy door open. Wooden planks screeched on the floor. Korgak had never added *Fix screeching door* to his list because it was the best way to put Krezul in a foul mood.

Korgak unhooked the prisoners and shoved them through the opening, one at a time. All but one struggled—the female had tied her long hair in a knot on her head, and she had a grin to match the smuggest of Grugrak's. Korgak slammed the door shut behind her.

The screams had already started.

Korgak checked off *Exercise the prisoners* and leaned on the door to wait, checking his watch from time to time.

As the end clicked closer, Korgak grew eager with anticipation. The prisoners were only too relieved when he finally opened the door and they spilled out in a steady trickle of smoke and pleasant smells of cooked hair and skin. None tried to escape. They never did. If they had the energy, they spent it putting out small fires in their clothes and beards.

Korgak forced them to their feet so they could be counted. He grinned when he reached the end of the line. Two missing. One male, one female. He checked off *Entertain the unicorn.*

"Stupid puny female. Too slow." He almost did a jig, but didn't want to risk appearing the fool in front of the prisoners.

He was about to close the door when one last knight came stumbling out of the unicorn's den. As the smoke cleared, Korgak's heart sank. The female had survived. He growled and adjusted his prisoner count, thinking again about adding *Prisoner has accident with gruel processor* to his list.

Korgak had just finished amending his list and tucking it away in a pocket when he noticed the wild grin on the female's soot-covered face, the streaks of purple blood all over her armor.

Confused, he ducked his head into the unicorn's den and rubbed his eyes, unable to believe what he saw. The great Krezul lay in a crumpled heap in the cavern, massive chest still and sword-pierced golden eye resting in a lake of viscous blood.

The female had slain a unicorn?!

He whirled on her, eyes wide. He opened his mouth dumbly.

How had the sword been missed? And how had a puny female managed to take down a *unicorn*? A unicorn that had burned a hundred villages and torched a thousand villagers?

As if reading his thoughts, the female said, "Retractable blade forged with Shadow Mountain magic. The only blade that could pierce unicorn flesh." Magic now spent, the blade dissolved, and the pommel clattered to the cavern floor. "And I'm faster than I look."

Korgak stared, stunned. Had the female *wanted* to be captured? And had Korgak fallen for her trap, even tossed her in with her quarry?

He couldn't believe it. The humans had succeeded in reaching the most closely guarded unicorn in the land. A purple unicorn released only to torch villages, to keep the humans scared. Korgak didn't care about politics. But he did care what the king would think.

The king would be most displeased, and Korgak knew who to blame.

He pulled his list from his pocket, a grin spreading across his face, and penciled in *Get Grugrak beheaded*, then checked it off. And since he was feeling especially generous given his upcoming promotion, he added *One free pass to prisoners after promotion ceremony.*

Dead Friends and New Horses

Sharon Dodge

I saw Macarty bobbing and weaving through the stable long before he saw me, and what I saw wasn't comforting. Even from this distance, I could see he was scared, moving too fast and catching the attention of all the horses and half the groomsmen. It was the south block, so it wasn't the busiest part of the stable, but a hundred horses is still plenty, especially with so many of them close to parturition.

The colony had six thousand members now, and it's not like we had the plasmass available to print out transports left and right. The horses ate up the local green matter just like it was hay, and they were fine so long as you supplemented and you made sure not too many got eaten by the local creatures. A good breeding program and a dozen mares, and twenty years later you had a nice organic transportation module that worked for old-school plowing, too. Not that we did that anymore, really, but there was a time.

"Belton, we got a problem," he said, stumbling into stride alongside me as I made my way down the line, checking on things generally: the state of tack, the freshness of hay, the number of available stalls.

"We do?" I asked. Sweet Bettie was getting along; we probably needed to move her soon. I liked to give the ones in foal a little extra space around their time. It's smarter, and safer, if a pain in the ass.

"Color's wrong," he said, and something about the way he bit at the word had me stopping short.

"What color's wrong?"

"The foal. She came early, way too early. Impossibly early, records must be wrong, and—and her color's wrong."

I swore and turned back where he'd come from. "Which?" I asked.

"Starmeadow," he said.

I swore again. We had some sixty mares in foal, but I knew Starmeadow wasn't close to time. "How early?" I asked. He wouldn't answer, so I moved faster, knees crackling with the effort.

Most animals had struggled to adapt to the change in days on the planet, but the horses had adjusted surprisingly well. The tour around the local star took almost two old Earth years, and with the change in the length of the day, the number of gestational days was shorter. Still, it took the same actual length, normally—the same hours, if you will. Gestation was still gestation.

"She premature, or just looking dysmature? You sure on gestation? We got jaundice?"

"I only saw her legs, though they weren't looking premature. Her days says she should be. But her color—" He went quiet again, though our feet were working even faster, and people and horses flowed out of our way, sensing the tension.

I didn't get much more out of him, not even the mare's previous gestational length, which would have given us a clue how bad this was. For some reason I couldn't pull it up on my flat, the thing insisting her files were all completed and unavailable.

Macarty meanwhile swore up and down Starmeadow hadn't been showing signs, no leaking colostrum, no vulvar laxity, no hint she was going into labor, though he also admitted they probably hadn't been looking too close since she was nowhere near term.

We finally rounded the corner, dropping to a slow walk as we did so. Macarty said that when they realized she was in labor, they'd moved her to the empty corner stall. He swore she'd barely gotten inside when she dropped the foal, and he'd gone running for me as soon as he saw the feet, which had me even more confused. Feet wouldn't show jaundice; how had he known her color was wrong?

The answer was clear as I looked over the stall door. I stood, a little stunned, watching everything. One of the corral girls, barely fifteen, was gently swabbing the foal's umbilical cord stump and clearing away a little of the afterbirth, carefully avoiding spooking the dam. I was surprised she was in there; normally, a proper hand would be handling the mare. The dam's placenta had already come out, and the foal was already standing, which wasn't normal.

The kid—Olympia?—was doing a good job, though, calm and gentle and methodical, and quick without seeming like it, too. I made a mental note to tag her in the logs; she was a good one, the kind of kid who belonged around here. She was out of the stall in a few minutes.

"Interesting horse, huh?" she said quietly.

"That's not a horse," I said, finally finding my tongue.

The thing in front of me had so many genemods I couldn't even count them. It had been a long time since molecular bio—everyone had to study it on the way over, back in the day; with a nine-year voyage, you were pretty lazy if you didn't have at least one PhD by the time you arrived—but even aside from the pale purple color, you had to be blind not to see the miniscule beard under its muzzle, or the leonine curve of that tail.

It even had a native block like the umph-bangs have embedded in the end of it, one of those weird mother-of-pearl things that some of the native creatures use to bludgeon prey to death while the larger of their mouths go in to crush the critter bit by bit into a nice, senseless, edible blob.

Its hooves weren't right, either, too slender, as were its legs, and the muscle that rippled along it seemed more like the impression of a horse than the real thing. The whole thing was too damn sinuous, too un-horselike, though its dam didn't seem to notice, nuzzling at it affectionately. It headed straight for her teats, too, none of this wandering-around nonsense that most foals do. No, this was pure programming, the jazzed-up dream of some nativist sympathizer, that was clear.

"It has a horn," Olympia said quietly, and I looked at her, disbelieving. I hadn't noticed one, and said so.

"It's just a little thing, a little … I don't know. A knob, kinda. But it's bigger than it was when it came out, and it's that same shiny color, like its tail. Like the umph-bangs have, you know."

I nodded; the kid wasn't slow.

"How did we not notice something in the medicals?" I asked, and Macarty crept up guiltily next to me.

"Ah, well, minor administrative issue," he said. "It seems quite a few of her appointments have been sort of missed. Signed off on, even though they didn't happen. And you know how it is, they get signed off, it's hell pulling up the old paperwork from the main server."

I groaned. I reviewed that paperwork, the summaries, anyhow, every month, but everyone knew I only glanced at the damn reports. It would have taken something big, usually an official red flag, for me to actually sit down and read. And no vet's going to look up old reports when there's no flagging. Not worth the trouble.

"How many days?"

"Two hundred twenty-nine."

Now that threw me; I sat down. Even with the change in day lengths, she should've made a good two-eighty, at least. This wasn't just tinkering with DNA; it was *really good* tinkering.

"I have to report this to the Standard," Macarty said slowly.

I growled. "Course you do. Just not today. I need to know where this came from. I'll send a notice about the pending investigation."

"I thought the nativists had all died off," Olympia said. She was watching the foal—hell, the damn unicorn—like it was the answer to her prayers. She'd laid her head on the stall door, a stupid kind of smile on her mouth.

"Mostly, kid," I muttered. "Mostly." The nativists had nearly brought us to a collapse twenty-some years ago, but believing you should be one with the planet's true nature had mostly led to a lot of suicides, or semi-suicides, depending on whether you believed they became one with the planet or just fertilizer. Kids Olympia's age barely knew anything about them, probably 'cause folks like me didn't like talking about them. As far as I was concerned, they were fertilizer, except one, and he was on his way.

I pulled up the records, looking for the sign-off. I groaned when I found it: it was my code. Well, the generic one, anyways, the one I gave out to a dozen administrators to use at some time or another when something failed and they needed to sign off on something. I shouldn't have been that stupid, but it had been a long time since I'd had to worry about security. I'd be real easy to hang for this.

"You should tell 'em to let her live," Olympia said. "I mean, maybe she could give the monsters a run for their money, protect the horses. She's going to have a horn, and she's got that tail. She could beat them at their own game. She could protect the herd." The kid started to get excited, turning to me. "My dad's on the Standard. I could tell him—"

"You just hold your horses, kid," I said softly but sharply, my tone reminding her to keep it down. Macarty snorted behind me. I forestalled her from speaking further, holding up a hand. "Macarty, I want you digging for whomever has seen this mare and signed off on any medical in the past four hundred days, and I want a thorough interview on each of them. Today. Go." He looked ready to protest, but with the look on my face, left after a minute.

Olympia looked at me with the wounded innocence only a kid her age could manage.

"Olympia, right?" I felt like a million years old as I said it.

She nodded grudgingly.

"Look, you may be the only thing between me and a real quick Excommunication," I said. "I appreciate it. But I need to be able to say more than I screwed up and whoops, we got a hybrid on our hands that we don't know anything about. A hybrid like they made when we first settled, when they were so sure we could modify our critters to live better here, but that ended up as Rollers and Killags and those horrible wounded rabbit-looking things that took so damn long to kill off. They don't take kindly to unplanned hybrids. I need a day or so, kid, and then you can throw everything you got at your father."

"Interviews won't help," she said. "They'll all find a way to blame someone else."

"Probably so," I agreed, amused. If I survived this mess, the kid was getting hired for real. "It's mostly busywork. I'm actually going to see an old friend."

❦ ✧ ❧

I still miss Joe. José Antonio Ramirez Suarez, really, but Joe to me. I talk to his widow, if that's what you should call her, now and again. She's getting her feet under her now, but there was a while when she was on the edge. Hell, I think we all were. Joe was one of the few that was almost as old as me, an old shitkicker picked off one of the last real working horse farms back on Earth. We knew he was sympathetic to the nativists, a lot of us old guys were, but no one ever really thought he *was* one. Least, I didn't.

He was right about it, though. While all the other nativists were doing crazy things like throwing themselves to the predators to become one with the planet ("One with shit," he'd say, and we'd all laugh), or jumping into the ponds of that glittering sludge covering so much of the planet, or even injecting themselves with the native microbes, he actually seemed to know what he was talking about.

If anyone was actually going to transition, the way to go about it would be through slow induction, like on one of those cliff faces where some of the birds we'd imported had been seized by the cliff sludge and integrated into it. They didn't always die straight off, you see; they were stuck like flies on sticky flypaper, desperately trying to escape. And the sludge didn't exactly eat them.

Joe had done a lot of studying en route to the planet and had become the most serious specialist we had on the planetary natives. He'd showed me once some of the data he'd pulled off the sludge. It was crazy—what little I could understand of it: wild perturbations in the brain and flesh of the poor little aves, comingling of DNA and thought and pattern. He figured they died only because they starved or dehydrated. A few of them had managed to nip a few insects from the air, and they survived much longer.

I figured that's where he got the idea. Like a lot of us here, Joe and Loua lost their youngest kid a few years back. Colony life is never easy: disease, and the native creatures (some say monsters), not to mention the wild wet season and the storms that come through. Truth was, her death was nastier than most. She survived the initial attack from a Roller, but was torn up bad. She didn't make it in the end.

After that, the fight sort of went out of them both. He'd done so much good work, fixing a lot of the mistakes some of those idiots had made on arrival. Made us all feel safe, really, even with what happened to his little girl. I think, stupid as it sounds, we all figured that just meant he'd conquer Rollers next. Only instead he went to the cliff.

By the time we found the note, Joe had strapped himself to the cliff face, a medical assist device under him, an IV in his hand, and a food tube at mouth level. Don't let anyone tell you different, that sludge moves fast. By the time we got there, it had moved over most of his body, dissolving what, I guess, it had identified as dead matter: his clothes, most of his hair and eyelashes, even some of his nails. It was pretty horrible.

He seemed surprised we'd found him so quickly. I guess he hadn't expected I'd remember where those birds had been, all those years before. We considered trying to pull him free, but he assured us he'd just die then, bereft of the greater Colony. He was a little out of it, and we weren't exactly sure what we could do, but we finally left him alone to talk with his wife.

Loua told me, later, that he said he'd wanted to learn whether there was a greater mind on the planet, didn't want to die without knowing if there was a real way to understand the alien—the unknown here on this planet. Said he didn't belong anymore there with her, as if he belonged strapped up there on the side of that cliff.

She'd gone back to visit him in the subsequent months, daily for a while even, though I heard she'd stopped about a month ago. I'd visited regularly, too, at first, but truth was I hadn't been in a long time. I wasn't even sure there was a him truly left to visit, but he was the only living nativist I knew of now, if living he was.

It's a short trip there with a good horse, and I was at the cliff that some call Mount Olympus in two hours. It was a tiny thing compared to the real thing, but most of the kids here had never seen anything resembling a mountain in this flat land. Folks like me, first-landers who knew what real mountains looked like, were mostly dead and gone now, one way or another.

I left my gelding far below the cliff's face; I didn't want to risk it touching any of the sludge, so I ground hitched it before I started up. Thankfully, Joe hadn't gone far. If it had been me, I'd have gone as high as I could, so I could have a good view for the rest of eternity. But he'd found an outcropping of rock that, I guess, he'd thought felt like a good seat to spend the rest of his life in, and it wasn't too far up. Easier to visit, at any rate.

I almost wished I hadn't found him when I got there. He'd assured me many times he felt no pain, and within two months of his transition's start, the tubes were long gone as he'd begun synthesizing his dietary needs. But his legs and arms had long been absorbed, and here and there parts of his bone were exposed. His torso was mostly veiled, for which I was grateful, but his head remained stubbornly visible, to our simultaneous relief and disgust. Joe still talked, in a way, though his vocal chords had developed a distinctly sappy sound, a wet smack, almost, in every word.

Now that I had him in front of me, his lips, and a lot of other parts, looked ready to go. He used to stand out from the wall, a little, anyhow, but now he was all sucked into it, head turned awkwardly so I could only see one eye really. I thought I could see part of his spinal column peeking out at the nape of his neck. I didn't meet his eye as I said hello.

"J-Joe," I stuttered.

"I had almosst givnup," he said, the words slurring together. His jaw barely moved. This was it, I realized, this was why Loua had stopped coming. "Wanted to say good-bye, old friend." The D was a whisper. I had a feeling there wasn't much tongue left. I shivered, then sucked it up and looked at him.

"Loua didn't tell me," I said, embarrassed, trying to pretend I didn't see what I saw. "Hell, Joe, I'd have come earlier. I'm sorry."

"Ah. May have felt it was … unfair to ask. Some disturbed. I told her you would not … mind."

I tried to act like I didn't, and nodded.

"You're going be even more annoyed when I tell you why I'm here," I said. I sighed and pulled out my flat. I leaned as close to him as I could make myself and showed him the picture of the unicorn. "Seems like an old friend of yours is doing some interesting things to my horses."

"Yesssss," he slurred, and I tried not to shudder as something dripped off his lip. My stomach churned, and I couldn't help myself; I looked away. "Fassscinating," he murmured, his eye moving quickly over the picture.

"You regret your decision?" I asked.

"You always ask," he hissed, though not unkindly, glancing toward me. I guess it was hard for him not to hiss now.

"I hate the thought of you suffering for however the hell long this shit lives. I could laser this whole damn cliff side, and you'd be gone. Over. Done."

"It isss beautiful," he said. That's what he always said. Sometimes I woke up in the night, wondering if it made him say that. Maybe he was right, and it was alive and conscious, but how did we know it was *good*?

"You like the unicorn?" I said abruptly, turning back to the picture.

"Horn?" he said.

"Yeah, I didn't see it either," I said. "There's a little nubbin. See?" I zoomed in on the head, then held up the flat again for him to look, and an *mmm* issued from his throat.

"Excellent. They will have good … defenssse."

"Yeah, and they used my code to get away with it. I'll be hanged for this. Maybe literally. We're talking Excommunication."

"No … problem. You ssstay at myplace," Joe hissed, and I laughed. His lip curled in something I was pretty sure was supposed to be a smile. "Hybrid is necessary to sssurvival. But if you are … thinking I can … tell you who … did this, do not know. I would have sssaid me. I sssuggested … horn implant. Defense."

"Oh." I felt deflated, and put the flat back in my pocket. "You were my big lead."

"Take sssampling. Review. Maybe … genetissist could guessss handiwork. Someone who liked my work."

It took me a second to figure out what he said with his words running together, but when I did, I brightened and mumbled a thanks, my eyes still on the much less unnerving-looking floor. I shuffled my feet nervously. It was hard to know what to say. Had Joe died that day he'd strapped himself here, or was he dying today? What do you say when someone's maybe not even the someone you knew?

"You really still you?" I asked. I'd never asked that before. It had seemed kind of rude, though Loua had told me she'd asked him many times.

"Yesss. And … no." He paused, seemed to think. "I am more me when we sspeak. I will soon be part of … greater. We will watch out for you. Wanted you … know. Not gone."

"I guess that's nice. Someone on this planet being on our side." It was kind of nice, actually. Better than thinking he was just going to be fertilizer, or under the control of whatever the hell the sludge was. I could almost believe it, him saying it like that.

"May I sssee hergain?" he asked.

I nodded, and pulled out the unicorn for him to see. After a second's thought, I managed to draw a live feed. You couldn't see all of her properly, but he could see her in action at least. The nubbin, I saw, had grown ever so slightly. I held the flat back up to his eye, closer to him than I'd ever risked before.

"Beautiful," he whispered, so quiet I almost couldn't hear. "Please do not let them end her," he said, each word gently drawn out. "If you bring … her, we will protect. We will bring her water, and not make her part of … usss."

"I don't think it'll be up to me, Joe," I said. "But I'll keep it in mind."

I paused a second, and then moved directly in front of his eye so he could see my face while I spoke. I didn't flinch this time.

"This is it, right?" I said.

"Yess. I was only waiting for … you," he said.

"You sure this is what you want?"

"Isss wanted," he said.

I nodded. I tried to think of the right thing to say, to tell him he was the best friend I'd ever had and I didn't want him to go, that these kids didn't remember the things we did, that no one would understand me when he was gone, but it didn't matter, because his eye imploded then, softly, the sludge shimmering gently over it to cover its crime.

"Oh, Joe, oh, man," I said, my words panicked and high. "You're sure, Joe? You're sure?"

"Isssokay," he said, the words barely comprehensible. "Goodfrien. Thank. You. Isss … beautiful." And with that, his jaw collapsed inward, a soft de-molding of his bones that the sludge gently embraced. The whole wall started to shimmer—I'd never seen that before—and I watched it for a second before I turned and got the hell out of there, racing down the cliff as fast as I could, half blind with grief.

By the time I got back to my horse, I couldn't see anything shimmering up on the cliff face, and I felt ashamed, but I also didn't go back.

ꕥ ✧ ꕥ

I went by Loua's as soon as I was back, and told her, in a gentle, somewhat censored fashion, what I'd seen. She nodded briefly, calmly, and I was surprised to notice a little gray in her hair. It'd had been a hard year, I knew, but in my head she was still that pretty young thing that Joe had somehow won over. Was she nearing fifty? I couldn't remember. I guess the years were catching up to all of us.

I didn't ask her why she hadn't told me he was waiting for me, though I wanted to. She looked too blank, lost. She didn't even notice when I stopped talking finally. I guessed she was losing him all over again, too. I left after that, heading back to the stables, where apparently the secret foal had been kept none too secret, and a crowd had gathered. I took one look and told them to leave or I'd call enforcement. A few troublemakers asked me if they thought that would keep my job, and I rounded on them quickly enough, still raw from Joe.

"Dam needs to bond with the foal. You screw that up and it dies, I'll hang you myself. Get out." That cleared them out fast enough. The colostrum is critical in horses, since foals are born without any kind of real immune system, so I wasn't being totally unreasonable, even if at this point I was pretty sure she'd had her fill. Still, I owed the creature a little privacy, and a chance. Maybe the Standard would declare it unacceptable, but I wouldn't have it die on my account.

It was steady on its feet already, suckling happily, and by all appearances was doing just fine. Still, I watched it for a few hours, albeit from a distance, and through the slats. I finally left to talk to some of the splicers about who might be a good candidate for its creator, which led to some interesting glances among the crew. Who had broken the rules? I got nothing for my trouble and gave up after few attempts.

Back at my place, I checked my flat again and saw that Olympia had written. *Sorry, talked to Father*, the message said. *The word was out. He's on your side. They'll convene tomorrow noon.* I sighed, though the news hadn't been entirely unexpected. Nice kid, that Olympia. Reminded me of my Allie, back in the day. Or at least the grandkid we might've had, if she'd made it. Macarty had finished a few token interviews, and I read through those, too, though I could tell he wasn't really trying. It was a needle in a haystack, and we both knew it.

I tried to sleep, but two hours later staring up at the ceiling, I realized I was an idiot. If I'd built a unicorn, I'd want to see the thing, wouldn't I? I swore, threw my pants back on, and raced to the stable, flat in hand, ordering the computer to pull up all the feeds and everyone who'd visited or had so much as checked out a script on simple genetics in the past seventy years. The list was long; it was kind of a hobby on the planet, after all.

I told the computer to drop the ones with only an interest in flora, and that cut the numbers pretty substantially. Vegetable farming was useful around here, and after the disastrous attempts twenty years ago, there wasn't much tinkering with the fauna. Too dangerous. The remaining list, crossed against the video feed, left only a few candidates, but in the end, none of it mattered. There was only one person besides Olympia who stayed to watch that unicorn for hours, dreamily, a mother's proud smile on her lips.

I'd been right all along, in a way. So had Joe. I should've seen it. I checked on the unicorn one last time before I started walking to Loua's. I was pretty annoyed she hadn't saved me the trouble initially, honestly.

When she opened the door, I started up fast. "You could have told me when I saw you before," I said.

"News of Joe kind of threw me," she said tiredly. She didn't even bother to pretend, the truth plain on her face. "I was going to tell him myself, you know. Show him. I'm glad he got see it. That why I didn't tell you he wanted to see you. I knew she was so close."

Surprised, I nodded. Not that I was happy, but at least I felt less betrayed.

"I'm surprised he didn't figure it was me, Bel. They were Vi's favorite. She used to say the umph-bangs used to be unicorns. 'Cause of their tails, you know?" She sighed and opened the door wider, letting me in. The smell of coffee was in the air, and she poured me a cup in short order.

I sat down across from her at the old standard-provision table, its legs almost as wobbly as my own back home. The fury radiating from me slowing to a trickle. She barely seemed to notice I was there, holding a cup of coffee, but not drinking it.

I wondered about what she'd said: if he had guessed. Maybe he'd been trying to mislead me, to protect her. I didn't want to think that, though I didn't want to think he'd betray her, either. Maybe he really hadn't guessed. I could be stupid, but I was pretty sure I wasn't the only one who had thought she was just your average microbial splicer, working on nice oxygen-producing algae, the kind of person everyone pushed paperwork off on. Paperwork. Of course. Everyone loved to ask good old Loua to finish off the paperwork.

"He didn't even ask about the other kids when I saw him last," she said sadly. "I don't think it was all him at the end, no matter his I'm-still-me crap. *Mi José habría preguntado.*"

"You planning to stand up behind this?"

"Why?" she asked calmly. Her eyes didn't seem quite focused. "Call it a mysterious accident. A wonderful permutation. That horn'll grow, you know. It'll be a hell of an impaler. I put in some killer instinct, protective instinct. And it loves girls. It'll take on a Roller before it lets one get hurt. I made sure Olympia was there, you know. Moved the schedules. It imprinted. Probably pretty fond of you now, too."

"Things don't work that way, Loua," I said, annoyed. "Nearly everyone here has a background in biology. It's nice work, but it's Earth-based. Any fool could see that." I put down the untouched coffee and sighed. She wasn't exactly doing me any favors.

"I guess so," she said. "Everyone's got too much time now. Twenty years ago, it wouldn't have mattered. The storms, and the Kyros proliferation. I guess I forget things have changed."

I snorted. Goslings acting like they were geese.

"What are you going to do?" she asked.

I sat a moment, waiting for an answer, thinking of Joe. Finally, I spoke. "Joe left around Herasios, right? Before the fall festival?"

She nodded. "A few days after, I think."

"Good," I said. "Do you think you can change a date?"

The Standard was fully assembled for the *graphe*, the public hearing, which was unsettling in and of itself. I couldn't remember the last time they'd all bothered to show up.

The live feed of the foal was up on a large flat as evidence, and everyone was eying it with interest. Talk fluttered up and down in waves of sound, *unicorn* and *purple* and *magical* and a hundred other silly words jumping out at me as I walked past the mass of attendants. The members of the Standard, unfortunately, were not the source of those comments. I was pretty sure which one was Olympia's father, based on cheekbones, but he looked just as severe as the others.

When it came time for me to speak, I laid it out slow and simple. People seemed to accept the administrative error pretty calmly, and we all agreed that the loophole would have to be closed, which was a relief. My hands stopped shaking after that part, at least. I verified the state of the foal's health, had its genetic history up on the wall—we'd taken a sampling that morning—and it was pretty clear from the tweaking that it wasn't a magic hybrid, as Loua had suggested I maintain. Too much Earth in that coding, too many biologists on the Standard.

"I can't say for sure where this originated," I finally said, *because you'd hang her*, I thought, sorting through my words as carefully as I could, "but it's clear it can be of use. If I had to guess, when I saw it, I thought this is very much like where Joe's line of work was. He opted for—well, everyone knows about his transition. I never heard of anyone who was as good a splicer as he was, who knew the planetary fauna like he did. He could've managed it, before he left. You can check the insemination log. It shows it was two days before his departure." It was a lie, but the paperwork confirmed it. I apologized, quietly, in my head to my friend. "He loved farewell gifts, grand gestures." True enough. "Unfortunately, he can't be questioned or held responsible, as he has truly passed, or transitioned, or whatever you want to call it. I went to the cave, and there's nothing left of him now."

Also true, if not what it sounded like; I didn't want questions about our last conversation. A gasp went around the room, and I tried not to show relief at their shock, at the distraction that would help me. I should've remembered I hadn't been Joe's only friend.

"I informed Loua already, in case you're wondering. You can check the cliff side yourself. I hope you'll give it—give her—a chance," I said. "The foal. She wasn't planned by the community, and she sure wasn't legal, but she sure is a pretty thing." I cleared my throat and sat down.

I was stuck there waiting, but thankfully it wasn't long. It was good none of them knew me closely, or they'd have seen in the stillness of my form how utterly terrified I was. About an hour after the Standard had gone into private session, a probationary offer was extended to the as-yet-unnamed foal of a limited life license. I idly wondered if I could get away with asking Loua what she'd like to call it.

I ducked my head to all the right people and got out of there as fast as I could, citing the foal's health. I felt eyes on the back of my head like a thousand buzzing flies I couldn't hope to swat away. I wondered how many people really believed me about Joe, and I finally decided I didn't care so long as I wasn't Excommunicated and the foal was alive.

Olympia and Macarty were at the stall when I got there. They both looked a little guilty. I turned off the video feed first thing so no one at the Standard could see us anymore. It wasn't legally required now.

"Ya'll planning on springing her if they voted her down?" I asked.

"Something like that," Olympia said, though Macarty harrumphed and said nothing.

The unicorn nickered and came up to me, its dam protectively right behind. I let it smell me, then gave it a good petting. It rubbed its head into my hands, leaving a barely visible hint of glitter in its wake that reminded me of the sludge Joe was now.

The lies I'd made, by implication at any rate, troubled me, though not as much as I'd have guessed. I'd been honest in a way. Loua had worked on the foundation Joe had left, after all. It was probably as much his baby as it was hers. I should have told them, maybe, about Loua. She wasn't exactly stable, and I'd have to make sure she didn't get into any more mischief, but then again, maybe she was done. Joe's passing had knocked her down again, maybe forever. We'd see.

"Did he say why he made her purple?" Olympia asked lazily, sidling up next to me with that earnest-kid look again.

"Oh, he didn't admit to anything," I said, then winced when I remembered I'd implied Joe had been dead when I arrived. She grinned proudly at me, pleased at having snuck the truth from me. "Damn. You're right, he was alive when I got there, though you don't need to go spreading that. But his kid's name was Violet. She died a bit back."

"Oh. That's sad," she said, a little of the smugness fading. "Guess that's how you figured it out. Smart."

I shrugged. It had only occurred to me while I was in front of the Standard. I was a quick one, all right. Any quicker and I'd turn to stone where I stood.

"It'll be fine," Olympia said, certainty in her voice.

"Glad one of us is sure," I said.

"No, it will be," she said, her voice gaining strength. "I was born here, too. We natives are strong. It's like … she was meant to be, kinda. We should call her Athena," she said.

I barked a laugh, unsettling Starmeadow briefly before I quieted down and we both stilled.

"That'll work, I guess," I said finally, softly. "I'm sure they'll love that." Loua would, I knew it. Joe would have, too. Maybe I'd even go back to tell him, on the off chance he could understand. Not sure words would matter much anymore to him, but you never knew. Things had a way of changing around here when I wasn't paying attention, people growing older, the world changing.

If nothing else, maybe I'd bring Athena on by to show her off, just near the cliff's edge, just so she could see where she sprang from. Everyone should know where they came from. Everyone should have a place where they belong.

The Godfairy

Quincy J. Allen

Small fists pounded on my front door, waking me out of what I wished had been a permanent coma. With a titanic headache pressed between my sweaty palms, I watched two dwarves in green police uniforms barge into my bedroom. They dragged me to my feet, informing me that my "old friend" Lumpy was calling in a solid I owed him.

"Lumpy, huh?" I managed over the cotton-swathed tongue wallowing in my mouth. I glanced at my cuckoo clock: six in the morning. I didn't care what Lumpy needed, getting me up at six would settle accounts … *like it or not.*

I was still dressed in a thoroughly wrinkled brown suit, so I was ready to go. My head spun from the previous night's bender. I'd been with three gruff but amiable elves who thought they could outdrink me. They were wrong, of course, but it took everything I'd had to be the last—and only—man standing. Hell, I was the only human in this godforsaken hellhole of cheery smiles, carefree dancing, and happy endings. Well, mostly happy. While I cursed daily the misbegotten deity of mischief that sent me here, I gave equal thanks that the place had a dark enough underbelly to keep me working, otherwise I would have blown my brains out a week after waking up in Fairyland.

It's a long story, and that was five years ago.

Anyway, the two little constables tugged at my arms, dragging me headlong out of my low-rent apartment. I was barely conscious, but I figured I'd wake up on the way to … wherever. They both kept idiot grins on their faces as they pulled me along. In Fairyland, nearly everyone walks around with sickeningly bright smiles all the time. At least in daylight. Except me, of course. I'm a curmudgeon. I generally do my best to avoid daylight—hence the drinking at night with gruff but amiable elves.

The constables poured me into a filigreed blue carriage pulled by four pink ponies that literally pranced the entire way. We bounced from the poor side of town through a few posh neighborhoods and out into the countryside. An hour later, the dwarves dumped me in front of a tall flight of stone steps that led to two massive oaken doors carved with a menagerie of mythical creatures. The doors were set into a bastion of white marble walls stretching high and wide. As the carriage pulled away, ponies prancing gleefully, one of the diminutive officers poked his head out the window, waved, and, I swear, winked at me.

I stood in the bright morning sunshine, a million colors reflecting off every surface. Dewdrops shimmered beneath the pregnant bellies of delicate petals. Bees trundled hither and yon. A troop of pixies in flowing gowns of yellow and green darted out from behind the castle. Their fluttering gossamer wings of gold carried them over a crystal blue moat full of dazzling koi and into the Whispering Wind Forest beyond.

What a load of crap, I thought, wishing my head would just come apart and get it over with.

I turned and stared up at the castle. It was right out of some fairy tale—no surprise—with pointy towers and broad turrets poking up into a cobalt blue sky. They made a hodgepodge skyline, suggesting the architect preferred form considerably more than function. Pinions of blue, pink, and white fluttered from each tower apex on a breeze that somehow didn't reach the ground.

A door opened, revealing a plump dwarf in a crimson suit. His purple boots seemed far too narrow to support his considerable girth as he trundled down the steps. He eyed me like I was a beloved dog that had just left a small carcass on his doorstep. I never moved. I figured this was his show. When he reached the bottom, he stared up at me with the SOP idiot grin, but it looked forced.

I stared down through fiercely bloodshot eyes. "So why the hell am I here, Lumpy?"

His smile straightened, albeit slightly, and he raised one bushy, brown eyebrow. "It's *Detective* Lumpy, Vincent," he said in a voice that reminded me of sucking on helium balloons.

"Right, right," I mumbled. "Detective." I tried to rub some of the hangover out of my eyes and failed. *Never underestimate the insidious power of faewine.* I made the mental note with the absolute certainty I'd lose said wisdom by lunchtime.

He looked at me expectantly with the understanding patience reserved for buddies suffering self-inflicted wounds. I'd given him the same look a few times over the years. I remember this troll he'd become enamored with—big girl, green, ugly as the south end of a warthog—but she floated his boat. She turned out to be a pro. I'd warned him, but he wouldn't listen until after she'd taken him for a quarter of his life's savings.

He kept waiting, that patient, forced smile as unwavering as a pixie's virginity. Through the haze of my hangover, I got what he was after.

"So, *Detective* Lumpy," I said slowly, my voice pressing into my skull, "why the hell am I here?"

"It's inside," he replied, his smile turning grim. He trundled up the stone steps and opened one of the massive double doors, stepping inside. In the distance, coming from some faraway room of the palatial interior, I heard a dwarf shouting, presumably into a phone. I heard another dwarf—smaller and female—wailing in another part of the house, sounding as if the sky had just fallen.

Ignoring the voices, Lumpy marched up the stairs that rose before us. I managed to keep up without stumbling, and we came to an open set of double doors. Beyond lay a bedroom the likes of which only the very wealthy ever see—unless a crime brings cops and private detectives like me bumbling about to put things aright.

There, on one side of the bed, covering most of what was certainly a downy pillow, was something I never thought I'd see.

I sighed and did my best to keep from emptying my stomach on the plush beige carpet. Five years since I'd crossed over into this insane asylum and you'd think I'd be accustomed to seeing unicorns.

Granted, this was only part of one, but still.

I glanced at Lumpy. I'd never seen him so angry. He couldn't take his eyes off the thing. Stuff like this wasn't supposed to happen in Fairyland.

"I take it you want me to find out whoever put that purple unicorn head where it doesn't belong?" I asked.

He nodded.

I stepped up to the bed and leaned over, examining the pale purple head and the deep purple mane that flowed over the edge of the pillow. Something caught my eye. I moved a few strands of mane aside and exposed several glittery flecks on the satin beneath. I licked the tip of my finger and pressed it against one of the sparkles. Drawing my finger back, I peered closely and watched the fleck disappear in a tiny flash of light.

Interesting.

"And the voice downstairs," I said, glancing at Lumpy. "The male one. He owns this place?"

Another nod.

I turned and walked past him, stepping through the double doors. Pausing, I said over my shoulder, "This makes us even, right?"

A final nod.

Without another word, I headed downstairs.

At the bottom, I turned away from the male voice, now speaking quietly enough that I couldn't make anything out, and headed towards the female voice. It's been my experience—in both worlds, mind you—that females, no matter the species, are more inclined to open up than males when something terrible has happened. Hell, most of my solved cases can be traced straight back to a lady who only wanted someone to put things right.

I turned down a hallway and spotted an office to the right. I figured I'd do a bit of snooping before tracking down the feminine voice. Stepping in like I owned the place, I headed over to a broad oaken desk, ignoring the books and bric-a-brac that filled the room.

I scanned the surface, skipping over an assortment of paperweights, and spotted a notepad next to what passed for a telephone in Fairyland. No wires, gem-encrusted, works on magic—but don't ask me to tell you how. There were faint impressions in the notepad, but I couldn't make them out.

On a hunch, I held my breath, carefully picked up the phone, and covered the receiver.

"… I'll pay you when Ulion freezes over!" the dwarf's voice hissed, and then the receiver slammed down. Ulion is the dwarven notion of hell, by the way.

I kept listening in case the person on the other end had some parting words. I wasn't disappointed.

"Stupid, Hammerhand," a squeaking, gravelly voice said, and then there was a click as another receiver went down.

Hammerhand? The name rang a bell, but I couldn't place it.

The second voice had been a fairy—an old female by the sound of it, perhaps with a smoking habit. I replaced the receiver and looked over the desk one more time. A quick glance in the wastebasket revealed a pile of discarded pages and one crumpled sheet from the notepad. Someone had been upset with whatever was on it.

I picked it out and un-crumpled it carefully. It had a single line of dwarven script. Fortunately for me, I could read dwarven.

Exacta—Jujubean Dream, Yellow Rose of the Whispering Wind

A satisfied smile crossed my lips. *This is going to be easier than I thought.*

"Nobody is supposed to come into my father's office," a feminine dwarf's voice said from the doorway. Her voice was soft, almost meek, and I picked up a trace of fear, as if being in the office was harmful to one's health. *Also interesting.*

She was short, dimpled, and around forty—roughly her mid-teens in human years. Her eyes were puffy, her cheeks still showing traces of tears. She wore a purple dress with little golden hammers embroidered at neck, cuff, and hem. A dainty milkmaid's hat held back a good portion of thick red curls.

"Hmm?" I asked innocently. "Oh! Sorry. I was looking for a pen." I reached down and picked one off the desk. I glanced at a cuckoo clock on the wall and scribbled the time on my palm. "There, see?" I held up my palm for her.

"What's that for?" she asked, confused.

"I'm on the clock now."

"For what?" Her head canted sideways.

"I'm working with the constables to help solve the—"

Her face paled, and it looked like she was going to start wailing. She'd clearly been close to the dismembered *Equus unicornis* whose head decorated the boudoir. I figured it was best to tap dance around the grisly particulars.

"—Errr … *problem* your family is dealing with." I stepped around the desk and held out my hand. "I'm Vincent Capaldi."

"Capaldi?" The imminent wailing retreated, replaced by a perplexed look. "That's a funny sort of name. I've never seen anyone like you before."

I smiled and shook her hand. "The name is Italian. So am I."

"What's an Italian?"

"It's a long story." I stepped out of the office and into the hallway. "Look, I don't want to upset you, but is there someplace we can talk? I really do want to help."

Her eyes started to tear up, but she sniffled once and put a brave face on things. "Yes," she said quietly. "The patio."

She stepped past me, and I followed her down the hall to a wide living room with a series of tall glass doors that opened up onto a lavish patio surrounded by flowers in every color of the rainbow. We stepped through an already open door, and I tried not to show my disgust with the multicolored vegetation. She sat at a low, wrought iron table surrounded by dwarf-sized chairs that would never hold my weight—or my butt for that matter.

She realized the problem and looked embarrassed. I smiled, despite all those colors pouring into my throbbing skull, and sat on the flagstones across from her.

"Don't worry," I said easily. "I'm used to it." I chuckled, which got a glimmer of smile out of her. "So, what's your name?"

"Darian."

"Hello, Darian," I said. "What can you tell me about last night? Was there anything that woke you up?"

"No." She frowned, and I could see her struggling to hold back tears. "I woke up this morning when Daddy started shouting. I ran to his bedroom to see what was wrong, and that's when I saw—" Tears flowed down her rosy cheeks, but she seemed determined to go on. "That's when I saw what they'd done to Dancer!" She sniffed once and covered her mouth. She was a tough kid, no doubt about it.

"I'm sorry, Darian."

"Father looked terrified," she continued, "and then he looked furious. At first I thought he was mad because of what they did to my unicorn, but father always hated Dancer. And Dancer hated him back. My mother gave me Dancer for my thirty-fifth birthday."

Thirty-five is sort of a "sweet sixteen" for dwarves. But something seemed odd about the way she'd referred to the matron of the family.

"Where was your mother?" I asked.

"She doesn't live here," she replied. No guilt or anger, just the matter-of-fact acceptance of how things are. I did pick up a twinge of regret, as if Darian preferred her mother's company to her father's.

"I see." Something didn't add up. The estate didn't match up with a guy who couldn't pay a gambling debt. Yes, gambling debt, but I'll get to that later. On a hunch, I said, "So, this is quite a place your father has."

"Oh, it's not his, not really," she said. "It belongs to my mother. She's the rich one. Daddy is just the governor, and that doesn't pay much."

Bingo! I smiled. I was going to have this little caper solved in no time. Hell, Lumpy was going to owe *me*.

"Can I help you?" It was the voice of the dwarf on the phone. His question had been gruff but not angry, like I was just some party crasher. I could tell that years of politicking had taught him to "maintain low tones" even when he finds a stranger on his patio the same morning someone puts a severed unicorn head in his bed.

I turned to see a middle-aged dwarf with slicked back red hair and what passed for an expensive suit in Fairyland: green silk, gold buttons, high collar, and black leather shoes with the toes curling up to a point.

"Good morning, Governor Hammerhand," I said. I rose to my feet, fighting off some spins and more pounding behind my eyes, and held out my hand. "I'm Vincent Capaldi. Detective Lumpy—I mean Detective *Ironsoul*—brought me in as a specialist on your case."

"Are you a specialist in dead horses?" he asked, his eyes narrowed suspiciously. There clearly wasn't any love lost between him and the unicorn.

"Not at all, sir," I replied easily. "I deal mostly with the more unsavory sorts who exist outside the boundaries of civil society." I locked eyes with him. "And I suspect you have some idea of the sort of people I'm talking about. Would you agree, sir?" I gave him my best *I-know-what-you've-been-up-to* smiles. "Detective Ironsoul also brought me in because I'm exceedingly *discreet*."

He hesitated and licked his lips. I watched him calculate risks and benefits, practically reading them fly across his face.

"Darian," he finally said, "would you go in and fix Daddy some breakfast?" His eyes never left mine. *He treats her like hired help,* I thought.

"Yes, Father," she replied and slipped past me with another sniffle. I suspected it was habit that made her close the door behind her, even though it had been open when I came in. I also suspected she recognized his tone: the one grown-ups use when they're going to talk business that doesn't concern children.

"Let me explain." He took a deep breath, like he was about to give a speech.

"Don't bother, Governor," I broke in. "I know just about everything I need."

"You couldn't possibly—"

"I'm very good at my job," I interrupted. I wanted to keep him off balance, mostly because it would be easier to get at anything he might try to hide, but also because I'd developed a mild disliking for him. What can I say? I'm ornery in the morning. "Would you like me to prove it to you?" I asked. I did my best to sound smug.

His face scrunched up dubiously. "I'm all ears."

I looked him up and down, as if sizing him up. "You like the ponies—not unicorns; you don't give a damn about them. You like the kind that go fast. The kind people bet on even when gambling is illegal for Fairyland's civil servants." His eyes grew wide, and I wondered if he was going to deny it. I pressed on like a freight train. "In fact, you bet on an exacta recently, and you bet *heavy*." I smiled as his denial turned to fright. On a hunch I added, "I'm guessing someone sold you an inside tip. Said it was a sure thing." I figured a guy like him—one who habitually spoke in low tones—wouldn't bet heavy on anything but a sure thing. "But the exacta didn't come in—and now you're on the hook for a cartload of gold, which is tough to come by on civil servant wages. Even a governor's." I'd destroyed him, but I felt like adding a little icing to the cake. "Does Mrs. Hammerhand mind you betting *her* money on ponies?"

He looked like he was going to pass out, and I was the one with the hangover. I stepped back and pulled out one of the little chairs for him. He moved forward, unsteady on his feet, and plopped down.

"How could you—?"

"Like I said," I interrupted again, "I'm very good at what I do." I sat down cross-legged on the flagstones in front of him and started in again. "I know you told the people responsible that you won't pay them, which means you won't ask your wife for the money, which also means you're more afraid of her than you are of them." I peered at him expectantly. "Why is that, Governor?"

"Because I won't divorce her," he said flatly.

It suddenly all made sense. "I see," I said. "If she files for divorce without due cause, you get half of everything." Let's just say I work on a lot of snoop cases that end in divorce. "But if you ask her to pay a gambling debt, she'll have your cojones over a fire—"

"My what?" he asked, bewildered.

"Umm … I mean that she'll have the leverage she needs to take everything *and* put you out of a job. A scandal like this ends careers. I take it you and the Mrs. aren't on good terms?"

"Orcs and elves get along better than we do." The disgusted look on his face was priceless. Rocks and hard places didn't hold a candle to where this poor sod found himself.

"Right," I said with an almost compassionate tone. "So now you get to choose between death at the hands of fairy mobsters or divorce, disgrace, and poverty." I managed to hold back the smile struggling to split my face. This guy had gotten himself into a real mess. "That's a tough call."

He just nodded.

"Where can I find the fairy?" I asked.

"Where else?" he replied. "At the track."

"She got a name?"

"The Godfairy," he grumbled.

"Seriously?"

"Do I look like I'm kidding?"

"No," I said. "Look, I think I can sort this out."

He looked at me hopefully. "Do you really think you can help me?"

"I'm not helping *you,* Governor." I watched his hope crumble like the burning timbers of a fire-gutted cottage. "I'm doing this to repay a debt I owe Ironsoul—and for a little girl who I suspect just lost her best and possibly only friend."

He didn't say a word.

I stood up and stepped past him, dusting off the seat of my trousers. I walked up to the glass door and opened it.

"Oh, and Governor," I said over my shoulder. "Don't *do* anything until you hear from me—probably later today."

"Don't worry. All I can really do is sit here and wait for an avalanche to hit me."

"That's a good way to look at it," I added and stepped through the door. As I walked down the hallway, I heard soft footsteps coming down the stairs. Darian met me at the bottom.

"Mr. Capaldi?" she asked meekly. I could tell she was embarrassed to ask for whatever she wanted.

"What can I do for you, Darian?" I knelt down so we were eye to eye.

She suddenly stiffened, and I saw fire in her eyes. "I want you to *get* the people who did this to Dancer!" she blurted.

It broke my heart to see a kid that young get her first desire for revenge. The world can be tough on the innocent, even in Fairyland.

"I'm gonna do my best to sort this out, kiddo," I said. "But don't get too wrapped up in revenge. It's a bad business, and once you're in, it's impossible to get back out again."

She tilted her head to the side, contemplating my words. "I think I understand."

"I hope so, Darian. And there's something you should always remember, *especially* in Fairyland. Not everything you see is real." I smiled as I rose and patted her on the head. "I'll see you later," I added and walked out the door.

As I strode down the stone steps, I saw a lavish, golden carriage coming up the long drive. Stopping at the bottom, I waited for it to pull up. A solid-looking dwarf in a smart-looking chauffer's uniform sat high in the driver's seat. He gave me a rather unfriendly sneer as he pulled back on the reins and set the hand brake.

Another dwarf opened the carriage door and stepped down quickly, pulling out a small stepladder as he bowed to a particularly plump female dwarf with stern features. Where I come from the only term that would describe her is *battle-axe,* but I knew enough about dwarves to know she was a real looker.

She looked at me like I was yesterday's garbage. Clearly she was not a dwarf to be trifled with.

"Who in Ulion are you?" she demanded as she approached, looking up at me.

"Vincent Capaldi, Mrs. Hammerhand."

"Don't call me that," she snapped. "It won't apply for much longer."

She brushed past me without another word. She'd obviously heard about the boudoir—probably from one of the staff keeping tabs on her husband. "I understand, ma'am," I said to her retreating backside. I had no doubt she was headed into the house to let the governor know her lawyer had been instructed to go for his cojones.

"The scandal is going to be rough on you, isn't it?" I asked.

She spun on me like a cobra. "What do you know about it?" she spat. Clearly Darian got those fiery eyes from her mother.

"Well, I know you love your daughter. I know your soon-to-be-ex doesn't like unicorns. And I know that females of your stature hate having dirty laundry aired out in public." I softened my tone the best I could. "Am I wrong?"

She hesitated, her eyes more calculating than the governor's had been. "No." She paused, and her demeanor changed from anger to worry. "Who are you, again?"

"Vincent Capaldi. That doesn't mean anything to you. *What* I am should interest you a great deal."

"And *what* are you?"

"I'm the private detective who is going to fix this."

"Oh, really?" she asked, incredulous.

"I think so." I smiled. "Detective Ironsoul brought me in because I'm good at what I do."

"You'd have to be to sort out this nightmare." She sounded angry and hopeless and disgusted.

"I figure I have a pretty good chance to do just that, ma'am."

"I'd be indebted if you did."

"I want to ask a favor, then, and the reason I'm asking is for a little girl who lost her unicorn today."

Her calculating eyes softened into motherly concern, just as I'd hoped. "What do you want?" she asked.

"Don't do anything hasty with the governor. Let him have it with both barrels—I doubt the gods themselves could prevent that—but don't give him any ultimatums until I get back."

"That's a rather large request, Mr. Capaldi."

I saw her weighing options.

"Just give me the day. I know you have no reason to trust me, but as I see it, you don't have anything to lose."

She paused for a moment, and then made her decision. "Alright," she said with finality. "The day."

"Thank you, ma'am. I'll be back in a few hours. How does that sound?"

"I was, in fact, going to suggest just that," she added, and her tone indicated it wasn't going to be a suggestion.

"Good. Now would it be possible for me to get a lift back into town in your carriage? The constables who dropped me off left me here."

"If you can do as you say, you can have the thing."

I raised an eyebrow. "Deal," I replied. "And thank you."

She nodded and marched into the house with a stiff back and a stern look. I pictured her with a double-barreled shotgun, breech open as she thumbed a couple of shells into the chambers. I didn't envy the governor's ears for the next few hours.

I stepped up to the door of the carriage. "Home, James!" I shouted to the driver, who was still sneering at me.

"My name isn't James," he growled.

"Yeah. Sorry. I just always wanted to say that." I smiled at him. "Take me to the nearest library."

His sneer transformed into surprise.

"Please," I added.

He shrugged once and nodded.

I got into a plush interior of blue velvet, felt the carriage lurch, and settled down to sleep off as much of my hangover as I could before we arrived.

☙ ✧ ❧

Standing there at the railing of the racetrack, looking out at a carnival of dwarves, elves, orcs, and trolls, I realized why I loved being there. Don't get me wrong. I love libraries too. I solve a lot of cases with the treasures buried within those sacred walls, which is why I'd gone there first. But a racetrack is a very special place. It's where people chase riches, where hope blossoms, and where dreams are generally crushed by the reality of long odds. And yet people keep coming back. It's like the gods boiled down the sum of existence into two minutes of thundering hooves, snapping whips, and screaming spectators.

I'd left the carriage—and the surly driver—in an open field outside the racetrack. I'd also left a copy of *Fairies: Their Culture and Traditions* sitting upon a bed of blue velvet. I'd gotten what I needed after flipping through it and was ready to deal with a fairy who could probably snuff out my life with the snap of her tiny fingers. One of the first things I learned in this place is that fairies are *dangerous*. Maybe that's the reason the place was named after them. It might also be the reason Lumpy gave me this gig—he knew where the bread crumbs led.

Most people in Fairyland joke about how it's bad luck to hurt a fairy. I didn't believe that when I first arrived, but I sure as hell believe it now. I'd learned the hard way, and the lesson cost me a pinky finger. I'd shot a fairy who'd gone bad back when I still had bullets for my .38. That's another long story, one I wish I could forget.

I rubbed the stub of my left pinky and considered what I was about to do. With a fairy. I have to admit, I felt fear creep in between the cracks of my hangover. And it's that fear—fear of instant and inescapable retribution—that lets the little bastards pretty much run the show when they want to.

Taking a deep breath to steady my nerves, I turned and headed for the restroom. After doing my business, I asked an old goblin selling hand towels where I could place a sizeable bet. I hinted that I was looking for a gruff little fairy that ran the show at the track. He held out his hand, whereby I produced a single gold coin, and he muttered a box number.

The box was, naturally, at the top of the grandstands. As I trudged up each flight of steps, my hangover took the opportunity to remind me that it could hang with the best of them. At the top, I scanned the doors and headed towards where a couple of gruff-looking elves stood on either side.

"Well, I'll be damned," I said as I approached. They both looked at me and smiled. They were two of my three drinking buddies from the night before. "How's the hangover, guys?" I asked.

"We don't get those," one of them said, a superior smile on his face.

"I wish I could say the same," I replied, chuckling painfully as I rubbed my temple.

"You look terrible," the other observed.

"Thanks." I stepped up, and they tensed a bit. *Bodyguards doing their job,* I thought.

"What can we do for you, Capaldi?" the first one asked.

I tried to remember his name but couldn't. "I'm here to see your boss, actually."

"Not possible," the second replied, and there was a fair amount of threat in his voice.

I looked around to make sure no one was within earshot. "Just tell her that I'm here for the governor." Their eyes went wide. I guess the hired hands were well-informed.

"Wait here," the second ordered.

I gave a nod, and he stepped through the door.

Thirty seconds later the door opened and a squeaky voice full of gravel said, "Please come in, Mr. Capaldi."

I let the elf standing just inside the doorway pat me down. Of course, he was feeling for wands and daggers, not concealed pistols, but this sort of thing is the same all over. There was a gigantic, gray orc in chain mail to my left, and I could just make out an elevated chair, almost a throne, behind him. The elf finished and nodded.

"It's alright, Griznok," the squeaky voice said.

The orc stepped aside, but his piggy, red eyes never left me.

I nodded to him with a smile and saw the Godfairy. She was old. I mean *ancient.* Her skin was gray and wrinkled like a prune. She couldn't be more than two feet tall, but she looked at me like I was her property. She wore a shimmering black dress with her tiny bare feet poking out the bottom. Her gray hair was pulled back into a tight bun, exposing wide, drooping ears that ended in sharp points.

"Godfairy," I said with a bow. "I'm sure you're busy, so I'll cut to the chase."

"Please do." She sounded bored. She probably figured I was there to make a threat.

"I'm here to make you an offer you can't refuse." I gave her a sly smile. I'm certain she didn't get the joke, but I thought it was pretty funny.

Boredom quickly changed to curiosity. "Oh, really?"

"Indeed," I said. "You have a problem—"

"I have a pain in the ass," she injected.

"I can't argue with you, but he's also the governor. Which is why you left him a present rather than just breaking his knees or whatever it is fairy mobsters do to deadbeats. There are too many eyes on him, right?"

"You're very astute," she said, raising an eyebrow. I couldn't tell if she was impressed or irritated.

"But after the phone call this morning, you're running out of options." I tried not to look too smug, remembering the sensation of my pinky getting blown off.

"What are you offering?" she asked, and there was no mistaking the menace in her voice.

"The balance due. Paid in full. Tomorrow."

She raised a small, jagged eyebrow. "I'm listening."

"Well, knowing what I do about these things, certain wheels may already be in motion." I figured she'd ordered either a hit or a kidnapping the moment she got off the phone with Hammerhand. "Which would probably get the attention of the authorities, right?"

"Probably," she said, and the chilly calm in her voice indicated she had an out. Maybe she had pull with the higher-ups in Fairyland. "I can weather a pretty big storm if it comes to that."

"I'm guessing it would be better for both of us if it didn't come to that. And if did, well, all offers would be null and void."

She smiled, and frankly, that smile scared the hell out of me. I'd seen less menacing sharks. She held up her hand and picked up the phone beside her.

"Get me Stoney," she said. Her hand never wavered as we waited. A minute later, I heard a deep, grumbling voice on the other end say something, probably a troll. "Hold," she ordered. "Twenty-four hours," she added and hung up the receiver. She raised an eyebrow expectantly.

"So, we have a deal?" I asked even though I already knew the answer.

"You have twenty-four hours," she snapped. "And if I don't get my money, I'll be adding *your* name to the dance card. Am I understood, *Mr. Capaldi*?"

"Yes, Godfairy. Perfectly."

"Good." She waved a dismissive hand in my direction and focused her attention on the gates where horses and pixie jockeys were being loaded.

As I stepped up to the door, I turned to her and narrowed my eyes. "There's something that's been bothering me."

"What's that, Mr. Capaldi?" Her eyes never left the track.

"Well, I read somewhere—I read a lot, by the way—that fairies consider unicorns to be sacred. That they'd *never* harm one. It's the same sort of bad luck as a guy like me gets when he shoots a fairy. Bad things happen, you know?"

"What's your point?"

"No point, really," I replied innocently. "But there's an innocent little girl in this world who lost her best friend. A purple one. I'd do something about that, if I could. It occurs to me that a Godfairy, even a mobster, might still be a fairy godmother somewhere deep down inside." I opened the door. "I did think it odd there was magical pixie dust on the governor's pillow." I gave the Godfairy a wink. "Pleasure doing business with you," I added and closed the door behind me.

☙ ✧ ❧

"It all comes down to fairies and unicorns," I said with satisfaction. "I've got a way out for everybody."

The battle-axe sat behind Hammerhand's desk, a dangerous look on her face. The governor was off to the side, sitting meekly in a carved wooden chair far too narrow for his ample hindquarters. When he'd come in, she'd silently pointed to the chair, like a master telling her dog to heel. It took everything in me not to laugh.

I looked at the governor. "How much do you owe the Godfairy?"

"Fifty thousand," he whispered, cringing. So did the battle-axe, but where his face turned red in embarrassment, hers was full of fury.

"And how much would it have cost you to divorce him before this all happened?" I asked her.

"More than I care to think about," she replied, looking at him like he was vermin to be exterminated.

I was worried. If she didn't budge on this, I was a dead man, and it would get ugly for their family. The book had been clear on fairies and unicorns, but it didn't say anything about fairies and dwarves, regardless of gender or age. I locked eyes with her. "So the two questions are, how much do you value avoiding a scandal and how much does your daughter mean to you?"

"What?" she shouted.

"He doesn't have the money, right?" I asked.

"Not even close," she growled.

"Well, he's in with some particularly dangerous fairies. If they aren't paid, they're going to come after *all* of you. Probably starting with your daughter. A kidnapping at the very least."

"You stupid bastard!" she hissed at her husband. And I'd thought the look she'd given him before was bad.

"Look, here's how this can work," I said. I looked at both of them, and for the first time I felt bad for the governor. The look on his face said it all. He'd had no idea of what he was getting into, and the reality of it was tearing him up. "Governor, you're going to give her the divorce. No settlement. You get to keep your job as long as you can hold it, which probably won't be long when she's finished cutting off your donations from all the wealthy folks who put you in office. You also get to stay alive, which you should consider a nice bonus." I turned to her. "And you get your divorce for a fraction of what it would have cost you otherwise—without any scandal. All of this stays neatly under the table."

"But—" she started.

"And neither of you," I interrupted, "has to worry about anything happening to your *daughter*."

Her mouth closed abruptly, and the room went silent, save for the ticking of the cuckoo clock.

"So," I said, turning to the governor. "Do you agree?"

"Yes."

I could barely hear him.

"How about you, ma'am?" I asked. I held my breath. I could see it eating at her. People like her didn't like to give away money, and she might be rich enough to think she was untouchable.

"Agreed," she said, biting off the word like rotten fruit.

"Then I believe the governor needs to call his fairy godmother, and you need to call your banker," I said, breathing a sigh of relief.

They both made their calls, and the arrangements were made. A cart full of gold would be delivered to the track in the morning.

"And with that," I said to them both, "I need to get home so I can finally sleep off this hangover. My head has been killing me all day." I stepped up to the door and turned. "Can I still keep the carriage?" I asked her. I figured she might go back on her offer since she'd just shelled out fifty grand.

She hesitated, and I could see her struggling with it. "It's yours." She paused for a heartbeat, finally adding, "And thank you. I *am* grateful you were able to sort this out, even with the price tag."

"It was my pleasure, ma'am."

"It's Miss Stoneshield. Why don't you stop by tomorrow afternoon? You can help me explain to Ironsoul that there's no longer a problem. I might even have other work for you."

"I'd like that. Thanks."

As I opened the door, she said, "You said something about fairies and unicorns. What did you mean?"

"I guess we'll see." I smiled and closed the door behind me.

Miss Stoneshield pointed me towards the patio and left me alone while she directed the movers to empty the house of the governor's belongings.

I sat in the afternoon sunshine, sipping a tall glass of iced tea as I lounged in a human-sized chair someone had thoughtfully placed on the patio. I stared out at the green acres rolling behind the white castle. The colors were still too bright, the bees still trundled, and another group of pixies drifted off towards the forest.

"It's still a load of crap," I muttered.

I heard the door open behind me but didn't turn.

"Capaldi!" Ironsoul shouted. "You'll never believe it!"

"The unicorn head disappeared, right? Replaced by something?"

"Yes! A sandbag! How did you—?"

As if on command, a redheaded lass astride a purple unicorn bounded over a nearby hill. I pointed, still not looking at him.

"How did you—?"

"Client privilege," I injected.

What I couldn't tell Ironsoul is that the Godfairy had pulled the oldest game in either world: a switcheroo. The dust on the pillow was the clue. Pixies working for the Godfairy had made a sandbag look like a severed head. But fairy godmothers are still fairy godmothers. Once I reminded the Godfairy of that, Dancer showed up in the barn late that morning—undoubtedly the same way he'd disappeared.

"Client privilege?" Ironsoul blurted.

"I'm sorry." I looked at him and smiled. "I can't tell you anything." I think I said it a bit too smugly, because his reply hit me hard.

"Well, if there wasn't a crime, any investigating you did doesn't count. Which means *you still owe me.*"

"Crap," I said under my breath.

"Come on, Capaldi. Off the record. Tell me what happened."

For a moment I considered spilling the beans. But I couldn't. I'd made a deal with *everyone,* and I kept my word. "All I can say is, 'Oh what a world it is that has fairy godmothers in it.'" I raised my glass to Ironsoul and closed my eyes to the brightness of Fairyland, thankful it had a dark underbelly.

The Faerie Journal

Megan Grey

I had just finished checking my faerie garden when I heard the rattle and thump of my aunt's rusty van pulling into the driveway. Normally, I'd hurry through the gate to the front yard to ask if she needed help with the groceries or whatever—Daddy was big on me repaying Aunt Lue's hospitality with "helpful hands"—but I hung back. Aunt Lue wasn't coming back from work or the store like usual. This time she'd brought my cousin home from war.

I eyed the bluebells as they trembled in a small gust of muggy Houston wind. Perhaps I should check that patch again. Papa Twilly always said faeries showed themselves more on important days, and today felt important. I parted the small petals carefully. This late in spring their blue was no longer as vibrant and pretty against the dark brown of my hands, the petals beginning to shrivel against the thickening heat of approaching summer.

Nothing. The flicker of a dragonfly, but no faeries.

I closed the journal that lay open beside me. Voices drifted faintly from the driveway: Aunt Lue, even Daddy. Which meant this was an important day for sure. I hadn't seen Daddy out of his bedroom in over three days. Another voice sounded, softer. Was that Janna? I didn't recognize my cousin's voice. I hadn't seen her since I was seven and we'd visited this very house for Christmas, back before Momma died. But that was five years ago. I wasn't a little kid anymore, and Janna probably wasn't the same teenage girl who'd put butterfly clips in my hair and taught me the words to a song that got me grounded when I sang it on Christmas Eve.

Back then I didn't even know about the faeries. It was only two years ago that Aunt Lue told me the stories of my grandfather, who everyone called Papa Twilly, and I'd started my very own faerie garden. Since then, I'd read every book I could find on the subject. That's how I knew the proper spelling for them—"faerie," not "fairy," which is a mistake a lot of books for little kids make. The serious ones, the ones that tell what kind of flowers and food attract them, the ones that have stories of people who've really seen them, always spell it right.

Daddy didn't believe faeries love cinnamon or are afraid of metal or that their leader is a majestic purple unicorn. Daddy didn't even believe faeries are real. Once I'd heard Daddy tell Aunt Lue that faeries were a white girl's foolishness. Which was ridiculous, even if the faerie books mostly did have stories about white girls. Papa Twilly saw faeries all the time, and he was a proud black man. He'd seen faeries in every color of the rainbow, and some besides. Many of them didn't have human skin at all, but were bark and leaves and moss with wings and limbs. So why would they care about human skin color?

"Lizzy!" Daddy called through the screen door. "You still out there? Luenna and Janna are here. Come in and see your cousin."

I brushed the loose dirt from my pants, though the knees on these jeans were so dirt-stained from days spent among my faerie garden that no amount of brushing or even washing would make them new again. I left the journal outside. On a day like today, I'd probably need to check again later.

Daddy squeezed my shoulder when I entered the kitchen. He was wearing the same clothes he'd been in last I'd seen him: his bathrobe over worn flannel pants. He didn't wear normal-people clothes much these days, but I guess that's not a problem if you never leave your room.

"Remember, Janna's been hurt, she's different. No staring," he said in a whisper.

"Yes, Daddy." I'd seen the pictures Aunt Lue had sent from the hospital.

But when I walked into the living room and actually saw my cousin in person, I ended up staring anyway. Janna wore a loose-fitting purple T-shirt with her high school track team logo on it and a pair of gray sweatpants that didn't manage to hide the fact that her left leg was missing, replaced by a fake metal leg that peeked out above her dirty white sneakers. She leaned on short black metal crutches that didn't look anything like the padded gray crutches I'd had the summer I broke my ankle. These didn't fit under her shoulders, but had handholds she gripped so tightly her knuckles paled.

Her face, though. The pictures had shown her head wrapped in bandages, so I'd been—like some dumb kid scared by a movie—kind of expecting my cousin to arrive wrapped up and shambling like a mummy, and maybe even drooling.

The truth wasn't worse, but it wasn't better.

The left side of Janna's once pretty face looked like it had melted under the Afghanistan sun. Her left eye was totally closed and nearly skinned over, the corner of it tugged down in a constant tearless weep. Her lip, too. Her black hair, cut close to her head, didn't cover the ragged hole where her ear should have been. My skin felt itchy all over looking at her.

"Hi, Lizzy," she said. Her voice didn't sound like the Janna of the dirty songs of Christmas past. It was too deep, too slurred.

Daddy patted my back, and I remembered my manners. "Hi, Janna. I'm glad you're back."

The right side of her lip curled up into a kind of smile, though her right eye didn't smile with it. Maybe the shrapnel had hit that muscle, too. "Me, too, Sugarcube."

Her calling me the nickname she'd given me that Christmas after catching me eating sugar cubes straight from the dish should have made me feel more comfortable.

I smiled so she would think it did.

"Let's get you to your room," Aunt Lue said. "I've kept up those posters you liked, except for that god-awful Kane one."

"Kanye," Janna and I said at the same time.

My aunt shook her head. "Either way, Lizzy's sharing the room with you now, and her momma, bless her soul, would never forgive me for putting her little girl in the same room with *that.*"

Janna slowly made her way to the bedroom. I didn't want to go in there, not yet, even though that's where all my books were. I went back to my faerie garden and peered into the patch of black-eyed Susans.

Daddy watched me through the screen door for a long time, but I pretended not to see him.

Papa Twilly's real name was Timothy William, which somehow became T. Willy, which eventually became just Twilly. Daddy's name was Timothy William, Jr., but everyone just called him Tim. I guess one Twilly's enough for any family.

I'd never met Papa Twilly, who'd died before I was born, but Aunt Lue told me all about him when Daddy and I moved in with her two years ago. Papa Twilly was a good man, fought in the Vietnam War and came home to a job working in plastics manufacturing. He married his high school girlfriend, my Nana Relia, and had four kids—Daddy and Aunt Lue and a set of twins who died soon after they were born. He also claimed his life was guided by faeries. "Life isn't easy, Luenna," he told my aunt one day after the twins died, "but my little friends are here, and we'll be okay."

Aunt Lue said he didn't tell many people about the faeries, because everyone he told thought he was crazy. Papa Twilly kept a journal, though, full of stories and descriptions and drawings of the faeries. Aunt Lue gave it to me a few months after I moved in, when I'd come home crying one day because the kids at school called me Orca. Even then I knew she didn't believe Papa Twilly's stories, especially since the Bible doesn't say anything about faeries. She just wanted to give me something so I'd forget about school and the whale sounds kids made when I walked by.

But when I read Papa Twilly's journal, I knew it was more than just stories. I knew the faeries were out there, and that one day I'd see them too. I just had to try hard enough, make them know I was here, waiting for them. The rest of the world may not believe in them, but I would believe hard enough to make up for everyone else.

A week after Janna's return, I sat in a patch of grass damp from the sprinkler Aunt Lue had turned on that morning. I looked back and forth between Papa Twilly's journal and one of my favorite serious faerie books. This book said faeries hated unnatural smells, perfumes and such, but Papa Twilly said a couple of his little friends used to only come out when he'd douse himself in Brut cologne. They'd perch on his shoulder like birds and whisper secrets of the forest into his ears.

Aunt Lue wouldn't buy me any Brut, so I'd snuck into her room after she left for work and sprayed on some of her drugstore perfume, coughing at the strong blast. It smelled flowery and not at the same time, like gardenia and roses rubbed with old pennies. Then I sat in front of the ring of stones I'd made for the faeries. Inside the ring were little bathroom paper cups filled with cinnamon and honey.

No faeries yet. I didn't blame them. I wrinkled my nose, still smelling the perfume on me even after a half hour outside.

The screen door banged shut behind me. Janna came out, using her crutches slowly on the steps down. She eased herself into the white plastic chair that was the only one left of the set of four Aunt Lue used to have out on the deck.

Though we shared a room, Janna and I hadn't talked much. She'd be sleeping when I went to school, and sometimes still be sleeping when I'd come home. Sometimes she'd just be sitting on the bed, staring out the window, tapping her fingers on her leg like there was an invisible keyboard. I'd started leaving my books out in the living room, so I wouldn't have to go into the bedroom very much.

Between Janna and Daddy spending all their days locked away, the house was very quiet until my aunt got home. I didn't mind. I was used to it by now.

"Mom says you're looking for fairies." The way Janna said it, I knew she wasn't spelling it right in her mind.

"Yes," I said, cautiously. I didn't know Janna's opinion on Papa Twilly.

"Found any yet?"

I looked down at Papa Twilly's journal, pages and pages of drawings and experiences. My notebook had pages and pages, too, but only of failed attempts. "Not yet."

She nodded, as if that confirmed something. "Did you take a bath in Mom's perfume? Maybe that's scaring them away." The side of her lip curled up like it had that first day. I was used to her new face now, but the difference between the two sides—one pretty and smooth, the other melted and scarred—still made my stomach a little floppy. Like my cousin was half herself and half someone else and neither version made a full person.

The smile on her face slipped when she caught me staring. I looked away guiltily and wiped sweat from my forehead. There wasn't much wind today, not that wind helped any this time of year. It just blew the heavy heat around. A fat bee buzzed near my ear, but I didn't bat it away. One of my books said bees were faerie scouts. Papa Twilly never mentioned bees, but who knows?

"How's school?" Janna asked. "Mom said you had a hard time when you first moved here."

"It's better," I said, though that wasn't really true. The kids didn't call me Orca anymore, but since I'd gotten boobs before any of the other girls, they started calling me Jugs and the boys laughed and tried to grab my chest in the hallway. But if my teachers couldn't stop it from happening, what was the point of telling anyone else? Daddy and Aunt Lue and Janna all had their own problems.

More silence, except for the twitter of a bird and the distant hum of freeway traffic two streets over.

"You can ask me, you know. About the war. About my face or my leg."

I looked back at Janna. "You want me to?"

She shrugged. "Better than no one talking about it all."

That made sense, I supposed. "Aunt Lue said you were driving a truck and a bomb exploded."

Janna let out a laugh, though it sounded more like a hiss. "I guess you know it all already, then."

"Does it hurt?"

"I take lots of pills. It's not so bad now."

I thought of Daddy since Momma died in the car accident, closed off in his room almost all the time. Writing his next book, he said, but he hadn't needed to be alone so much to write the first three. I wished there were pills that took away the pain of losing people like there were for losing legs. I wished even more that the faeries would come.

Janna watched me expectantly, a kind of challenge in her good eye.

I sucked in my lip, thinking. "Did you ever see someone die?"

She blinked, staring back at me, and for a minute I thought I'd failed at some test I didn't even know I was taking. Then, softly, "Yeah. Lots of people. My friends."

In Papa Twilly's journal, he talked about the Vietnam War. The faeries came to him there, too, though they weren't the same ones he knew from Texas. They were creatures of reeds and water, with wings of palm fronds and bodies slim as blades of grass. They'd whisper to him in a language he didn't understand and watch over him when he slept. He'd see them flutter over the bodies of the dead no matter what country they were from, saying good-bye to friends who'd never even known they were there.

I wondered what the faeries in Afghanistan looked like.

Janna must have gotten bored waiting for me to ask more questions, because she kept talking all on her own. "We were doing a supply run when we hit a land mine. When *I* hit a land mine. Then they attacked, pinning us down. Carter, Brooks, the LT, Rice, and Millaney—all of them but me died. Well," she said, barking out another of those not-laughs, "Rice is still alive, but he's worse off than me. He's a vegetable, pretty much. They'll pull the plug on him eventually. Probably better that way."

Didn't sound better to me. I turned back to the ring of stones. A roly-poly crawling around the base of the cup of honey curled into a ball when I touched it.

"You know Papa Twilly was totally bat-shit, right?" Janna said, sounding angry all of a sudden. "Mom told me all those stories when I was a kid, too, and I even believed them for awhile. But mental illness runs in our family. Papa's mother went to a sanitarium and her sister killed herself. Even your daddy ..." She trailed off, then shook her head.

"Daddy's not crazy. He's working on his book!" I yelled. Warm liquid spilled onto my fist, and I saw I had crushed the tiny cup of honey. I drew in a shaky breath. Best manners. Anger scared faeries. "And Papa Twilly wasn't crazy, either. The faeries are out there."

"Then why haven't you seen them?"

"Go away, Janna." I carefully set down the crushed cup, my fingers sticking together at the knuckles. Maybe the faeries didn't like DollarCo store-brand honey. I should ask Aunt Lue to buy a different kind.

I didn't look back as the plastic chair scuffled in the dirt as she got up, or as the crutches creaked and her pretend foot dragged across the ground. Then the sounds of her walking stopped.

"I remembered those stories after the bomb hit," she said. "There was all this movement and heat and pain, but no noise at all. And walking through it all I saw a giant purple unicorn, coming right up to me. Had the horn and everything. It watched me and I watched it. Then the noise came back and all the screaming and the gunfire, and the unicorn was gone."

My anger disappeared, replaced by pure shock. "You saw the purple unicorn? That's … that's …" I was going to say "impossible," because even Papa Twilly had never seen the purple unicorn that ruled over all the faeries. But if the faeries were real, that meant the unicorn was, too. Joy and envy pulled my thoughts in different directions like kids at tug-of-war.

"There was no purple unicorn," Janna said quickly. "The therapist said your brain does strange things in situations like that. It's like a coping mechanism or something."

But I didn't care what some therapist who'd probably never even read any serious faerie books thought.

"Maybe the unicorn saved you," I said.

Janna blinked her good eye, once, twice. "Maybe it shouldn't have."

Without another word, she went into the house, the screen door slamming shut behind her.

I spent days poring over every reference to the violet unicorn, ruler of faeries the world over, in Papa Twilly's journal. There wasn't much, really, since he'd never seen so much as a mystical hoofprint, but he'd drawn a picture based on what the faeries described to him. I traced that picture with my finger until I worried I'd rub the old ink right off.

I was happy the unicorn saved my cousin. But it chewed at me, deep in my gut. Why her? Why, when she didn't even believe, would she see the most rare of all the magical creatures?

Why couldn't I?

"Hey, Jugs," called a boy biking past with his friends on the way home from school. The boys pulled their bikes around to block me on the sidewalk.

My heart hammered in my chest. There was only a week left of school. Why wouldn't they just leave me alone? My hands tightened around Papa Twilly's journal, palms sweating into the black leather.

"Do a dance for us, Jugs. Shake that fat ass," another of the boys said. His name was Andre, and he was the biggest and meanest of them all.

"Leave me alone," I said, looking around for a way out. There were four of them, enough to surround me. A car drove past, but didn't stop.

"We'll let you past after we see those big ol' titties dance," said Andre's puny shadow, Tyler. He had a face like a ferret and smelled like one, too.

"Go away." I tried to keep my voice firm and normal, even as I clutched the journal in front of the jugs they wanted so badly to see. I read once that bullies respond to direct statements said without emotion. That they only wanted a reaction and if you didn't give it to them, they'd leave you alone.

Maybe these bullies hadn't read that article.

Andre grabbed the journal from my sweat-slick hands and opened it.

"Stop it!" I cried, jumping at him to get it back, but Javier, the boy who'd first spoken, shoved me to the ground.

"Shit," Andre said, laughing. "There's like fairies and shit in here. Juggies likes that Barbie Snowflake stuff."

Tyler snickered.

Tears pricked at my eyes, and my knees stung from scraping against the sidewalk. "I'll scream! I'll scream and scream and you'll go to juvie where you belong if you don't give me back my book and leave me alone!"

But fear rooted me to the sidewalk, to the pebbles digging into my skin.

"Maybe Jugs will dance to get her book back," Andre said.

The fourth boy, Leon, turned from watching the far intersection. "The bus will be here soon. We'd better go." He lifted the front wheel of his bike from the ground a couple times. Nervously.

Hope flowered in me. The next bus stop was close by. If I screamed, surely someone would chase them away.

Andre flipped him off. "Dance for your book, Jugs." He ripped a page from the journal, and the sound was like my chest being torn open.

"No!" I shrieked, stumbling up to grab at Papa's journal.

"That's it," he laughed, ripping another page, crumbling it in his fist. I saw a flash of color, greens and browns and metal gray. The self-portrait of Papa in his war fatigues.

I rushed at Andre, intending to use every ounce of my body and my rage to knock him down, to shove his face into the pebbles, but Javier dropped his bike and grabbed me, followed right behind by Tyler. His stick arms were stronger than they seemed. I howled as Andre ripped another page free, making another crumpled ball of Papa Twilly's words and pictures.

"Andre ..." Leon warned. The blue city bus had stopped two streets down. Still too far away.

What if the bus didn't stop here? What if it did and no one who got off helped me?

Why were the faeries letting this happen?

I struggled and kicked and even tried to bite, but the boys swore and laughed and pinned my arms so far back I thought my shoulders might break.

Andre ripped and ripped, page after page, tossing the crumpled balls into the street, then with one final tear and crumple, he tossed the journal onto the sidewalk. He stepped up to me, avoiding my flailing kick, and brought his nasty face within inches of mine.

"Thanks for the show, Jugs," he said. His breath smelled of Doritos and root beer.

He took the last ball of wadded-up pages and stuffed it down my shirt. Then, with a final laugh, he gestured and the boys shoved me back onto the sidewalk. The four of them were halfway down the street on their bikes by the time the bus drove past.

It didn't stop. I watched the pages of Papa Twilly's journal bounce around the street in its wake.

☙ ✧ ❧

When I got home, I had already wiped the tears from my face on my shirt. Aunt Lue would ask questions I didn't want to answer. The remainder of Papa Twilly's journal, along with the balled-up pages I'd gathered from the street and from my shirt, was in my backpack. I couldn't stand to look at it, to discover which pages would always carry the marks of what Andre had done, no matter how much I re-taped and smoothed.

To my surprise, it wasn't my aunt who greeted me when I walked in the door, but Daddy. He sat in my aunt's ugly avocado-colored armchair.

"Hey, Lizzy." He didn't look at me as he spoke, just kept staring out the window.

I followed his gaze. Nothing was out there, just the small brick ranch houses across the street that all looked like Aunt Lue's.

"Hey, Daddy."

I dropped the backpack on the entryway tile with a thunk. Aunt Lue would have been all over me about leaving my things laying around where people could trip over them, but Daddy didn't so much as raise an eyebrow.

I started toward the kitchen for a snack, but paused after a few steps.

"Are you okay, Daddy?"

He turned and looked at me for the first time in days. I'd forgotten how handsome my daddy was. Even more so in person than on his book jackets. Momma used to say his smile could charm the quills from a porcupine. He hadn't smiled in so long, I couldn't remember if that was true.

"What happened to your knees?" he asked.

"I tripped on the sidewalk."

He stared at me for a bit, and I couldn't tell if his dark eyes read the lie on my face or not.

"My publisher dropped me," he said.

I blinked. "But the book you've been working on—"

"They don't want it."

I didn't know what to say. My knees still ached, and so did my shoulders and my right elbow, though I didn't remember hitting that. "Maybe another publisher will."

He turned to the window again. "It's not done. I've barely got three chapters."

My chest turned hollow. He'd already started the book when Momma died. Two years in his bedroom, two years with the door closed on me and everyone else, and he hadn't even been working on the book, not at all.

"I'm going to check my faerie garden," I mumbled. I didn't want to go back outside, but I wanted to be inside with him even less.

"They're not there, Lizzy," he said with a sigh. "Papa Twilly was wrong. We don't all have little friends looking out for us."

I walked numbly to the backyard. Bees crawled over the cups of honey, and tiny red fire ants scurried around a new hill they'd opened near my ring of stones. The bluebells hung low in the afternoon heat, dead white petals dropped onto the dirt.

I knelt down on the ground and stared at the flowers, not even seeing them. I began to sob, giant, racking sobs that shook my too-big stomach and my too-big breasts.

No little friends came to comfort me. Daddy had been right all along.

☙ ✧ ❧

School finally ended, and summer cast its muggy blanket over the world. I only went out into my faerie garden one time, when Aunt Lue asked me to pick up the little cups of cinnamon and honey after she saw a raccoon rooting around our backyard.

I threw them away and kicked the stones around until there was no trace of a ring left. Just rocks scattered in the dirt.

I kept indoors like Daddy, like Janna. Aunt Lue would come in the house and peek into our bedroom and see Janna lying in bed, sleeping as usual, and me sitting on my bed reading something that was not my faerie books. I'd picked up some manga from the library, which I liked. Manga didn't ever pretend to be real.

Aunt Lue would sometimes ask if we wanted to go to the park or the museum, though we always said no—or I always said no and Janna kept sleeping. Sometimes, my aunt wouldn't say anything at all. She would just smile in a way that wasn't really smiling, but sad.

One day, after bringing Janna home from physical therapy and helping her back into bed, Aunt Lue said she hadn't seen Papa Twilly's journal around in awhile.

"It's in my backpack," I said.

"Still?" Aunt Lue glanced to where my backpack slumped under my chair like a deflated balloon.

I shrugged. I didn't dare mention the torn and still-crumpled pages. Aunt Lue might know better than to believe in Papa Twilly's faeries, but he was still her daddy and she'd be mad that I'd let that happen to his journal.

"She's twelve years old, Mom," Janna said. "She's over the fairy thing." She swallowed two blue pills and rolled over.

Aunt Lue watched me expectantly, and I turned another page in my manga book. She didn't even bother fake-smiling this time. She just looked sad, though I didn't know why.

Hadn't they all wanted me to see the truth about the faeries? About Papa Twilly?

That night, I woke to a strange scratching noise. I peered around the dark room. Enough moonlight seeped through the one broken blind that I could see that Janna's bed was empty, her sheets tangled. Her prosthetic leg, usually propped up against the nightstand, was gone.

"Janna?" I called quietly. Had she gone to the bathroom? And if so, why would she put on her leg? She would use just her crutches for that.

The scratching sounded again, louder, with a hint of the squeal chalk sometimes made on a chalkboard. Or like branches against glass.

Only we didn't have any trees by our room.

My heart beating erratically in my chest, I padded over to the window and opened the blinds. At first all I saw was light, white and so bright it seemed the moon itself had fallen into our window-well. Then the light dimmed, drawing to a point, and I realized that the actual moon was a tiny crescent mostly hidden by clouds. All the light in the window had come from this one narrow point, this one slim, spiral horn that had been scratching at the glass.

And that horn was attached to the head of a horse. A horse standing outside my bedroom window, with a mane and body so gray that … No. Not gray. As the horse stepped back from the window, the light from its horn gently illuminated a coat that was deep violet. Flickers of shadows with the shape of flowers and insects darted around it, just outside the light.

The purple unicorn had come. The faeries had come.

I trembled, barely able to think or breathe. I didn't bother pinching myself. I didn't dream much, and never like this. This was real. It had to be real.

I pressed my fingers to the window, the glass cool from the constant blast of AC. The unicorn bobbed its head twice, pawing at the earth with a glimmering hoof. Then it turned to the right and walked out of view.

"No," I whispered, afraid to say anything louder, afraid the trailing light from that mystical horn would burst like a bubble and leave me back in my faerie-less life. "Come back. Please, come back."

The light began to fade. I scrambled past my bed, stubbing my toe on a stack of library books as I ran to the kitchen and from there into the backyard.

The unicorn stood there, glowing serenely in the night, perfectly still against the flurry of tiny wing beats on the very edge of the light. Under the gaze of those coffee-dark eyes, my heart filled my whole chest, the warmth of light and hope and giddy joy spreading all the way from my bare feet to my bed-mussed hair.

I wished Papa Twilly could see this.

I reached my hand out slowly, carefully, hoping against hope that one of the faeries would come sit on my fingers or whisper forest-secrets in my ears, but froze partway. The unicorn pawed the ground and snorted, as if distressed. As if …

And then I saw her. Janna, lying on her side on the dying grass, the plastic chair knocked over beside her. An empty pill bottle peeked out from her curled fingers, and another sat a foot or so from her, half-hidden in a dandelion patch. The pretty side of her face was turned up to the light, her good eye closed.

"Janna!" I shrieked. The rustle of wing beats grew more frantic at my terror, and those at the outskirts of the unicorn's light fled.

I rolled her over, shook her shoulders. "Janna! Janna, wake up!" Her skinny body felt as heavy as the giant sacks of flour Aunt Lue got from DollarCo. Her head bobbed on her neck.

"Help her!" I cried, turning to the unicorn. "Please help …"

The unicorn was gone. The faeries were gone. The only light shining on Janna's face came from the back porch bulb.

I blinked, stupidly, then gathered Janna as close to me as I could. "Daddy! Aunt Lue! Help! Help!"

I screamed until the screen door banged open and Aunt Lue ran out in her nightgown and wailed and Daddy followed in his bathrobe and flannel pants and called 911. Then I held Janna until the ambulance came, and they pulled her from my arms and whisked her away.

☙ ✧ ❧

I didn't go to sleep even after Daddy and I returned from the hospital. I pulled Papa Twilly's journal out of my backpack. I stroked the soft, worn leather of the cover and ran my fingernail over the ragged edges of ripped pages. Then I set to work with the crumpled balls of paper I'd managed to collect, smoothing out each one as gently and lovingly as if I'd been running my hand over the gleaming coat of the purple unicorn.

I didn't hear Daddy come in at first, but I did smell the hot chocolate. He set a steaming mug on the desk in front of me.

"She's going to be okay, they said. You found her in time."

I nodded. I already knew this. I'd been there when the doctors told him and Aunt Lue, and he'd said it at least twice in the car. Maybe he needed to keep saying it to believe it.

He sat on my bed, staring at the mug in his own hand. He lifted it as if to drink, but then lowered it again. "Your aunt, she knew Janna wasn't doing well. But she didn't know … I mean, none of us knew how bad it was."

I paused in my paper smoothing. This page talked about how when Papa Twilly's babies died, the faeries wove a beautiful wreath of Texas prickly poppy and starlight for the gravestone.

"You're a hero, Lizzy," Daddy said. "She's alive because of you."

"She's alive because of the purple unicorn. And the faeries. They probably told the unicorn what was happening."

Daddy took a drink then, a long one even though it probably burned his tongue. He set the mug down on the carpet and leaned forward so his elbows rested on his knees. He looked me in the eye, really looked at me, and I was reminded of the unicorn's eyes, dark and mysterious and full of a kind of love too deep to understand.

"I'm sorry, baby. I'm so …" His voice broke, and he looked away for a second and then back. Red rimmed the edges of his eyes. "I'm so sorry. I've been a terrible father. I've been so lost since your momma died. And I've shut you out. I can't lose you, too, baby girl. I won't."

My throat felt thick, tight. I wanted to run away and I wanted to bury myself in his strong arms all at the same time, and so I didn't move at all.

He took my hand and enfolded it in his own, warmed by the hot mug and soft like bluebell petals. "I know I need to earn back being your daddy. And I will. I will be there for you from now on. The thing is, I don't know if I can believe in faeries or unicorns. But I believe in you. I believe in us."

I didn't forgive him, not then. Not yet. But he was my daddy. I dove into his arms and let him hold me. I breathed in the smell of him, the sweet of hot chocolate and the musky scent that was uniquely him, a scent I'd loved and forgotten. I sobbed into his chest, releasing the pain of the bullies at school, the fear of seeing Janna's body on the ground, the ache that had never left since Momma died. It hurt and felt good, all at once.

I knew then that it didn't matter if he didn't believe in the little friends. It didn't even matter if I ever saw them again. They were there.

And we'd be okay.

The Greggs Family Zoo of Odd and Marvelous Creatures

Kristin Luna

A patch of sky over the neighbor's acreage turned a milky purple, like an old, healing bruise. Fourteen-year-old Alice watched the odd occurrence from the fence line, her legs resting between the dry, wooden beams.

Then, a peculiar-colored horse fell from the opening. Its weight met the earth with a muffled crack. The great horse whined, its eyes wide with shock. It attempted to rise, but only fell back down.

Alice scrambled to the top of the fence for a better look. She watched in horror as the horse panted and writhed on the ground. She wrestled with herself if she should help the creature. Back in Chicago, she wouldn't hesitate to help a hurt bird or dog. But things seemed different in Nebraska, where a dark, indigo horse with a broken, splintering horn between its inky eyes fell from the sky.

She gritted her teeth and hopped over the fence. Her grandparents wouldn't be happy to know she'd trespassed onto the neighbor's property.

The unusual horse seemed wary of her presence, so she knelt within a few feet of its head. The horse's eyes followed her cautiously. Its mane showed strands of silver between the deep purples and blues. The hair continued down around its neck and onto its chest.

"You sure are hairy, aren't ya?" she muttered.

The horse's ankle swelled rapidly. Alice moved a little closer, slowly bringing her hand to the horse's shoulder. She hesitated briefly before laying it on the soft, indigo hair.

"It's gonna be alright," Alice cooed.

The sound of approaching hoofbeats drew Alice's gaze upward. A cowboy directed his jet-black horse close to the great, indigo beast without glancing at Alice.

Under his weatherworn hat, the old man's face was like a crude mask with small, blue marbles peeking out of the folds as eyes. A rolled cigarette rested in the corner of his mouth, a small chimney for smoke to move in and out.

Despite the cowboy's leathery appearance, he jumped off his horse with surprising agility. He walked toward the girl and the bluish-purple creature.

"Now ain't this somethin'," he mumbled. His voice was low, and his cigarette bounced with every word. "You know what you're lookin' at, kid?" The blue marbles looked directly at her.

"Looks like a unicorn to me," Alice said casually, staring right back into the old man's eyes.

"Sure is." The old man's eyebrows arched. "Can you keep a secret?"

"Depends." Alice shrugged.

"Depends?" The old man repeated incredulously.

"What's it worth to you?" Alice asked. If she'd learned anything from her poor neighborhood in Chicago, it was how much secrets were worth.

"I like your style, kid. Reminds me of a smart aleck I used to know." The man smiled, revealing two rows of browning teeth.

"Is it broken?" Alice asked, looking at the swelling leg.

The old man considered the horse. "Nah. Just a sprain, looks like."

Alice sighed with relief.

"Where'd you come from? You with the Wamsleys or Zimmermans?" the man asked, rolling up his flannel sleeves. He bent down to the indigo horse and put a toughened hand on its thick neck. The unicorn's body relaxed under the man's touch.

"Wamsleys. Betsy and Ralph are my grandparents."

"They puttin' you to work for the summer? Detasslin' or some such?"

"Yeah, that's what they want me to do." Alice hung her head and sighed. She imagined how boring it would be to break the tips off of corn in the summer heat.

"Not what *you* want to do, is it?"

"No."

"What's your name, kid?" The old man extended his hand.

"Alice," she said, taking his hand.

"I'm John Greggs. And I got me an idea, Alice. My knees aren't what they used to be. How about you help me out on my farm for the summer?"

Alice smiled.

"I'll take that as a yes. I'll come by later to talk to Ralph and Bea. You go on now and tell 'em you found yourself a job, and I'll fix this old girl up."

☙ ✧ ❧

Alice woke with the sunrise the next morning. She pulled on a pair of pants and her orange West Communities YMCA Summer Day Camp T-shirt. The shirt was starting to get tight across her shoulders, and moth holes let the light in on one side. She had received it with a free summer camp membership, an anonymous donation for underprivileged youth in her neighborhood. It was the best summer Alice ever had.

She snuck down the stairs and shut the front door quietly behind her. Alice walked down the gravel road to Greggs' brick house.

Greggs sat on an old, wooden rocking chair on the front porch, smoking a cigarette and holding a steaming mug.

"Mornin'," Greggs hooted.

"Morning," Alice replied.

"Those the best shoes you got?" Greggs asked, scratching under his cowboy hat.

Irritated, Alice replied, "These are the only shoes I've got."

Greggs shrugged. "Those'll have to do. I'll get you a pair of boots when those wear down in a week or two."

Alice bit her lip, feeling heat brush her cheeks. The girls at school made fun of her raggedy tennis shoes. She had to put duct tape on the laces to keep them from breaking.

A cloud of dust ushered in a new, green pickup truck on Greggs' drive. A sharply dressed, heavyset man got out of the cab. His stomach spilled over the top of his jeans, and his face was the color of a cherry tomato. He carried a hunting knife about the size of her forearm on his belt.

"Hi there, John. How're y'all doin'?" The man approached, tipping his hat.

The man gave Alice a curious look and leaned closer. Alice noted that he smelled like mint and chewing tobacco. "And who are you, little lady?"

"She's helping me for the summer, Artie." Greggs' bones creaked as he pushed himself from the rocking chair. He moved down the steps and stood next to Alice.

"Taking care of the unicorns?" The man winked at Alice, who stiffened at the mention of the creatures.

Greggs' face remained ornery and cold. "You know I ain't got no unicorns, Mayor. Those were nothin' but parlor tricks my daddy put on for out-of-towners."

"Really? Was it a parlor trick that killed my daddy's brother when he was just a boy?"

"He was drunk and trespassing on our land. Wisdom says he was lookin' for trouble. Besides, it was half a century ago. I think it's time you stopped beatin' that dead horse."

Mayor Artie's face soured.

"What can I do you for, Artie?" Greggs grumbled.

"I know you've heard about the coyotes eating the local cattle. The Browns' farm was attacked just last night. I'm stopping by all the farms out here, making sure your livestock is safe."

"Okay," Greggs mumbled.

"I've been talking to Sheriff Martell. We've been thinkin' about paying all you farmers a courtesy visit. Checkin' on your fences, securing them up for you."

"Well that's mighty kind of you, Mayor. But I'd rather no one come on my property without due cause." Greggs folded his arms in front of his chest.

"Coyotes gettin' at your livestock ain't proper cause?" Artie raised an eyebrow.

"Nothin' I can't handle myself."

Artie narrowed his eyes, taking a step back toward the truck. "I don't suppose one of your animals have been making a mess of those cattle? I wouldn't be surprised."

"I don't got any animal that could've done that. Besides, I've talked to some of the other farmers. They say the marks are too clean to be coyotes."

"Maybe you've got animals on that farm of yours that could make some clean marks. In fact, I'm sure you do. We'll see what the other farmers think of that. I'll be back, John, and I won't come alone. You can count on that."

The mayor hopped into the cab, kicking the truck into reverse. A cloud of dust followed as it barreled down the gravel road.

"What's stuck up his butt?" Alice looked to Greggs.

Greggs sighed and uncrossed his arms. "That is one meddlin', schemin' man. Always looking for an excuse to poke around my land. C'mon, I'll tell you about it around back."

He put out his cigarette, eyed Alice's shoes once more, and walked into the house, holding open the door behind him.

The sparse walls and mostly empty rooms made every footfall echo. The few items in the living room to the right—a couch, a folded-up blanket, a coffee table—trapped the smell of stale cigarette smoke.

A white blur of dog came reeling from the hallway and jumped up on the old man.

"Down, you damn dogs," Greggs grumbled, although he gave a gentle pet on each of the two heads.

Alice's eyes went wide. "That dog's got two heads."

"Sure do. This here is Charlies."

The white bulldog set upon Alice with reckless abandon, almost knocking her over. The two heads licked at her arms and hands with their stinking, slobbery tongues. Alice cringed at her coated hands and wiped them on her pant legs.

"Keep a'walkin', or they'll just keep lickin' at ya."

Alice followed Greggs as Charlies jumped against her back legs, making her knees bend with every other step.

Greggs paused briefly in the kitchen, where he gathered six apples, a stalk of celery, a pack of Pall Malls, and five boxes of black hair dye in a basket.

When they reached the back door, Greggs quickly shut the screen behind Alice, trapping Charlies in the house. Both of Charlies' heads whined, and its front legs scratched at the door. Greggs ignored him and continued into the backyard.

A big, brown barn stood in front of an overgrown field, the paint peeling from its aging wood. A molding billboard rested against the side of it.

"All right, now," Greggs said, stopping her before he opened the gate to the field. "You strike me as the type that's seen some things. Didn't even look shocked to see the unicorn in the back yesterday."

Alice thought of her mother, who was often passed out from taking and mixing too many drugs. "Yeah, I've seen a few things."

"An old soul. That's what you got. I can always tell when someone's got one." Greggs studied Alice with his beady, sky-blue eyes, and Alice tried her best not to squirm.

"See that sign over there?" Greggs pointed to the aging but still colorful sign propped up against the side of the barn.

Alice looked at it and squinted. "I can't make it out."

"It says *The Greggs Family Zoo of Odd and Marvelous Creatures.*" Greggs leaned against the fence and lit a new cigarette. "My daddy bought this land for cheap from the government way back when. Wanted to make a name for himself raising cows, chickens, pigs, and the like. So he got this land, and he started clearin' it out and puttin' up this fence.

"One day, he was workin' as the sun was just settin' down. He told me he felt a chill all down his backside, and when he looked up, a little bit of the sky had turned black right above him. Daddy cleared out of the way—no tellin' if that was gonna turn into a tornado or some such. But he kept watchin' it. A creature with big ol' wings fell from that black smudge of sky. Damn near died on its way down. Daddy took it to the barn and nursed it back to health, and the thing just stuck around. Not a friendly creature by any means, but it didn't go nowhere. So Daddy named him Wayne and let him stay.

"Not a few months later, and Daddy found a strange horse runnin' around on his land. Its hair was purple in the sunlight. And you can guess what it had stickin' out of its head."

"A horn," I offered.

"Yep. It was a unicorn," Greggs confirmed. He shifted his weight from the fence, sucked on the end of his cigarette, and opened the gate for Alice.

"Now, my daddy was no dummy. He knew them cows and pigs were gonna cost money, but he spent all he had buyin' up the land. See, he and my momma came up with the idea of this little roadside zoo.

"You'd see backyard zoos all over Nebraska and Missouri back then. People had one or two jungle cats, maybe a bear. But there wasn't a zoo quite like this one. No, sir. These strange creatures kept on fallin' from the sky, and Daddy kept right on collectin' 'em. He took good care of 'em, and so did me and my brother. Daddy made a lot of money on the zoo, at first.

"But the thing is, people don't believe what they ain't never seen before. The zoo became a laughingstock in town. People called us crooks. Said we put cheap things on regular animals to make 'em look funny.

"One night, some local boys got drunk and hopped the fence. They wanted to see how we put the horns on the unicorns. They wanted to see how we fooled everybody.

"Well, it was no joke. One of them boys spooked a unicorn so bad that it stabbed him. Went clean through his stomach." Greggs shook his head. "That was Mayor Artie's uncle. Of course, Artie wasn't even born at that time. But he's still got to remind me of the event as if he had been. He's been obsessed with that story ever since he was a boy. He's taken it on himself to investigate. He thinks I'm housing hellhounds or something evil. I've never seen a man so convinced of something in all my life.

"Anyway. Daddy had to close down the zoo after that boy died. Daddy died a few months after that. We had enough money to keep the farm goin'. And these creatures keep comin' from that same spot in the sky."

"That's amazing, Mr. Greggs," Alice said.

"Just Greggs, kid." He looked amused.

"Okay, Greggs. Did your dad ever figure out what that thing is? Up in the sky?" Alice asked.

"Nobody knows what it is. It's like some other place started throwing their trash through it. All these unwanted animals and such. I think my daddy figured it was our job to take care of these dysfunctional creatures. So that's what we continued to do after he died. Now it's just me, as you can see. And I'm so old I'm practically growin' cobwebs."

Greggs started toward the barn, carrying the basket full of odds and ends.

"So you've got all these unicorns in your barn?" Alice asked.

"Most of 'em. Can't keep 'em locked up all day, though. So I got the idea to dye 'em. You know, with hair dye?" Greggs shook a box of dye in the basket. "As soon as a new one comes through, I color the purple coat black. If anyone sees one of 'em from the road, all they see are black horses. You can't even see the bone on their heads from that distance." Greggs smiled in satisfaction.

"Clever." Alice wondered if Greggs didn't have one or two screws loose.

"I know," Greggs said, turning toward the barn.

A hissing sound stopped them both in their tracks.

"Careful, now," Greggs whispered.

Alice noticed a dark figure on the barn roof, blocking the sun. The figure spread its enormous, black wings and jumped from the roof. It made a twirling and hissing sound as it dove. Then it screeched.

Greggs casually pulled Alice clear from the dark creature's path.

Alice clutched Greggs' muscular forearm in panic.

The creature smacked into the ground face-first.

"And that's Wayne," Greggs said, leading Alice closer to the incapacitated creature.

"What the hell is that thing?" Alice grimaced.

"Daddy took to calling him a werebat. You know those stories about werewolves? Well, one of those mixed with a bat. Don't he look just like that?" Greggs squatted next to Wayne and carefully rolled the creature onto its back.

Alice's stomach turned with disgust. Wayne's body, where it wasn't covered in matted, black fur, was slick and shiny like plastic wrap. Dark dents and scars lined its hairless head. The bridge of its nose was ribbed, and huge nostrils flared at the base.

No matter how repulsive the werebat was, Alice felt a pang of pity for it. "What's wrong with it?"

Greggs sighed and gathered Wayne in his arms. "Can you grab that basket, kid?" he said over his shoulder as he walked to the barn.

Alice grabbed the basket and jogged after him.

Greggs raised his voicc. "I think ol' Wayne here is supposed to be one of them horrific creatures. Like the ones on *The Twilight Zone*."

"What's *The Twilight Zone*?" Alice asked.

"Oh, hell," the old man laughed, "never mind. Can you grab the door?"

Alice slid open the enormous barn door.

"Anyway," Greggs said going into the barn, "Wayne can't fly. I think he's supposed to, but I ain't sure. He keeps tryin'. And he keeps on fallin'. So your first chore is to keep an eye out for Wayne. Can you do that?" Greggs plopped the creature onto a large, wooden worktable.

"What if he lunges at me again? I can't carry him around," Alice said, evaluating Wayne's weight.

"He's actually pretty light. See?" Greggs hooked his finger around one of Wayne's ankles and half-lifted the creature from the table. "Don't worry, kid, he's all scream, no bite. Knocked all his teeth out from fallin' so many times, anyway."

"Okay," Alice said, still unsure. "Just carry him in here if I find him like that?"

"Sure thing. Oh, and he gets six apples a day. Only the red ones, no Granny Smiths. Just mush 'em up real good and leave 'em out somewhere easy to find. I don't think he sees real well." Greggs unloaded the apples next to the worktable. "Now, ready to see some geese?"

"I guess so," Alice said, following Greggs as he exited the barn.

Greggs led them to a chicken coop the size of a playhouse. Alice peeked inside. Gray, long-necked geese sat on nests. The white males flapped to the doorway, threatening Alice and Greggs away from the females.

Something clanged down a metal shoot below the coop. Bending over a bucket, Greggs picked up a marbled, brown egg. He rapped his knuckles on it. "Solid wood. About as useful as a sixth toe."

Alice reached for the wooden egg in wonder.

"I don't know what else to use 'em for but my whittlin'." Greggs grabbed a second egg from the bucket and stuck it in his pocket. "Just put 'em on the table on the back porch. Also, feed the geese a couple handfuls of grain a day." Greggs pointed to a large, broken-down ice chest. "Feed's in there."

Alice took note of the feed, and then quickly followed Greggs past the geese. He walked quickly, taking them to the edge of a small, smelly lagoon.

"And these"—he pulled out the pack of Pall Malls from the basket—"are for the merlady. I call her Marilyn."

"Merlady?" Alice's eyes bulged.

Greggs whistled. The soupy surface of the lagoon broke, revealing the ratty, orange hair of the merlady.

As she pushed the top half of her body onto the small, grassy bank, Alice couldn't help but curl her lips in disgust. Marilyn's face wrinkled with extreme age. Bags of skin sagged from her arms and waist. Her breasts hung down to her bellybutton like deflated party balloons. Three slits on either of her cheeks opened and shut. Gills, Alice realized.

"Hey there, Marilyn," Greggs cooed at the wretched crone. "This is Alice. She'll be bringing you your cigarettes from now on. But don't you worry. I'll be here at sunset for our evening smoke, like usual."

Greggs squatted next to the merlady. He stuck a smoke in her mouth and lit the end for her. Marilyn sucked in deep. Using her brown fingernails, she plucked the cigarette from her lips and exhaled. She let out a satisfied-sounding sigh.

"I don't know if she knows what I'm saying, but she sure likes her Pall Malls." Greggs pulled one out for himself, lighting the end.

The two flicked the tips, letting the wind carry the ash, and looked out at the land. Alice sighed, crossed her arms, and watched the lagoon.

As she watched, the murky water parted again, this time revealing a three-headed snake twice the size of Greggs. Greggs' head was turned away from the lagoon, and the snake came closer and closer to the bank.

"Greggs," Alice whispered sharply to warn him.

He turned his head to the snake. The heads hissed, their green scales and black eyes sparkling in the sun. "Oh, don't worry, kid. They're vegetarians. Throw some celery to 'em."

Alice's hands shook as she peeled ribs of celery off the stalks. She limply threw the pieces in front of the snake. The three heads darted to the celery in the water, snapping the crisp ribs in their mouths. When they finished, the heads turned to Alice and hissed.

"Well, keep goin'," Greggs encouraged.

Alice threw the ribs carefully until the stalk was gone. The hydra hissed once more at Greggs, then slid back into the lagoon.

Greggs put out his cigarette stub, stood up and brushed off the back of his jeans. "Why don't you light another one for Marilyn before we go? Takes her no less than ten minutes to do it on her own with them webbed fingers."

Alice exhaled, dreading the experience. Her hands still shook from feeding the hydra. As she flicked the flint to ignite the cigarette dangling from the merlady's lips, Alice remembered lighting cigarettes for her mother. She asked Alice to light them when she was too strung out to do it herself.

"You okay, kid?"

Alice shook her head. "Yeah. It just smells out here, is all."

"Yeah, it does. But they seem to prefer it." Greggs held up his hands. "Don't ask me. I don't get it."

Greggs started back toward the barn, leaving Alice to one last, lingering look at the saggy merlady.

Alice ran to catch up with Greggs just as he opened the barn door. Greggs pointed to the empty table where he had set Wayne. "See? Gone already. Sneaking off, doing his sneaky werebat things."

Alice nodded, surprised that the werebat survived his earlier plunge.

Greggs pointed beyond the table to two long, wooden rows. They walked farther into the barn. In each stall, a black unicorn stood. Most contently chewed on hay, absently watching the old man and young girl.

"I've got thirteen unicorns. A few of 'em pass away when they fall, but most of 'em make it out okay."

Alice squinted at one of the unicorns. An unusual creature slept peacefully on its back. "Is that a cat or something?" she asked.

Greggs clapped his hands, waking the creature. Its yellow eyes opened lazily, then the little dragon rose and stretched out its wings and legs.

"Just a little whelp. We've got a quite a few of 'em around here. They seem to prefer the unicorns. Cute little things just curl up on 'em and sleep all day."

"That's a dragon, right? Don't dragons breathe fire?" Alice wondered. "Isn't that dangerous for the unicorns?"

"Not these little guys." Greggs reached over the gate and scratched the whelp on the head. The dragon rubbed Greggs's hand affectionately. "Can only puff smoke every now and again. That is, when they aren't sleepin'. And that's about all they do."

Greggs moved down to the next gate and opened it. Alice recognized the unicorn that had fallen from the sky the day before. It lay on a blanket, its ankle wrapped.

"How is she?" Alice asked.

"She'll be fine in no time."

They studied the unicorn. Its eyes watched them passively as a dragon whelp curled up by its chest.

"So that's it? Those are my chores?" Alice asked.

"Well, not quite. I'll handle the jackalopes today. Poor things are blind and have antlers that go on for miles. Get tangled in just about everything. Then there's Glen, the turtle about the size of my living room. He mostly just burrows underground, though. Just gotta check on him every now and again, make sure he's still breathin'. The donkeys can be a handful. Not real donkeys. I just call 'em that because they look like a cross between a dog and a monkey. They hang in the trees in the middle of the field out back. But I'll show you all that later." Greggs turned back to the unicorn. "Your job for the rest of the day is to dye this old girl black."

Alice swallowed. "I don't know how to do that."

"It's okay, I'll do it with you. It's really as easy as readin' the back of the box."

Greggs opened the box and handed Alice a pair of plastic gloves.

☙ ✧ ❧

Every day except Sundays for the next three weeks, Alice met Greggs on his front porch at seven o'clock in the morning.

Greggs provided her with a pair of sturdy, leather cowboy boots, just as he promised. Every day, Alice would put on her boots and pick up the wooden goose eggs and deposit them on the back porch. She cleaned the unicorn stables and touched up the coats when purple started showing through. Charlies joined her on most days, their heads nipping at her calves. She learned to wear jeans early on, saving her legs from the constant slobber.

Alice became more comfortable with feeding the hydra. She lit the merlady's Pall Malls without comment, watching the old, withering creature puff. Marilyn shrieked at her when she wanted another one, and Alice lit them all without complaint.

Wayne kept jumping from high places. Sometimes from the loft in the barn. Sometimes from the roof of the house. And every time, Alice picked up his surprisingly light body and took him to a soft, shady area to regain consciousness. She became fond of the strange thing and his determination to fly.

Alice helped untangle the jackalopes, checked up on Glen the giant turtle every few days, and put up with the donkeys' antics.

The unicorn that fell from the sky recuperated quickly, with the help of daily injections of bute. Alice wrapped the sprain every few days, enjoying the excuse to spend time with the magnificent creature.

Greggs would walk around the farm, patting each of his creatures happily. The animals loved him and purred under his touch. When Charlies wasn't following Alice, he was by Greggs' side, pleading for scratches and adoration.

No new creatures had appeared since Alice had joined on as a farmhand. Every night, before Greggs smoked a cigarette with Marilyn at the lagoon, he'd ride out to the fence separating his land from Alice's grandparents' land. He'd wait an hour, and when no dark clouds appeared, he'd ride back.

After Independence Day, the coyote attacks picked up considerably. Farms to the south and to the west regularly reported dead or considerably torn up cattle, and the deaths kept creeping closer to Greggs' farm.

Alice and Greggs spent four days reinforcing the fence. Alice spent so much time hammering, her hands still vibrated when she went to bed at night.

ଓ ✧ ଓ

Just as he had promised, the mayor returned two weeks into July. And he was not alone.

Alice had just finished collecting the eggs. As she set the last one on the table, she heard rapping on the front door. She felt a sense of foreboding, as no one had called on Greggs since she started working on the farm. Knowing Greggs was out in the barn with the unicorns, Alice hurried to him.

"There's someone at your door," she called, unable to hide the alarm in her voice.

Greggs shuffled up to the house, Alice following close behind. Charlies tried to get through the back door behind them, but Alice nudged him with her foot, forcing the two-headed dog to stay in the backyard. Both faces whined in unison. "It's to keep you safe, Charlies. Now hush up!"

They walked wordlessly to the front door. Turning back slightly to Alice, Greggs exhaled and opened the door.

Mayor Artie, pudgy as ever, stood in the doorway just outside the screen door.

"Told you I'd be back, John."

"What's this about, Artie? I'm in the middle of something."

"So are we." Artie turned to the side, revealing Sheriff Martell. The sheriff kept a thick, brown mustache and wore aviator sunglasses. His arms were muscled, and a tan line peeked out from his short-sleeved uniform. Behind the sheriff was a crowd of about twenty local farmers, all wearing scowls.

"What's all this about, Sheriff?" Greggs asked.

"Afternoon, John. It looks like we have a problem." The sheriff pointed to Gregg's driveway. Alice squinted, just making out bloody cow parts lining the gravel road. A cow head lay closest to the front porch, its eyes watching the house lifelessly.

"Holy Hannah," Greggs mumbled, covering his mouth.

"And it all points back here. To your farm full of creatures, John." Artie smiled slyly.

"That's not possible," Greggs said, shaking his head. "Nothing I have could've done a monstrous thing like that."

"And are we supposed to just take your word for that? Your family's been keeping those creatures a secret for years. We need to know what's back there, Greggs. For the safety of everyone and their livestock." Artie turned back to the farmers. "Don't you want to know what John Greggs has been hiding on this farm of his?"

They confirmed that they did.

Greggs looked at Alice by his side. His eyes looked old and watery. "It's hopeless."

"Show them," Alice said boldly.

"They'll take one look at 'em, and think they're dangerous," Greggs spoke quietly. "They won't understand, kid."

"Then we make them understand. *I'll* make them understand," Alice assured him. She opened the screen door and addressed the mayor, sheriff, and farmers. "Come on. I'll show you the animals. You'll see that nothing on this farm could've hurt those cattle."

Alice led the people through Gregg's living room and out the back door. Charlies whined at the unfamiliar faces, and Alice patted both of the dog's heads.

"This is Charlies. Watch out, he'll lick you until there isn't a dry spot left on you."

The farmers peered over each other's shoulders. They stared at the two-headed dog, mouths agape. The mayor stood still, his arms crossed in front of his chest, sneering at the dog.

Alice smiled smugly. "Follow me. What you're really here to see is in the barn."

She led them to the fence and opened the gate. Charlies galloped next to a burly-looking farmer. The farmer patted their heads and chuckled, seeming to take an immediate liking to the dog.

Greggs put his leathery hand on the barn door. He looked at Alice, and she nodded at him. He slid the door open.

"Here's where we keep the unicorns," Alice said, matter-of-factly. She walked up to the first stall and pet the unicorn's mane.

Gasps sounded from the party.

"Is this really a … a …" a woman stammered.

Alice approached the woman, gently took her hand, and led her to the first stall. She placed the woman's hand on the unicorn's black mane.

"Yep. It really is a unicorn. See? Just as gentle as can be."

The woman's face lit up, and she watched the creature in awe.

The mayor yelled. "What in the world is that? There on that one's back?"

All eyes landed on a little dragon whelp, which was licking itself unceremoniously on the backside.

Greggs cleared his throat. "That's a little whelpling. Go ahead, they love gettin' pet."

The woman moved slowly toward the dragon whelp. She lifted her hand to the creature, and the whelp stood and brushed its body against her hand.

"Aw," the woman cooed. "Look at you, so sweet."

Their fears subsiding, the farmers gathered around the stalls, admiring the unicorns and the dragon whelps.

Alice smiled at Greggs triumphantly.

An older farmer who was petting a whelp looked over to the mayor. "You told us John had dangerous creatures back here, Artie."

"These little things are as gentle as house cats," the woman said, tickling a whelp's back.

"Are we looking at the same things, here? Look at these freaks! Who's to say they won't kill something or someone if they got out?"

The old farmer jiggled the lock on the stable door in front of him. "Looks secure to me. And if they did get out, I don't see what kind of harm they'd do anybody. And these things sure didn't rip up my cattle. Those cuts were too clean."

"Go ahead and have a look around if you're still not satisfied, Artie. All the animals on this farm are safe, kind, and secure." Greggs smiled at the mayor confidently.

The farmers looked around the barn, some going outside to look at some of the other creatures.

Mayor Artie looked around incredulously. Alice slipped behind him and slid the knife off his belt. She handed it to Greggs, who nodded at her knowingly.

"Artie." Greggs motioned the mayor over.

The mayor's face was red and sweaty with rage. "These animals need to be destroyed. They're dangerous, and it's just a matter of time before they kill again."

"The way I see it, it's only a matter of time before *you* kill again."

"Don't you wish you could prove that." The mayor smiled.

"You and I both know what killed all those cattle."

Artie sneered. "Yeah, one of your freaks here."

"No, I don't believe so." Greggs looked to the mayor's knife in his hands. "This is your knife, isn't it?"

"Hey, where did you—"

"You're always showin' this thing around. Awful proud of it, aren't you?" Greggs slid the blade out of the leather hilt. "It doesn't look like you had a chance to clean it recently. I can just make out some blood in the ridges. Oh my, is that cow hair in some of that blood, there?"

Mayor Artie swallowed and balled his fists.

"I'll tell them, Artie. I'll tell these folks their own mayor's been cuttin' up their cattle, just so he can get a peek at my animals. And now you've seen 'em. You're lookin' at my big secret. Now what do you say you stop this whole thing between us? Let sleepin' dogs lie?"

Artie relaxed his fists, staring at his bloodied hunting knife. "All right. I'll leave you alone." Artie pointed his finger in Gregg's face. "But if anything happens to anyone visiting this freak show you call a zoo, you better believe I'll be all over you like white on rice."

"And so will I," Greggs said, holding up Mayor Artie's knife. "You'll leave me, Alice, and this zoo alone, or everyone will hear what you've done."

Mayor Artie swept his hand across his sweaty brow. He nodded once and turned to leave.

"Wait," Alice called. "Don't you think you should say something about the dead cattle and all those cow parts on Mr. Greggs' driveway?"

Greggs held up the mayor's knife. "What's this secret worth to ya?" He winked at Alice. She chuckled, remembering the first time they met when the unicorn fell from the sky.

Artie wheeled around and faced the farmers. "For all you still here, I just wanted to formally apologize to John. I was wrong." He flashed a contemptuous look at Greggs, and then turned back to the people. "You all can still count on me to track down the beast that killed your cattle. I'll find it, don't you worry about that."

The farmers watched Artie skeptically as he walked out of the barn. He didn't look back at Alice or Greggs.

Alice threw her arms around Greggs, and Greggs patted her back. "You're just what this place needs, kid. Someone who believes in it.

Someone who thinks these creatures ought to be loved and admired, and not kept a secret. Now, c'mon. We've got a lot of work to do."

"What do you mean?" Alice asked, pulling away from Greggs.

"I mean we're gonna reopen The Greggs Family Zoo of Odd and Marvelous Creatures. You and me—whaddaya say, kid?"

Alice looked at the remaining farmers in the barn. They laughed with one another, petting the unicorns and the dragon whelps while they chatted. The joy on their faces was undeniable. Alice even caught a glimpse of Wayne in the rafters, watching the people. She loved the farm more than she had loved anything else.

"You belong here, kid," Greggs said, smiling proudly.

"I think I do."

"All right, then. Let's show these farmers the rest of the animals." Greggs started toward the door. "And tomorrow, we begin renovations. I need you here at six o'clock sharp, and not a minute later. We've got plenty of work ahead of us."

Alice smiled as they walked out of the barn. "I'll be here. Six o'clock. Not a minute later."

Ménagerie Violette

Colette Black

A fantastical medley had come to life, the diverse array of fae, werewolves, leprechauns, vampires, and others, including some sorceresses like myself, paraded down Paris's Champs-Élysées. I stood amongst the crowd, observing the spectacle's belly slither onward, its tail not far behind. The beast's rowdy head began to circle the still-incomplete Arc de Triomphe, cymbals clanging and trumpets blaring in time with the supernaturals' acrobatics.

My father would be furious if he knew I'd come, but at seventeen, I was of age, and he had no right to deny me attendance to such a popular event. And if I succeeded, the name Floressa Pietregalla would be an inspiration to sorceresses the world over. The thought gave me a little thrill as I nestled more determinedly into the surrounding crowd.

The people smelled of sweat and acrid perfumes, but the scent wafting from the street held even less appeal. The majority of supernaturals exuded chemicals that reminded humans of fresh orchards, but to a sorceress they all smelled of rotting fruit. I gave thanks to whatever power had created my kind that I could emit any perfume I desired, sweet or foul, enticing or repugnant.

For now, I chose to have no smell at all. The better to observe while remaining unobserved. I did so without awe, though I was disturbed at the participants' willingness to display themselves like circus animals. Unlike the surrounding mortals only recently made aware of the uncomfortable veracity of their legends, I focused solely on claws and implements. Someone would be murdered tonight, and the murderer was a supernatural.

A male faerie doffed a top hat nearly half his size. Meant, perhaps, to compensate for his lack in height? He spread incandescent wings through the slits in his frock coat, vaulted into the air, and performed a quadruple somersault before size and gravity brought him to an unsteady landing. The crowds roared, but the young man's eyes shifted toward the young lady to his right. Demure as a comtesse in our own Louis XVIII's court, she averted her gaze. With porcelain skin that made faeries the envy of every courtier, she turned rosy pink along her high cheekbones.

"The ol' fop of a fairy managed a nice trick there, I do say."

Recognizing Jack of Krinlock's voice as he came beside me, I suppressed a sigh. I meant to give him my attention for but a moment, however he presented a stunning form in a chestnut redingote coat snug to his wide shoulders, tapering to his narrow waist, then draping in slim folds to his knees over dark trousers. It accented brilliantly with a well-tailored waistcoat and simple cravat held in place by a single pearl pin. He topped the ensemble with a d'orsay hat of conservative height and sensual curves. With his stature, he needed neither tall hats nor padded coats, for he filled the less extensive versions admirably.

He returned my observations with intelligent eyes that bowed to no one and would not be dictated to by the opinion of others. It was something I liked about Jack. I pursed my lips at his all-knowing smile, set in unusually tanned skin for an Englishman, framed by a quite ordinary mop of brown hair accented with less-than-ordinary streaks of reddish-blond that followed into his rugged sideburns.

I supposed him to be less informed concerning the fae, to think a simple trick would attract a faerie lady's attention. "La, monsieur. Most fae find physical displays of prowess, while they are being watched by mortals, stuck as they are at full size, embarrassing. I do not think his efforts accomplished what he had hoped."

"Would you mean the attention of the woman with the becoming mauve dress and the ruffled collar?"

Turning back to the parade, I watched with surprise as the fae woman sidled close to the man, the disparity between their wings emphasizing the woman's extremely petite frame. Tilting her mauve parasol to one side, the lace edge fluttered in the slight breeze below its sharp ebony tip. She took the young man's arm, the black-patterned hem of her cone-shaped skirt brushing against his ankles.

Jack smirked. "Come now, Miss Pietregalla, even you cannot dispute love when it is right in front of your eyes."

I didn't miss the double meaning, as *he* was standing before my eyes more than the fae couple. Since my coming-out soiree a year ago, despite all my efforts to show a distinct lack of interest in any mortal, Monsieur Jack Krinlock, two years my senior, had become an infrequent suitor. Since my seventeenth birthday a month ago, infrequent had turned to persistent.

I flipped open my fan, letting the ornate silver frame and yellow taffeta fabric hide my embarrassment. "Infatuation is all I see standing before me, and I prefer you use my Christian name. Pietregalla is much too Corsican."

"Ah," said Jack. "You don't want to be associated with your exiled Bonaparte."

"Of course not." I fanned my face. The very idea! "Not only was he a vampire, but the rumors say he adhered to traditional feeding practices on mortals. Until the outrage dies down, I believe it best not to flaunt our shared Corsican heritage."

Jack's eyes twinkled in delight, as if I'd invited him to use my name out of familiarity. "So what brings you to the Ides of March parade, Floressa?"

Though I tried, I couldn't hide the excitement in my voice. "I am here to catch a murderer."

His amber eyes darkened. "I thought your father told you to stay out of it."

"*Mais bien sûr,* of course." I snapped my fan shut. "I may be young, but I am as capable a sorceress as another. My father is away from town, taking care of business across the channel. I will show him what I can do."

Jack fumbled with his waistcoat, fingering the edges with nervous energy. "It might be best for you to wait. Surely your father won't be gone more than a fortnight."

"I did the divinations," I said. "The Violet Unicorn is striking tonight."

As if in mockery, a unicorn clopped its amethyst hooves against the gravel road, its horn sparkling the same color. Its silken coat, a deep damson purple, shimmered like spun sugar. As it approached, it whinnied, seeming to goad me for my inability to find the killer with a similar namesake. Its long-bearded handler glared in our direction—dwarves weren't capable of anything besides glares, I thought—tugging the unicorn forward. The little man's mulberry coat appeared almost too coordinated with the unicorn's gemlike hues. Dwarves rarely bothered with fashion. He took care around the horn swishing above his helmeted head. Even an accidental swipe of that horn could draw blood.

Smirking, Jack watched it pass, understanding the irony. "Do they really think he could be a unicorn? They're as docile as kittens."

I succumbed to an unladylike snort, the kind my father always chastised me for. "Of course the killer is not a unicorn. Some *imbécile* from the Americas was at the scene after the first murder. He commented that the slash across the victim's neck appeared as if something from a violent unicorn. With his strange accent, it sounded like 'violet unicorn.' The appellation has continued."

"Still, I don't see what you hope to accomplish at a parade of the supernatural. The murderer isn't going to reveal himself during a parade."

I gave Jack a genuine smile. "Father says people leave clues about themselves everywhere they go, especially when watched by a sorceress. I have a suspect, already. I must only test my theory."

"Test where?"

Tapping my fan against Jack's chest, I shot him a flirtatious smile from under my long lashes. "That, *mon ami,* is something you need not know. You are human, and I'll not put you in harm's way."

Of course, my sweet and chivalrous Jack refused to take no for an answer. "Regardless of your destination, you must at least have a gentleman's escort. Will eight thirty be soon enough?"

I gave a demure smile befitting a girl my age. "*Bien sûr,* I will await you at my home in Paris." I gave a short curtsy and wished him well. "*Bon après-midi.*"

Jack managed a flourishing bow, despite the crowd. "A good afternoon to you as well, Floressa."

Before I could turn and leave, he took my hand in his, leaving a lingering kiss across my knuckles.

In an attempt to hide the fluttering rising from my stomach to my cheeks, I bowed my head and make a quick escape. Raising my yellow-and-white parasol above my less-than-desirable olive complexion, the silver tip capable of stopping werewolves and worse, I strode through the crowd and away from Jack's heady influence. He had the good sense not to follow. As I used bright smiles and sharp elbows to force my narrow frame through the masses, I directed my thoughts toward Jack as if he had a palm reader's gift, which was how it sometimes seemed.

And, monsieur, you had best not follow when you discover I am not at home.

☙ ✧ ❧

Perhaps Jack did have a palm reader's gift, for rather than follow, he outmaneuvered me. By appointing half past eight as the time he would arrive with his carriage, he manipulated my predictable arrival to the Jardin Tabille gardens at 8:15.

Leaning a muscular shoulder encased in a plum tailcoat against one of the many pillars near the garden's entrance, he tipped a short top hat, the black sheen matching his simple Hessians, his cravat tied much as it had been earlier in the day, but now with a black pearl pin encompassed in gold filigree. Unlike most men his age, his most obvious adornment wasn't a fob or an oversized button, but his all-knowing smile, set above a well-sculptured jaw and perfectly symmetrical features.

He pushed off from the pillar, taking easy strides to stand beside me. "You look beautiful, Floressa. You should wear periwinkle more often."

Self-conscious of my gown's wide neckline, I pulled a cream paisley shawl over my shoulders before changing my matching parasol to my other hand and tucking my free one through the crook of Jack's arm, noticing the taut muscles beneath my fingers. I let him accompany me between hedges sprinkled with tiny white flowers and ornate urns overflowing with pink tea roses that muted the smell I'd come to associate with Jack: human male, eau de cologne, and something familiar that I couldn't quite place.

I sighed with false exasperation. "You, monsieur, are a trickster." I wasn't sure if I wanted to slap him or laugh, but I couldn't remain angry. "How did you know where to find me?"

"Where else would you find a gathering of the supernatural and the mortal, but the Ides of March Integration Ball?" Leaning his head close to mine, Jack's warm breath tickled my neck. "I also had Humphrey wait along the Rue de Maubeuge with my carriage. He followed you, in case I was wrong."

We passed a tall elm, the damson unicorn from the parade eating lazily at the long grasses near its base. The glaring dwarf gave us a perfunctory glance and a disgruntled sniff, as if we were the ones with hygiene offenses. Most of the supernatural set recognized me as a sorceress by my wide, large eyes and the streak of silver above my left ear. Otherwise, however, I looked human and in these dimly lit walkways, he likely mistook me as such.

Spotting my objective, I urged Jack to the far end of the dance floor, well away from the orchestra grating their strings into a raucous waltz. We sat at a table near a tall hedge that led into a labyrinth filled with alcoves perfect for lovers' rendezvous.

I took his long fingers into my own. "You should stay here, mon ami. As I said before, you are too human and could easily become a target."

Jack bristled, his back straightening in English indignation. "I'm not letting a beautiful young lady such as yourself roam a place of such dubious reputation as the Jardin Tabille alone. It is not done, my dear."

An inebriated dandy, his cravat untied and hanging loose around his neck, took his giggling companion by the hand and ducked into the shadows of the labyrinth. As I'd suspected, the fairy girl and her supposed "newfound" companion from the parade followed.

As much as I adored Jack, this was no job for a mere human. "Stay," I ordered, coming to my feet.

He pushed his chair back, intent to follow. I'd sworn to Jack early in our friendship that I would never use sorcery on him, but he left me no choice. Pulling from my reticule what appeared to be smelling salts, I tossed a pinch between us and spoke a quick incantation. The lavender flakes sparked, and Jack froze, seeing nothing, hearing nothing. Guilt made my heart heavy, but I couldn't stand the thought of putting my dear Jack in danger.

Hurrying into the labyrinth, I did a final check behind me. The duration of the spell depended on the subject's willingness to be lulled versus their determination for freedom. Jack's interest in me was likely more diversionary than true affection, so he wouldn't fight too hard to remain by my side. I should be well done with this entire escapade before Jack blinked.

Following the scent of rotten berries, I found the faeries standing before the drunken couple. The dandy's jacket and shirt lay draped over one edge of the bench. The woman's arms crossed her breasts, her look of horror following the diminutive faerie woman's substantially tipped parasol.

"Stop!" I yelled. "You're not going to kill another innocent."

The faerie woman turned. We faced one another, fashion accessories raised like dueling swords, my parasol of periwinkle flowers against her mauve with ruffled edging.

"Who do ye be?" said the faerie, her Irish accent so strong I could scarce make out the words. "I may be a thief, but no mortal lass dare call me a murderer."

Shocked, I finally took in her companion's pale expression, the deep green coin purse dangling from limp fingers, and the slack jaw of a novice.

My parasol felt suddenly heavy. "You're not the Violet Unicorn."

"Congratulations, my dear," Jack's voice drawled from behind. "You've broken your promise to me, and unveiled a petty thief."

Jack mocked me, but I sensed an underlying anger. And with good reason.

I dropped the tip of my parasol, digging it into the moist dirt between bits of gravel. "I'm sorry. I didn't want you to get hurt."

"So you left me sitting at a table, stiff as stone, unable to defend myself?"

I hadn't thought of it that way. I'd only wanted to keep him from danger. "But there were people. If anyone had tried—"

Jack growled, a sound I'd never heard from him before. "Nobody here would lift a finger for a mortal who suddenly disappears into the shadows. Your only thought was to prove yourself to your father. Nothing else. Now that this ridiculous charade is at an end, I presume you can find your own way home."

He turned on his heel, disappearing between dark hedges and darker shadows.

I reached out a hand. "But ..." There was nothing else to say. I'd betrayed his trust, and he had every right to condemn me for it.

"Come on then, Harold," said the faerie woman to her companion. "I be thinking we're done here for the night."

With a curt nod, he followed the woman's quick steps. "Yes, Tianna."

I followed a few paces behind, wiping at the tears in the corners of my eyes. The faeries had only made the first turn toward the main pavilion when I overhead Tianna.

"And what be the treasure here?"

As I turned the corner, Harold squinted down at the item in her hand. "A cravat pin. Nice workmanship."

I threw myself between them, grabbing Tianna's fingers with my own. "That's Jack's pin."

"The man blustering at you a moment ago?" asked Tianna.

"I deserved it," I said. "Now what has happened to him?"

The woman raised frightened eyes. "Something bad, lass. I sense it. Be best if ye get yourself away."

"*Non.* Jack's life is in danger, and it is my fault."

Nearby broken branches evidenced a struggle. I searched until I spied the drag lines of a man's heels turning the labyrinth's corner. A few paces farther, two deep footsteps took its place then disappeared into the thicker gravel.

"Good luck to ye, lass." Tianna took Harold's hand and dragged him in the other direction, toward the labyrinth's entrance and away from Jack's tragedy.

I straightened my shoulders, lifted my chin. *I am Floressa Pietregalla, daughter of the best sorcerer-detective in all of France,* I told myself. *I must find Jack. He may be a mere mortal, but I love him.*

The admission shocked a gasp from my lips. I couldn't lose him, especially not now that I'd finally realized how much he meant to me. And he'd broken my spell almost instantly, which proved the affection must be reciprocated.

With quivering hands, I pulled my ingredients pouch from my reticule, retrieving my satchel of dried hydrangea. Upending the sparse contents onto the footprint, I uttered my spell. This time I felt the magic's cost. Weariness dragged at my bones. The footprint glowed a pale blue, followed by the next print and the next, overlaying the seemingly undisturbed rocks and dirt, leading me farther into the labyrinth. After a nervous glance behind, I gripped my parasol in sweaty palms, and followed the footstep's iridescent lead.

The faint glow brought me deep into the labyrinth's belly, farther than even the lanterns reached. Eventually I stepped between two hedges that had almost grown together, obscuring my path if not for the magical footprints. I found myself in a small meadow, seemingly closed off by rectangular hedges, and screamed. Blood slicked the fresh grass. It poured like a stream from the dead man leaning against the far hedge, his head angled to one side as if it might topple. His life leaked across his magenta coat, so similar in color to Jack's.

A familiar voice slithered from the shadows, chilling me more than the cool spring air, or even the sight of the stranger's life spilled between us. "His name is Pierre Francois Hercule de Serre," said Jack. "The Minister of Justice, Keeper of the Seals."

I swallowed back the bile threatening to add its stench to the dead minister's.

Stepping around the dead man, Jack held up his murder weapon, a broad branch in the shape of a unicorn's horn. It glowed a pale amethyst. "In the name of justice, he performed horrible atrocities against our kind. What he orchestrated behind the scenes of his political façade was even worse. I'm afraid he had to die." Jack rested a white-gloved hand, somehow pristine despite the murder, upon my shoulder. "I assumed you would go home. I promise, I had no intention of subjecting you to such a sight."

His touch warmed me, despite the icy fear running through my veins. How could he do that, even as I stood there, staring at his handiwork?

"*Un moment.* You said 'our kind,' but you're … you're mortal," I stammered.

Jack's all-knowing smile illuminated his face. "Is it so hard to exude the scent of a human male, to color a streak of silver hair, or use just a touch of artistry to make one's eyes appear smaller rather than larger? I'm sorry I deceived you, but I had to appear mortal in order to do my job."

Gathering my courage, I stepped back, straightened my shoulders. "My father will know of this. He will stop you."

Jack grabbed me by the arms, turning my head away from the minister and lifting me as if I weighed no more than a child's doll. He took me to the opposite corner, as if not seeing the corpse would change what had happened.

"Why do you think the investigation into the Violet Unicorn hasn't gone anywhere?" Jack asked, gaining my full attention. "Monsieur Pietregalla already knows who I am, what I do, and why."

A haze filled my mind. It was like someone had taken my vision of the world and twisted it into something unrecognizable.

Jack shifted, and I caught sight again of the dead minister.

"No!" I yelled, shoving Jack back, using more magic than I intended. "My father would never condone this."

Jack slipped, dropping his weapon where it transformed into an ordinary branch. This time he kept his distance, holding up his hands as if harmless. "It's a political assassination, ordered by the British Supernatural Consulate and in coordination with key French officials."

"I don't believe you," I said, but my words were weak. I wanted to believe him. "I screamed when I came in here. Someone will be coming soon, so it would be best if you tell me the truth."

Seeming to sense my indecision despite my words, he came close, pulling my shawl around my shoulders. "I'm a sorcerer, my dear. Until I leave, no one can enter this glade without the use of sorcery." He enfolded me in an unexpected embrace, somehow making me feel warm and calm. "I swear to you, this is the truth. I was waiting for your father to return so I might request your hand in marriage, but your insistence at being here threw everything askew."

"My hand in marriage?"

Jack chuckled. "Yes. I love you, and I think we would make a good team, in more ways than one."

Could it be true? He'd resisted my spell, but then he was a sorcerer. Did he really care for me or was this a ruse to keep me quiet?

Jack stepped back, taking my hands in his. "You're always talking about defending the rights of the supernaturals. You'll still be a detective, but you can also be a spy, helping me find those who are preying on the innocent."

Marrying Jack, working alongside Jack—the idea held appeal, until I took another glance at the dead minister. "I won't kill anyone."

"No need," said Jack. "This was the end of my assignment. The Violet Unicorn is headed to Italy." I opened my mouth to protest, but Jack held up a hand, forestalling me. "Only to gather information. As a married man, assassinations will no longer be my task."

He took my arm in his, and we walked back through the bushes. I wasn't sure what decision I'd made, but I couldn't turn Jack over to the authorities. But did I want to live my life with someone who was either a murderer or an assassin? Did I dare trust him?

After leaving the labyrinth, weaving through tables, and making our way to the gardens, we stopped in a shadowy copse of trees. The dwarf stepped out, his rictus frown almost as terrifying as the dead minister's. I screamed, but Jack's hand over my mouth quieted my outburst to a squeak.

"All is well, Floressa." He released my mouth and pointed to the beautiful creature that appeared as nothing more than a shimmer.

I couldn't hide my awe. "The unicorn. It belongs to you?"

Jack nodded. "Which is why the sticks I ensorcell become like unicorn horns. Almost as sharp, too."

Stepping forward, he ran a gentle hand along the unicorn's neck. The unusually docile beast nuzzled Jack's shoulder, careful to keep its horn turned away from him. My fears dissipated like dirt washed clean in a spring rain. Unicorns were docile, and throughout history they were defenders of the innocent. The animal's loyalty meant that Jack had indeed extracted righteous justice, even if I didn't agree with the method. Otherwise, no unicorn would tolerate his presence, let alone show such affection. Relieved, I took my first deep breath since I'd stepped between the hedges. I might still have reservations, but I could trust *mon amour*, my dear Jack.

Sprinkling nightshade across the unicorn's buttocks, Jack whispered a spell.

"Nightshade?" I asked. "That's for causing illness."

Jack lifted me by the waist, his hands warm through the fabric, and placed me on the unicorn's back. "Not when combined with the unicorn's natural magic and the right spell."

He vaulted up behind me, wrapping his arms around my waist and holding to the lustrous mane. I arranged my parasol across my lap, holding it in my left hand and gripping a tuft of mane with my right. The dwarf removed the halter, and we stepped into the garden, in full view of the patrons. Nobody gasped, nobody so much as looked in our direction.

Whispering into my ear, his lips caressing my neck, Jack sent chills down my arms that had nothing to do with the night air.

"Nightshade on a unicorn makes him and his riders invisible," said Jack.

As he urged the unicorn forward, I asked one more question. "If you are the Violet Unicorn, and I become your partner, then what will that make me?"

With a glance at the parasol in my lap, he flashed his familiar smile. "You, my dear Floressa, will be the cunning, ever-daunting, Periwinkle Parasol."

The Unicorn Prince

Gama Ray Martinez

Death greeted Anteus as he stepped out of the forest. Blackened earth stretched out before him as far as the eye could see. What had once been cultivated fields were now lifeless. Even the insects and other creatures that fed on dead things were absent. Above, the full moon shone red, a phenomenon that only happened once every thirteen years. Terrible things came out under a blood moon, and even good and noble creatures could be driven insane by its power.

In the distance sat a cluster of simple wooden houses with thatched roofs. Though Anteus had been called here, he suspected the houses were all but abandoned. He closed his eyes and tried to sense any hidden life in the dead vegetation around him. A heartbeat later, his eyes shot open and his blood went cold. This land hadn't just been killed. It had been drained of even the potential of life. All his power wouldn't be enough to restore a single blade of grass. Nothing would ever grow here again, not unless what had been taken could be restored. Anteus suppressed a shiver as he began walking toward the buildings, dead grass crunching under his feet.

He was still a ways off when a thin man in loose-fitting robes ran out of one of the houses to meet him. Dark circles showed under his eyes, and his gaunt face sported a patchy black beard. The image of an oak, the ancient symbol of the druids had been embroidered on his chest. Opher was only twenty-three but worry had aged him at least a decade.

"Well met, servant of life," Anteus began with the traditional greeting between druids.

"Well met, fellow servant." Opher's voice wavered as he spoke, and sweat ran down his face. "Thank the Mother you're here. I'm glad you came so quickly. You wouldn't happen to have a panacea, would you?"

Anteus raised an eyebrow. "The universal antidote is a myth."

"I had hoped I was wrong about that."

"Calm down, Opher. Tell me what happened."

"It went mad." Opher's words tumbled over each other. He glanced at the sky. "It must have been the blood moon. I had to reach into the land itself to draw enough power to stop it. All I could think to do was a transformation."

"Well, that explains this." Anteus surveyed the scorched land. "It doesn't say why though. What exactly did you transform, and why didn't the power return to the land once the spell was complete?"

"You wouldn't believe me unless I showed you. Come with me."

Opher trembled as he walked and a strong grassy aroma hung about his person. Anteus recognized it as maypop, a powerful sedative. His heart began to race.

Opher was a cultivation druid, responsible for helping farmers with their crops and ensuring they respected the land. He'd spent years pouring power into the earth to make it fruitful, and that had given him a vast reservoir of power to draw from should he ever need it, but this far from the wild, he rarely had to deal with anything more dangerous than a fox. There was nothing in twenty leagues that should've been able to frighten him like this, much less force him to draw so much power from the land.

Opher's house on the outskirts of the village was the only one still inhabited. Like most druids, he preferred to be outside when he could and so his dwelling was a simple place with a single room. It had a dirt floor so he could always feel the earth beneath him. A small table and a single chair sat against the wall opposite the door, just below the house's only window.

A box sat in the center of the room. A variety of herbs hung from the ceiling, and symbols of power had been inscribed not only on the ground but also into the wooden box. Anteus looked at Opher, and the younger druid nodded.

Anteus stepped up to the box and looked inside. In the center sat a potato. A pearly white spiral horn rose from one end. He blinked several times. For a moment, his mind refused to accept what he was seeing. Then he looked up at Opher. It was almost a full minute before he found his voice.

"You turned a unicorn into a potato?"

"Anteus, he was mad. He was attacking people."

"Unicorns are peaceful."

"It gets worse."

"How could it get worse?"

"The unicorn was purple."

Anteus sputtered. Human nobility wore fabric of blue or purple as a symbol of status, but few realized the custom had originated as an imitation of the ruling family of the unicorns.

"You turned a *royal* unicorn into a potato?" A chill ran down Anteus's spine. As far as he knew, there was only one royal unicorn anywhere nearby. "By the Mother, is this Prince Ekel? Did you transform the unicorn's heir?"

"I'm a cultivation druid, Anteus. I didn't know what else to do. I didn't have a wide range of options. All I know is crops." He swallowed. "Why didn't the horn change?"

Anteus took several deep breaths to calm himself. When he finally spoke, he'd regained his composure, or at least as much as could be expected. Opher's actions could throw the world into chaos.

"A unicorn's horn is pure magic. I don't think it can be transformed. In fact, it should be working to counter your transformation."

Anteus extended a hand. Where the field outside had been devoid of life, the potato teemed with it. It practically hummed with power. It was actually trying to change back, but something was preventing it. He closed his eyes and concentrated. It was there, just beyond his reach. He stretched his senses out.

It was like touching a bolt of lightning.

He found himself on the ground, leaning against the wall. The wood had cracked behind him, and his back pulsed with pain. He picked himself off the ground and looked at Opher.

"What did you do?"

"I'm not sure. It was instinct."

"You have to undo it. We might have been able to use the madness of the blood moon as an excuse if it were a normal unicorn—but for the royal family? There will be war."

"I've been trying." Opher waved his hands at the symbols around the potato. "I'd invested power in these fields for years, and I used it all. I can't just undo it."

Anteus shook his head. "I don't think the transformation is complete. The power you used is trying to finish it, but the unicorn's horn is countering it. It's a stalemate."

"Can you break it?"

Anteus considered for a second. He was a stronger druid than Opher by a considerable margin, but breaking another druid's spell was an order of magnitude harder than undoing one's own work. Finally he shook his head. "It has to be you. Have you tried a reagent?"

"Fairy dust and leprechaun gold."

"Those wouldn't do it, not unless your power was already close to what you needed."

He pulled a pouch from his belt and spilled half a dozen crystal vials onto the table. He picked up one containing a powdery white substance: ground dragon teeth. It was stronger than either of the reagents Opher had mentioned, but not by much. They needed something specialized instead of raw power.

He put down the vial and went through the others. Harpy feathers. Gargoyle scales. Griffin milk. Manticore poison. Finally, his fingers closed around a vial containing black dust. He handed it to Opher.

"Vampire ash from an elder nearly five hundred years old. They're shape-shifters, so this might give you what you need to undo a transformation."

Opher held the vial up to the light. He shook it once, and the ash swirled inside. For a moment, Anteus thought he heard screaming, but he knew it was only in his mind. The creature that ash had once been had caused death and pain before it was taken down, and the psychic resonance of such things lingered long after the creature itself had been destroyed.

"This is incredibly rare," Opher said.

"If it helps prevent a war, it's worth it." Anteus noticed the younger druid shiver at his words, though he tried to hide it.

Opher nodded. He uncorked the vial and spilled the contents into his hand. He muttered a few words, and the runes around the box glowed deep red. A gentle humming filled the air, and the light spread to the potato, pulsing in time with Opher's breath.

He reached out and touched it with his left hand. The glow crept up his fingers and vanished into the ash, which shone brightly for a second before disappearing entirely. Sweat beaded on his brow, and a vein pulsed in his forehead. After several long seconds, he let out a breath. The glowing potato and runes both went out, and Opher shook his head.

"I thought I had it, but once I actually got my hands on it …" He shook his head again. "The vampire ash is the closest I've come, but I need something stronger."

"I was afraid of that. Vampires can change, but there's more to them than that. What you need is a pure shape-shifter, or at least as close to one as we can manage."

"A pure shape-shifter?" Opher's voice wavered. "What do you mean?" Even as he asked the question, his eyes focused on the blood moon just above the horizon. He looked back at Anteus, who nodded.

He ran his finger along one of Opher's hanging herbs. He could sense the power running through it. Something like this could only be gathered in a very specific way.

"Holly harvested with a silver sickle under the full moon's light?"

Opher nodded slowly. He'd gone several shades paler, and sweat covered his forehead.

"I assume you still have the sickle?"

Opher nodded again.

"Good. You'll need it. Tell me, have you ever hunted werewolves?"

ꝏ ✧ ꝏ

A snapping twig interrupted the nocturnal sounds of the forest. Opher jumped and waved his weapon in the general direction of the sound. "What was that?"

"Be quiet," Anteus said. "Werewolves are twice as dangerous under a blood moon, and there are worse things than them out tonight."

"Sorry. It's just I've never done anything like this."

Anteus nodded. A chill wind rustled through the forest. A spiderweb brushed against his face, and he resisted the urge to cry out as he threw his arms in front of him. The tree the spiderweb hung from drew back in response to his power. Its branches pulled the stray strands away from him, and he let out a breath of relief when he saw the spider scurrying along one of the branches.

Opher looked at him, surprised by the strong reaction, but Anteus only shrugged. His affinity with the wild normally made him immune to the venom of snakes and spiders, but the blood moon could enhance their potency tenfold, and even his powers might not be enough to protect him.

Opher bit his lower lip, trying to be brave. Anteus understood his anxiety. Druids often participated in blood moon hunts, serving as a shield between the people under their charge and the terrible things that walked under the crimson glow. He himself had participated in half a dozen, but those groups had been trained for battle. Having only a cultivation druid by his side to hunt a creature that drew its very power from the moon had him even more worried than the younger druid.

Anteus knew that Opher had spent his life close to people, and had very little idea of the wild things that walked the earth under the blood moon. Though Opher had lived through one blood moon before, thirteen years ago, he couldn't have been any older than ten. He wouldn't have been old enough to fight. Tonight would be his first time, and the first time was always the worst.

They moved through the forest like ghosts. Even Opher, with his limited exposure to the wild, had mastered the skill of moving silently through the forest. The hours passed, and a mist crept into the woods. The blood moon infused it with a red light. As it thickened, Anteus cursed under his breath. Almost anything could be hiding in that fog.

"What exactly are we looking for?" Opher asked.

"Claw marks on the trees, particularly those big enough to do the tree serious harm. Some werewolves can make marks in rocks too. Teeth that are too sharp to come from any local animal. Heavy footprints that look more beast than man." Anteus moved his hand through the red mist. It had grown thick enough to obscure the ground below. "Though I suppose we won't be seeing much of the last."

Opher nodded. His knuckles whitened as he tightened his grip on his sickle. "Maybe we should wait until we can bring more people to help."

Anteus shook his head. "Maybe if it were someone other than Prince Ekel. If the unicorns discover where he is—and *what* he is—and that you did it, we won't be able to avoid war. We certainly can't afford to wait for another full moon, blood or otherwise."

Opher started to speak but stumbled. He reached into the fog, and when he withdrew his hand, tendrils of mist clung to his fingers. At first, Anteus didn't recognize the blood on Opher's hand. Anteus directed his power at the earth. Some of the nearby trees quivered, and a second later, a platform of gnarled roots emerged from the fog.

The doe's body atop the roots had been mangled almost to the point of being unrecognizable. Her throat had been ripped out, and her legs bent at odd angles, the bones jutting out. Blood matted the fur, and a slash across her face had blinded the creature. Most of the flesh was still there, however, and Anteus suppressed a shiver. This was not the work of a predator. Of all the creatures in the world, only man killed for pleasure. Or something that had once been a man.

Anteus waved a hand, and the roots lowered the body to the earth. He briefly considered directing them to bury the creature, but he rejected the idea. Few animals buried their dead, and it would be no honor to the doe to treat it as a human. Instead, he opened his mind to the trees around him and concentrated.

He tried for only a few seconds. There was too much blood and there had been too much violence for him to sense anything useful. He stepped away from the corpse and began to move around it in a circle, dragging his hand on the ground until his fingers found the trail of blood. He closed his eyes and focused until he felt the faint echo of the life that still remained in the blood. His sense of it only extended a few feet, but it was enough. He met Opher's eyes.

"Let's go."

Leaves crackled under the younger druid's feet, but he clenched his jaw and regained his grip on the magic keeping him silent. He nodded once, but it was a slow, unsteady motion, and he seemed unaware of the death grip he had on his sickle.

The blood trail continued for several yards before fading beyond Anteus's ability to sense. He tried to rely on more conventional senses, but the night foiled him. The smell of tree sap hung heavy in the air, masking any scent. Insects chirped, and somewhere in the night, a frog's song rumbled through the forest. Even his sense of the plants felt muted as if the fog was a blanket covering a sleeping world.

They looked for another half hour, but they found no sign of the beast. Finally, Opher threw up his arms.

"What are we going to do, Anteus?" he asked, almost in tears. "I don't want to be the druid who caused a war with the unicorns." In the quiet of the night, Opher's voice sounded like a thunderclap.

Anteus shushed him and listened to the wind, searching for any sign of the werewolf. The forest was quiet in a way living woods rarely were. Even the insects had gone silent. In a cold panic, he directed the trees to form a wall upwind of them, the direction from which an animal would strike. Oak and ash bent down and stabbed their branches into the ground just before the werewolf leaped through the air.

The huge beast crashed through the braches, leaving a shower of splinters in its wake, but they trees slowed it just enough.

Anteus threw himself to one side, and the werewolf flew over the top of him. The wind of its passage carried the scent of rotting flesh, and the beast's razor-sharp claws tore a rent in his cloak.

Opher screamed, but Anteus ignored him and rolled to his feet, meeting the creature's eyes.

If death had tooth and claws, it would've looked like that.

The creature stood nine feet tall. Blood dripped from a muzzle filled with teeth sharp enough to bite through steel. Its arms were a solid mass of muscle that rippled under the thick coat of blood-matted fur. The moonlight painted the creature's fur black, and its feet vanished into the red carpet of fog.

It tensed and prepared to attack again, but Anteus threw out his hand and the nearby branches lashed at the werewolf, wrapping themselves around it. For any ordinary creature, that would be enough, but a werewolf was ten times stronger than a man so Anteus had to concentrate on his enchantment to keep the werewolf from tearing itself free.

"Opher," he said through clenched teeth. Sweat dripped into his eyes, and every breath was a struggle as he allowed his strength to flow into the trees. "Kill it."

The younger druid shook violently, and he took unsteady steps toward the bound creature. The werewolf's growl made the leaves vibrate. Opher paled and froze midstep. He looked at Anteus with wide eyes. His lower lip quivered, and all color drained from his face.

The monster's muscles tensed, and Anteus felt cracks forming in the wood. The trees screamed in his mind. His arm shook from the effort of keeping the branches in place.

"It really wants to rip out our throats," Anteus managed. "If you could do something to prevent that, I'd appreciate it."

Opher nodded, practically tripping over his own feet as he stumbled to the wolf. He delivered a weak slash.

Anteus feared the attack hadn't even made it through the fur, but then a thin trickle of blood ran down the beast's chest, passing over some of the branches.

A howl escaped its throat, and Opher dropped his weapon. He fell back. The werewolf roared, and the trees' cries of pain tore at Anteus' mind. The earth trembled and wood splintered. With a lurch that sent pain shooting through Anteus, the werewolf broke its bonds.

Its cry of triumph reverberated through the fog. It took a lumbering step toward Anteus, but he lacked the strength to do anything. He prepared himself to die, but suddenly, the werewolf's form rippled.

Off to one side stood Opher, his arm extended toward the beast and his face twisted in concentration. For a second, Anteus thought he'd actually do it, but when Opher had transformed the unicorn, he'd had all the power he'd invested in the land for years. Now, all he had was the strength of his own will.

The werewolf closed its eyes and growled. Its form solidified.

Opher raised his other hand.

It was an empty gesture. Two hands wouldn't increase the power of the enchantment, but the werewolf didn't know that. Its eyes widened, and fear flickered across its face. A heartbeat later, it had disappeared into the woods.

Opher ran over to Anteus and knelt down before him.

"Are you alright?"

Anteus was breathing heavily, and it took several seconds before he found his words. "We failed."

"We ..." Opher took a deep breath. "We could go after it."

Anteus shook his head. "I'm exhausted, and you can't do much more than annoy it. We need to inform the council to prepare for war."

Opher closed his eyes and a tear rolled down his cheek. "I'm sorry."

He helped up Anteus. Before they left, Anteus touched the trees that had held the werewolf. He closed his eyes and endowed them with what strength he could, hoping it would be enough for them to recover from their wounds. Each of the trees swayed against the wind in a gesture of thanks.

A single leaf tumbled from one and brushed Anteus's nose. He caught it before it disappeared into the fog, and his fingers felt the sticky blood on it. He looked up. One of the branches was little more than a splintered remnant, but Anteus remembered the shallow wound Opher had inflicted and the blood that had dripped onto one of branches. He held the leaf out to Opher.

"Maybe not."

They rushed back to town as quickly as they dared. Opher's door creaked as they pushed it open. The silence in the air carried an eerie calm that seemed at odds with the gravity of the situation.

Opher held the leaf covered in werewolf blood in his left hand and began to chant. The blood emitted an angry glow, and Anteus heard roaring in his mind. The runes around the box glowed and the horned potato vibrated. Opher shook, sweat streamed down his face. He went to one knee but held his arm toward the potato. The horn began to hum, emitting a soft white light that flowed into the potato. The skin rippled and writhed. A heartbeat later, it stilled.

"I can't." Opher's breathing was labored and his voice was strained. The light from the werewolf blood began to fade as its power waned. "It's taking everything I have just to hold the enchantment. I can't unravel it."

They locked eyes and Anteus nodded, extending his hand. He had precious little power to give, and lending strength druid to druid didn't work the same way as offering strength to the trees, but Opher was so close. Even a fraction of power might be enough.

Opher took in a sharp breath. Strength flowed out of Anteus. He closed his eyes; he could feel Opher's struggle. Even their combined powers fell short. Opher held the spell in his hands, and Anteus sensed the flicker of a thought. Their power wasn't enough to undo the transformation, but with Anteus' added power, Opher could snap its link to the unicorn. It could work, but the enchantment would need a new host.

"No." Anteus's voice was barely a whisper. His eyes opened, and he tried to rise, but he didn't have the strength. Opher was lost in his efforts.

The potato bounced in the box. Its skin bulged, and Opher began to shrink. His arms and legs shriveled, and his face flattened. The potato bounced out of the box and grew, sprouting violet hair as its round form melted away.

A few seconds later, Opher was gone, and in his place sat a potato. A shadow fell over it. Anteus looked up.

In the light of the blood moon, the unicorn's purple fur seemed to shimmer. Its eyes were deep blue pools that he could lose himself in. It inclined its head and touched its horn to Anteus's heart. Images of flowers blooming and a sunrise flashed through Anteus's mind as strength returned to his body. He bowed his head.

"Prince Ekel," he said. "Forgive us. Druid Opher tried to protect his people the only way he knew how."

The unicorn inclined his head, and Anteus heard a voice in his mind. "He saved me."

"What?"

"It is a terrible thing to take a life. Few unicorns can do so and survive."

"But you have soldiers. We worried your transformation would lead to war."

"I said few, Human, not none. Our warriors sacrifice much to defend us." He looked at the potato. "I owe him more than I can repay. First, he stopped me from killing. Then, he cured my mind."

"The vampire ash," Anteus realized. "He said he felt something. I never considered he was affecting your mind."

A tear flowed down the unicorn's long face before falling to the ground. It made a peculiar musical sound when it hit, and the note lingered in the air. "I would help him if I could."

"He took the curse on himself," Anteus said, "and no magic can heal wounds that were self-inflicted."

The unicorn inclined his head. "Precisely so, but there is one thing I can do. I can complete the transformation."

He waved his horn, and light erupted from the potato. The ground shook once, then all was still. Ekel walked out without another word.

Anteus gasped when he stepped outside. A wave of green flowed outward from the house, restoring the grass to life. Flowers emerged, and crops sprouted in the nearby fields. Anteus knelt and ran his fingers through the grass. Power coursed through the field—all the power Opher had invested in it, restored.

Ekel didn't look back as he walked into the woods and the sun peeked over the horizon. Dawn spread across a land that lived again.

The Girl with the Artist's Eyes

Nathan Barra

I had given up on subtly glancing at my watch an hour before, about the same time I'd sweat through my red-and-white Comic-Con staffer's shirt. *¿Dónde estás, George?* I thought, as I paced across the washed-out carpet that marked the entrance of the Olympia Convention Center's basement Exhibitor's Hall. *Please, make good on your promise.*

Having bolstered myself with thoughts of Papi, I had braved the labyrinth of the black-cottoned souk, searching through books and buttons, crafts and comics, collector's pieces and geeky paraphernalia until I found a Makoto Shinkai art print. Papi loved his work, and Shinkai was a guest at the Con. If I could get away fifteen minutes early and haul some serious tail, I could, in theory, catch the legend himself after a panel and beg an autograph.

Elbow-to-eyebrow crowds were a tradition for the Saturday of Olympia Comic-Con. Though record-breaking attendance was good for the Con, all wasn't so *bueno* for the *chica* too broke to buy a full Con pass. Papi had offered to cover my convention pass in apology for not being able to make it this year, but I had refused. Being the door guard for the Exhibitor's Hall on Con Saturday was a rough gig, but I had grown out of being his geeky little princess who drew her own comic books for fun. I wanted to work for my own way, even if that meant keeping the crowds from congealing and blocking the flow of the convention's financial heart's blood.

Truth was, he needed the money as badly as I did. Yeah, I had double jobs as a barista and at the art store, but Papi had the new baby my stepmother had given him. Perhaps, in hindsight, I should have caved and let Papi, or my oldest friend, George, pay my way.

When I heard the sound of a large, angry dog barking behind me, I nearly wet myself. As I spun to face the beast, I threw a hook kick where I estimated its head should be, but only managed to stagger George. He was tall, with the mesh of unwieldy limbs and budding muscle that signaled an end to his growth spurt. He was a ginger, except for his pale amber eyes, which glistened with mixed amusement, and to my pride, pain. "What was that for, Catalina?"

"For being a jerk," I said, punching his shoulder for good measure. "You know how I feel about dogs."

He grinned and straightened, rubbing his hip. "For sure, but that's what makes it fun, chica." He dodged my next smack and bent to pick up his phone.

It had only been a sound clip. My heart still raced though. "I hope you broke your screen."

"Hey, no need to be hateful." Standing, he pocketed the phone and held out his fist. "No hard feelings, eh? Especially since I am relieving you early and all."

Rolling my eyes, I obliged him, bumping fists. "Of course not, *mi hermano gringo*."

"If you would pardon me, Citizens," an unfamiliar voice interrupted, "but I am seeking Stan Lee." He put the same emphasis on the name that a medieval knight would have used for "my lord" or "the king." It wasn't the sort of reverence one heard in the modern day.

"Of course you are," I said, turning. "And how can we help … you?" At first glance, he was a man in need of a great deal of help.

Standing in a dramatic pose, the man's costume was an abomination. It had been made from two main materials, spandex and a shag rug, with a color palette inspired by a neon purple highlighter and the contents of a can of Mountain Dew. The tops of his black wading boots were wrapped in furry, purple shag. A pair of furry briefs fashioned from the neon rug topped plum-colored spandex bike shorts with a green stripe down the sides. A violet Under Armour shirt clung to a body that wasn't meant for formfitting materials.

His faux leather belt bore a giant brass buckle emblazoned with the monogramed letters "PU" in a toxic green lacquer. He had dyed a wig to wear as a mane, atop which he had tied a burnished ivory horn that looked to have been bought at a Renaissance festival to drink ale and feel manly.

Glancing at George, I saw the blank expression he wore when trying really hard not to laugh.

He shrugged. "There's no wrong way to do costuming."

"There are limits to 'cosplay and let cosplay,' George," I whispered back.

"I am the Purple Unicorn," the man proclaimed. "Defender of Peace and Justice."

"Right," I said, not seeing his Comic-Con badge. "This is a paid event. You can only come in if you have a badge."

The man fished for a lanyard tied to his belt. "Of course. Your diligence is admirable."

Scanning his badge, I asked, "You're Walter Sams?"

Holding up a finger to shush me, he winked. "I can neither confirm nor deny the Purple Unicorn's secret identity."

"Right," I said, drawing out the word. I accessed the Comic-Con scheduling app on my phone. "Well, Mr. Sams—"

"Please, the Purple Unicorn." He lowered his voice. "You aren't very good with the concept of a secret identity, are you miss?"

I decided not to argue. "Well, um, Mr. Unicorn," I said as George made choking noises. "Stan Lee is scheduled to be at his photo booth for the next hour. That's in the twenty-five hundred block." I gestured. "Go in through these doors and take a right." Looking at him with a straight face, I added, "The furry track is in the north building, second floor. You know. In case you're interested in that sort of thing."

"I thank you for your assistance," the unicorn said in an artificially deep voice.

"Wait a second," George said. "Why, exactly, are you looking for Stan Lee?"

I sighed and rolled my eyes as I elbowed my friend. "Why are you encouraging him?"

"Because, Catalina," he said with gravitas. "The world must know."

"I am going to be an Avenger," Sams declared.

"An Avenger?" George repeated.

"Indeed," Sams boomed. "I spoke to Stan Lee in San Diego, and he said that his people would get in touch with my people. Then, when I got home, I remembered that I don't have people yet and so I must meet him in person. Again."

"Did you wear *that* costume?" I asked skeptically.

"That's understandable," George said, shushing me.

Walter Sams was gawk-worthy, but the stream of attendees into the hall had shrunk to a trickle. I ignored a man in a full Guy Fawkes-*V for Vendetta* getup in favor of the men who sauntered behind him. They were a group cosplay, a dozen men dressed in black tactical gear with the red-and-white patch of Umbrella Corp on their shoulders.

"Hey," I shouted, "you guys hold up for a second." The props they carried caught my eye. Their realism, when combined with the face-concealing gas masks, made me uneasy. Most of the guys ignored me and held up their single-day badges as they streamed past.

"Cool costume," I said, cornering one of the cosplayers. "Those guns look really real, though. Has someone from Con security cleared those? The props inspection table is upstairs."

Nodding, the costumed attendee pointed to the zip tie that locked back part of the prop, and then to the pale blue plastic band stamped with "OCC Security" wrapped around the grip. I had thought this year's bands were green, but I wasn't positive. The staffer's orientation had been long and mind-numbing, a thousand regulations and details condensed into an hour. This year could be blue again; it was hard to keep track.

The guy waited to see if I would take issue, watching me through the windows of his gas mask, but when I heard George call my name, I let him pass. If security had vetted the prop, it should be okay. "Go on, and enjoy your con."

Nodding, he swaggered into the hall and disappeared into the crowd.

Turning back, I found George holding his phone out to me. Alas, the screen wasn't broken. "Hey, chica! Can you take a picture with me and the Purple Unicorn?"

I snatched the phone and backed up as they posed. Glancing at the time on the display, I saw that my window to catch Shinkai for an autograph was closing. I hurriedly snapped the picture and handed the phone back. "Gotta go."

"Wait!" George said. "Can I borrow one of your Sharpies? Do you have a purple one in your backpack?"

"I do. Wait, why?"

"I want the Purple Unicorn to sign my chest."

Sams looked thrilled at the notion.

"Give it a rest, *tontito,*" I said as I rushed towards the escalators. Rounding the corner, I nearly ran into a man in a maintenance uniform erecting a barricade. "Hey, what's this?" I demanded.

The man shrugged, looking bored. "One of the safety alarms tripped, so we need to shut down the whole bank of escalators for an inspection."

"In the middle of Con Saturday? Are you serious?"

"How many of you people have been up and down these escalators today?"

"Ten of thousand? Maybe twenty?" I guessed.

"Right. Makes this alarm a bit more important than your nerd party. Sorry, lady, you'll have to wait. The escalators are down for maintenance until further notice."

Fuming, I turned and rushed back towards the Exhibitor's Hall, passing George and the Purple Unicorn taking a selfie. It was best to ignore them. There were elevators were tucked into a recessed corner by the hall's entrance. As a Comic-Con veteran and a staffer I knew they were there, but few others did. Not as fast, but they would have to do.

As I approached the hall's entrance, I glanced at the projector screens mounted on the far wall of the Exhibitor's Hall. They scrolled leisurely between upcoming convention events and sponsors' logos, oblivious of my hurry.

I wish I had the time for the Zombie 5K Fun Run/Shamble. I thought. *Next year.*

I froze as the screens went black, followed a heartbeat later by the lights. The reverberation of thousands of voices escalated into cries of startled annoyance.

"Seriously? It's just not my day!" Growling in frustration, I pulled my phone from my pocket to use as a light and started toward the doors to the hall. If no one controlled the situation, the irritated crowd could stampede. Shinkai would have to wait.

I had only taken two steps when the screens flickered back to life, bathing the hall with illumination. All the projector screens, which before had been set to different channels, now displayed a single gray scale image. The words "Stand by for a Public Service Announcement" bracketed a circle with a rotating bar. Bold numbers counted down from five each time the bar passed the twelve o'clock position.

At zero, the screen went black and then came to life with a flare of color.

Two men stood in Stan Lee's photo booth. The man in the Guy Fawkes costume held a knife to Mr. Lee's throat. The trickle of blood meandering down Stan Lee's neck meant the blade was real. It shouldn't have made it past security.

"Ladies and gentlemen of Olympia Comic-Con, I require your immediate and undivided attention," Guy Fawkes said in a calm voice. "I am the leader of this group. We are now in control. We call ourselves the Protagonists. We, unlike the masses of sheep, seek to maximize our own impact in the world and be the active force in our own lives."

One of Stan Lee's bodyguards broke free from the Umbrella Corp soldiers. He was gunned down well short of his charge, however. The screams of the crowd were short-lived as one of the goons let loose a spray of gunfire overhead.

George's voice broke into my awareness. "Is this even real?"

"They're kidnapping Stan Lee," I said as I unlocked my phone. There was no reception in the convention center's basement, but I did have a very faint connection to the Wi-Fi.

"Now, ladies and gentlemen," Guy Fawkes said over the hall's loud speakers, "we find ourselves in need of some investors. In order to facilitate our growth, we have decided to crowdsource our efforts. As your first stretch goal, I present to you Mr. Stan Lee. Tweet, post, blog, or otherwise get the message out. Geekdom only has one chance to do this right." He shook the terrified comics legend. "If donations exceed the amount specified on this website in the next eight hours, he will go free." A URL appeared below his face on the screen. "If not," he said as he nicked Stan Lee's throat with his knife, "well, let's not go there, shall we?"

Walter Sams puffed with excitement and bravado. "Well, Citizens, it appears to be time for my debut. If you'll excuse me, my greatness awaits."

"No! Walter, stop! It's time for the police," I said as I messaged my convention coordinator.

"You fail to understand, miss. I am a *real* hero," Sams said as he reached up to untie the string that secured his horn to his head.

"Seriously, Walter," George said. "Now isn't the time."

"Now is the ideal time," Walter disagreed, a grin splitting his lips as he struck a dramatic pose. "The time for a few heroes." With that, he brought the horn to his lips and blew.

I didn't hear the sound the horn made, but I will never forget that moment. My vision went black, and my eyes expanded in their sockets, fit to burst from the pressure. I felt as if my brain had transformed into thousands of angry wasps, buzzing through my sinuses as they sought to burrow their way out of my skull. My skin crawled and stung, a white-hot acupuncture needle digging into each of my pores. I couldn't say how long it lasted. I had no sense of time, but when the world did return, it was with a new reality.

Blinking, I waited until my eyes refocused, praying that the pain hadn't left me blind. The first thing I noticed were the colors. Where before everything had been slightly washed-out under the halogen glow, now all the colors were vibrant, somehow idealized and perfect. The curtains separating the booths were black as night, but there was never a darkness so complete. The yellow walls, which had looked like anorexic daisies before, now provided physical comfort, calming my mind and sharpening my focus. I could sense the life held in the red of Stan Lee's blood, and the menace in the gray of the knife. I itched to get to my watercolors and try to capture the hues. Although it might have been impossible, I yearned to immortalize the perfection of the moment.

I staggered to a nearby booth and picked up a comic book at random. The art spoke to me, enticing me to both read the story and understand the depth of the artist. How he struggled, poor and unappreciated, but proud of his work. How he believed he might make a difference with his art and his desire to entertain one boy in particular—his son. Dropping the comic, I reeled. How in the world could I possibly have known all that from a single look?

A strong hand on my shoulder turned me. "Chica. Catalina? Catalina!"

I blinked up at George. He was beautiful. The lankiness of his movements and the seeming incompleteness of his teenage body had evened and filled out. He didn't have the pretty muscles like in the magazines, but rather the slabs that came from years of hard work. His goatee had filled out from the wisps he refused to shave, but his eyes were unchanged, still the pale amber I had known for years.

"Oh, wow," I said as I stared.

A small wrinkle appeared between his eyes, another point of concrete memory in the sea of surreal flooding the Exhibitor's Hall.

"Catalina, what happened to your eyes?"

My eyes? All the colors darkened. *Something had happened to my eyes?* I dropped my backpack to the floor, ripped it open, and dug through the assorted junk looking for my makeup kit. Pulling the small compact out of the bag, I flipped it open.

The white part of my eyes had deepened, looking like pools of milk; the pink tinge that too many double shifts and exhaustion had left behind was completely gone. Instead, the pale green irises had burst, and swirls of colors began to seep into the fresh medium. Not just green, but any color I could imagine, some of which I couldn't even name. It was like looking at my watercolors as I cleaned my brushes, except they maintained their pure tones and clean lines instead of fading and mixing into the inevitable ruddy brown.

Pantone, eat your heart out.

Shaken, I glanced at George, but couldn't form a coherent sentence. Seeking calm, I focused on the warm yellow walls for a moment and was finally able to gather my thoughts. "What happened?"

A booming, eminently heroic voice answered me. "The horn brings the ideal into the real. It makes what we imagine ourselves to be into who we are. You, for example. You see the world as an artist, so the horn has given you an artist's eyes." His voice drew my attention, and my jaw dropped at the sight.

It was as if the Purple Unicorn had stepped off the pages of a Golden Age comic.

Walter Sams had transformed into a man who was epic in proportions, built with muscles on his muscles. His boots had transformed into actual hooves, and the shag rug had smoothed into an elegant coat. His mane flowed faintly as if in a breeze. The strong curves of the horn parted the silken strands, jutting from his forehead like a banner proclaiming his allegiance to justice. The color scheme was still hideous, but I supposed that the magic of the horn could only go so far.

"Wait," George said, "you have a magical horn of wish fulfillment?"

If my eyes have changed, what about the rest of me? I looked down, hoping to see my ideal figure, but groaned.

"What is it?" George asked me.

"This is not fair. You get to be hot. Unicorn guy attains the superpowers he's always dreamed of. I gained weight."

"What are you talking about, chica?" George asked.

"This is not the time for petty concerns, Citizen," the Purple Unicorn said. "I must rescue Stan Lee and take my place amongst his chosen heroes."

"Well, at least his priorities haven't changed," George muttered.

"Heroes!" the Purple Unicorn boomed. "A group of villains, posing as the protagonists in this story, have taken one of our greatest progenitors.

I scanned the faces of the crowd around me. Many of the exhibitors were largely unchanged, slight alterations of their actual selves. The cosplayers, however, had come to life, transforming into their costumed counterparts. I realized then that Walter Sams had made a horrible miscalculation.

"I call upon you to stand against these antagonists," the Purple Unicorn said, pointing, "and free Stan Lee!"

People don't just cosplay the heroes. Villains were just as popular.

The ringing silence of the seconds following the horn's transformation and the address of the Purple Unicorn was shattered by the voice of a single undead: "BRRAAAAIIIINS!"

The hall seemed to pause for a deep breath and then all hell broke loose. Sith lightning flashed over the booths as the hum and crackle of lightsabers filled the air, the Hulk punched Superman through a section of booths, and the Joker began cackling. As the imaginings of thousands of fans came to life to do battle, those who hadn't come in costume fled for their lives.

"Oooookay. This is bad. Really, really bad," George said in what I thought was a profound understatement.

"Wait a moment, Citizens!" bellowed the Purple Unicorn as people bumped him in their single-minded focus to flee. "You are perfectly safe in my aegis."

"No one is listening to him," I shouted.

"How smart of them," George replied.

"George, people are going to get killed if they keep stampeding," I shouted over the growing cacophony. Ducking, I scurried out of the way as Iron Man and Boba Fett flew overhead, fighting several members of the Green Lantern Corps. I rushed into a break in the crowd and began dragging my weight against the Purple Unicorn's huge biceps. "Hey! Unicorn guy!" When he looked at me, I continued. "This is the opposite of helpful. How do you make it stop?"

"Stop? But—"

"Yes, stop!" I yelled, pointing to the Exhibitor's Hall. "Look at them! They're killing each other. And innocents." Appealing to his interests, I said, "What if Stan Lee gets caught in the cross fire?"

The Purple Unicorn looked pained, and a bit of Walter Sams shone through. "But I can't," he said. "The effects will last as long as the disk of the sun is in the sky."

I slapped him, but nearly broke my hand on his jaw. "Six hours!"

"More or less."

George had pushed his way through the stampede in time to hear the last bit. "Does the effect move with you?"

"With the horn, yes."

"Allons-y!" I shouted in my best Doctor impersonation as I dragged George and the Purple Unicorn into the crowd.

"But Stan Lee! This is my chance!" shouted the Purple Unicorn.

"Look," I yelled as George and I tried to tow his mass, "there is no way you'll get through that melee in time. The Protagonists can't get back this way, either. There is a service corridor with a staircase in the back. It'll take them upstairs to the loading docks. If you want to catch them, we need get there before they do."

My logic seemed to appease the Purple Unicorn because he took the lead and began to part the crowd. George and I grabbed onto his belt, to be towed in his wake and avoid being trampled. Even being knocked to the ground in a crowd like this could prove fatal.

With a bit of effort, and a few helpful pulls from George, I was able to ignore the colors that tried to draw me in. Blocking them out proved easy enough to master. At least something was working in my favor.

As we crested from the Exhibitioner's Hall, I threw my weight against the Purple Unicorn. "Elevator!" I shouted. I doubted the maintenance guy, even if he was legit and not in league with the Protagonists, would have stood against the stampede. My shout seemed to make it through. As the Purple Unicorn veered, the few people crowded around the elevators saw him coming and fled.

Luckily, the doors slid open after short pause. We piled in, and a group of frightened exhibitors and fans surged toward us—until they saw the costumed mass of the Purple Unicorn.

The Purple Unicorn had to turn sideways to fit through the door, and he had to kneel to keep his horn from poking the ceiling tiles, but eventually the doors closed and the noise died off to a rumble.

George panted as the elevator slowly ascended. "What's the plan?" he asked me.

"I don't know. This situation isn't exactly covered in the volunteer manual," I snapped back.

"Well, no, but there'll be cosplayers upstairs too."

"Right." I thought quickly. "Hey, unicorn guy. What's the range on the horn?"

"A couple hundred yards, I think? I am its guardian, so I have never gone far enough from it to be sure."

"Right," I said, turning back to George. "Where did they set up the TARDIS?"

"Uh, the south hall?"

I cursed. "That would have been way too cool. Alas, plan B. Get him outside and away from the costumes. Head east for five or six blocks, someplace where his magic wish fulfillment horn won't give someone superpowers."

"Sounds like as good a plan as any," George said.

"But what about Stan Lee?" the Purple Unicorn demanded.

"We'll take care of that on the way. Save him, take him with us, and you two will have a little under six hours to talk. Sound good?"

When the Purple Unicorn nodded eagerly, I took a deep breath.

Focusing, I tried to remember the exact shade of the walls downstairs and found it wasn't that difficult to recall the pigment and bathe myself in its calm.

"Alright," I said as I glanced at my phone to check the time. My heart sank. Panels had just ended, so the halls would be crowded with people making their way to the next thing on their schedule. I was unsure as to what cosmic force wanted to make today as bad as humanly possible for me, but it must be cackling to itself by now.

"When the doors open, we run. Better that we give bumps and bruises than prolong the battles." Looking to George, I asked, "Are you ready, Robin?"

He grinned at me. "I want to be Batman."

I tilted my head at the Purple Unicorn. "Look at what wanting to be a superhero gets you. Plus, I called it first."

He stuck his tongue out at me, and I retaliated in kind.

As the doors opened, I slipped through the crack and began sprinting. "This way to the service corridor and Stan Lee," I called over my shoulder to the Purple Unicorn. I dodged and weaved, channeling years of rushing between back-to-back panels to help me navigate the crowds.

Chaos reigned around bubbles of intense violence as nonsuperpowered fans fled the superpowered showdowns. In one pocket, River Tam faced off with Neo. In another, four Harley Quinns were overwhelming Batman. Two groups of Spartans were facing off in a wide space they had cleared in the food court, a phalanx from *300,* and a pair from the Halo games.

How are they not being slaughtered? No! Focus. To stop this, I need to run. I can't stop to watch, no matter how awesome the show.

I dodged and ran, making my way back to the service corridor and the loading bays through which I had helped unload the vendors' wares the day before. Reaching the swinging double doors, I pulled them open and ushered the Purple Unicorn and George through. Pushing the doors closed behind myself, I yelled to George, "Take your belt, and tie these doors shut!" I grabbed the Purple Unicorn's elbow. "You! This way." Leading him deeper into the complex, we were almost to the loading docks when he stopped me. When I started to protest, he clamped a hand over my mouth.

"What the hell, boss?" a man in hysterics yelled from ahead, voice muffled. "This was supposed to be easy. It was supposed to be bloodless, for us at least."

"Shut up," the cultured voice of Guy Fawkes snapped. "Our way out is not far. Get Stan Lee into the trunk and get in the car. It's only a setback. A regroup, not a retreat."

"Stan Lee," whispered the Purple Unicorn.

You have to be kidding me.

"But boss," the first man started. The muffled sound of a blow silenced him.

"Do what I say." The leader's voice was cold. Lethally so.

"Stan Lee!" bellowed the Purple Unicorn as he released me to charge after his goal. "I'll rescue you!"

I would have fallen if George hadn't caught up to us then. "Come on, the belt won't hold for long," he barked as he pulled me into a run. "How did you know they'd come this way?"

"I didn't," I admitted. "I just told the unicorn guy what I thought he needed to hear. But, I mean, it makes sense. What else were they going to do?"

"Well, it worked. On both counts."

Sounds fighting echoed around the upcoming corner. Gunshots, grunts, and the wet thump of skulls hitting concrete. I pushed myself harder, hoping I wasn't too late.

We rounded the corner to find the Purple Unicorn kneeling on the chest of the Protagonists' leader, his Guy Fawkes mask lost somewhere. A strangled wheeze escaped the superhero's grip on his lower face. He began to thrash and scream as the Purple Unicorn began to squeeze. Around them lay the crumpled bodies of three of the Protagonists, Stan Lee's unconscious form against the wall.

"Hey, Purple Unicorn!" George shouted as we ran towards the scene. "Didn't you learn anything from comics?"

I ran to check on Stan Lee.

Eyes still on Guy Fawkes, the Purple Unicorn growled, "What do you mean?"

"It is the choices that separate the heroes from the villains. You stand on the edge of a cliff. Leave these guys to the police. Please."

Looking up from my limited first-aid, I shouted, hoping to tip the balance. "Purple Unicorn! Stan Lee will be okay. Whatever you do now, Walter will have to live with, just like all those poor people behind us will have to live with the destruction they caused while under the horn's influence. What would Walter want?"

The Purple Unicorn looked at his captive with disgust, but released him, standing and backing away a few steps. Banging echoed down the hall, desperation clear in the rhythm. Screams of pain and terror were faint, but clearly audible. Grief and regret crossed the self-made superhero's face.

"Enough," he said. "What I have done is enough." Turning to the lead Protagonist, he said, "Run. Try to survive the next six hours. I sincerely hope you live long enough for the police to catch you."

As the man scrambled to his feet and ran, the Purple Unicorn approached. "Catalina," he said, eyes downcast. "How do I make this right?"

Standing, I gestured to the unconscious form at my feet. "Pick him up and follow us. We need to get the horn away from here." We jogged, backtracking to the loading bays. As we approached, I signaled for a stop. The bay doors vibrated as fists pounded on the other side. Cries of terror and pleas for help could be heard over bestial growls, groans, and the creak of chain link.

"Catalina," George asked as he came up next to me, breathing hard, "What's out there?"

"Uh … Fifth Street." Wait. Wasn't something supposed to be happening at two o'clock on Fifth Street? It took me a moment to remember, but when I did, I began cursing in a stream of steady Spanish. "It's the Zombie 5K Run/Shamble. We've unleashed the zombie apocalypse on the convention center."

George stared at me for a full minute before saying anything. "Now what?"

The Purple Unicorn answered. "Now, I go let those people in." He set the unconscious form of his idol on the floor. "I let those people in, and we hold out as long as we can. Hopefully, until the sun goes down."

"We could also not do that," George said in a panic.

As solemn as I had ever seen him, the Purple Unicorn evaluated George. "It is our choices that make us who we are. I choose to do this."

Sighing, George nodded, and we followed. When the Purple Unicorn lifted the bay door, the humans desperately scrambled for the opening, only to be dragged back by the zombies. George and I helped pull as many through as we could, but eventually, the Purple Unicorn was forced to close the door. Sensing the life within, the horde shoved fingers and arms through the gap and tried to pry it open. The Purple Unicorn bore down on the sliding door and held it closed, stomping on zombie hands and fingers with his cloven hooves.

However, I'd seen every zombie movie ever made. It was only a matter of time until the living were overwhelmed.

I backed to the far wall and slid down until I could rest my head on my knees. I was unsure how long I sat like that, but eventually, I looked up, pulled out my phone, and rubbed the tears from my eyes. I contemplated the text message for a long moment. In the end, I sent only the simple truth: "I love you, Papi."

George slid down the wall next to me, his arms scratched and bruised. I saw a bite. I wondered how long it would take him to turn. "Hey, chica," he said, "it'll all be okay."

"Yeah, Mr. Ray of Sunshine? In what way will it be okay?" When he didn't respond, I asked, "How are those people we rescued?"

He shrugged. "Battered, terrified, and in shock." He adopted a cheesy British accent. "No one expects the zombie apocalypse!"

I couldn't help but laugh. "It's 'No one expects the Spanish Inquisition,' you dork."

"Psssh. I wish. The Spanish Inquisition would take longer than sundown to kill us." He glanced at his wound, uncertain. That was sobering. As much as I wished he could be anywhere else at that moment, it was good to have a friend.

After a pause, George asked, "Why weren't the Protagonists transformed by their costumes?"

It took me a moment to reorient. "I dunno. Does it matter?"

He shrugged. "Maybe if we knew, we could figure out how to stop the horn."

Focusing on the yellow again, I thought about it. "Maybe the costumes weren't what they imagined themselves to be," I guessed. "Or maybe Walter Sams didn't imagine them to be superpowered when he blew the horn."

George turned to me. "Do you think you could reverse it? Unimagine all this?"

"I'm not sure it works like that."

"How do we know? Do you think Sams ever tried?"

"Well, no." I didn't want to try, because I didn't want to fail. "Why don't you do it?"

"Because," George said, "I don't have the focus. I can't see the world that clearly. You are the girl with the artist's eyes." When I scoffed, he continued. "No, seriously. The Purple Unicorn had that part right. You see the world, all of it. You come alive when you have the brush in your hand. C'mon, chica, I've seen it. You can do beautiful, delicate things with your watercolors. Things I wouldn't even imagine were possible. You're wasted as a barista and at the art supply store." It was an old argument.

Looking away, I asked, "What does it matter now?"

"What matters," George said with renewed confidence, "is how you paint. It's not just the light and bright and happy. That's the ideal, the world that Sams has built for himself and, by extension, the rest of us. You also paint the dark, the shades of gray you love so much. No one understood that when you mixed black into the other colors when we were kids, it was on purpose. It's what this reality is missing, and what only you seem to be able to see."

I gestured to the door. "There's plenty of dark out there."

George shook his head. "That's the dark and gritty of horror novels and comic books. It's not the gray of life," he insisted.

I paused, thinking. "And if I do this," I said, "and we survive, then what?"

"Then you do what makes you come alive. You quit one of your jobs, cut back on your expenses, and paint."

"And if I fail?"

He looked at me significantly. "You can still fail doing what you don't want to do, you know?"

"Why does that sound familiar?" I asked.

"When I asked your Papi if I should try engineering, if I was smart enough to make it through the schooling or if I should be an electrician like my dad, he told me much the same thing."

Smiling, I said, "My Papi's a remarkable man." Putting my hands on my knees, I levered myself to my feet. "Eh, Purple Unicorn." He looked back at me, the strain of holding the door closed evident on his face. "I need to borrow your horn."

"Why?" he asked.

I tried to force a smile. "Please, what can it hurt?" He hesitated, but eventually nodded and bent his head. I crossed to him and reached to take the horn. It came free with an ease that surprised me, as if the horn was eager for the feel of my hand.

I studied it, delving into the colors, the lines, and the textures of its surface with my unique vision. I saw the horn's ancientness, and, for the briefest of moments, I understood the scope and purpose of its power. A twinge in the back of my mind, like the entirety of a migraine condensed into an instant, forced my gaze away. Swallowing, I closed my eyes and turned my face to the ceiling to plead for the intervention of any benevolent force willing to help.

I pictured my city, Olympia. Not just the Olympia that was on postcards and the tourism website, but the Olympia with homeless residents and dirty sidewalks. The reflection of a sunrise in windows covered with fingerprints, the faint smell of sewage in the morning mist.

I pictured the Comic-Con, with its teaming mass of passionate humanity, the failing air-conditioning, and the sense of confinement the crowds lent to even the largest rooms. I remembered the sore feet, aching shoulders, and the thrill of being in the same room as some of my heroes. I tasted sweat that wasn't mine; I felt the bruises of accidental elbows to the face. I remembered the tarnished pictures of my very first Con: Papi squatting next to my stroller that was decorated with cardboard wings fashioned to look like an X Wing fighter.

I pictured George, not as the idealized man he was now, but as George the engineering student. I added roughness to his edges, bags underneath pale amber eyes from sleepless nights spent studying. The pain of failed tests, his doubts if the struggle was worth it, the heartbreak he felt when his fiancée had cheated on him. Within that cocoon of pain was both the pride of being the first in his family to earn an advanced degree and the jealousy that fact garnered from his cousins. The courage to push forward into grad school regardless.

Last of all, I imagined myself. Still Papi's little geeky princess despite how much I've grown. An adult with an art degree and two jobs. Working in an art supply store for the discount—and to be close to the people who actually practice what I dreamed of doing, but was too afraid to pursue. Barely sleeping and lying awake next to a man I didn't love because I had grown comfortable with the relationship and because living with someone helped pay the rent. I looked into myself, saw the dark alongside the light and accepted myself for not only who I was, but who I yearned to be.

Who, I resolved, I *would* be. Just because the world could be painted in gray didn't mean it should be accepted that way. Sometimes, it was necessary to reach through the gray and touch the ideal. Otherwise, all you'd ever see is black and white.

In my mind, I painted the world in shades of gray and in color, using both to impart meaning. Lifting the horn to my lips, I took the deepest breath of my life. I made a choice and blew through the horn in an effort to remake my world.

This time, the shift in reality didn't come with blackness and pain. My eyes lost focus until all that remained was a shifting haze of colors. My body prickled, as if every inch of my skin had fallen asleep simultaneously. The horn grew immense, gaining a psychic weight that drew in my will with the inexorable force of a black hole. The energy folded and built upon itself, my soul vibrating in time with each surge.

In the moment of resonance, It became aware of me.

The bond was tenuous and tentative, like the brush of fingertips across eyelids, but I knew that was for my protection. Its ancientness and otherworldliness were entirely beyond my comprehension and would crush the relative insubstantiality of my existence.

It, in return, comprehended my entire being in an instant.

There is a price to will shaping. There were no words, no thoughts, but rather simple understanding.

What price?

Memory. Destiny. Vitality.

All of these things?

As much as is necessary.

There was no sense of time. I could have paused for a moment or a lifetime. *I will pay.*

As I regained awareness, the world changed. The silence was broken by the distant cries of shock, confusion, and trauma. Zombies no longer clawed at the bay doors, the moans of the undead shifting into confused, but coherent, questions. The Purple Unicorn had once again become Walter Sams, absurd costume disheveled, face twisted with effort and remorse, sweat dripping from his hooked nose.

I spun to George. He was restored, delirious and grinning. "Damn, chica," he said. "You did it."

I had done something, enough for now. The shrill of police sirens grew closer as I collapsed to my knees, clutching the horn tightly to my core.

Conner Bright and the Case of the Purple Unicorn

Robert J. McCarter

The ringing of the phone is like a dentist's drill to my sodden consciousness. I groan, realizing I hadn't managed to get undressed when I tumbled into bed. Again. I feel for my cell phone on the nightstand, my hand connecting with a half-eaten microwave burrito before finding it.

"G'day, you got Bright," I say, remembering even in my hungover state to use my B-movie quality Australian accent.

"Got a job for you, but you've got to get here quick." The voice is feminine and a tad husky. Detective Trisha Sanchez. Why the hell is she calling me? After that jacked-up stakeout, I'm her least favorite private investigator in the Phoenix metro area.

"What kind of a job?" I say, my voice rough from too long in a noisy bar working as a bouncer and too many cheap beers afterward. I look around my shit hole of a bedroom. Dirty laundry, trash, the spring heat of the desert morning flowing in the open window. "And can they pay?"

An Australian accent is easy. Just elongate your vowels—"paay" instead of "pay"—and throw in the occasional "mate" and "g'day." In the desert southwest, that and changing my name to Conner Bright, keeps my past at bay.

"They can. It's a murder, Bright, so get your ass out here now. No booze or I'll throw you in the drunk tank."

"Aces. Happy to help."

"Texting you the address now." She hangs up.

After some mouthwash for breakfast, I stop by the old cookie tin that sits on the top of my little entertainment center. It's got a shameful layer of dust on top and holds the ashes of my father inside. "Hey, Dad," I say, without a trace of an Australian accent. "I've got a case. An important one."

Sitting next to the tin is a DVD of *Crocodile Dundee*. My dad took me to that movie in 1986 when it came out. I was thirteen and loved it, but not as much as he did. When we exited, he'd said, "Now that's a man, son. That's a man."

☙ ✧ ❧

I get out of my 1976 El Camino, my cowboy boots crunching on the dry ground as I approach the murder scene. It's a hot day, and since the El Camino doesn't have air conditioning, I'm already sweating. I'm at a little ranch in the desert between Phoenix and Wickenburg, Arizona. This is a big deal. There's lots of cowboys and lots of guns around here, but not that many murders in the sticks.

I get the usual assortment of looks as I duck under the yellow tape. Looks of surprise from folks that don't know me, looks of recognition or disdain from those that do. The disdain belongs to Trisha Sanchez, the detective who called me in.

And the looks from the others, it's what I expect. I'm tall and slim; at 6'5" and 170 pounds, some people call me scarecrow. I've got a bowie knife with an eleven-inch blade on my belt, a crocodile claw hanging around my neck, and a wide-brimmed bush hat on my head, all to go with my Australian accent.

"G'day, Detective," I say, tipping my hat to Sanchez as she strides away from the murder scene. She's in her late-thirties, short and wiry, wearing reflective sunglasses.

"Your client's in the house," she says, grabbing my arm and pulling me away. I resist a moment, watching Helen Montana, one of the medical examiners, leaning over the prone form of a gray-haired Mexican man that has a ragged hole in his chest.

"Where we goin'?" I ask.

"To see your client, Irene. She asked for someone to help her solve this murder."

"And you called me?" Something isn't right.

She pauses, her hand still locked around my bicep, her head jabbing back to the scene. "At this point we're ruling it an accident. The victim, Edwardo Campos, has got a big hole in his chest, and we found a bull running loose with blood on his horn."

She starts to pull me forward again toward the one-story ranch house. It's small with blue vinyl siding that was popular in the seventies. The blue has started to fade, and the house looks like it has seen better days.

"Then what the hell am I doin' here?"

Sanchez smiles, showing her perfectly white teeth, looking something like a shark. "The kid says she saw it happen."

I shrug.

"She says it was a man riding a purple unicorn that killed her great-uncle."

☙ ✧ ❧

I almost don't go in. I almost march back to my El Camino until Sanchez says the magic words. "She's got cash." I think of the delinquent notices stacked on my little kitchen table. I think how I'd love not to buy the cheapest damn beer in the store.

It's surprisingly neat inside the house. Not fancy, but everything's put away, the wood floors swept, the old throw rugs shook out. The living room isn't much—an old couch with a brown blanket thrown over it, a wooden rocking chair, and a shelf full of books. No TV, no stereo. It looks very much like what this house probably looked like a hundred years ago.

Sitting awkwardly in the rocking chair is a tall deputy with blond hair. He gives Sanchez a brief look of relief before scurrying out.

And then I see the girl. She's got long black hair, big brown eyes, and is maybe eight years old. I almost leave again.

"Irene," Sanchez says, "this is Conner Bright. He's the private detective I was telling you about. He's got a reputation for dealing with unusual cases."

With that Sanchez leaves. I stand there awkwardly, my hands shoved into my jeans, wishing I hadn't answered the phone this morning.

The girl's wearing a purple shirt and has a stuffed unicorn on the couch next to her. On the table in front of her is a battered hardcover of *The Last Unicorn.*

Great. Of course she saw a purple unicorn. She's obsessed with them.

"Where are you parents?" I ask.

She just shakes her head. Ah hell, she's an orphan too.

I lower myself into the rocking chair, wishing the hard seat was padded. The room smells of must and wood polish. "You got any family?"

She shakes her head again, her hands sitting placidly in her lap.

"I'm sorry about what happened to your great-uncle out there."

Her brow furrows and she stares at me a moment before saying, "Where you from?" Judging from her uncle and her appearance, I expect her to have a Mexican accent, but she doesn't. Not a trace.

"Australia," I lie. But it's a lie I tell everyone. "A little place called Scatterwood deep in the outback."

"You don't believe I saw a unicorn." She says it straight up, her voice steady, her eyes clear.

I shake my head.

"I did," she says, her voice too hard for someone so young. "And you have to prove it." She pulls out a wad of hundred-dollar bills from her pocket and slaps them on the coffee table in front of her. I notice light red stains on her hands and I imagine them pressed against her dead great-uncle's chest.

I know I should say no, but three thousand is a lot for me. A whole lot. I rub my suddenly sweating palms on my jeans. I'm dying for a drink. That would clear my head. Help me think this through.

"Well?" she asks.

I get up and start pacing. "Why don't you tell me what you saw."

꧁ ✧ ꧂

The girl talks, I pace, my feet finding squeaky boards in the old floor. The money is in a jumbled pile on the coffee table in front of her. I want it even more than I want a drink.

"Been here for a few months," she says. "Came after the accident …" Her face darkens, and she blinks several times. "We moved around a lot, Mama, Papa, and me. We picked grapes in California, pecans in Oregon."

"Your parents were illegals?" I ask.

She nods. "But I was born here. After the accident, Uncle Ed came and got me. He was afraid they'd send me back to Mexico."

"Tell me about your great-uncle," I say.

She shrugs. "He raises cows, rides horses."

I look at the wad of hundred-dollar bills and then back to her, doubting that was all he did.

"And last night?"

Irene pauses, her hands finally leaving her lap as she wraps them around her chest and shivers. "Uncle Ed was so happy. Said things would be changing today, like a birthday party but better. Said it would be good. We were reading when the animals started making noise. He took his gun and told me to stay.

"I wasn't scared until I heard a shout. I went to the window and peeked through the curtain. That's when I saw it."

"The unicorn?" I ask, keeping my tone as even as possible.

She nods. "The moon was full so I could see good. At first I thought it was a horse with a man riding it. But then I saw the horn and the dark purple fur. Uncle Ed was real surprised. That man spurred the unicorn hard, and it ran down my uncle, its horn hitting him … right in the … He … I …" She trails off into soft sobs. I feel for the kid. She's suffered way too many losses in the past few months.

The tears don't last long. She takes a deep breath, holds it for a few beats, and slowly lets it out. She wipes the tears from her cheeks, her eyes hardening. "The man got off the unicorn and came in here."

"What did you do?"

"I hid behind the door. He walked in like he had been here before. Went right to the kitchen. I hid behind the couch and watched. I couldn't see much. There was banging, crashing, and a bunch of beeps. He marched out holding some papers."

"Did he see you? Did you get a good look at him?"

She shakes her head. "He had a bandana over his mouth. I don't think he saw me. He walked right out, got on his unicorn, and rode away."

I nod and walk into the small kitchen. One of the plain handmade wooden cabinets is open, cans spilling out onto the counter and the floor. In the cabinet is a small metal safe embedded into the wall. The door is ajar, and the safe is empty.

"Is that where you got the money?" I ask after I walk back into the living room.

Irene nods, her hands back onto her lap, her eyes way too calm.

It's a hot day and the corpse of Edwardo Campos is going to stink to high heaven soon. The smell of blood and urine and horse manure is already overpowering.

"It looks like a horn did this," Helen Montana says, pulling away the bloodied cowboy shirt that used to be a powder blue. There's been a lot of foot traffic, but I did find a few fresh hoofprints leading to the corpse. She gets up, brushing absently at her ponytailed blonde hair. Helen is a tall, big-boned woman with blue eyes and a great smile. She's my age at around forty. There's been sparks, and we've briefly dated a few times, but never a sustained flame. Working with her is always a bit awkward.

She walks several paces back to a yellow CSI marker where I located the hoofprints right next to a shotgun. "It looks like he was hit here and thrown back."

"The bull did it?" I ask.

"I'll know more when I do the autopsy."

I nod, glancing back to the faded blue ranch house.

"Sorry, Conner," she says, and I hear that sweetness in her voice that makes work hard.

"Did they get a blood sample from the bull's horn?" I ask.

She chuckles and looks over to a corral where two deputies are trying to get a rope around the bull. He's a big Hereford and doesn't appear to be cooperating. "Maybe you should go show them how it's done."

I shake my head, feeling uncomfortable. Helen was born in upstate New York and has a thing for cowboys. Could explain her interest in a mess like me.

Sanchez walks up, her arms folded. "You taking the case?"

"Any other witnesses?" I ask, pointing at a smaller building back behind the blue house.

Sanchez shakes her head. "Campos used to have a ranch hand living there. The neighbors told us he left a few months ago before the girl got here. Said they were close, that the old man treated him like a son, but something happened."

"Did you call CPS, Child Protective Services?"

She nods. "Doesn't look like they can get out here today."

"Why the hell not?"

"Budget cuts. Short staffed. You know the drill."

"And what about Irene?"

Sanchez chuckles and smiles at me again. "You take the case, you take the girl." She walks away looking like she's having the time of her life, paying me back for that stakeout with this mess.

☙ ✧ ❧

I go help the deputies with the bull. Not that I want to get into the corral with a ton of pissed off beef. I need to think. And to think, I need to move. Everyone, including Detective Sanchez, knows I need the cash. But taking a little girl's money on a wild-goose chase doesn't seem proper.

I climb over the fence and hop down onto the churned brown dirt of the corral. It stinks of horse and cow, but at least it doesn't smell of death. The jolt of the hop doesn't do my sacrum any good, and I feel each and every one of my old rodeo injuries. I rode bulls for a while, but mostly worked as a rodeo clown—keeping other riders safe was the right kind of crazy for me.

"You're just makin' the old boy mad," I shout to the two deputies. One is the lanky blond from the house. "Back away." They comply promptly.

I scrape some oats out of the bottom of the feed trough and get the specimen collection swab from the tall deputy and amble over toward the bull.

Those deputies may have been born and raised in Arizona, but they ain't no cowboys. They were afraid and trying to overpower an animal that's five times their weight. Stupid.

"Hi ya, boy," I say gently as I approach, the hand with the oats outstretched. I keep my eye on the bull and walk slowly. This is no rodeo bull used to bucking guys like me off. This fellow's older, probably kept around for stud duties. He didn't want to fight, but he didn't want to be bullied either.

People think cows are dumb, but they ain't. They seek safety and comfort just like the rest of us. The bull's big brown eyes finally leave mine and flick to the handful of oats. I'm two paces away and I stop walking, the final choice has to be his.

My left hand has the swab in it, and I hold it just back from the oats. I'd be a fool to spring it on him while he was eating. His nostrils flair and his eyes flick to the swab and back to the oats. He doesn't like the sharp alcohol scent of the swab, but he wants the oats.

I stand there like I don't care and just keep talking to him. He eventually takes two steps forward, his soft mouth in my hand as his rough tongue licks up the oats. I wipe the swab against the red stain on his horn, and when he's done eating, I back slowly away.

A crowd has gathered, and there's a smattering of applause. When I'm clear of the bull, I look back and see Helen holding Irene on the other side of the corral. Detective Sanchez is there, a question on her face.

☙ ✧ ❧

"The girl is traumatized," I say to Sanchez. We're out of earshot of Helen and Irene, who are both staring at us as we walk the dirt driveway. "She needs a professional."

"The system sucks," she says, "but the girl needs something to do, and running around with you trying to find a purple unicorn might be better than her hanging out in the sheriff's office."

I'm about to say something stupid when it occurs to me that this must be Sanchez's way of looking out for the girl. But why me? "What about the robbery? There's somethin' that ain't right."

She shrugs and points towards the bull. "I've got the killer right there. As to the money, the old man just realized he bought a bunch of Home Depot stock on a whim back in the eighties. He's suddenly rich, that explains the money, and besides, the safe wasn't forced open. Until I have evidence to the contrary, I'm done."

I nod and look back at the girl. Helen has her by the hand and is walking her away from the crime scene and towards the pasture. The girl needs someone, that much is certain. But me? A mostly drunk, past-his-prime cowboy pretending to be Australian?

"Look, Bright," Sanchez says. "Just take the girl for the day. Take any clue you can find and run it down with her. I'll call you when the social workers are ready for her."

Sanchez walks away and starts barking orders. I don't fight it. I owe her.

I keep Irene in the house while Helen finishes with the corpse and hauls him away.

It's odd that the murderer wanted those papers, but didn't care about the money. And that damn unicorn keeps tripping me up. Maybe there was no robbery. Maybe Irene knew the combination and got into the safe herself.

I'm standing in the mess of a kitchen staring off into space when I notice Irene looking at me. Her eyes have that too-wide look of shock. That's why she's been so restrained. The poor kid is in shock. Sanchez was right, she needs something to do.

"All righty then," I say, stooping down and picking up a can. "Get over here and help me clean this up."

"Clean?" Irene says.

I nod. "There could be a clue here, so we're gonna clean up this mess and see what we can find."

While Irene is in the kitchen, I go searching Edwardo's bedroom. It's small and neat, with a twin bed, an old wooden chest at the end, a small closet, and a cross on the wall.

I start in the closet, going through the pale blue cowboy shirts—the man liked to dress the same every day—and patting down the two dark blue blazers. Each of them has a matchbook from the same place. The Sugar and Spice, a "gentlemen's club" in downtown Phoenix.

So the old man liked to look at young women.

"Did your Uncle Ed go out much?" I ask Irene back in the kitchen.

Irene nods. "Every Saturday night. He didn't think I knew, but he snuck out after I went to bed. Stayed out real late. He always came back smelling like smoke." She wrinkles her nose.

It's Monday morning, Edwardo was killed Sunday night. Maybe something happened at Sugar and Spice. I show Irene the matchbooks.

"What is it?" she asks.

"A clue, Irene. It's a clue."

☙ ✧ ❧

The Sugar and Spice is a pinkish building with bright neon that sits between a bank and a fast-food joint off a busy street in central Phoenix. I shift uncomfortably in the seat of the El Camino as I drive by for the fourth time. It's Irene sitting next to me that makes me feel uncomfortable.

The fifth time I drive by, Irene sighs and says, "Just pull in."

I park behind the building.

"Are we going in?" Irene asks.

"You're kiddin', right?"

"I know what goes on in there. Men look at girls." She ends by rolling her eyes.

My reputation's bad enough without dragging an eight-year-old into a strip club right before turning her over to CPS. "Not gonna happen, love," I say as I get out the car. I walk over and open the door for her. She looks puzzled, but gets out and follows me to the McDonald's next door. As I do this, I'm convinced that I'm not the only man that's dropped off a little girl at this McDonald's before ducking into Sugar and Spice.

She doesn't complain, but she grabs my hand and holds it as we cross the hot asphalt. Her hand feels so small in mine, and I look down at her and she's looking at me with a tiny smile on her face. That look of trust scares the hell out of me.

The inside of Sugar and Spice smells of desperation, with a bored blonde dancing and a few rumpled men watching. I give the bartender a twenty and show him the picture of Edwardo Campos that Irene gave me. He tells me Edwardo was there the night before last, buying drinks and celebrating like he'd just won the lottery or something.

On the way out of Sugar and Spice, I'm confused. I have no motive for murder, and no idea why a robber would leave behind a wad of cash—or ride a purple unicorn, for that matter.

I'm not looking and collide with a man on his way in while I'm on the way out, the Phoenix heat swirling around us.

"Sorry, mate," I say, looking at the stranger. He's got on alligator-skin cowboy boots, a Stetson hat, sharp green eyes, and a sneer. He's almost as tall as me, but a lot beefier.

"Watch it, buddy," he grumbles, moving past quickly. I'm distracted by his boots, which would make a fine addition to my Australian cowboy look.

I get halfway to the El Camino when Irene runs up and wraps her arms around me. "That's him," she whispers between gulping breaths. "The man that came into my house. That killed Uncle Ed."

"How do you know?"

"The boots. The eyes. I'll never forget them."

An El Camino is a crappy car to tail someone in. Especially mine. With its shiny blue paint job and tricked-out rims, it stands out. This car is the one thing in my life that I truly take care of. I love it. It's a car, but it's got a bed like a truck. It's rare. It used to be my dad's.

Irene is sitting right next to me, eyes wide. She smells of cheap beef, french fries, and fear. Her closeness feels strangely good.

We follow Alligator Boots in his red Ford F-150 from Sugar and Spice to a Circle K where he stops for gas. I pull into the carpet place next door. When he ducks into the Circle K, I make to get out of the car, but Irene grabs me.

"Don't go," she says. "Please."

I get lost in those big brown eyes of hers. I'm not used to someone needing me.

"I'll be right back. No worries." Those eyes don't look like they believe me.

I walk casually over to the truck and place my cell phone in the back. What I see there makes me gasp. It's a long horn with spiral ridges running its length. It's an honest-to-god unicorn horn. I'm dizzy for a moment. Did Irene really see what she thought she saw?

As I look closer, I see that the tip of the horn is rough, as if it broke off, and the other end has an odd leather harness on it.

I rush back to the car, my heart pounding hard.

☙ ✧ ❧

It feels strange, like I'm missing something. I've left Irene with the morgue's receptionist. I had called in on a burner phone I bought at the Circle K to have Sanchez trace my cell so I could keep tabs on Alligator Boots. She told me Helen needed to see me and it was urgent.

Helen is pacing when I walk in. Her blue eyes are a bit wide and remind me of Irene's. Does Helen need me too?

The corpse of Edwardo Campos is laid out on a metal table, the wound to his chest all that much more shocking being exposed—no shirt to hide it, no blood to mask it. It's a big, red hole near his heart.

The morgue is pretty small. A couple of shining tables for the dead with bright lights mounted above. A wall of drawers for bodies to be stored in. Except for the ragged wound in Edwardo's chest, the place is spotless and smells strongly of antiseptic.

Helen's biting her lip and stands me next to the body, showing me a stainless steel tray. In it is what looks like a piece of bone about the size of an almond. Like a piece of rib or something.

"So?" I ask, shrugging my shoulders.

"The blood you got from the bull's horn is his. But … I pulled *this* out of him," she says, like she's telling me the Pope is secretly a woman or something.

I give her a blank stare. I'm clueless.

She drags me over to big round magnifying glass and holds the tray underneath it, giving me a pointed look. I lean close and look at the little piece of bone. It's pointed and has a distinct spiral ridge. When I look back at Helen, I'm smiling. She looks worried.

"That ain't no cow horn," I say.

She shakes her head.

"Good on ya, Helen," I say, kissing her on the cheek. "You just made my case."

"What? Conner, unicorns don't exist. How can this be?"

I shrug. "Don't know. What I do know is I just saw the mate to that piece in the back of an F-150."

☙ ✧ ❧

We're back in the El Camino heading out of Phoenix towards my place. I'm tired and hungry and don't know what else to do. Sanchez won't go after Alligator Boots. Won't tell officers to look for an F-150 with a unicorn horn in the back, says she'd be risking her reputation and won't do that for me. She wants more evidence.

Irene's smile is a mile wide. She looks so much more like a kid now. She's happy because I told her what Helen found and what I saw in the back of that F-150. Told her that I believe her. Her smile warms my wilted old heart.

It's near rush hour and the Phoenix traffic is thick as ants on honey. We're moving slowly forward in the stifling heat.

Phoenix is a flat and boring expanse except for the occasional outcrop of craggy stone. The city streets are a monotony of urban sprawl with strip malls, cookie-cutter houses, and the ubiquitous Circle Ks.

"So do you think it was a real unicorn?" Irene asks, her voice all bubbly and light.

I shrug my shoulders. Given the harness that was on the horn, I doubt that. I didn't get to telling her that part, and with her lit up like this, I just can't.

In the rearview, I catch a flash of a bright red truck weaving its way through traffic. My face falls.

"What's wrong, Conner?" Irene asks.

"Nothin', love," I lie. I point at the glove compartment. "There's a bottle of water in there. You best drink in this heat."

She nods and dutifully pulls out the water bottle and takes a drink. My eyes keep flicking to the rearview mirror looking for that red truck. Maybe it's Mr. Alligator Boots. Maybe he got wise to me following him.

At a stoplight, I pull out the burner phone and text Sanchez, *Check location of both phones.*

A minute later, as the traffic is finally starting to ease up, she texts back. *Same location.*

☙ ✧ ❧

We didn't have the tail long. I saw him briefly right behind me and then he was gone, talking a left and speeding off.

When we're past the city and closer to my house, we pull into yet another Circle K, my stomach grumbling and my head pounding. I needed food and a drink. A stiff drink. I take Irene in. She holds my hand the whole time while I pick up a few microwave burritos and some cookies for us, and she picks out some potato chips.

I stop in front of the refrigerated section. I have to let go of Irene's hand to open the door. My hand's shaking a bit, my body screaming for alcohol. And there it is. Row after row of beer, an obscene number of choices. Dark beer, light beer, fancy beer, cheap beer, foreign beer.

Beer reminds me of Tommy Wilkins. Of the sickening sound of his scream when I ran him over. You'd think it would make me drink less, but it's done just the opposite.

I was sixteen and at a high school party near Globe, Arizona, where I grew up. Tommy and I fought over a girl whose name I can't even remember. We were both drunk, and I was trying to leave and he wouldn't get out of the way, banging on the hood of my old Toyota pickup and screaming at me while I revved the engine. My foot slipped off the clutch and ...

It was big news in Arizona. I did my time in the juvenile system, had my records sealed, but people around here remember my name. That's why I changed it, even though it broke my dad's heart. That's the reason behind the whole fake Australian thing. That's why my life is such a—

"What?" I ask. Irene had just said something.

She smiles and points at the vitamin water. "Can I have one of those? The purple one, please."

I blink at her a few times and nod, grabbing two of the plastic bottles and handing them to her. I turn my back on the obscene array of alcohol. Maybe tonight I can sleep without the beer.

I'm not thinking well. I drive right to my ten acres, a few miles from the Circle K, and pull in. Irene is babbling on like happy kids do, her words bright shards bouncing around my car. My fatigue and her happiness seem to lull me into a peaceful state. She goes on and on that when she grows up she's going to make a "My Little Unicorn" toy for girls, like the one already made for horses. That since unicorns are real, and once she finds one and gets her picture taken with it, everyone girl in the world will want one.

I still haven't told her about the harness.

"Maybe instead of 'My Little Unicorn,'" she says as I unlock the door to my dingy single-wide trailer, "I will name it after you." She's beaming at me now, like I'm someone important. "I'll call it 'Unicorn Bright.' That's a wonderful name."

I step into the house and am nodding when the clenched fist of Alligator Boots connects with my jaw, fiery pain radiating through the left side of my face. He was waiting behind the door.

As I go down, I curse my fatigue. He had tailed me long enough to get a look at my license plate. From there it wasn't hard to get my address or break in.

Irene screams and our food goes tumbling to the floor. On my way down I get a look at the chaotic mess of my living room. Dust covering the flat screen, piles of clothes, trash, dirty carpet.

I have a horrible realization: If I can't take care of my own living room, how am I going to take care of Irene? The thought doesn't last long. My head bounces off the carpet with a sharp crack and darkness descends.

I wake up with a start, the light of the full moon shining above me, hard ground below me, and cool air on my skin. My head is pounding and my jaw aches. My mouth is dry and my stomach clenches. I roll over and try to vomit, but there's nothing in me.

I hear the snort of a horse and bolt upright, the motion making my stomach try to empty itself again.

"Stand up," Alligator Boots says. He's mounted on what looks like a purple unicorn, a white horn jutting from its forehead, its coat a dark purple. In the moonlight it's hard to see the harness on the horse's head, but I know it's there.

"Why might I be doing that?" I ask, trying to hide the pain and desperation in my voice.

"Because if you don't, it will go badly for the girl."

We're back behind my trailer. It used to be a horse corral, back when I could afford to keep a horse. Now it's a falling down fence and a weedy expanse of dirt. Back behind the horse and Alligator Boots, I see the trailer, my El Camino, and his F-150 with a horse trailer attached.

"What?" I ask, trying desperately to get my mind to turn over.

Alligator Boots staged Edwardo Campos's death as an attack by a unicorn. Why? So Irene, a little girl obsessed with unicorns, would see it. Would talk about it. Would be dismissed. He put Edwardo's blood on that bull's horn. He also took something from the safe, just papers and not money.

This was all about Irene. The way her great-uncle had died had been a show for her.

Alligator Boots points to his right and I see Irene. She's tied to one of my cheap plastic chairs. She's gagged and her eyes are wide, her cheeks stained with tears.

I nod, make a show of getting up, and then slump back to the ground with a grunt. "What is it you needed from that safe?" I'm leaning on my right side, where my bowie knife should be, but he's taken it.

"Stand up!" he yells.

"You're the ranch hand Mr. Campos had a recent falling out with, ain't ya? The one that was once like a son to him."

He pulls a gun from his side and points it at Irene. "Stand. Now." He's not yelling anymore and that's a bad sign.

I slowly get into a squatting position. I feel in my right boot. That knife is still there.

I remember what Sanchez had told me about Edwardo Campos's recently remembered stock. What the bartender at Sugar and Spice had said when I showed him Edwardo's picture. How Edwardo had hinted to Irene that things were about to change for her.

"He wrote you out of his will," I say as I pull the knife from my boot and hold it behind my back, shakily standing up. "That's what ya took, the will that left everything to Irene. I'm guessing he hadn't signed it yet, but was about to. He had told all his buddies at Sugar and Spice about his windfall, about how he was leaving it all to his delightful niece that loves unicorns and the color purple. Someone there told ya."

Alligator Boots doesn't speak. He spurs the horse hard, and it leaps forward. As I stand there, I have empathy for Edwardo Campos. He came out in the middle of the night under the bright moonlight expecting a coyote and saw a galloping unicorn bearing down on him. He had the shotgun in his hand, but he didn't use it. His grandniece had been babbling about unicorns, and now seeing one made him dumb for an instant, just one small instant.

Adrenaline dumps into my bloodstream, my heart pounding in my ears in time with the thundering of the hooves. But I don't move. I stand there swaying, still trying to get my bearings, hoping my body still remembers my time at the rodeo.

I wonder what Detective Sanchez will do if she finds my body just like Edwardo's, if she has a hysterical girl that talks about yet another man being run through by a purple unicorn. Once, she might brush off, twice, never. It's all over for Alligator Boots, even if I don't survive. This thought gives me comfort. Briefly.

But what of Irene? I remember how she clung to me outside Sugar and Spice, how she sat so close to me in the El Camino, how she held my hand in the Circle K. It felt strange, but good, to be depended on. My eyes flick to her. I can't hear her over the pounding hooves or through her gag, but it's clear she's screaming.

The unicorn is upon me. I smell dust, paint, and its sweat. I quickly rotate my body around, moving just to the side. I pull the knife from behind my back. I do what I need to do.

ꕥ ✧ ꕥ

I wake up slowly and groan, realizing I'm fully dressed again. I'm slumped in a half-seated position, my lower back and my neck aching, my mouth dry as the desert.

"Take it easy." I'm not sure who it is at first, a woman with a sweet voice. Helen.

And then the events of the last day tumble onto me like a monsoon cloudburst. I bolt upright and open my eyes. "Irene," I croak.

"She's fine," Helen says, putting a hand on my back, a gentle smile on her lips.

"Where is she?" Part of me feels silly. I hardly know the girl. Another part of me is desperate for her to be okay.

"CPS came while you were sleeping. She's just fine, Conner."

I nod and rub at my face, trying to wake myself up, feeling several days of stubble. I remember the charging unicorn. I remember rotating out of the way and jamming my knife through one of those alligator skin boots. I remember him screaming and falling off that spray-painted horse, struggling to get up. Me punching him in the face. Him lying still. Untying Irene. Her sobbing and clinging to me while I call Detective Sanchez.

"They took her," I mumble, mostly to myself.

Helen is looking at me, her soft blue eyes searching my face like I'm not the man she knows.

I remember what it had felt like as Irene clung to me while we waited for the sheriff's deputies to arrive. How the ambulance had come and I had refused it and Irene had refused to leave me. How they had hauled Alligator Boots away. How Helen had finally come and we had gone into the trailer. I had given Irene my bed and held her hand for hours until she fell asleep and then stumbled out to the couch. Helen had insisted on staying.

"That horn," Helen says, pulling out her phone and showing me a picture that looks like a whale with a unicorn horn sticking out of its head. "It was real. This is a narwhal, that tusk is some crazy tooth."

It all makes sense … except for how I feel.

I look up to the tin of ashes on top of my entertainment center. I lever myself up, stumble over, and say, "Hey, Dad. The girl's safe." I reach down, my head screaming at me, and pick up a stray piece of paper, a microwave burrito wrapper.

"What are you doing?" Helen asks.

"I'm cleaning up." She's staring at me, like she doesn't know me. Like we've never danced or touched or had meals together. "Will you help me?"

The door is a faded yellow and the neighborhood's somewhat faded, too. It might have been cheery three decades ago, but now it's looking a little sad.

It's been ten days since I met Irene, and two days since I've had a drink. I would have come sooner, but I swore to myself I wouldn't do it unless I had been dry for at least two days. My hand is shaking as I knock.

A plump woman with a pinched face answers the door.

"I'm here to see Irene," I say. "I called earlier."

She nods, lets me in, and leaves me in the living room. There's a TV playing loudly with strange blue creatures on it dancing around. There's a couple of kids, much younger than Irene, watching it, their eyes wide.

And then she's there. This time I'm expecting it and kneel down before she gets to me. "You okay?" I whisper.

She hugs me hard. She nods and sniffs. I can feel her tears on my shoulder. I can feel my own tears on my cheek. "What took you so long?" She says it gently but it feels like a horse kicked me in the chest.

"I was … I …" I stammer. "I was trying to …" I can't finish. I can't tell this girl that I was trying to be worthy of her. That I have been ever since we met. That I will be as long as she'll have me.

I don't know if she understands, but she hugs me even harder and that's enough.

My Hero

Mark Ryan

Based in the VilleAnne universe created by Peter J. Wacks and Steven L. Sears

"Do really think you'll find anything for him here?" Jill asked.

Christine shrugged and let loose a sigh. "He's always been a fan of *Star Wars,* but you just can't find the original collectibles anymore." She gestured to a cheap plastic *Millennium Falcon* that was missing several pieces. "He goes on and on about the ones he had when he was younger."

"Good luck finding any in a thrift shop." Jill lifted a piece of a china set to examine the price.

Christine smiled as she picked through the shelves of collectibles. The thrift store was huge and filled with all manner of junk, or treasure, depending on one's perspective. A set of giant, hot cocoa mugs caught her attention.

"Alora, what do you think of these?" She turned with one of the mugs in hand. "Where did she run off to?"

"Probably looking for Supers toys." Jill scanned the store. "Though, I doubt she'll find any of those, either."

Christine let out another sigh. "I'd better find her before she breaks something that just went up in price." She weaved her way back to the main aisle of the store and started scanning the offshoots.

It didn't take her long to find her daughter once she saw the giant banner labeled TOYS. Jill was right about the Supers toys. They were expensive to say the least, and some were incredibly rare. It was no surprise when all the money from the merchandise of heroes like Darkest Knight went to charities, for education or something like that.

She came up behind her daughter and put her hands on her hips. "I believe I asked you to stay close."

Alora turned and looked at her with an innocent smile, holding up a toy. "Mommy, what's this?"

Shock hit Christine, making her heart skip a beat. Sinking to her knees, she gently took the soft plastic toy. It was a Twilight Sparkle purple unicorn. Its left hind leg was warped from heat, and strands of its glittery mane and tail were melted into clumps. The left eye had been lovingly, though poorly, painted back on the slightly drooping face.

"What's wrong, Mommy?"

Tears splashed on the purple unicorn.

☙ ✧ ❧

The smell of pancakes filled the air as the cheer of the crowd blared out of the tinny-sounding speakers mounted into the giant wooden television.

"Christine, breakfast is ready," her father called from the kitchen.

She barely heard him, continuing to watch the televised parade with fascination. Yesterday was Supersday, and Xonometer—her favorite Super—had been front and center. To top it off, today was her tenth birthday. Xonometer raised a muscled arm and waved at the crowd, his silver, power-augmenting armor—highlighted with crimson and blue—glinting in the bright sunlight.

"Christine?" her father called again.

"Just a minute," she said absently.

"Come and eat now, before your pancakes get cold," her mother added.

Heaving an oppressed sigh, she tore her eyes from the screen and plodded into the kitchen.

"Good morning, birthday girl," Jim said as he curled the newspaper in half and peered over it through his thick spectacles at his daughter's wild, sleep-messed hair. He was already showered and clean-shaven, his wavy dark hair neatly combed and parted.

Christine tried to hide her smile as she rubbed her brown eyes. He hadn't been home for breakfast in longer than she could remember; he was usually at work before the sun rose. She pulled a chair away from the table and sat, savoring the sweet smell of pancakes that hung in the air, mingling with the tang of freshly cut grass. The droning of several neighbors mowing their lawns before the summer day grew too warm hummed a slightly dissonant harmony that drifted in through the open windows alongside a cool breeze.

Slipping a third small cake on the top of a stack, her mother set the plate on the table in front of Christine. She was an Englishwoman. Blonde-haired, blued-eyed, and as beautiful as the day her father had met her, or so he always said.

"Thank you," Christine said drowsily as she reached for the syrup. She usually got only two pancakes, but she was ten now.

Her mother leaned down and kissed the top of her head. "Happy birthday, honey," she said as she smoothed her daughter's dark, curly hair. "What are you two going to do today?"

"You're not joining us?" Jim asked, his eyes following her as she returned to the stove and placed the pan back on the burner before adding a dollop of batter.

"I have to get the house cleaned up before my parents arrive, or were you not listening when I told you they were coming?"

Jim's mouth hung open for a moment, making him look slightly imbecilic. "That's right. I'm sorry, Diane. It slipped my mind."

Diane brought the coffeepot to the table where she filled his empty mug, kissing him on the top of his head. "How many pancakes would you like?" she asked as she turned away.

"Three sounds about right." He stirred a spoonful of sugar into his coffee.

Pancakes now thoroughly saturated in syrup, Christine cut away a large bite and stuffed it into her mouth. The rich buttery taste of the cake, mixed with the sweet caramel of the syrup, made her eyelids droop with pleasure as she chewed blissfully. Pancakes were her favorite.

The telephone's obnoxiously loud ringing rattled the end table in the family room. Christine stopped chewing and her eyes locked on her father. Her mother's eyes did the same. The phone rang several more times and went silent.

"Did you hear something?" Jim said as he looked up from his paper. Christine started giggling as she began to chew again.

"Chris, honey, don't laugh with your mouth full," Diane said, smiling happily at Jim. She flopped a cake onto a plate and added more batter to the sizzling pan.

"What do you want to do today?" Jim asked as he set his paper aside.

Christine swallowed and peered around the room, searching. "We could start with opening presents."

"Presents?" her father teased. "What presents?"

Christine rolled her eyes and looked at her mother, doing her best to imitate the expression she had seen on her face so many times. Jim took a drink of his coffee, hiding his grin as he looked at his wife, who rolled her eyes from Christine to him in the same fashion. Coffee splashed from his mug as he nearly choked.

"Serves you right for teasing her like that, Jim." Diane flopped another cake onto his stack.

"What did you get me?" Christine asked.

He dabbed at the coffee soaking into his shirt with a napkin. "I'll go get them," he said and rose from the table.

Diane flashed her daughter a grin.

Jim returned a few moments later with two presents. One that was haphazardly wrapped with what appeared to be as much tape as paper, and another that was so perfectly decorated it seemed almost a shame to tear the paper. "Which do you want first?"

Christine eyed the presents, scrunching her nose, trying to decide which of her parents had guessed her desires more accurately. Going against her instincts, she took a chance and pointed to the disastrously wrapped present. The grin on her father's face widened as he handed over the gift he had picked for her.

Her mother settled the last pancake on her father's stack and brought the plate to the table, setting it in front of him. She put her hand on his shoulder as he sat.

Christine pushed her pancakes aside and tore into the wrapping. The excessive tape actually made removing the paper a small challenge. When the last of the wrapping had torn away, a small purple unicorn with sparkling hair sat on the table before her. Christine stared at it in disbelief.

"You like it?" her father asked.

"My Little Pony, Twilight Sparkle Unicorn?" Christine said flatly, rolling her eyes again. "I'm ten now, Dad. I haven't played with ponies since I was eight."

"Oh," her father said, crestfallen.

"I told you, dear." Her mother shook her head. "Open the other one, honey." She pushed the other present toward Christine. Paper tore again and revealed a large red and blue robot.

"Optimus Prime!" Christine shouted with excitement.

"Optimus … what?" Jim asked.

"It's a Transformer, dear. She watches the cartoon every Saturday."

"A Transformer?" He came around the table, abandoning his pancakes, and watched as Christine opened the box. He sat beside her and helped pull the pieces out of the packaging.

"Your cakes are getting cold, Jim," Diane said as she took what little was left of Christine's breakfast to the sink. "You still haven't said what you want to do today, Chris."

"Optimus Prime is the leader of the Autobots," Christine explained to her father as they put together the toy. "I love it, Mom! He looks kinda like Xonometer!"

Her mother smiled. "How about going to a movie?" she persisted.

"Wait," Christine said too late as her father pressed a button on the arm of the toy. A small piece of black plastic flew across the kitchen and bounced off the cabinet to her mother's right.

"It even shoots rockets!" Jim said excitedly.

Diane sighed, shaking her head when Christine giggled.

"Optimus protects the people of earth, like Xonometer," Christine added. Her father's hands withdrew from the toy, and she looked at him. Her smile vanished. Talk of the superhuman always seemed to change her father's mood.

"He's just like everyone else you know." Jim's voice had a distant tone.

"He's a hero," Christine said heatedly.

"Maybe you could go to the museum, or see the new Xonometer tribute?" Diane suggested as she flipped a pancake, oblivious to the look on Jim's face. His eyes strayed to the now-silent telephone.

"You promised," Christine's voice was little more than a whisper.

Her father's eyes came back to hers, and he seemed to return from wherever it was he had gone. "Yes, yes I did. Today is your day." Smiling, he patted her hand and moved back to his own chair. He began consuming the pancakes almost mechanically, clearly still distracted.

Diane joined them at the table and drenched her pancakes in syrup. "I think that would be a great idea. You've hardly talked about anything other than Xonometer for the last year, Chris."

It was true. Kids everywhere were all about the superhuman. And why wouldn't they be? He could create KEFs—Kinetic Energy Fields, dubbed "plasmight" by the corporations—that enabled him to control lightning and manipulate matter. Christine had even seen footage of him using his power to lift a carload of children to safety when the vehicle was hanging, probably soon to fall from a bridge. He was even trained by and succeeded Magnificent!, the first of all the Supers. If there was a kid who didn't like Xonometer, Christine had never met them, or heard of them for that matter.

But it wasn't just his powers that fascinated Christine, there was something familiar about him. Maybe it was his voice, or the fact that he often refused payment for his deeds, but she felt she knew him and that they would be great friends if they ever met. A thought occurred to her: Optimus Prime reminded her of Xonometer. She could likely make the Autobot look like Xonometer with the right adjustments.

"Did you forget to eat again yesterday, Jim?" Diane asked, staring at him quizzically.

Christine giggled more as her father halted his inhalation of his pancakes.

He swallowed the mouthful he was chewing. "No, no, I was just thinking."

"Well think about slowing down before you choke yourself."

Jim chuckled and took another, exaggeratedly slow, bite.

Diane shook her head and looked at Christine. "Don't encourage him."

Christine couldn't help herself and continued laughing.

"Why don't you go get washed up and dressed so you two can go?"

Christine clutched Optimus to her chest and hopped down from her chair.

"Don't forget your pony," Diane said before taking a bite of her pancakes.

Christine fetched the purple unicorn from the table with a roll of her eyes and a smile for her dad, which he returned, displaying a mouthful of pancake. "Ewwww!" Christine cried out, running from the kitchen and up the stairs to her room.

Standing Optimus Prime carefully on a shelf in perfect battle pose, and tossing the unicorn to her bedroom floor, she headed to the bathroom. She showered more quickly than usual and put on her favorite blue sundress that her parents had given her for Christmas the year before. It matched perfectly with the blue dress shoes they gave her for Hanukkah and the blue socks they gave her for the Winter Solstice. Christine didn't really understand all the different holidays, but that didn't bother her; they all came with presents.

Normally she wore jeans and a shirt, but she wanted to look her best for Dad today. Of course, that didn't mean she would go without her periodic table ball cap. Being a pharmacologist, her father smiled whenever he saw her wear it. She pulled it over her damp hair and settled it into place.

After a glance in the mirror, she nodded to herself in satisfaction and ran to the stairs.

"Don't forget the sunscreen," her mother said, handing Jim a small bottle at the bottom of the stairs.

The phone rang. Christine stopped on the stairs, but didn't take her eyes off her father. He stared at the phone as it rang again, then grinned and looked at her.

"You ready to go, kiddo?"

Christine tried to suppress a grin and nodded, continuing down the stairs as he opened the front door.

The passenger door to the forest-green and wood-paneled Wagoneer groaned as he opened it for her. Inside, the jeep smelled of stale bread and dust, the foot area of the middle seat full of wadded-up fast-food wrappers and empty paper coffee cups.

"Sorry, I haven't had time to clean it out," Jim said ruefully as he climbed into the driver's seat. After a few stubborn splutters, the engine started up, and the radio blared with the voice of a newscaster reporting on what sounded like an accident. Jim quickly pushed in the Def Leppard tape sticking out of the deck.

The drive into Denver was little more than an hour. They listened to *Pyromania* the whole way while Christine occasionally hung her arm out the window, letting her hand carve serpentine waves through the wind.

The downtown area was overflowing with people, and they were forced to park a good distance from the memorial. Christine didn't mind. They walked along the crowded Sixteenth Street mall, making note of the places they would stop by on the way back, in between his questions about school and her friends. She didn't remember taking his hand, but didn't mind once she realized she had.

"Thanks, Dad," she said, looking up to see him smiling at her. They took a right onto Wynkoop and continued on until they came to a street vendor.

"Jim! How are you?" the vendor said as they approached.

"I'm good, Ramesh. Yourself?"

"I am doing great! I graduate next week," Ramesh said with a proud grin.

"That's fantastic! You need to come by the lab in a few weeks then. I'll put in a good word for you."

Ramesh's eyes widened. "You—you would do that for me?"

Jim nodded, and Ramesh seemed at a loss for words. His attention eventually settled on Christine. "Your daughter?"

"This is Christine." He nodded again. "Today is her tenth birthday."

Ramesh clapped his hands together. "Her birthday!" Christine smiled shyly. "Well then, lunch is on me today!"

"Thank you, Ramesh, but you don't have to do that," Jim protested, reaching for his wallet.

"Nonsense, I want to," Ramesh forestalled. "Sanjay, come help me." A young boy who looked to be about the same age as Christine stood from a chair and joined them. "Meet my son. Sanjay, this nice man is my friend, Jim Gonzalez, and his daughter, Christine."

"Hello, Sanjay, it's nice to meet you," Jim said, reaching out a hand.

Sanjay shook it. "Likewise, Mr. Gonzalez." He turned to Christine and grinned. "Hi."

"Hi," she replied, returning his smile after a moment.

"What will you have today?" Ramesh asked them.

"I'll have a bowl of the chicken masala with the curried rice," Jim ordered.

"So what are you doing for your birthday?" Sanjay asked Christine.

She looked across the street to the memorial. The head of the black iron Xonometer tribute statue soared above the crowded plaza. "We're going to the memorial."

"Have you been there before?"

"No."

"It's the bomb," he said, flashing her another smile. A cute smile.

"Sanjay," Ramesh said, holding out a bowl of light yellow rice. "Chicken masala. What would you like, Christine?"

"I don't know." She liked what she smelled, but was unsure what to order.

"How about the same as your father? And a cup of iced chai?"

Christine nodded, smiling shyly.

A man rushed past the cart, knocking Jim's lunch from Sanjay's hands. The man didn't even notice what he had done.

"Can you believe the nerve!" Ramesh shouted.

A large group of people was gathering around an electronics store nearby. Many more rushed by the cart to join them.

"What's going on?" Christine asked, looking up at her father. She felt a sudden sense of panic. He seemed almost in a trance and started moving with the flow of people toward the store, pulling Christine along. Ramesh and Sanjay followed after them.

"Can you turn it up?" someone shouted from the crowd and a store clerk obliged.

"—the scene now, and there is still no word on the estimated forty miners trapped inside. Officials have sealed off the area as more collapses are imminent—"

"Where is Xonometer?" another voice in the crowd shouted.

"Oh no," her father whispered.

"Dad?" Christine said softly, slipping her hand into his.

He looked down at her and gripped her hand tightly. He started back for the cart, Ramesh and Sanjay following.

"Dad, what is it?"

"I'm so sorry, Chris."

His tone scared her. She hadn't ever seen him like this. Not that she could remember.

"Ramesh, I must ask you the biggest favor."

"Yes. What do you need? What is wrong?"

"I can't explain now, but I need you to watch over Christine."

"Dad, no!" she protested.

"Honey, I'm sorry. I—There isn't any time."

"For how long, Jim? I still have to run my cart—"

"I'll call her mother to come and pick her up. It shouldn't be more than an hour or two."

"No, Dad! You promised!" Christine began to cry.

Jim knelt to look her in the eye. "I know I did, Chris. Someday, I hope you will understand, but I must go. Right now."

Tears flowed freely down Christine's cheeks as he stood and turned away.

"You promised!" she said again.

Jim stopped and looked back at her. "I'll make it up to you." He turned and pushed his way through the crowd.

"I hate you!" she shouted angrily at his back. Hesitating again, his back stiffened before he continued. "I hate you!" she repeated , to no avail.

"Look!" a voice from the crowd gathered around the electronics store cried out. "It's him! Xonometer is there!"

Christine lost sight of her father and moved to sit at the base of a concrete planter with a shade tree growing out of it. She pulled her knees to her chest, her arms wrapped around them, and rested her head on them. Sanjay sat beside her.

How could he do this to her? On her birthday of all days. Did he even love her anymore? Did he care at all? The questions only brought more tears, and she cried for what seemed an eternity until she went numb to everything around her.

"Christine?" Her mother's voice cut through the noise of the square.

She raised her head and squinted against the bright afternoon light. Diane was hurrying toward her, deep concern on her face.

"Oh, Christine!" her mother said gently. Christine rose to her feet and ran to her mother. Tears threatened to flow again as her emotions surged, mixed with the comfort of her mother's embrace.

"Ramesh?" Diane asked.

"Yes, Mrs. Gonzalez."

"What happened?"

"I—I'm not sure. Everything seemed fine until we saw the news about an accident. Then your husband looked … afraid, and he said he had to go."

Christine managed to regain her composure.

"Thank you for watching Christine, Mr. Banerjee," Diane said.

"Of course, Mrs. Gonzalez. Is everything alright?"

"I'm not sure. Let's go, Chris." She took Christine's hand.

They walked to the car her mother had parked a short distance away. Christine crawled into the backseat. Diane started the car and turned to look at her.

"I'm so sorry, Chris …" Her words faded as Christine turned to face the back of the seat. "That bastard," she muttered as she pulled out of the parking spot.

☙ ✧ ❧

"Why don't you go inside and rest, honey?" The question woke Christine from her slumber. Diane held the car door open, looking down at her with sadness.

Christine wiped her cheek and peeled herself from the fake leather seat, saying nothing as she moved quietly inside and upstairs to her room. Upon opening the door she saw the Twilight Sparkle unicorn laying on its side, staring up at her, oblivious to her pain. Motionless, she stared back at it. The quirk of its indented smile seemed to mock her.

Diane's voice drifted up the stairs. "I don't care what he's doing.…What do you mean he isn't there?" She was nearly shouting. "He left Christine in the square with a man she barely knows and called me to come and get her!"

"He promised," Christine whispered.

"Of course it had something to do with work. It always has something to do with—" A door slammed, cutting off her mother's words.

Christine grabbed the unicorn roughly by its mane. Turning with purpose, she marched down the stairs and out into the garage where she collected lighter fluid and matches. The door that opened from the garage into the backyard banged against the wooden siding as she threw it open. Stalking to the makeshift fire pit, she opened the bottle of lighter fluid and doused the charred remains of the logs leftover from the last time she and her mother had used it, yet again without Dad.

She struck a match and tossed it into the pit. Flames leaped toward the sky, and she backed away, startled. Regaining her resolve, she lifted the unicorn to eye level.

"What good are promises?" she asked it. The lifeless painted eyes and indented smile still laughed at her.

"Christine! What are you doing?" Diane shouted from the patio door.

She flung the unicorn into the fire before her mother could stop her.

"What on earth!" Diane shouted again and grabbed the grill tongs from where they hung next to the fire pit. "What were you thinking?" She gingerly plucked the smoldering unicorn from the fire.

"I hate him!" Christine started crying.

Diane tossed the smoking toy onto the concrete patio and dropped the tongs. She frowned at Christine, seeming unsure what to do.

The sobs only strengthened. "I hope he never comes home!"

Diane knelt in front of Christine and hugged her tightly.

Christine couldn't stop crying no matter how hard she tried. She felt like she was six again, and she didn't want to cry like a little kid, which made her even angrier, which made her cry harder.

Arms wrapped around her, lifting her from the ground. She could hardly remember the last time her mom had picked her up. She didn't care, and she let the sobs continue to wrack her body. It was so unfair, just so unfair. Mild awareness of being put into bed faded quickly as she cried herself to sleep while her mother gently caressed her hair.

☙ ✧ ❧

She awoke to the sound of the TV turned up loud and rose, kicking aside the sheets on her parents' bed. Diane stood in the living room with her arms crossed, watching the recorded aerial footage as the news anchor explained.

"... here you can see Xonometer using his powers to enter the mine. And here, a little later, you can see when he reached the blockage in the mine, the side of the mountain bulging from what can only be Xonometer's plasmight—My God, would you look at that? Wait, play that again for the folks at home."

A lone figure—little more than an ant from the camera's altitude—entered the mine, even as the mountain above it undulated.

"It looks like one of the emergency crew risked entering the mine as well. It takes true courage to go in there without a Super's powers, folks. Oh my, this must be when it happened."

The side of the mountain suddenly buckled and caved in upon itself. Christine stopped next to her mother and watched the spectacle. Xonometer would be fine. He was always fine, even if a little banged up.

"We can only hope that Xonometer was able to withstand the collapse, and maybe protect the miners as well. It's at times like this that I like to ask for the thoughts and prayers of our viewers at home. Every little bit helps—Wait! We're going live now to our eye in the sky with some new developments."

The picture returned to the aerial view only moments before the collapsed side of the mountain heaved upward, a wedge of crackling plasma pushing it to either side of the slope in a massive display of raw power. Miners began to emerge from the cloud of settling dust, most of them helping one another or limping with haste. Emergency workers swarmed around them with stretchers and offering aid.

"He's done it, folks! Xonometer has rescued the miners! I have to admit, I was afraid there for a moment. And there is the Super himself! He seems to—Wait a minute. Something's wrong. It appears that Xonometer is injured. Not to worry, folks, emergency workers are there. And he is a Super, after all. Hold on—he's waving them into the mine. Oh dear. There must be casualties. I heard it years ago from Magnificent! himself that this is exactly what every Super Hero fears, folks."

Diane finally seemed to notice Christine standing beside her. "Go change out of your nice dress, Chris. I'll make us something to eat." She muted the TV.

"Xonometer wouldn't leave me on my birthday....and he saved all those people."

"How about I order a pizza?" her mother said, trying to cheer her up.

Christine shrugged. She did like pizza. "With extra cheese?"

"Of course." Diane ran her fingers though Christine's curls. "Go on."

Christine did as she was told, putting on her favorite Xonometer T-shirt and some shorts. Hurrying back down the stairs, she stopped halfway when the phone rang just as her mother was about to use it to order pizza.

"Hello," Diane answered, making a silly face. Christine giggled. "Yes. This is she." The silly look melted away. "Wha ... What?" The sudden change in her mother's tone made Christine grip the banister. "I—I don't understand. Was there an accident at the lab?" Diane looked at her, fear plain in her eyes. "Is—" She choked on her words and put her free hand over her mouth as tears welled. "Is he alive?"

"Mom?" Christine asked, scared now herself.

The tears streaked down her mother's cheeks. "Thank you," she said softly and hung up the phone. She stood silently, one hand still on the handset.

"Mom?" Christine said again, more urgently.

Diane seemed to come back to herself. "Put on your shoes, honey. Dad was in an accident. He's in the hospital."

"What happened?"

"Just put on your shoes!" her mother said sharply. She immediately softened her tone. "We need to hurry."

In minutes they were in the car and on their way back into the city. Christine had never seen her mother drive so recklessly: honking, shouting, swerving, and without a doubt, speeding, she made the drive in record time. They reached the hospital, parked, and were on the third floor at the ICU station before Christine could think to ask any questions.

"Jim Gonzalez?" Diane asked the nurse.

"And you are?"

"His wife."

"Right this way, Mrs. Gonzalez." The nurse exited the station and motioned for them to follow. She led them to a waiting room. "Please wait here. A doctor will be with you shortly."

The room was filled to overflowing with families. Christine reached her hand into her mother's for reassurance. Diane weakly smiled down at her, though Christine could see that her mother was equally frightened.

They didn't wait long before a doctor stepped into the room. "Diane Gonzalez?"

"Yes?"

The doctor offered his hand. "I'm Dr. Stanzek."

Diane took his hand. "How is my husband?"

"Walk with me to his room?" Dr. Stanzek motioned toward the door.

Christine held tightly to her mother's hand as they left the waiting room. The halls were bustling with busy staff.

"Your husband suffered a crushed rib cage, a collapsed lung, a concussion, several broken bones, and massive internal hemorrhaging," Dr. Stanzek explained.

"How—how did this happen?"

"He was caught in a rock slide, part of the mining accident that occurred this morning."

Christine's heart crawled into her throat.

"This morning? He had breakfast with us this morning. And brought his daughter into the city for her birthday...."

"Yes, well, the miners trapped in the collapsed mine weren't rescued until almost an hour ago," Dr. Stanzek explained. They came to a door inside the ICU. "Regardless of the details, he is lucky to be alive." The doctor's voice became hushed as he pushed open the door and led them into the room.

Christine fought the tears that threatened to fall once again. The figure lying in bed couldn't be her father. Sections of his thick, curly, dark hair had been shaved from his head and a visible patchwork of stitching crisscrossed his scalp. The rest of him was covered in bloodied bandages and a bouquet of tubes sprouted from all over.

"Lucky to be alive?" Diana said, dazed.

"Yes. If he hadn't been brought to us so quickly, he would not have lasted long."

Diane looked at the doctor. "The mines are at least an hour away. How did he get here so quickly?"

Dr. Stanzek nodded toward the corner of the room. "You can thank him for that." A figure rose from the darkness, large, formidable, and masked. "I'll leave you to talk, but your husband needs to know that you are here. He needs to hear that you love him." He looked at Christine. "Both of you."

The door closed behind him, and only the sound of the machine breathing air into her father's lungs and the occasional beep filled the quiet. Stepping into the light, the figure raised his head to reveal bloodshot eyes.

Christine's breath caught in her throat. It was him. Xonometer. His armor was battered and scuffed, some pieces even missing. The crimson and blue suit he wore beneath the armor was torn in many places. Stitches were visible under some of the larger tears, and dried blood stained the tough fabric, darkening the hue.

"Dia—Mrs. Gonzalez … I am so sorry." Even his soft words had power to them.

"I don't understand," Diane replied.

"I couldn't—I wasn't strong enough."

"What was my husband doing there?" Diane asked forcefully.

Xonometer looked at the bed. "He was helping me."

"Why?"

The Super looked to the bed again. "Very few know this, but a side effect of using my powers is radiation. It causes rapid damage to my cells. It didn't occur to me that it would be amplified inside the mine when my plasmight was centered around me. I—I should have known better."

Christine overcame her awe and took a step forward. "You're my hero."

Xonometer squatted before her and smiled sadly. "I'm no hero. I'm no different than anyone else. I just have some nifty tricks."

"Why was he helping you?" Diane demanded.

The hero's smile vanished. "For the last two years, Jim has worked tirelessly to help me," he explained, looking back and forth from mother to daughter. "I know he has neglected you to do so, and I am sorry for that, too."

"To help you what?" Diane pushed.

"Stay alive."

Christine's breath caught in her throat.

Diane shook her head. "You are superhuman. How could he help you?"

"His serums have kept my powers from destroying me. They stabilize my cells and allow them to repair. He promised that he wouldn't let the plasmight kill me. He wanted to tell you but, we knew if word got out that he was keeping me alive, you two would have become targets for my enemies." He smiled again at Christine. "He came into the mine … I could hear the emergency workers shouting at him to stay back."

Diane gasped, and Christine realized the truth. The lone figure running into the mine had been her father.

Xonometer rose and turned to face the bed. "Everyone would have died in that mine today if it hadn't been for him, including me. So you could say that he is *my* hero."

"Why are you telling us this if it puts us in danger?" Diane instinctively pulled Christine closer to her.

Xonometer turned to face them. "My world can't know who the real hero is, but Jim told me once that you are his world. We probably should have told you long ago. There should be no danger, if you tell no one."

Looking at the bed, Christine remembered the last words she had said to her father as he had left her. Left her to go save her hero.

☙ ✧ ❧

"Mommy?" Alora said again, distraught.

Christine's mind returned to the present, brought back by the worry in her daughter's voice. Smiling, she wiped the tears from her face. "I never thought I would see this again." She sat back, and Alora snuggled up next to her.

"What is it?"

"It's a purple unicorn your grandfather gave to me on my tenth birthday. I lost it when your father and I moved, shortly before you were born. I don't know how it ended up here, of all places."

Alora reached out and toyed with the clumps of melted plastic hair. "What happened to it?"

"A misunderstanding." Christine handed the unicorn to her daughter. "I want you to keep this safe for me. It was the best gift Grandpa ever gave me."

Alora took the toy and examined it more closely. "What was Grandpa like, then?"

"He was a hero." Christine's voice wavered as she tried to suppress her tears. "My hero."

Of Unicorns and Pie

Nathan Dodge and Sharon Dodge

"No returns," he growled at the customer at the counter as I watched nervously from near the shop door. You never think you're going to be sneaking into a semi-legal exotic pet emporium, but when you realize you've forgotten your kid's sixth birthday, you find yourself doing drastic things.

"You didn't tell me it would get so crazy," the guy whined, the pimply face adding no further weight to his case. He sounded like my daughter, Katie, when she didn't get dessert.

"If you'd followed directions, you wouldn't have a problem. Go clean up your mess. Not my problem."

The guy started to protest, but the man just leaned in, like he was listening. It didn't look threatening to me, but the guy stopped, his pale features turning another couple of shades lighter, and finally he ran out. The man behind the counter sighed. I gave him a minute before I approached him.

"Uh, I was wondering about your exotics," I said, stumbling out of the gate. "I mostly see, like, turtles and fish. I heard you had weird stuff. My—"

"Do you bake?" he barked at me.

I blinked. I didn't.

"Sure," I fibbed. "Great rhubarb pie." Grandmother Nettie used to make that, back when I lived in the proper South, not here in the dusty desert.

"Where'd you get the rhubarb? Don't grow around here." He stared me down, daring me to lie, again like Grandmother Nettie. But heck, I'd always risen to a challenge. A tiny smile found its way to my lips, and the story just came tumbling out.

"Grocery. Nowadays, they sell it just about anywhere. Plenty of sugar on top for a nice crisp crust. Put in just a touch of strawberry, but you shouldn't overdo it. The pie loses its sense of self, otherwise." That's what my grandma used to say, anyhow.

The man nodded gravely, as if this conversation had anything to do with pets. For a second, I wondered if he had some sort of weird barter/trade thing going on, but his next words filled the gap.

"Can't trust anybody to follow directions anymore. You bake, you can come look at 'em. Just follow the directions. Read it through first, ahead, plan it out. Then you make a nice pie."

I nodded with him, oddly pleased with myself.

And then we entered the back room.

At first, I thought it was a bizarre aggregation of stuffed animals, like teddy bears, only not. There were a few dozen glass terrariums, the same kind as up front that held the turtles and fish, only here they were filled with other things. Everywhere I looked there was something unreal: tiny tigers with people faces, three headed dogs, a harpy the size of a small chicken, and all sorts of other things. Only they weren't stuffed. They moved and shimmied and coiled. Nasty things, things that seemed cool in textbooks, things that looked almost funny and quaint, only here they were in miniature with bright, beady eyes that watched me, weighed me, assessed me.

"Wow," I said.

"Yeah, I mix it up," he said calmly. "Whatcha looking for? Got a nice little salamander loves to cuddle—"

"It's for Katie," I interrupted. "Katie, my daughter. Got anything—sweet? Not so … dangerous?"

"Daughter?" he said, a frown twisting his lips. "Listen, these things are high-maintenance—"

"It'll be taken care of," I said. "I promise. It's just … the harpy's a little intense."

"Yeah, Griselda always gets passed over. Such a sweet girl, too," he sighed. "Hmm. I think I know the perfect pet—for a daughter. Come with me."

Near the back, he stopped before a wire-mesh cage. Not a terrarium, or a fish tank—a cage like for a dog or a litter of kittens. I stopped, fascinated, feeling a warm tingle inside.

In the cage stood a unicorn. A *real* unicorn. No more than twelve inches high, light pink, its tiny, soft-looking horn covered with a haze of white fuzz, sort of like new deer antlers on a young buck.

"She's very sweet and gentle," he told me. "Thing is, she takes a good deal of care. She comes with a manual."

"How much?"

"I've had her a while, and I need to move her, so she's on sale. Normally fifteen hundred, but you can have her for half that, including the manual."

I fretted. The budget I had in mind didn't approach even the sale price. And yet … She—he'd said "she"—was so delicate, so comely, with large, dark eyes, delicate lines, and diminutive hooves, that I was quite taken. As I looked at her, she moved close to the metal mesh and made a sound not unlike a horse's nicker, only about an octave higher.

"All right," I said.

The store owner provided a small travel cage that braced her and held her in place, though considering the amount of cash I was putting down, it seemed only fair. As he took my credit card, he frowned and gave me a barrelful of last-minute advice.

"Be sure to read the manual. She takes a lot of care, like I said. All the way through. Feed her organic oats regularly, fresh and uncooked. I'll throw in five pounds, but you will need to warn me in advance to order more. No more than an ounce a day at first, adding proportionately as she grows. And add just a pinch of sugar in her oats for flavor; she likes that. She'll need more fruit and flowers as she grows. And make sure she has plenty of water at all times."

He helped bundle us out to my car, carrying the oats, and adding one last tidbit. "One thing. She can't handle negativity or fighting or conflict. She needs a calm household, lots of love and attention. Give her that and she'll flourish." For a moment, I felt kind of insulted; it's not like we walked around hitting one another at home or anything.

But as I nodded to him and turned the engine, my stomach tightened. Katie and I didn't have words often. Did we?

My worries vanished under the hero's welcome I got at home. Katie loved her, took to her immediately. Named her, of course, an absurd name, like most children pick out: Maryella. A name you might give a child. Not Spot, or Fluffy, or Pinkie, or even some racehorse name like Pride of Arizona. Maryella.

"Are you sure?" I asked. Silly question.

Things went well that first month. Maryella this, Maryella that. She was all Katie could think or talk about. Katie's pet quickly became potty-trained, acclimating to a cat box of litter, and being careful never to make a mess.

I was pleased with myself; I read the manual, mostly, and drove out to the farmer's market to pick up some of the flowers the book mentioned—nasturtiums and dandelions, even some broccoli flowers. They weren't organic, but I figured close enough. Katie braided Maryella's hair and then fed the flowers to her petal by petal, Maryella rubbing up against her like a cat after each one.

After that, however, Katie began to forget feedings, so I had to remind her. She still forgot, or stubbornly pretended to forget, perhaps hoping that I'd pick up the slack and let it slide. I covered for her during the next few weeks, and mostly kept the grumbling to myself, though the flowers were tossed in the bucket and I didn't have time to measure the oats. But I did it, and close enough. After all, Katie seemed happy with Maryella.

I did have to remind Katie to be careful, because Maryella, at twelve inches high, resembled a toy terrier or Chihuahua in size, with delicate bones and tiny, fragile ankles, and a little rough play could be dangerous. Most of the time, Katie remembered.

Then Katie started to school—not kindergarten, but all-day school. While first graders don't have a lot of homework, she was practicing addition and reading simple sentences, and though she'd greet Maryella happily every day when she got home, she'd also complain whenever I reminded her of Maryella's care.

A couple of times, I'd stare down at Maryella's bowl, trying to tell whether Katie really had fed her or not, like she'd said. Would my Katie lie? I didn't have much time to wonder. I started going to PTA meetings and somehow was signed up for a fundraiser on top of work hours, and then a new kid moved in down the street whose mother wouldn't let her come over, which irritated me to no end. So between school and the new kid whose house Katie had to go to, and homework and just plain daily life, she began to spend less time with Maryella.

I checked the manual again a month or so later, vaguely horrified to see we'd already missed the critical parsley and violets feeding; I threw some dried parsley in her dish that night. The manual also said she needed to be fed blackberries or fresh-picked raspberries, then have her hair braided and her teeth and horn brushed. It also recommended releasing butterflies in the house to help ensure proper coloration, though it thankfully said that wasn't absolutely necessary.

I told Katie to at least brush Maryella's hair, but she just said "I'm busy." I resorted to nagging and tried to make sure at least the poor thing had her oats, and occasionally, I did a quick braid. Only I forgot the sugar in her oats and the water one night, and the next morning Maryella got sick all over the couch. Katie blamed me and I yelled at her, furious, reminding her of all the promises she'd made.

Maryella crawled behind the sofa as we argued, whimpering softly.

You'd think after that, Katie would've have done better, but she didn't, and eventually I quit asking, although I wasn't happy about it. And I tried. I tried to follow the directions, tried to think of it like following the directions to Grandmother's rhubarb pie.

I drove across town to buy fresh-picked berries, got them home, and then left them out in the car. By the time I remembered two days later, they were half-covered in mold. I ended up giving Maryella some frozen berries that she eyed dubiously before delicately crushing them between her teeth.

And while I didn't forget the water, I overlooked the feeding schedule at times, especially after a long, hard day. When I forgot, Maryella would make a piteous sound the next morning, and guilt made me add a bit extra to her food—overfeeding in compensation for my sins.

The long nights at the office began to multiply. I went in straight after taking Katie to school at seven thirty, and by the time I left work, I was already exhausted. After picking up Katie from the after-school care—whose owner I had to pay extra to keep her until almost eight o'clock—sometimes I barely got her clothes changed before I put her straight to bed.

And since she wasn't playing as much with Maryella, sometimes I forgot the unicorn completely.

No matter how hard I tried, life seemed to get in the way of any sort of organization I'd try to achieve. Worse, Katie began having problems at school, particularly with math. English was okay, because she liked words and word play, but numbers of any sort, as she would continually tell me, were "boring."

Eventually, the inevitable school conference resulted. Katie's math teacher, solemn and concerned, kept his voice in a monotone, his pale, round face neither smiling nor frowning. At the end of the meeting, all I had really been able to gather was that he was unhappy about something.

Next came a far more serious meeting with the principal, who said that Katie paid little attention in class and had failed to turn in several assignments. She asked if there were problems at home. Her soft, motherly face reminded me of nothing so much as my own mother lecturing me as a child. When we got home and I asked Katie why she couldn't pay attention in class, trying to be sympathetic, she screamed at me and ran to her room in tears. That night she wet the bed.

It was about this time that Maryella began to change. She had never grown, or hardly at all, her tiny, delicate horn polished and shiny but small and delicate. Abruptly, Katie told me, "Maryella isn't pretty anymore."

I hadn't been paying attention to our pet, and as I did, I saw she was no longer a light, baby-girl pink, but a darker fuchsia. Her horn had grown as well, no longer shiny white with a trace of pink, but matte-surfaced, the color a deep cream or maybe ecru. Maryella kept to herself more as well, hiding behind the bed or under the sofa in the den.

Once when Katie fed her, she barked a harsh neigh, almost a snarl, and struck out at Katie with her horn. It was too dull to do any harm, but I yelled at Maryella, and she looked angrily at me and fled her food bowl. Later, I tried to make it up with soft words and a sugar cube, but she hid behind the sofa making a noise that sounded almost like a growl.

Then Grandma Nettie, she of the rhubarb pie, and my last living relative, died. I got the call on my way to work and pulled over to the side of the road and sat there for an hour before I managed to make myself go on in.

Somewhere between the teacher meetings, the hours at work, the funeral plans, and trying to find a second tier of childcare because the after school daycare owner was tired of staying open so late, my feeding schedule for Maryella cratered completely. I'm not sure if Maryella had four meals in five or six days. When we came back that awful day from the funeral, I piled on the oats and sugar and threw in a handful of wilted nasturtiums for good measure.

I hadn't looked at the manual in a long time.

A few days later, when I had been delinquent in attending to her, I found that Maryella had somehow slipped from the house and through the fence and was eating the neighbor's cat food. When the cat, a big pumpkin-colored blob named Orange Crush, objected, Maryella, not half her size and weight, turned her horn on Orange Crush and brought blood to one paw.

Orange Crush fled with indignant cries, and I ran frantically toward them, scooping up Maryella and retreating to our yard before the neighbors came to the scene.

I discovered two things that day. First, Maryella's horn was two inches longer, razor sharp, and now the color of moss. It smelled a bit like it as well. Second, her color had also continued to change, evolving through violet to a much darker purple. She had grown no larger, but considerably more aggressive, and I began to worry if it was safe for Katie to be around her anymore.

For all my worry, my care grew even more shoddy. Maryella's hair grew tangled in knots; my daughter stopped playing with her. Maryella began sneaking outside, and once, when I went to fetch her, I caught her following Orange Crush, who stood on the opposite side of the fence, as though she were stalking him.

For a few days, I managed to get it right with her. But then I forgot about the next meeting with Katie's teacher. Katie's attention had gone from terrible to worse, and my boss, his black eyes and Hitleresque moustache vibrating with anger whenever I didn't arrive at my desk an hour early, had progressed from simply overbearing to abusive. Layoffs were in the air.

By the time I met with Katie's math teacher, swearing to my boss I'd work that night *and* be in on the weekend, I was huffily informed that with support like mine, it was no wonder that Katie continually had troubles. He had a picture on his phone of Katie the day before, hair greasy and tangled, wearing the same clothes as the previous day. He wondered aloud if perhaps he or the principal ought to contact child protective services.

My whole body froze, and when it thawed, I put on a fraudulent smile and poured out simpering, bootlicking words. I went home instead of back to work. After putting Katie to bed, I pulled out a half-bottle of Irish whiskey father had bought fifteen years ago and drank myself into a maudlin crying jag.

Life should be easier, I told myself as I watched an old soap opera on cable, bleary-eyed. Just understand the rules, follow them, and everything should turn out okay. Like making a rhubarb pie. You measure the ingredients, mix them properly, and bake. And there you have a pie. Don't forget the hint of strawberry, of course.

In the morning, Katie off to school with two coiled braids and a freshly washed dress I'd woken at four to iron, I arrived at work and sat down at my desk only to realize that Maryella had not eaten in twenty-four hours and I had left her no food.

The sudden feeling of nausea surprised me—the fact that I'd eaten far too little and drunk way too much had not completely registered—and the retching onto the carpet by my desk occurred too rapidly for me to reach the restroom down the hallway.

My tyrant surprised me by his reaction. Instead of screaming at me for throwing up at work and damaging his carpet, he shooed me out, telling me, "I don't want to get whatever that is. Go home and don't come back 'til you're well."

I drove home slowly. Once there, I collected the current bag of oats, some sugar, the carry case, and finally Maryella. My mind had made itself up sometime between the office and home. Maryella wasn't turning out the way she was intended, and if I didn't do something quickly, the poor animal had no hope. I resolved not to say a word that evening. Katie noticed Maryella so little any more, I wasn't sure she'd miss her.

When the shop owner saw me enter with the carrier, his eyes narrowed, and he shook his head slightly. Then he came to meet me at the front of the store.

"I'm sorry," I told him. "I did my best. I really did. Especially at first. Then things got—complicated. My daughter is having trouble in school, and my job is a nightmare, and—and—" My eyes teared up, and I tried to explain about Grandmother Nettie, and her death, and the pie instructions, and how the recipe just didn't seem to work, all the words flooding out at once so that it wasn't making much sense. I stumbled to a halt, my hands in a prayerful grip in front of me.

"I'll pay you to take her back," I said. "She just doesn't look good anymore, and Katie won't feed her, and I'm so busy, and I'm worried about her." Meanwhile, in the carrier, Maryella had begun to whimper and make anxious little noises.

I remembered how he had treated the customer in front of me on my first visit, and I shrank back, expecting a stream of invective accusations about everything from my lifestyle to my IQ.

Instead, he took the case, staring through the holes in the side, sizing up little Maryella. His face had a strange look, a bit sorrowful, and pitying, perhaps even with a tinge of sympathy. Maryella continued to whimper, and he whispered soft words that I couldn't understand until finally she fell silent.

He lifted his eyes, placing the case on the counter, the same expression on his features. "You did okay, I guess," he told me. "They're hard to care for. Everybody's busy nowadays. I'm sure you … did the best you could."

I left him there, standing beside Maryella's case on the counter, looking after me with that sad-solemn face, seeming to sense things inside me that I hadn't said. On the drive home, I wondered—or hoped?—if everyone had secrets like mine. If they tried an exotic adventure like going to a far-off tropical island, or hiking across a foreign land, or perhaps just trying to raise a toy hydra or a miniature griffin or a small, fireless dragon—doing something, anything, to get away from the failures and frustrations of this life.

Perhaps none of us has the time for such frivolities anymore. Maybe no one has time to bake a pie properly, to remember the sugar crust at the top and bottom of the fruit, to cut the butter in cold, to make the slits in the crust for venting. Maybe we don't have room for that simple kind of magic in our cluttered, chaotic, desperate modern lives.

Katie was still at school when I got home. At first, I just sat at the kitchen table, staring at nothing and trying to make my mind blank as well.

Finally, I rose and stepped to the drawers in the kitchen counter, digging slowly through each, exploring the contents. I found it finally under a pile of pots and lids, beside an odd collection of tongs and dull bread knives and an old hand-propelled eggbeater. Grandma Nettie's recipe book, with the rhubarb pie recipe on the very first page, and tiny notes on almost every line in her small, even hand. Sitting at the table, I laid it in front of me to read. I started with the ingredients, and then the directions, and finally Grandma's notes, absorbing every word.

Then I stood up and went to check the pantry.

Gateway Blood

Ezekiel James Boston

"Pa?" Mother called. Dressed for the ball, she hiked her long baby blue dress carefully as to not cause wrinkles. "Pa?"

Still in my smoking robes, I leaned on the fireplace. It crackled with soothing blue freeze-fire chilling the room nicely. My gaze returned to the trophies of hunters long since past. For some reason, Kam's silver stake kept my attention. "Yah, Mother?"

"Oh, good. You're not in your suit."

That was strange. Normally she'd be griping up a blue streak. The change brought me from my thoughts as she shuffled closer. I set down my pipe with the fine Turkish blend old Carl had sent me and turned away from the jars of moonshine. After two hundred years with her, I knew the source of the matter and shook my head.

"What'd Junior done now?"

"Oh, Pa." She pressed me with a hug. "It's horrible. Just horrible."

I embraced her wonderful satin-clad, grave-cold body. Our first century had been dictionary definition perfect. Then we decided to have a child. The following decades had grown steadily worse. "Just tell me what he done."

"Little Kev, he's—" Whatever the thought, it made her fangs retract. She slap-covered her mouth. I looked elsewhere in the room while she composed herself. She did soon enough. Her incisors relaxed back into full extension, she continued. "He's—"

And whoop, up they went again. "Where is he?"

She kept her mouth covered. "Down to the mill."

I rubbed her back until her fangs eased back out. She helped me out of my smoking robes, and I went to find my boy.

☙ ✧ ❧

Taller than me now, he stood on the mossy side of the water mill between the waterwheel and where the crick kinked. I couldn't help but pause to admire his dead pale complexion in the moonshadows. A smile crept to my face. He was a chip off the old block. One day, he was gonna give some lucky girl a real fright.

"Don't, Dad."

He didn't turn or glance over his shoulder. Impressive. I approached along the crick to see what had him so transfixed. "Don't what, son?"

Though I hadn't seen it before, now, in the moonshadows, all wrought with inner-conflict, I finally understood why the judges gave him top honors in both Pensive and Brooding. While both traits had their merits, it would've been nicer if he would've placed in Lurking or Creep.

He shook his head. "Just, don't."

"Fine, son. Fine," I said and eased along the bank. "I—" My incisors shot up into my gums.

By his feet, bound in some sort of trap made of ropes and leather straps, a unicorn lay on its side, legs kicking weakly. Where the moonlight touched it, its coat shone a glittery lilac. "Now, son—"

He turned a palm toward me. "I said *don't.*"

I froze. His fangs were out, but they trembled. He was scared, and he had all rights to be. While that kid down the way bragged about juicing mythicals, one look at 'em and anyone over one-fifty knew the brat was just spouting words. "Did I ever tell you—"

Little Kev cut me off to finish my sentence. "“'Bout the time I drank werewolf blood?”" His dead eyes—so very dead—rolled. "Yeah, Dad. Dozens of times."

"Well." My voice came out muffled. Reflexively, I'd cover my fangless mouth. "I wasn't bragging about it none. No, I told ya so much as a warnin'."

Kev didn't say anything. Just kept staring at it.

My fangs refused to come down. The whole thing got me that deep. "Sometimes, some creatures just seem to want to be bitten, and you can't help but wonder, what kind of power lies in their blood? Am I right, son?"

He nodded absently.

"To this day, I regret drinking from that wolfman." I spied my wife easing along the mill roof. We both began to creep closer to him. "And you know what? So does Mother."

"Ma?" He turned. His gazed passed over me. "Ma drank werewolf?"

"Yah," I answered.

He found me and stared with great intensity as not to lose me as I slunk along the gurgling waterline.

"We both did when we were dating." Ready to spring, Mother crouched on the mill's pitch. "Was good fun for a bit. We were stronger. Our fangs, thicker. Good fun in all."

His brooding eased. He remained pensive. "What happened then?"

"A full moon."

"You mean." His own gasp surprised him. I'd told him about the drawbacks hundreds of times. Realizing the potential curse in our blessing, he softly spoke, *"Drink the blood, gain the flesh."* He gulped. "You mean, Mother goes all hairy, too?"

"Yah, every full moon, which comes faster than yah'd think." I could see nerve building in his eyes. His fangs extended further. "Mother!" I yelled.

Kev sprung.

Mother blocked him from the unicorn.

He tried to move around her, and the moment's hesitation was all we needed.

I sped up the bank, drove him through the water mill's stone wall, and we rolled on the dusty wooden planks.

"Let me go!" he wailed. "I'll risk it."

Mother dropped on us in a flash. She knocked me away and had him pinned before I could fully recover. Having drank more wolfman, she'd always been stronger and faster.

"Let me go! Let me go! Let me go!"

I hustled over to the unicorn and undid the major binding.

It heaved to its hooves and sped away.

"Nooooo!"

It pained my unbeating heart to hear my son wail like that. Still, I picked up one of the lengths of leather and tested its strength. "First, unicorns. Then what? Griffins?" It'd hold out through a whippin'. I had to set him straight or he'd become a no good shine-head like my brother. "Let that Eddie Cullen kid drink all the unicorn he wants." My fangs eased back down. I sounded the belt across my hand. "But ain't no son of mine's gonna sparkle."

The Monoceros

Lou J Berger

My initial mistake was going to the employee lunchroom to heat up my noodle soup.

McDavity was holding the door of the staff refrigerator open, staring at the contents, and grimacing. It isn't that I don't like McDavity … Well, it is, actually. He's my supposed "boss" and although I don't believe that I actually *need* a boss—I can come up with research assignments myself, without being prompted by sub-intellectual cretins like McDavity—I do admit that he dealt with the upper-level non-technical people for me.

So I sidled over to the microwave, shoulders hunched and creeping silently, hoping he would ignore me. No such luck.

"Johnson!" he barked, without even turning his head in my direction. "Who's Mary Sue?"

I straightened up.

"She works in the chemistry lab. She's the department chair?" I shook my head in disgust, opened the microwave door, popped my soup on the glass tray, slammed the door, and pushed the large number "3" on the keypad. The microwave whirred to life and the light lit up, displaying my soup turning in a slow pirouette. I faced McDavity.

"She's only been working for you for the past two years," I said.

McDavity grunted, leaned forward, and retrieved a red, plastic container with a bit of tape on top. The name MARY SUE had been scrawled on it. McDavity frowned, cracked open the lid and brought the container up to his nose. He took a deep, suspicious sniff and grumbled in appreciation. Turning his head in my direction for the first time since I'd entered the lunchroom, he allowed a broad, gap-toothed grin to split his face. "Spaghetti and meatballs!" he bellowed. "My favorite!"

I held up a finger to protest, since the container was clearly labeled, and Mary Sue would probably mind that he was sniffing her food, but it was too late. He ripped off the lid, tossed it into the sink, grabbed a fork from the counter, and began gobbling down the contents, slurping at the cold noodles and stuffing entire meatballs into each cheek.

I watched, horrified, for as long as it took me to become thoroughly disgusted: about fifteen seconds, and that's being generous.

"Johnson!" he mumbled around a mouthful of pasta, then waved me over with his red sauce-stained fork. "I have an assignment for you."

"I really can't," I protested. McDavity had a reputation for assigning his scientists to research assignments on exotic planets, and I was more interested in going home to my nice bed every night.

Besides, I'd begun an on-again, off-again romance with the waitress at the corner diner two blocks from my house. Every night, at 10 PM, I'd walk over, across black asphalt streets glowing with reflected streetlight, sit in the same booth, and order a glass of milk and a slice of coconut cream pie.

Natalie would swish over, her skirt flowing around her generous thighs, and bring me the pie, the glass of milk, and a fork, then arrange it all in front of me. Sometimes, if I was feeling particularly frisky, I'd look up at her face as she arranged things. A week ago, a tendril of hair had escaped her severe hairdo and fallen in front of her eyes, but I wasn't courageous enough to reach up and brush it aside.

Most of the time, I just watched her hands as they moved across the table. Sometimes, when she was finished, she'd touch my shoulder and say "Enjoy!" before walking away.

I say on-again, off-again, but that's not entirely accurate. I think I'm on-again when I can look her in the eye. The rest of the time, we're off-again. It's entirely up to me to take the next step, and I simply won't be rushed into love. It isn't proper.

McDavity was still waving the fork at me and saying something, so I stopped daydreaming about Natalie long enough to listen.

"... and you'll go to Kepler-186f to document the existence of the *monoceros purpurea.*"

"What?" I squeaked. "I can't go, Mr. McDavity. I have obligations, experiments I'm not finished running yet. A lecture to give. So, you see, it's impossible."

McDavity tossed the empty container into the sink, along with the fork he'd used, looked around for a napkin and, failing to find one, wiped his hands on his trousers. He finished chewing the food left in his mouth and swallowed it in a big gulp.

"Nonsense, Johnson. You're going. Have my assistant draw up your travel papers." He walked out of the room, whistling tunelessly. I stared after him.

This was ridiculous. I didn't have to tolerate this.

Mary Sue walked in from the hallway and made a beeline for the refrigerator, but froze halfway when she spotted the empty container in the stainless steel sink. She scowled at me and pointed at the sink.

"You did that?" she screeched. "I can't believe you ate my lunch! It's labeled with my name! I am going to HR about this." She whirled around and stomped from the room, her short, cropped hair swaying angrily.

I stared after her, openmouthed. I hadn't even had the opportunity to deny it.

Behind me, the microwave beeped. With a muffled pop, the noodle soup exploded, coating the inside of the microwave oven with moist, sticky noodles.

I sighed. Maybe finding a *monoceros purpurea* wasn't such a bad idea after all.

Then it struck me. *Monoceros purpurea* means "purple unicorn."

I groaned aloud.

☙ ✧ ❧

My second mistake was not quitting, right then and there. There's something indubitably wrong when your boss is an unethical twit like McDavity, somebody who steals another's lunch and then lets me take the blame. I won't describe how painful the discussion with HR was or how long it took for the travel papers to be drawn up, and I certainly won't mention the horrible conditions on the FTL ship I took, the *USS Driving Miss Daisy*.

It was an older model, with subpar shielding, and I spent the first week of the trip wishing I enjoyed the taste of alcohol and the second week of the trip in soused bliss. When we disembarked on Jungle, the heavily forested Earth-like planet orbiting in the habitable zone around Kepler, I had a monstrous hangover and what felt like fur growing on my tongue.

I had absolutely no interest in finding a purple unicorn and resented being sent away from my lab. Most importantly, I hated being apart from Natalie. My stomach growled, thinking of coconut cream pie, as I stumbled off the shuttle into the bright sunlight of Jungle, or Kepler-186f.

A tiny, cheerful man with a scarlet face stood in the receiving line, holding a small sign that said JOHNSON on it. I assumed he was my driver, so I walked up to him, dropped my suitcase at his feet, and said, with all the dignity I could muster "I am Johnson, you diminutive tomato."

He smiled up at me, folded the sign, and said "Come with me." He turned and walked away, ignoring my luggage.

Grumbling, I picked up my suitcase and followed him. We walked through a pair of glass doors and into a cool, air-conditioned terminal crowded with dozens of different aliens in transit from one place to another, with Jungle being a stopover.

I was ogling a three-breasted, orange-furred woman when my driver stopped short, causing me to bump into him. Hard.

"Whass the *deal*?" I bellowed, swaying above him and trying to focus well enough to see what had caused him to stop.

With a grandiose gesture, he indicated a completely empty bike rack. I frowned, pointed a shaky finger, and said "Very nice. You have bike racks. Now are you going to drive me to my hotel?"

His smile never faltered, and he gestured again at the bike rack. I began to grow annoyed. I just wanted a nice, cool, dark hotel room with a bed that was connected to a concrete floor that was, in turn, connected somewhere below to solid ground. I didn't want to sleep on a ship's bed again anytime soon.

So I did the honorable thing and squinted once again in the direction of the bike rack. And, this time, I noticed something I'd not seen before. At the end, wedged into the last slot, there was a bicycle.

A dilapidated, rusty, oval-wheeled bicycle.

"Whassat?" I demanded, drawing myself up to my full five foot seven height. "I am expected to convey myself on *that*?" I pointed and, in so doing, dropped my suitcase on his foot.

His smile disappeared, and he spent the next fifteen seconds or so hopping around on the other foot, yelling words that I couldn't understand. When the ruckus died down, my headache was worse, and, to my chagrin, a police officer stood in front of me.

He held a cudgel in one hand and kept whacking it against the horny callus on the palm of his other hand. Several highly inappropriate jokes came to mind, making me giggle.

The next thing I knew, I was staring in wonder at the very shiny patent leather shoes the police officer was wearing, and I'd completely forgotten about my headache. Because my stomach felt like a mule had kicked it.

I opened my mouth to protest and all the lunch I'd eaten on the ship slithered out and coated the tops of the very shiny patent leather shoes in front of me.

In the cold, dark, lizard portion of my brain, I found this shocking. But I wasn't using that part of my brain at the moment, so I laughed.

When everything was straightened out and I'd apologized to everybody, I found myself riding down a busy street on the oval-wheeled bicycle, rising up and down, my suitcase strapped securely to a rack mounted over the rear wheel. The police officer had spoken English well enough to send off my driver—who, it turned out, was only there to greet me and extort a massive gratuity—and give me directions to the hotel and the tour guide I was supposed to be using during my search.

After navigating the streets of Jungle's main city, Brazil, I finally found my way to the location the officer had described.

It was not, as I'd hoped, a modern hotel with dark, cool rooms and clean crisp sheets on the bed.

It was a thatched hut with a hammock and about a million small green lizards. I spent my first night in Jungle sweating profusely and knocking curious lizards off my face. The damn things flew.

☙ ✧ ❧

The next morning, I drank about a gallon of water and looked for my guide. An older woman met me and introduced herself as Khalif.

"Khalif?" I said.

She frowned at me and crinkled her nose. "Yes," she said in broken English. "My friends call me Khalif. You call me Miss Ocking-Klark."

I grinned at the audible hyphen. "Are you divorced?"

She shook her head. "No, he dead. Annoyed me." She waggled a warning finger at me. "Don't annoy me, you."

I ducked back into my lizard den to fetch my suitcase.

We climbed into a small truck, and she drove me into the back country. I'd done some reading on the way to Jungle and had learned that 90 percent of the planet was still unexplored. The *monoceros* I was seeking had been rumored to exist, but nobody had ever photographed one or captured one. Sure, other unicorns existed, of all shades, and they roamed everywhere, but nobody had documented a purple one.

We trundled our way down an almost-invisible dirt path, pushing aside vines and the clutching branches of countless bushes. The jungle reeked of warm, moist death, pungent and sharp one moment, flowery and sweet the next.

I tried to strike up a conversation with Ocking-Klark, but she refused to converse. "We be there soon!" she kept singing out, every time I asked how long it would be.

It was just turning dark when she finally stopped the truck. "Now you get out," she said.

I looked around. "Where are we?"

She smiled at me, but no part of that smile touched her eyes. "You get out," she said again. But this time, there was a snub-nosed automatic in her hand.

I got out.

She started the truck again and drove directly into a bush. I stared at her. Had she crashed, leaving me alone, in the middle of the jungle? White lights lit up on the rear of the truck and a horrible beeping sound began.

I scratched my head and then, without warning, the truck zoomed directly at me. Acting purely on instinct, I dove to the side, away from the truck and into a thorn bush. Dozens of thorns pierced my skin; one almost got me in the eye.

"Hey!" I shouted. The horrible beeping stopped and Ocking-Klark's voice said sweetly, "Sorry!" There was a thump as something hit the dirt, then a loud grinding sound, and the truck pulled away from me, twin red lights disappearing down the path we'd followed, fading into the gathering darkness.

I crawled out of the thorn bush, dusted myself off, and tried to stanch the bleeding.

"Hey!" I yelled after the disappearing red pinpricks but they were gone, swallowed up in the growth.

I was alone.

I kicked the bag she'd thrown from the back of the truck and spent the next few moments hopping on one foot, clutching at the other one I'd used to kick the bag. I sat down and pulled off my shoe and sock to examine my foot. Nothing was broken, but it certainly ached.

The bag was a Jungle survival kit, and it included water, freeze-dried food, cooking utensils, a sleeping bag, a folding cot, a gas stove, and a large black block that seemed to be some sort of folded tent. It had a yellow button on the side that said PRESS ME AND STEP BACK.

So I did.

With a hiss, the black block split, then split again, lurched up, and then split a third time.

Giant wings lifted up from the center, reached for the sky, and then slowly settled to either side. When the noise had abated, I found myself staring, openmouthed, at a nice four-room tent, complete with zippered mosquito netting and a functioning bathroom.

"Huh," I said, which was as close to intelligent as I felt at that moment. I dragged everything into the tent and zipped it shut as the last of the light drained from the sky.

The tent had a clapping light mechanism that would turn on when you clapped once, then turn off when you clapped twice. I found that out by accident, never mind how, but I soon had the lights on and the equipment stashed in one of the rooms.

The tent was remarkably spacious, but I couldn't figure out what powered the lights. There didn't seem to be any batteries and, eventually, I gave up looking. I unrolled my sleeping bag and went to sleep, surrounded by the sound of millions of whirring insects.

❧ ✧ ❧

The next morning, I awoke to sunlight peeking through the trees around me. A fine mist floated in the air, and the chattering of the insects from the night before was merely a memory. I went inside the little bathroom, ran some water in the sink, and washed my face. Then I unpacked my toothbrush and brushed my teeth, wondering, as I spat, where the waste water would go.

A crunching sound from outside drew my attention, and I stepped to the screened wall of what I had decided to call the living room to peer out.

I gasped. I'd flown across the dark depths of space to find a purple unicorn and, bejeweled in dew and regal in a shaft of early morning sunlight, there stood one, resplendent and majestic.

I whirled around, grabbed my datapad, and fumbled with the zipper on the tent wall. Ripping it straight up, I stepped outside and walked slowly through the underbrush, datapad held at arm's length, trying to record this beautiful creature. It was sixteen hands high, which in horse terms is really tall, and it allowed me to approach within ten meters without trying to escape.

The high-definition camera in the datapad worked flawlessly, and I crept even closer. I hadn't imagined that my quest would turn out to be so easy. I began to narrate as I moved, hoping to capture the information I was seeing, just in case the video portion didn't come through.

"It is approximately nine in the morning on June 25, 2157, and I am on Jungle, deep in the backwoods. I awoke this morning and found the elusive *monoceros purpurea* standing outside my tent. It's approximately a hundred and sixty centimeters high, weighs approximately four hundred and fifty kilograms, and appears remarkably tame. The horn is spiral in nature and emanates from the beast's forehead, extending out about fifty centimeters."

I had approached within three meters, and I imagined that my calm, relaxed voice was instrumental in maintaining the unicorn's placid demeanor. I stepped closer and continued to narrate.

"The coat is a deep shade of aubergine, silky in appearance and without knots or matting. The unicorn appears very tame and, as I approach, has not become skittish or changed its rate of respiration."

At this point, I was a mere meter away. I could see the whites of its eyes and the casual flaring of its nostrils as it breathed. I kept one eye on the long, spiral horn, wondering what the lethal radius for such a menacing weapon might be.

The unicorn swung its head around and looked directly at me with its left eye. It opened its mouth. I moved the datapad closer, trying to film its teeth, wondering if close examination of the molars would allow me to, later, assess the age of the giant, eggplant-colored beast.

The unicorn leaned forward a bit, clamped its teeth on the top of the datapad, and, whinnying, galloped away from me, ripping the datapad right out of my hands.

The sounds of its crashing through the bushes faded as I stood there, mouth agape, in utter disbelief.

"Hey!" I shouted.

I must have stood there, frozen in place, for five full minutes, staring in the direction the unicorn had gone, hoping against hope that it might return and give me back my datapad.

Mentally, I kicked myself for having not thought about the danger inherent in approaching a unicorn so closely. I should have known better and, foolishly, I had let my scientific curiosity override common sense.

"Idiot," I whispered, then turned around and began trudging back to my tent. I hadn't gone three meters before I heard a slight sound, an extra crunch of greenery. I stopped. There was a half-step sound after I'd stopped moving. I strained my ears.

Something was amiss. I took three more steps, then stopped again. For the second time, I heard that odd half-step sound. As if I was being followed.

Frowning, I took two more steps and then whirled around.

Two meters behind me stood the purple unicorn, datapad firmly clamped in its teeth, stalking me. Its eyes flew open with a merry twinkle, and it spun around and galloped away.

We played this game for the better part of the morning, me giving chase, screaming to the unicorn to drop the datapad and it bounding joyously into the brush every time I drew close.

By the time midday rolled around, I was exhausted and in no mood to continue. I stepped into the tent, turned on the cold water faucet, and soaked a washcloth. Pressing the washcloth against my forehead, I collapsed on the bed and stared up at the ceiling.

Stupid unicorn. I didn't want this assignment anyway and now McDavity was going to charge me for the lost datapad. I moved the washcloth from my forehead and wiped it across my neck, cleaning off the sweat that had accumulated there in the jungle heat. I ran it along my arms and across my face, feeling the cool dampness revive and refresh my spirits.

Then I sat bolt upright. Bed? I scrambled off the bed and looked around for the sleeping bag I'd slept in the night before. It was nowhere to be found. I looked under the bed and then behind it, just in case it had fallen between the wall and the bed.

I stopped short. Wall?

With trembling fingers, I touched the cool plaster of the bedroom wall and then ran them across the soft, cotton sheets. I scratched my head, unable to explain what I was seeing. Had I been so obsessed with the unicorn that I had missed somebody replacing my tent with a walled room?

I heard the beep of a horn outside and scurried to the front door, which I opened and stepped through, even more confused. Hadn't it been a zipper just moments before?

Ocking-Klark roared toward me in her truck, slammed on the brakes and slid to a halt a mere half-meter from me. I took an instinctive step back and pointed an angry finger at her.

"You left me here!"

"Shut up," she said kindly, and got out of the cab. "I brought lunch. You eat. Stop complain."

I settled down and walked with her to the back of the truck, which was empty save for a picnic basket. I grabbed the handles and lifted it up and out, then, staggering under the weight, stumbled to the picnic bench beside the gazebo. I put the basket on the bench and sat down, drawing the back of my hand across my forehead.

Yes—a picnic bench and a gazebo. I had no idea where they had come from, but I was too hungry to care.

"You eat," repeated Ocking-Klark. "Stop complain."

We ate. The basket held fried chicken, mashed potatoes, gravy without lumps, biscuits, corn on the cob, and, for dessert, a blackberry pie and a gallon of vanilla ice cream.

Ocking-Klark ate an enormous amount, glancing at the house and the gazebo from time to time, admiring the lawn. Sucking on a chicken leg, she popped it out of her mouth and used it as a pointing device, which she aimed at the house. "This yours?"

I bristled. "I thought you were going to explain it, actually. Last night I opened up that tent thing you left for me and, today …" I waved a hand helplessly. "I don't even know how you did this. Did you do this?"

She shook her head and smiled, showing me teeth like tombstones. "Not I. You did. Changed surroundings to match desires."

"You have drugs here on Jungle, do you?" I scoffed, a sarcastic grin playing on my face, but with an ice-cold knot of fear in my gut.

I couldn't explain these changes, the way the tent had vanished, only to be replaced by what looked like a comfortable three-bedroom Tudor-style house, complete with a manicured lawn and the aforementioned gazebo and picnic bench.

Opening my mouth to speak, I snapped it shut again. While I'd been admiring the house, the purple unicorn had returned. It nickered and walked over to the picnic table, laying the datapad gently on the wooden surface.

I looked at the unicorn, then at Ocking-Klark, then at the gazebo and the flower garden, thoroughly confused. I took a deep breath and said the smartest thing I've ever said.

"I have no idea what is going on."

Ocking-Klark stopped munching on a biscuit and shrugged. "You Earthman. You spoiled. Nobody need all this." She waved at the garden, at the pond and the small dock. "You are idiot."

She went back to eating the biscuit. The purple unicorn stretched its neck and nudged my shoulder, then looked intently at the picnic basket.

My head hurt. I wondered, briefly, if I was simply hallucinating, if perhaps I was actually still in my sleeping bag, overcome with heat exhaustion and panting in the midday heat, slowly dying.

The unicorn nudged me again and returned its gaze to the picnic basket.

Unless … An insane idea formed in my mind.

I closed my eyes and imagined what a perfect Granny Smith apple would look like, imagined sunlight on the green skin, the brown stem, the clever flowerlike starburst on the underside. I imagined how it would feel cupped in my hand, the cool, smooth skin against my palm. I opened my eyes and reached into the picnic basket, just knowing it would be there, and closed my hand around a cool, green Granny Smith apple.

It lay there in my hand, in the sunlight, looking just as I'd imagined. I slowly extended my hand and the unicorn lipped it off. He crunched it happily and then extended his neck for another.

"No," I said, standing up quickly. "You'll get fat."

I looked down on Ocking-Klark, who was cutting a wedge from the blackberry pie. "Khalif?"

She glared at me, holding a knife. "Dessert. You shut up."

"Fine." I went inside the house, down the front hallway and into the study, with a view overlooking the lake. "Computer, establish contact with Earth." I gave the vid coordinates to McDavity's office and, after a moment, the wall-screen lit up.

McDavity stared at me from his desk, an irritated scowl on his face. "What the hell do you want, Johnson?"

I ignored his bluster. "Sir, I found the *monoceros purpurea*." I held up the datapad. "I'm transferring the data I collected to you now."

He shook his head. "Didn't I tell you to go there in person?"

I nodded. "Yes, sir, you did. I am standing on Kepler-186f as we speak."

He snorted. "Impossible. We're having a real-time conversation. Where are you, in somebody's house nearby? I'll have you fired for insubordination, Johnson!"

My datapad chimed softly. "Data transfer complete, sir. You may check your in-box."

He leaned to the side, did something with his desk. "Yeah, I got it. Come into my office, Johnson. I'll hand you your termination papers personally."

"No, sir," I replied, as calmly as I could.

He slammed his open hand down on his desk. "What did you say, Johnson?" His eyes bugged out, and his face turned red.

"Consensus reality, sir," I said quietly.

He paused, then frowned in confusion. "What?"

"Consensus reality," I repeated. "There is something about this place that gives you whatever you dream of. I can't explain it, because I don't understand it, but this"—I thumped the wall—"wasn't here this morning. I awoke in a tent, and now I have a house. A purple unicorn stole my datapad and played tag with me all morning. I just ate a picnic lunch of fried chicken with a woman who has probably never even tasted chicken before. If she even exists." I pondered that for a moment, but discarded it.

"Johnson," said McDavity, his voice calmer. "Let's not hurry to conclusions here. Tell me where you are."

I sighed. "Orbiting Kepler, on 186f, in a house that reminds me of my grandmother's, next to a lake." I looked out over the lake at the floating boathouse and the tail end of a twin-diesel cabin cruiser poking from within. Fred, the mechanic, waved at me from the pier. I waved back.

"Basically," I said, turning back to McDavity. "Whatever I want, whatever I imagine, I get. So, I quit."

He spluttered. "But … why?"

I shrugged. "I don't need the job. I have everything I could want right here."

McDavity opened his mouth to say something more, but I cut the connection. His picture faded away to nothing, and the wall went dark.

"Computer," I said, a grin creeping across my face. "Connect with Mac's Diner." I gave the vid coordinates. The wall sprang to life, and I stared into the interior of the diner. It was late afternoon there, and I could see Natalie working behind the hostess.

"Yes?" asked the hostess.

"Could you put Natalie on, please?"

She looked at me oddly, then said, "Please hold."

I waited for Natalie to come on the line, wondering if she knew how to make coconut cream pie.

Outside, the purple unicorn whinnied.

The Last Dregs of Winter

Scott Eder

S*tupid sheep.* Kayden shooed another of the escaped livestock into the pen with the tip of a muddy boot. The fierce wind from last night's storm had knocked the rails out of several sections of the old wooden fence, providing an easy escape route for the spooked animals. *It's a good way to get yourself eaten by a wolf, dummy.*

"Git." He slapped another one on the rump. "Move it."

The black-faced sheep, its woolly coat full and ripe for shearing, glanced back. "Baa."

"Don't give me your sass, you little booger. Scoot." He kicked it gently, and it scampered into the pen with an indignant bleat. Securing the gate with a rope loop, he scanned his father's homestead for fluffy escapees. The swells of the surrounding hills made his search more difficult. Thankfully, the animals' white coats stood out like tufts of cotton against the winter-brown landscape.

Most of the sheep had stayed in the pen, clinging to the well-trodden and familiar despite the storm's fury. A few roamed close to the two-room shack Kayden shared with his father and sister. Others strayed near the dilapidated barn with the missing front doors. Several others had braved the elements and trod the brown grass less traveled, ending up way … over …

Kayden groaned.

"How did they get…? If they step on her, I'll …" The woolly boogers had wandered fifty yards across the property to take shelter within the outer curve of a thick copse of aspen—the only windbreak for miles. It also served as the resting place of his mother, marked by a simple wooden plank carved with her name, Summerlyn. They'd buried her after the ground thawed last winter. Until then, they'd laid her on a plank in the barn draped in the best of their threadbare linens.—

Kayden tried not to think about her. He didn't want to cry, not anymore, not after he caught the back of his father's hand the last time—the only time his father had hit him. But it was hard, not thinking about her, especially when his younger sister was around. So alike they were. Golden hair, green eyes, milky skin, all the same, as if in giving birth to Violet, his mother had recreated a tiny version of herself, in body as well as in temperament. Both of the Monroe girls embodied the warmth and joy of spring—bubbly, quick to laughter, and overflowing with life. Until, of course, that all ended.

Kayden shook his head, trying to banish the gloom that settled over his soul. He almost convinced himself that he let the weather get to him, that the dregs of winter, with its gray skies, leaden air, and low clouds clinging to the tops of the trees, brought out his melancholy, but today something felt … different, wrong. The feeling settled in his stomach like a shard of ice.

After a last glance at the runaways, Kayden inspected the closest section of fence with one end of the middle rail ground in the mud. He raised his foot to block a sheep from getting out through the gap.

"I guess I'll fix the fence before I round up your brothers and sisters." He hoisted the rail and shoved it back into its socket. Sliding a wooden mallet from the loop on his belt, he fit a wooden peg from his pocket into the post, and smacked it home, securing the beam.

One down, infinity more to go. Kayden frowned, estimating the repairs would take all day without help. The worst part was that shoving the rails back into place simply delayed the inevitable. Most of the posts tilted one way or the other, some held up only by a random accumulation of dirt and debris. Once his father scraped enough money together, they'd replace the whole sodden mess, or so he promised, but until then …

Hoist. Shove. Fit. Smack. *And that's two.*

A tinkling laugh drifted out of the barn.

"Kayden!" His father, Simon, a powerful man nearing his middle years with his mouth drawn down in a perpetual scowl, strode out of the barn leading an old nag. Violet sat on its back, digging her heels into the tired old horse's flank, urging her to jump, to run, to do anything other than walk sedately at the end of its lead.

Beside her rode Petre, from the Kravens' farmstead several miles away. Atop a great draft horse, the slight boy reminded Kayden of a skinny frog hunched upon the back of a tree trunk. Small for his fourteen summers, he barely filled out the sackcloth shirt and hand-me-down britches. His hands trembled upon the reins.

Simon shoved leather gloves onto his hands and yanked the wood ax from the stump near the barn door. "Young Petre here has brought a tale of wolves. His family lost half their flock and are asking for help. Maybe if we thin out the wolves' numbers, Missy Kraven and her kin can hold their own." He shook his head and eyed the heavy clouds creeping across the sky, blocking access to the sun. "Take care of your sister, fix the fence, and collect the sheep. We don't want them attracting any predators. We have enough to worry about."

Violet held up her hands as her father lifted her off the nag. She squealed in delight, holding him close before he deposited her on the ground. Simon's smile vanished when she left his arms. Only Violet had the power to crack the man's stony demeanor anymore. No more than six, she skipped through the milling sheep, greeting each by name in a lilting, high-pitched song as she passed. Dressed in a warm brown overcoat and threadbare mittens, she slid in the mud, but quickly righted herself. Tousled blonde curls bobbed in counterpoint to her steps, partially obscuring the small horn she'd tied to her forehead with a purple ribbon.

Simon rode close to Kayden, eyes fixed on his little treasure dancing about the livestock. "Careful," he whispered. "She's a unicorn today."

"Great. Another animal to watch over." Kayden smiled, feigning annoyance. Violet charged into each day as if it were a new challenge to be conquered. Very rarely did she do it as a little girl. Most of the time, she saw the world through the eyes of some animal. Birds. Dogs. Sheep. One day she pretended to be a snake and hissed every word.

More often of late she donned the horn and purple ribbon of her favorite.

"Kaykay!" Violet skipped to her brother and rubbed her horn along his arm until he knelt beside her and opened his arms wide for a good morning hug.

Holding the precious bundle tight, Kayden realized how much light and color she brought to his drab existence, especially this time of year. When the colors all melted into dead browns and tans, her splash of gold and tinkling laugh brought a ray of sunshine wherever she went.

Violet grabbed two of Kayden's fingers in her little hand and pulled him toward the center of the yard, scattering sheep with a "yip yip" and a light swat to their dirty rumps. "Kaykay, we need to save the farm."

"Oh?" Kayden pretended to look worried, scanning the horizon for signs of danger. "Save it from what?"

She grew wide-eyed, and leaned close. "The stone dragon. He wants to eat us."

Kayden picked up his sister and rolled her over his shoulder, tickling her belly. "Not the *stone* dragon. I thought we killed him last week."

She scrambled out of her brother's grasp. "No, silly. You can't kill stone."

"Violet," Simon spoke up. "Leave your brother alone. He has chores to do."

Violet rubbed her horn against her father's waist and galloped off to torment the sheep.

Simon smiled at his daughter, and then glanced wistfully toward the stand of aspen on the far side of the field outside the fence.

Kayden caught the glance. "I see Mom in Violet more every day … that hair."

Simon grunted. "Keep your eye on her. I'm sure the wolves are on the prowl, and not just keeping to our neighbors' land." He rode off, Petre in tow, waiting until he hit the muddy ground away from the kids to give the horse his head.

Kayden worried about his father and the other steaders in the area. Second- and third-generation farmers and livestock owners all, and not a warrior in the crew. Strong and proud, they could put up one hell of a fight, but when confronted by several hunger-stricken killers, pride wouldn't keep them alive. Still, his father had done this before, and always came back.

Kayden banished his worry, looked to the fence, and sighed.

It's not going to fix itself.

He checked on his sister. She wound in and out of the sheep, talking their black woolly ears off about who knew what. Her high-pitched babbling reached him as a gentle, constant chirp. Satisfied, he set to work. After checking his supply of wooden pegs, he socketed a rail and secured it with a solid smack of his mallet. Though cracked down the center, the thick-headed tool had seen many winters and still hit square.

The next section of fence had two rails down. He fixed one, and then the other, humming a tune the Kravens' daughter, Winnie, had taught him during the harvest dance. She was a pretty one. Red hair. Full lips. Eyes like the spring grass, and her curves … ooh, the curves. He stood up, stretching his back and taking a deep cool breath to slow his pulse. He and Winnie had stepped out on occasion, but nothing formal. He planned to remedy that once the winter needs had been met.

Kayden noted the absence of his sister's chirping and glanced over his shoulder. He spotted her several feet outside the gate, picking the first lavender wildflowers struggling through the ground thaw.

A pang of fear gripped him. "Don't stray too far, Vi. A wolf's favorite dinner is leg of unicorn."

Violet glanced back, lips pursed in a duckbill as if to say "Who me?" She continued picking her flowers, while Kayden moved to the next section of fence. One of the sheep sneaked out. He tracked it down and shuffled it back into the relative safety of the pen. With all this activity, he doubted any marauding wolves would descend upon them. Just in case, though, he did a quick scan, looking for movement among the hills.

A shiver crawled up his spine.

Where's Violet? Further out into the field, farther than she should have gone without him, and trundling toward the aspens and their mother's grave.

"Violet!" Kayden yelled, but she continued moving. He slid the mallet into its loop on his belt and jogged toward her.

At the gravesite, she picked a few additional flowers and knelt before the grave.

In the open, beyond the pen and the area surrounding the farmhouse, Kayden felt exposed. Even though the fence itself provided little protection, it bolstered his confidence and provided a sense of security. Out in the open field, running away from the sanctuary of his home felt wrong, but he attributed that to slacking off, and not working on the fence.

Halfway to the trees, the sickly sweet smell of decay punched Kayden in the nose. He gagged and stumbled, but recovered and picked up the pace.

The trees rustled behind the grave, though the air was still. Something dark moved behind the first line of gray-barked boughs.

Nonono. His world flipped. Kayden sprinted, covering the ground as fast as he could, but he was too far away.

Violet squealed.

A long face the color of a bone-deep bruise—a vicious clash of deep purple, black, and blue—shoved its way between two thin trunks. With eyes the dull blackness of death, and a grease-slick mane to match, it pushed its way into the clearing, snapping the young trees. It stood over Violet and nickered. Nostrils flaring, it turned its head, revealing two feet of spiraling bone sticking out from its forehead like a spear, tapering to a sharp, lethal point.

"Kay, Kay, it's a unicorn. A for reals, for true, unicorn. Look!" Violet stood up and pointed. "He has a horn like me." She touched the horn strapped to her head for emphasis.

"Vi, honey, come away from there." Kayden's mother had called Violet honey only when she wanted to keep her safe, and it had worked, but Kayden lacked her motherly magic.

In her excitement, Violet ignored him.

Kayden slowed his pace, not wanting to spook the creature. *Could it really be a unicorn?* He had believed them nothing more than myth, creatures born of fancy and rainbow-lit dreams coated in shimmering white purity. This, this … *thing* seemed to absorb the light, drawing it into itself as if to cloak the world in night.

The stench Kayden noticed earlier intensified. Its near physical presence repelled him, urged him to come no closer.

But he had to, for Violet.

Kayden inched closer and grasped Violet's hand. He tugged, trying to move her away, but she fought him.

"Gr-off me, Kay." Violet jerked out of his grasp and stepped forward.

The unicorn bent low, touching its horn to hers, examining her unnatural appendage. With a casual flip, it knocked the false horn clear, yanking Violet's head to the side and snapping the ribbon.

"Hey," Violet glared up at her visitor. "That wasn't very nice."

Wisps of black smoke curled from between the unicorn's dark, heavy lips. Open sores wept foul ichor down its legs and across the prominent outline of its rib cage beneath sweat-slick skin. It wobbled as it took a step toward Violet.

Violet coughed and waved her hand in front of her nose. "Phew. He smells icky."

"Come on, Vi." Kayden felt for her hand again, his eyes never leaving the creature's horn. With one lunge, it could pierce them both. "I don't think it's in the mood to play. Let's leave him be. He looks ill."

"But if he's sick, Kay, we should help him." She slipped Kayden's grasp again and moved forward. She reached out to the creature's muzzle. Kayden snatched her hand back as the creature snapped its gnarled teeth.

This time, Kayden clenched his sister's hand tight and pulled her back. Despite the unicorn's obvious ill-temper, Violet still fought her brother, digging in her heels.

"Stop, Kay. Stop. Please."

Not this time. "Dad would be angry if he knew you'd wandered this far from the house on a day like today, especially with him away. What if a wolf appeared? What then?"

At the invocation of her father's disappointment, the child relented and allowed herself to be guided toward the farm. She didn't turn around, for that would require her to lose sight of her creature. Instead, she walked backward, guided by Kayden's hands on her shoulders. The awkward arrangement slowed their speed.

"Kay, why isn't he white?" Violet asked. "I thought unicorns were supposed to be white. And smell like sugarcane. It looks sad to me, like Daddy does when he thinks we're not watching."

"Like I said, he's sick." He tried to pull her along faster, but she tripped and landed on her butt.

The darkling beast raised its head and pawed the ground. It sniffed the freshly picked flowers sprinkled over their mother's grave, and ate them.

"Hey!" Violet yelled. "Leave those alone. They're for my mommy." She looked up at Kayden. "I don't like him. He makes my tummy feel funny."

The unicorn advanced several steps then danced to the left as if to better align himself with his prey.

"Mine too. How 'bout we leave him alone and head back." He spared a quick glance over his shoulder, gauging how much open ground he had left to cross.

Still too far. If it wanted, the creature could be upon them within ten long strides.

The unicorn dipped its head. Once. Twice. And blew out foul gas with a snort.

Mouth suddenly dry, Kayden picked up Violet and turned. Fighting the urge to run, he kept his pace slow and deliberate. In the muddy conditions, it would be easy to slip. If that happened, they'd be at the creature's mercy.

Slow and steady. He increased his pace, walking heel to toe, focusing on the ground ahead, directing his feet as best he could to surer footing.

The unicorn neighed.

Violet, looking back toward the beast over Kayden's shoulder, whispered in his ear, "It's coming." She trembled in his arms and gripped him tighter, burying her face in his neck. "Run, Kay, run." Her voice faltered.

Heart drumming, breathing rushed and heavy, Kayden ran as fast as he dared. Footing treacherous, he slipped, twisted his ankle, but maintained his forward momentum.

Hoofbeats squelched behind him, getting closer.

Kayden felt the vibration in the soles of his feet, the heavy thump of the creature chasing them. He glanced over his shoulder, the one not covered in golden ringlets, but the move cost him. The treacherous mud slid out from under his foot. He went down, sliding on the side opposite his sister to spare her the brunt of the fall.

The timely slip saved them.

With its horn leveled at Violet's head, the creature thundered past. It tried to stop, but slid into the yard in front of the house. Its front hooves splayed wide, it went down, spearing an unfortunate sheep in its path. Righting itself, the unicorn turned toward the brother and sister, raising its head as if the impaled and struggling sheep weighed less than air. Blood from its victim leaked down its muzzle and dripped into the mud.

The unfortunate sheep bleated in terror and pain.

Blocked. In the span of seconds, the creature had stolen their path to sanctuary and now held the high ground.

With a quick snap of its head, the unicorn tossed the injured sheep across the yard, where it tumbled a few feet before lying still.

The unicorn's soulless black stare seemed fixed on Violet. Whenever she adjusted her position, the creature's head moved a fraction. It flicked its ears whenever she made the slightest sound.

Why her? I thought unicorns revered the pure, the virgins, and yet this one seems bent on Violet's destruction.

Rooted to the spot, Kayden tried to figure a way out of this dire situation. Open ground stretched around him, and he didn't have the speed to reach cover before the creature could spear him. The way it watched, the way it waited, he knew it would charge if he made a movement in any direction.

Stalemate.

Violet grew heavy in his arms. As he set her down, his arm brushed a bulge on his hip. *The mallet. I forgot about that.* Against this brute, how effective would a small wooden hammer be? Maybe if he bashed it in the eye, he could distract it enough to run past, reach the house, and lock themselves inside.

Grandfather's sword is in there, a relic from his service in the High Lord's army. Hope swirled in his chest at the thought of getting his hands on a real weapon. Not that he'd ever used a sword, but the promise of wielding a sharp blade instead of a measly hammer seemed far more appealing. Unless his father took it, but Kayden didn't remember seeing the sword's pommel riding high over his father's shoulder. No. His father had taken the ax. He was sure of it.

The unicorn watched them, silent and still, a bruised and abused equine abortion.

Violet sat on Kayden's right foot. "I'm tired, Kay, and hungry. I'm scared too. What does it want? Why is it here?"

"Good questions. I've been asking them myself, but I don't have any answers."

I wish I did.

The sheep gave the creature a wide berth, moving to the other side of the house as if sensing the wrongness, the vile nature of the creature. Even those dumb brutes couldn't tolerate its presence.

Can I use them somehow, the sheep? Nah. They're nothing but lumps in the way at this point.

By the position of the sun, Kayden judged he'd stood in the mud with his sister clinging to his leg for over an hour. The unicorn showed no lessening in focus or intensity.

Do these creatures even get tired? Thank goodness we're not in the middle of winter or the blaze of summer.

He spun the hammer in his hand, judging the weight, gauging the heft. He could throw it, but then what? Would it buy them a precious few seconds to slip by and get into the house?

"Vi," Kayden whispered. "Get up."

Violet pulled herself up using his trouser leg.

"Let's get a little closer," he whispered.

Violet panicked, breathing fast, and dug her little fingers into his thigh. "Why?"

"Come on." He shuffled forward. Violet clung to his leg, but followed, taking the steps as slowly as he. "Granddad's sword is inside."

"But the unicorn is so big, and …" Violet's voice dropped to barely above a whisper. "And I think it wants me."

She realizes it too. "No, baby, I don't think so." He tousled her hair, running his fingers through strands of gold. "It's just confused. The sickness has driven it mad, that's all. Don't think like that."

Swallowing hard, she rubbed her nose. "I know it does. I can feel it in here." She tapped her chest and looked up at her brother, eyes big and moist. She bit her lip. "Please don't let it get me."

Kayden mustered his bravest smile. "No chance, Vi. He'll have to go through me first, and you know how tough and stubborn I can be." He tried to joke around, tried to set her mind down some other path, a nearly impossible task considering the beast stared right at them.

"I love you," Violet said.

Anger welled in Kayden's breast, hot and fast. *How dare this thing just materialize and threaten to blow apart our world? It's bad enough the last winter took our mother, I will not lose any more. Not now. Not ever.*

His grip on the mallet tight, he took a large step forward. Eyes fixed on the unicorn's horn, watching it wave from right to left, he took another step. And another. Violet clung to his leg and mirrored his steps, taking two for each of his one.

The closer Kayden crept, the more intense, and focused, his anger became.

The unicorn waited no more than fifteen paces away. Tense. Ears twitching. Nostrils flaring.

And safety lay just beyond. The trouble was that the thing Kayden needed to be safe from blocked his way. If only he could trick it into thinking they fled in one direction, while sprinting in the other.

The unicorn's chest heaved. Thick mucus flowed from its eyes, smearing the deep purple coat and drawing darker lines down its cheeks. It switched the few strands of hair remaining in its tail, waiting, watching … hunting.

Hunger overriding fear, several sheep wandered between Kayden and the unicorn, picking at sporadic blades of dead grass.

Is this the time? Kayden knelt in the dirt and pulled Violet around to face him. He cupped her cheeks and whispered, "I'm going for the house."

Violet stiffened and shook her head, gulping breath in short, rapid gasps.

"When I do," Kayden continued, watching the unicorn over Violet's shoulder, "I want you to duck behind those sheep."

Violet turned slightly, looking at the closest sheep. They came up to her shoulder. Kayden hoped his ruse would buy her the opportunity to duck out of sight behind her woolly friends.

She nodded.

"Ready?" He directed her to his right side, out of his planned path.

"Go." Kayden jumped toward the door, waving his arms, and yelling at the unicorn. *"Hey!"*

His sudden charge startled the unicorn, and it reared.

Kayden hurdled the sheep and sprinted for the door, expecting at any moment to feel the horn pierce his back, but it never came. He also didn't feel the beast bearing down on him. In fact, he didn't feel or hear anything.

Kayden turned, dread gripping his bowels and coursing through his limbs. *Wait. It doesn't want me. It never did. It wants her.*

Violet hid behind the sheep as instructed, but the unicorn wasn't fooled. It must have been attuned to her in some way. The yard was full of sheep, and yet the sickly creature walked unerringly toward his sister's hiding place.

Violet peeked over the sheep's back, catching a glimpse of her stalker. She whimpered and hunkered down, pretending it didn't see her.

No more than five feet separated them now. Kayden had to do something. He didn't want to be the one to tell his father he'd lost his golden girl. He knew how much his mother's death had cost his father, had cost them all, and now to lose Violet?

This will not happen.

Across the field and riding hard from the direction of his neighbor's farmstead came his father. He whooped and hollered, trying to get Kayden's attention. He waved the ax in one hand and gripped the reins in the other. While the sight warmed Kayden's heart, gave him a tiny glimmer of hope, his father was too far away. He wanted to believe his father had arrived in time to save them, but that kind of happy coincidence only happened in fairy stories.

The reality was someone was going to die in the next few minutes, and Kayden's decisions, his actions, would dictate who. The thought didn't scare him. He was beyond that now, and he accepted the inevitable with cold practicality. No matter what, he would do whatever he could to save his sister.

He slipped the mallet into his hand. Acting on instinct, he threw it at the creature. It bonked off its head, just above its right eye.

"Come on, you beast. Come get me," Kayden yelled, stomping in the mud.

The unicorn snapped its attention to Kayden and whinnied.

Kayden wanted to believe his attack at least hurt the beast a little, but the sound reminded him more of a laugh, or a snort of disdain.

Kayden charged the unicorn, trying to hold its attention so Violet could run to the house. As he did, he angled toward his sister, cutting the distance, trying to put himself between them.

The unicorn shrugged him off like a fly and focused on Violet.

She screamed as it approached, startling the sheep. It bolted, leaving her alone and exposed.

Kayden ran as fast as he could, but the mud tripped him up, and he couldn't make the progress he needed. Closing the distance, the world seemed to slow around him.

The unicorn tossed its mane and raised its horn for the killing blow.

Too late. Too late.

Violet screamed and shook her head in denial, golden ringlets bouncing and bobbing, like sunlight spilling across her shoulders.

Kayden dove.

The unicorn lunged, horn aimed at Violet's heart.

Violet raised her arms to ward off the blow and turned her head. She screamed.

The unicorn's horn punched through bone.

Kayden's bone. The spiral horn tore through his ribs, spearing his heart, and snapping through his shoulder blade to exit the other side. His heart beat one last time, a mighty thump that vibrated against his violated chest, and stilled. Legs failing, the only thing keeping Kayden upright was the strength of the purple beast.

With its horn through Kayden's chest, the beast's eyes were only inches from his own. And in that deadened stare, Kayden saw the loss that ravaged the once majestic creature. He saw the pain, the suffering, and the despair to which this poor thing had fallen after no more than a single turning of the season. Once a grand monarch of nature, now a wasted heap of blighted sinew clinging to the last vestige of life.

Like me, clinging to life. No. Wait. My heart stopped. I'm dead, right? Then why …

A tingling sensation began in his heart. Not a beat per se, but the quiver of movement, the tremble of an attempt. And then a flutter around the unicorn's horn, grasping, clutching, drinking.

Kayden felt a pull on his very soul. What had been his and his alone since conception, now fed another. Everything that made him Kayden trickled into the beast. His memories. His hopes. His dreams. His desire for Winnie. His love for his mother. His love for his father. His love for his sister.

The unicorn drained him in less than a second.

Kayden felt the cold in his fingers first. It gnawed at his fingertips, climbed to his knuckles, spread quickly over his hands and up his arms. His toes went numb, or he couldn't feel them anymore, or ... what? His mind grew fuzzy. Thoughts slowed as if traveling through syrup. Darkness closed in, narrowing his vision, blurring the scene around him.

The unicorn shuddered, once. It made eye contact with Kayden's dimming sight. A spark ignited within that dead stare. It flared, bright and strong, burning away the sickness, the blight that afflicted the creature, traveling across its being, healing whatever it touched with the benevolent fires of Kayden's love.

Kayden's vision sharpened. His heart beat again. Not to feed the other creature, but to pump blood through his body.

With a tooth-grinding scrape, the unicorn pulled back, withdrawing its horn through its bone-shattered track and out of Kayden's chest. The once blackened shaft glowed a pristine ivory white. As the tip cleared, a golden flash blinded Kayden for a moment. Spots danced before his eyes.

When his vision cleared, the unicorn's form blurred. The deep purple bubbled and seethed, until like mud from the banks of a swiftly flowing river, it slid down the creature's skin, leaving great swathes of shimmering white. The process continued until not a smudge of darkness remained, and the proud creature stood whole and unblemished. Even its emaciated form had filled out, removing all trace of the illness that had ravaged it near to death.

Simon thundered into the yard. He leaped off the horse, sliding in the mud until he found his footing, and raised the ax over his shoulder.

The unicorn bowed its head, prepared to take the strike it had earned.

The gesture, one of atonement, freed Kayden from his stillness. Though not recovered, he had enough strength to stagger between his father and the unicorn, forcing his father either to continue the stroke or catch him before he fell face-first in the filth.

Simon dropped the ax and caught him. With a strength Kayden had never realized the man possessed, his father lifted his weakened body and cradled him to his breast.

Kayden's left hand swung free, until he felt another, small and warm, grab hold.

Violet. She kissed the back of his hand and held it against her lips.

A tear rolled down Kayden's cheek.

The unicorn rose from its pose of attrition and lifted its head. It stared first at Violet, and dipped its head. It then met the stare of Simon, and dipped its head again. When its eyes met Kayden's, the creature bent its forelegs and bowed, touching the tip of its horn gently, reverently, to Kayden's forehead.

Though he felt like death, that touch renewed Kayden's spirit and bolstered the love and hope in his soul. It also promised that his body would mend, stronger than ever.

Unable to speak, Kayden nodded slightly to acknowledge their understanding, their shared loss, and their renewed outlook for the future.

The unicorn stepped around the family and walked through the gate. Once clear of the mud, it trotted across the field, leaving in its wake a trail of wildflowers blooming in a riot of bright colors. At the grave of Kayden's mother, it bowed once again. As it rose, a single rosebush grew and blossomed at her head.

After a last glance at the gathered family, it turned and vanished into the trees. At its passing, the sun burst from behind the clouds, bathing the three in glorious golden light.

"Come." Simon kissed his son's forehead, something he had not done since Kayden had turned five, and carried him toward the house.

Violet held tight to Kayden's hand, determined to maintain her grip, no matter what.

Professor Gottesman and the Indian Rhinoceros

Peter S. Beagle

Professor Gustave Gottesman went to a zoo for the first time when he was thirty-four years old. There is an excellent zoo in Zurich, which was Professor Gottesman's birthplace, and where his sister still lived, but Professor Gottesman had never been there. From an early age he had determined on the study of philosophy as his life's work; and for any true philosopher this world is zoo enough, complete with cages, feeding times, breeding programs, and earnest docents, of which he was wise enough to know that he was one. Thus, the first zoo he ever saw was the one in the middle-sized Midwestern American city where he worked at a middle-sized university, teaching Comparative Philosophy in comparative contentment. He was tall and rather thin, with a round, undistinguished face, a snub nose, a random assortment of sandy-ish hair, and a pair of very intense and very distinguished brown eyes that always seemed to be looking a little deeper than they meant to, embarrassing the face around them no end. His students and colleagues were quite fond of him, in an indulgent sort of way.

And how did the good Professor Gottesman happen at last to visit a zoo? It came about in this way: his older sister Edith came from Zurich to stay with him for several weeks, and she brought her daughter, his niece Nathalie, along with her. Nathalie was seven, both in years, and in the number of her there sometimes seemed to be, for the Professor had never been used to children even when he was one. She was a generally pleasant little girl, though, as far as he could tell; so when his sister besought him to spend one of his free afternoons with Nathalie while she went to lunch and a gallery opening with an old friend, the Professor graciously consented. And Nathalie wanted very much to go to the zoo and see tigers.

"So you shall," her uncle announced gallantly. "Just as soon as I find out exactly where the zoo is." He consulted with his best friend, a fat, cheerful, harmonica-playing professor of medieval Italian poetry named Sally Lowry, who had known him long and well enough (she was the only person in the world who called him Gus) to draw an elaborate two-colored map of the route, write out very precise directions beneath it, and make several copies of this document, in case of accidents. Thus equipped, and accompanied by Charles, Nathalie's stuffed bedtime tiger, whom she desired to introduce to his grand cousins, they set off together for the zoo on a gray, cool spring afternoon. Professor Gottesman quoted Thomas Hardy to Nathalie, improvising a German translation for her benefit as he went along.

> *This is the weather the cuckoo likes,*
> *And so do I;*
> *When showers betumble the chestnut spikes,*
> *And nestlings fly.*

"Charles likes it too," Nathalie said. "It makes his fur feel all sweet."

They reached the zoo without incident, thanks to Professor Lowry's excellent map, and Professor Gottesman bought Nathalie a bag of something sticky, unhealthy, and forbidden, and took her straight off to see the tigers. Their hot, meaty smell and their lightning-colored eyes were a bit too much for him, and so he sat on a bench nearby and watched Nathalie perform the introductions for Charles. When she came back to Professor Gottesman, she told him that Charles had been very well-behaved, as had all the tigers but one, who was rudely indifferent. "He was probably just visiting," she said. "A tourist or something." The Professor was still marveling at the amount of contempt one small girl could infuse into the word tourist, when he heard a voice, sounding almost at his shoulder, say, "Why, Professor Gottesman—how nice to see you at last." It was a low voice, a bit hoarse, with excellent diction, speaking good Zurich German with a very slight, unplaceable accent.

Professor Gottesman turned quickly, half-expecting to see some old acquaintance from home, whose name he would inevitably have forgotten. Such embarrassments were altogether too common in his gently preoccupied life. His friend Sally Lowry once observed, "We see each other just about every day, Gus, and I'm still not sure you really recognize me. If I wanted to hide from you, I'd just change my hairstyle."

There was no one at all behind him. The only thing he saw was the rutted, muddy rhinoceros yard, for some reason placed directly across from the big cats' cages. The one rhinoceros in residence was standing by the fence, torpidly mumbling a mouthful of moldy-looking hay. It was an Indian rhinoceros, according to the placard on the gate: as big as the Professor's compact car, and the approximate color of old cement. The creaking slabs of its skin smelled of stale urine, and it had only one horn, caked with sticky mud. Flies buzzed around its small, heavy-lidded eyes, which regarded Professor Gottesman with immense, ancient unconcern. But there was no other person in the vicinity who might have addressed him.

Professor Gottesman shook his head, scratched it, shook it again, and turned back to the tigers. But the voice came again. "Professor, it was indeed I who spoke. Come and talk to me, if you please."

No need, surely, to go into Professor Gottesman's reaction: to describe in detail how he gasped, turned pale, and looked wildly around for any corroborative witness. It is worth mentioning, however, that at no time did he bother to splutter the requisite splutter in such cases: "My God, I'm either dreaming, drunk, or crazy." If he was indeed just as classically absent-minded and impractical as everyone who knew him agreed, he was also more of a realist than many of them. This is generally true of philosophers, who tend, as a group, to be on terms of mutual respect with the impossible. Therefore, Professor Gottesman did the only proper thing under the circumstances. He introduced his niece Nathalie to the rhinoceros.

Nathalie, for all her virtues, was not a philosopher, and could not hear the rhinoceros's gracious greeting. She was, however, seven years old, and a well-brought-up seven-year-old has no difficulty with the notion that a rhinoceros—or a goldfish, or a coffee table—might be able to talk; nor in accepting that some people can hear coffee-table speech and some people cannot. She said a polite hello to the rhinoceros, and then became involved in her own conversation with stuffed Charles, who apparently had a good deal to say about tigers.

"A mannerly child," the rhinoceros commented. "One sees so few here. Most of them throw things."

His mouth was dry, and his voice shaky but contained, Professor Gottesman asked carefully, "Tell me, if you will—can all rhinoceri speak, or only the Indian species?" He wished furiously that he had thought to bring along his notebook.

"I have no idea," the rhinoceros answered him candidly. "I myself, as it happens, am a unicorn."

Professor Gottesman wiped his balding forehead. "Please," he said earnestly. "Please. A rhinoceros, even a rhinoceros that speaks, is as real a creature as I. A unicorn, on the other hand, is a being of pure fantasy, like mermaids, or dragons, or the chimera. I consider very little in this universe as absolutely, indisputably certain, but I would feel so much better if you could see your way to being merely a talking rhinoceros. For my sake, if not your own."

It seemed to the Professor that the rhinoceros chuckled slightly, but it might only have been a ruminant's rumbling stomach. "My Latin designation is *Rhinoceros unicornis*," the great animal remarked. "You may have noticed it on the sign."

Professor Gottesman dismissed the statement as brusquely as he would have if the rhinoceros had delivered it in class. "Yes, yes, yes, and the manatee, which suckles its young erect in the water and so gave rise to the myth of the mermaid, is assigned to the order *sirenia*. Classification is not proof."

"And proof," came the musing response, "is not necessarily truth. You look at me and see a rhinoceros, because I am not white, not graceful, far from beautiful, and my horn is no elegant spiral but a bludgeon of matted hair. But suppose that you had grown up expecting a unicorn to look and behave and smell exactly as I do—would not the rhinoceros then be the legend? Suppose that everything you believed about unicorns—everything except the way they look—were true of me? Consider the possibilities, Professor, while you push the remains of that bun under the gate."

Professor Gottesman found a stick and poked the grimy bit of pastry—about the same shade as the rhinoceros, it was—where the creature could wrap a prehensile upper lip around it. He said, somewhat tentatively, "Very well. The unicorn's horn was supposed to be an infallible guide to detecting poisons."

"The most popular poisons of the Middle Ages and Renaissance," replied the rhinoceros, "were alkaloids. Pour one of those into a goblet made of compressed hair, and see what happens." It belched resoundingly, and Nathalie giggled.

Professor Gottesman, who was always invigorated by a good argument with anyone, whether colleague, student, or rhinoceros, announced, "Isidore of Seville wrote in the seventh century that the unicorn was a cruel beast, that it would seek out elephants and lions to fight with them. Rhinoceri are equally known for their fierce, aggressive nature, which often leads them to attack anything that moves in their shortsighted vision. What have you to say to that?"

"Isidore of Seville," said the rhinoceros thoughtfully, "was a most learned man, much like your estimable self, who never saw a rhinoceros in his life, or an elephant either, being mainly preoccupied with church history and canon law. I believe he did see a lion at some point. If your charming niece is quite done with her snack?"

"She is not, " Professor Gottesman answered, "and do not change the subject. If you are indeed a unicorn, what are you doing scavenging dirty buns and candy in this public establishment? It is an article of faith that a unicorn can only be taken by a virgin, in whose innocent embrace the ferocious creature becomes meek and docile. Are you prepared to tell me that you were captured under such circumstances?"

The rhinoceros was silent for some little while before it spoke again. "I cannot," it said judiciously, "vouch for the sexual history of the gentleman in the baseball cap who fired a tranquilizer dart into my left shoulder. I would, however, like to point out that the young of our species on occasion become trapped in vines and slender branches which entangle their horns—and the Latin for such branches is *virge*. What Isidore of Seville made of all this…" It shrugged, which is difficult for a rhinoceros, and a remarkable thing to see.

"Sophistry," said the Professor, sounding unpleasantly beleaguered even in his own ears. "Casuistry. Semantics. Chop-logic. The fact remains, a rhinoceros is and a unicorn isn't." This last sounds much more impressive in German. "You will excuse me," he went on, "but we have other specimens to visit, do we not, Nathalie?"

"No," Nathalie said. "Charles and I just wanted to see the tigers."

"Well, we have seen the tigers," Professor Gottesman said through his teeth. "And I believe it's beginning to rain, so we will go home now." He took Nathalie's hand firmly and stood up, as that obliging child snuggled Charles firmly under her arm and bobbed a demure European curtsy to the rhinoceros. It bent its head to her, the mud-thick horn almost brushing the ground. Professor Gottesman, mildest of men, snatched her away.

"Good-bye, Professor," came the hoarse, placid voice behind him. "I look forward to our next meeting." The words were somewhat muffled, because Nathalie had tossed the remainder of her sticky snack into the yard as her uncle hustled her off. Professor Gottesman did not turn his head.

Driving home through the rain—which had indeed begun to fall, though very lightly—the Professor began to have an indefinably uneasy feeling that caused him to spend more time peering at the rear-view mirror than in looking properly ahead. Finally, he asked Nathalie, "Please, would you and—ah—you and Charles climb into the backseat and see whether we are being followed?"

Nathalie was thrilled. "Like in the spy movies?" She jumped to obey, but reported after a few minutes of crouching on the seat that she could detect nothing out of the ordinary. "I saw a helicopiter," she told him, attempting the English word. "Charles thinks they might be following us that way, but I don't know. Who is spying on us, Uncle Gustave?"

"No one, no one," Professor Gottesman answered. "Never mind, child, I am getting silly in America. It happens, never mind." But a few moments later the curious apprehension was with him again, and Nathalie was happily occupied for the rest of the trip home in scanning the traffic behind them through an imaginary periscope, yipping "It's that one!" from time to time, and being invariably disappointed when another prime suspect turned off down a side street. When they reached Professor Gottesman's house, she sprang out of the car immediately, ignoring her mother's welcome until she had checked under all four fenders for possible homing devices. "Bugs," she explained importantly to the two adults. "That was Charles's idea. Charles would make a good spy, I think."

She ran inside, leaving Edith to raise her fine eyebrows at her brother. Professor Gottesman said heavily, "We had a nice time. Don't ask." And Edith, being a wise older sister, left it at that.

The rest of the visit was enjoyably uneventful. The Professor went to work according to his regular routine, while his sister and his niece explored the city, practiced their English together, and cooked Swiss-German specialties to surprise him when he came home. Nathalie never asked to go to the zoo again—stuffed Charles having lately shown an interest in international intrigue—nor did she ever mention that her uncle had formally introduced her to a rhinoceros and spent part of an afternoon sitting on a bench arguing with it. Professor Gottesman was genuinely sorry when she and Edith left for Zurich, which rather surprised him. He hardly ever missed people, or thought much about anyone who was not actually present.

It rained again on the evening that they went to the airport. Returning alone, the Professor was startled, and a bit disquieted, to see large muddy footprints on his walkway and his front steps. They were, as nearly as he could make out, the marks of a three-toed foot, having a distinct resemblance to the ace of clubs in a deck of cards. The door was locked and bolted, as he had left it, and there was no indication of any attempt to force an entry. Professor Gottesman hesitated, looked quickly around him, and went inside.

The rhinoceros was in the living room, lying peacefully on its side before the artificial fireplace—which was lit—like a very large dog. It opened one eye as he entered and greeted him politely. "Welcome home, Professor. You will excuse me, I hope, if I do not rise?"

Professor Gottesman's legs grew weak under him. He groped blindly for a chair, found it, fell into it, his face white and freezing cold. He managed to ask, "How—how did you get in here?" in a small, faraway voice.

"The same way I got out of the zoo," the rhinoceros answered him. "I would have come sooner, but with your sister and your niece already here, I thought my presence might make things perhaps a little too crowded for you. I do hope their departure went well." It yawned widely and contentedly, showing blunt, fist-sized teeth and a gray-pink tongue like a fish fillet.

"I must telephone the zoo," Professor Gottesman whispered. "Yes, of course, I will call the zoo." But he did not move from the chair.

The rhinoceros shook its head as well as it could in a prone position. "Oh, I wouldn't bother with that, truly. It will only distress them if anyone learns that they have mislaid a creature as large as I am. And they will never believe that I am in your house. Take my word for it, there will be no mention of my having left their custody. I have some experience in these matters." It yawned again and closed its eyes. "Excellent fireplace you have," it murmured drowsily. "I think I shall lie exactly here every night. Yes, I do think so."

And it was asleep, snoring with the rhythmic roar and fading whistle of a fast freight crossing a railroad bridge. Professor Gottesman sat staring in his chair for a long time before he managed to stagger to the telephone in the kitchen.

Sally Lowry came over early the next morning, as she had promised several times before the Professor would let her off the phone. She took one quick look at him as she entered and said briskly, "Well, whatever came to dinner, you look as though it got the bed and you slept on the living room floor."

"I did not sleep at all," Professor Gottesman informed her grimly. "Come with me, please, Sally, and you shall see why."

But the rhinoceros was not in front of the fireplace, where it had still been lying when the Professor came downstairs. He looked around for it increasingly frantic, saying over and over, "It was just here, it has been here all night. Wait, wait, Sally, I will show you. Wait only a moment."

For he had suddenly heard the unmistakable gurgle of water in the pipes overhead. He rushed up the narrow hairpin stairs (his house was, as the real-estate agent had put it, "an old charmer") and burst into his bathroom, blinking through the clouds of steam to find the rhinoceros lolling blissfully in the tub, its nose barely above water and its hind legs awkwardly sticking straight up in the air. There were puddles all over the floor.

"Good morning," the rhinoceros greeted Professor Gottesman. "I could wish your facilities a bit larger, but the hot water is splendid, pure luxury. We never had hot baths at the zoo."

"Get out of my tub!" the Professor gabbled, coughing and wiping his face. "You will get out of my tub this instant!"

The rhinoceros remained unruffled. "I am not sure I can. Not just like that. It's rather a complicated affair."

"Get out exactly the way you got in!" shouted Professor Gottesman. "How did you get up here at all? I never heard you on the stairs."

"I tried not to disturb you," the rhinoceros said meekly. "Unicorns can move very quietly when we need to."

"*Out!*" the Professor thundered. He had never thundered before, and it made his throat hurt. "Out of my bathtub, out of my house! And clean up that floor before you go!"

He stormed back down the stairs to meet a slightly anxious Sally Lowry waiting at the bottom. "What was all that yelling about?" she wanted to know. "You're absolutely pink—it's sort of sweet, actually. Are you all right?"

"Come up with me," Professor Gottesman demanded. "Come right now." He seized his friend by the wrist and practically dragged her into his bathroom, where there was no sign of the rhinoceros. The tub was empty and dry, the floor was spotlessly clean; the air smelled faintly of tile cleaner. Professor Gottesman stood gaping in the doorway, muttering over and over, "But it was here. It was in the tub."

"What was in the tub?" Sally asked. The Professor took a long, deep breath and turned to face her.

"A rhinoceros," he said. "It says it's a unicorn, but it is nothing but an Indian rhinoceros." Sally's mouth opened, but no sound came out. Professor Gottesman said, "It followed me home."

Fortunately, Sally Lowry was not more concerned with the usual splutters of denial and disbelief than was the Professor himself. She closed her mouth, caught her own breath, and said, "Well, any rhinoceros that could handle those stairs, wedge itself into that skinny tub of yours, and tidy up afterwards would have to be a unicorn. Obvious. Gus, I don't care what time it is, I think you need a drink."

Professor Gottesman recounted his visit to the zoo with Nathalie, and all that had happened thereafter, while Sally rummaged through his minimally stocked liquor cabinet and mixed what she called a "Lowry Land Mine." It calmed the Professor only somewhat, but it did at least restore his coherency. He said earnestly, "Sally, I don't know how it talks. I don't know how it escaped from the zoo, or found its way here, or how it got into my house and my bathtub, and I am afraid to imagine where it is now. But the creature is an Indian rhinoceros, the sign said so. It is simply not possible—not possible—that it could be a unicorn."

"Sounds like *Harvey*," Sally mused. Professor Gottesman stared at her. "You know, the play about the guy who's buddies with an invisible white rabbit. A big white rabbit."

"But this one is not invisible!" the Professor cried. "People at the zoo, they saw it—Nathalie saw it. It bowed to her, quite courteously."

"Um," Sally said. "Well, I haven't seen it yet, but I live in hope. Meanwhile, you've got a class, and I've got office hours. Want me to make you another Land Mine?"

Professor Gottesman shuddered slightly. "I think not. We are discussing today how Fichte and von Schelling's work leads us to Hegel, and I need my wits about me. Thank you for coming to my house, Sally. You are a good friend. Perhaps I really am suffering from delusions, after all. I think I would almost prefer it so."

"Not me," Sally said. "I'm getting a unicorn out of this, if it's the last thing I do." She patted his arm. "You're more fun than a barrel of MFA candidates, Gus, and you're also the only gentleman I've ever met. I don't know what I'd do for company around here without you."

Professor Gottesman arrived early for his seminar on "The Heirs of Kant." There was no one in the classroom when he entered, except for the rhinoceros. It had plainly already attempted to sit on one of the chairs, which lay in splinters on the floor. Now it was warily eyeing a ragged hassock near the coffee machine.

"What are you doing here?" Professor Gottesman fairly screamed at it.

"Only auditing," the rhinoceros answered. "I thought it might be rewarding to see you at work. I promise not to say a word."

Professor Gottesman pointed to the door. He had opened his mouth to order the rhinoceros, once and for all, out of his life, when two of his students walked into the room. The Professor closed his mouth, gulped, greeted his students, and ostentatiously began to examine his lecture notes, mumbling professorial mumbles to himself, while the rhinoceros, unnoticed, negotiated a kind of armed truce with the hassock. True to its word, it listened in attentive silence all through the seminar, though Professor Gottesman had an uneasy moment when it seemed about to be drawn into a heated debate over the precise nature of von Schelling's intellectual debt to the von Schlegel brothers. He was so desperately careful not to let the rhinoceros catch his eye that he never noticed until the last student had left that the beast was gone, too. None of the class had even once commented on its presence; except for the shattered chair, there was no indication that it had ever been there.

Professor Gottesman drove slowly home in a disorderly state of mind. On the one hand, he wished devoutly never to see the rhinoceros again; on the other, he could not help wondering exactly when it had left the classroom. "Was it displeased with my summation of the *Ideas for a Philosophy of Nature*?" he said aloud in the car. "Or perhaps it was something I said during the argument about *Die Weltalter*. Granted, I have never been entirely comfortable with that book, but I do not recall saying anything exceptionable." Hearing himself justifying his interpretations to a rhinoceros, he slapped his own cheek very hard and drove the rest of the way with the car radio tuned to the loudest, ugliest music he could find.

The rhinoceros was dozing before the fireplace as before, but lumbered clumsily to a sitting position as soon as he entered the living room. "Bravo Professor!" it cried in plainly genuine enthusiasm. "You were absolutely splendid. It was an honor to be present at your seminar."

The Professor was furious to realize that he was blushing; yet it was impossible to respond to such praise with an eviction notice. There was nothing for him to do but reply, a trifle stiffly, "Thank you, most gratifying." But the rhinoceros was clearly waiting for something more, and Professor Gottesman was, as his friend Sally had said, a gentleman. He went on, "You are welcome to audit the class again, if you like. We will be considering Rousseau next week, and then proceed through the romantic philosophers to Nietzsche and Schopenhauer."

"With a little time to spare for the American Transcendentalists, I should hope," suggested the rhinoceros. Professor Gottesman, being some distance past surprise, nodded. The rhinoceros said reflectively, "I think I should prefer to hear you on Comte and John Stuart Mill. The romantics always struck me as fundamentally unsound."

This position agreed so much with the Professor's own opinion that he found himself, despite himself, gradually warming toward the rhinoceros. Still formal, he asked, "May I perhaps offer you a drink? Some coffee or tea?"

"Tea would be very nice," the rhinoceros answered, "if you should happen to have a bucket." Professor Gottesman did not, and the rhinoceros told him not to worry about it. It settled back down before the fire, and the Professor drew up a rocking chair. The rhinoceros said, "I must admit, I do wish I could hear you speak on the scholastic philosophers. That's really my period, after all."

"I will be giving such a course next year," the Professor said, a little shyly. "It is to be a series of lectures on medieval Christian thought, beginning with St. Augustine and the Neoplatonists and ending with William of Occam. Possibly you could attend some of those talks."

The rhinoceros's obvious pleasure at the invitation touched Professor Gottesman surprisingly deeply. Even Sally Lowry, who often dropped in on his classes unannounced, did so, as he knew, out of affection for him, and not from any serious interest in epistemology or the Milesian School. He was beginning to wonder whether there might be a way to permit the rhinoceros to sample the cream sherry he kept aside for company, when the creature added, with a wheezy chuckle, "Of course, Augustine and the rest never did quite come to terms with such pagan survivals as unicorns. The best they could do was associate us with the Virgin Mary, and to suggest that our horns somehow represented the unity of Christ and his church. Bernard of Trèves even went so far as to identify Christ directly with the unicorn, but it was never a comfortable union. Spiral peg in square hole, so to speak."

Professor Gottesman was no more at ease with the issue than St. Augustine had been. But he was an honest person—only among philosophers is this considered part of the job description—and so he felt it his duty to say, "While I respect your intelligence and your obvious intellectual curiosity, none of this yet persuades me that you are in fact a unicorn. I still must regard you as an exceedingly learned and well-mannered Indian rhinoceros."

The rhinoceros took this in good part, saying, "Well, well, we will agree to disagree on that point for the time being. Although I certainly hope that you will let me know if you should need your drinking water purified." As before, and so often thereafter, Professor Gottesman could not be completely sure that the rhinoceros was joking. Dismissing the subject, it went on to ask, "But about the Scholastics—do you plan to discuss the later Thomist reformers at all? Saint Cajetan rather dominates the movement, to my mind; if he had any real equals, I'm afraid I can't recall them."

"Ah," said the Professor. They were up until five in the morning, and it was the rhinoceros who dozed off first. The question of the rhinoceros's leaving Professor Gottesman's house never came up again. It continued to sleep in the living room, for the most part, though on warm summer nights it had a fondness for the young willow tree that had been a Christmas present from Sally. Professor Gottesman never learned whether it was male or female, nor how it nourished its massive, noisy body, nor how it managed its toilet facilities—a reticent man himself, he respected reticence in others. As a houseguest, the rhinoceros's only serious fault was a continuing predilection for hot baths (with Epsom salts, when it could get them.) But it always cleaned up after itself, and was extremely conscientious about not tracking mud into the house; and it can be safely said that none of the Professor's visitors—even the rare ones who spent a night or two under his roof—ever remotely suspected that they were sharing living quarters with a rhinoceros. All in all, it proved to be a most discreet and modest beast.

The Professor had few friends, apart from Sally, and none whom he would have called on in a moment of bewildering crisis, as he had called on her. He avoided whatever social or academic gatherings he could reasonably avoid; as a consequence his evenings had generally been lonely ones, though he might not have called them so. Even if he had admitted the term, he would surely have insisted that there was nothing necessarily wrong with loneliness, in and of itself. "*I think*," he would have said—did often say, in fact, to Sally Lowry. "There are people, you know, for whom thinking is company, thinking is entertainment, parties, dancing even. The others, other people, they absolutely will not believe this."

"You're right," Sally said. "One thing about you, Gus, when you're right you're really right."

Now, however, the Professor could hardly wait for the time of day when, after a cursory dinner (he was an indifferent, impatient eater, and truly tasted little difference between a frozen dish and one that had taken half a day to prepare), he would pour himself a glass of wine and sit down in the living room to debate philosophy with a huge mortar-colored beast that always smelled vaguely incontinent, no matter how many baths it had taken that afternoon. Looking eagerly forward all day to anything was a new experience for him. It appeared to be the same for the rhinoceros.

As the animal had foretold, there was never the slightest suggestion in the papers or on television that the local zoo was missing one of its larger odd-toed ungulates. The Professor went there once or twice in great trepidation, convinced that he would be recognized and accused immediately of conspiracy in the rhinoceros's escape. But nothing of the sort happened. The yard where the rhinoceros had been kept was now occupied by a pair of despondent-looking African elephants; when Professor Gottesman made a timid inquiry of a guard, he was curtly informed that the zoo had never possessed a rhinoceros of any species. "Endangered species," the guard told him. "Too much red tape you have to go through to get one these days. Just not worth the trouble, mean as they are."

Professor Gottesman grew placidly old with the rhinoceros—that is to say, the Professor grew old, while the rhinoceros never changed in any way that he could observe. Granted, he was not the most observant of men, nor the most sensitive to change, except when threatened by it. Nor was he in the least ambitious: promotions and pay raises happened, when they happened, somewhere in the same cloudily benign middle distance as did those departmental meetings that he actually had to sit through. The companionship of the rhinoceros, while increasingly his truest delight, also became as much of a cozily reassuring habit as his classes, his office hours, the occasional dinner and movie or museum excursion with Sally Lowry, and the books on French and German philosophy that he occasionally published through the university press over the years. They were indifferently reviewed, and sold poorly.

"Which is undoubtedly as it should be," Professor Gottesman frequently told Sally when dropping her off at her house, well across town from his own. "I think I am a good teacher—that, yes—but I am decidedly not an original thinker, and I was never much of a writer even in German. It does no harm to say that I am not an exceptional man, Sally. It does not hurt me."

"I don't know what exceptional means to you or anyone else," Sally would answer stubbornly. "To me it means being unique, one of a kind, and that's definitely you, old Gus. I never thought you belonged in this town, or this university, or probably this century. But I'm surely glad you've been here."

Once in a while she might ask him casually how his unicorn was getting on these days. The Professor, who had long since accepted the fact that no one ever saw the rhinoceros unless it chose to be seen, invariably rose to the bait, saying, "It is no more a unicorn than it ever was, Sally, you know that." He would sip his latte in mild indignation, and eventually add, "Well, we will clearly never see eye to eye on the Vienna Circle, or the logical positivists in general—it is a very conservative creature, in some ways. But we did come to a tentative agreement about Bergson, last Thursday it was, so I would have to say that we are going along quite amiably."

Sally rarely pressed him further. Sharp-tongued, solitary, and profoundly irreverent, only with Professor Gottesman did she bother to know when to leave things alone. Most often, she would take out her battered harmonica and play one or another of his favorite tunes"—"Sweet Georgia Brown" or "Hurry on Down." He never sang along, but he always hummed and grunted and thumped his bony knees. Once he mentioned diffidently that the rhinoceros appeared to have a peculiar fondness for "Slow Boat to China." Sally pretended not to hear him.

In the appointed fullness of time, the university retired Professor Gottesman in a formal ceremony, attended by, among others, Sally Lowry, his sister Edith, all the way from Zurich, and the rhinoceros—the latter having spent all that day in the bathtub, in anxious preparation. Each of them assured him that he looked immensely distinguished as he was invested with the rank of *emeritus*, which allowed him to lecture as many as four times a year, and to be available to counsel promising graduate students when he chose. In addition, a special chair with his name on it was reserved exclusively for his use at the Faculty Club. He was quite proud of never once having sat in it.

"Strange, I am like a movie star now," he said to the rhinoceros. "You should see. Now I walk across the campus and the students line up, they line up to watch me totter past. I can hear their whispers—'Here he comes!' 'There he goes!' Exactly the same ones they are who used to cut my classes because I bored them so. Completely absurd."

"Enjoy it as your due," the rhinoceros proposed. "You were entitled to their respect then—take pleasure in it now, however misplaced it may seem to you." But the Professor shook his head, smiling wryly.

"Do you know what kind of star I am really like?" he asked. "I am like the old, old star that died so long ago, so far away, that its last light is only reaching our eyes today. They fall in on themselves, you know, those dead stars, they go cold and invisible, even though we think we are seeing them in the night sky. That is just how I would be, if not for you. And for Sally, of course."

In fact, Professor Gottesman found little difficulty in making his peace with age and retirement. His needs were simple, his pension and savings adequate to meet them, and his health as sturdy as generations of Swiss peasant ancestors could make it. For the most part he continued to live as he always had, the one difference being that he now had more time for study, and could stay up as late as he chose arguing about structuralism with the rhinoceros, or listening to Sally Lowry reading her new translation of Calvalcanti or Frescobaldi. At first he attended every conference of philosophers to which he was invited, feeling a certain vague obligation to keep abreast of new thought in his field. This compulsion passed quickly, however, leaving him perfectly satisfied to have as little as possible to do with academic life, except when he needed to use the library. Sally once met him there for lunch to find him feverishly rifling the ten Loeb Classic volumes of Philo Judaeus. "We were debating the concept of the logos last night," he explained to her, "and then the impossible beast rampaged off on a tangent involving Philo's locating the roots of Greek philosophy in the Torah: Forgive me, Sally, but I may be here for awhile." Sally lunched alone that day.

The Professor's sister Edith died younger than she should have. He grieved for her, and took much comfort in the fact that Nathalie never failed to visit him when she came to America. The last few times, she had brought a husband and two children with her—the youngest hugging a ragged but indomitable tiger named Charles under his arm. They most often swept him off for the evening; and it was on one such occasion, just after they had brought him home and said their good-byes, and their rented car had rounded the corner, that the mugging occurred.

Professor Gottesman was never quite sure himself about what actually took place. He remembered a light scuffle of footfalls, remembered a savage blow on the side of his head, then another impact as his cheek and forehead hit the ground. There were hands clawing through his pockets, low voices so distorted by obscene viciousness that he lost English completely, became for the first time in fifty years a terrified immigrant, once more unable to cry out for help in this new and dreadful country. A faceless figure billowed over him, grabbing his collar, pulling him close, mouthing words he could not understand. It was brandishing something menacingly in its free hand.

Then it vanished abruptly, as though blasted away by the sidewalk-shaking bellow of rage that was Professor Gottesman's last clear memory until he woke in a strange bed, with Sally Lowry, Nathalie, and several policemen bending over him. The next day's newspapers ran the marvelous story of a retired philosophy professor, properly frail and elderly, not only fighting off a pair of brutal muggers but beating them so badly that they had to be hospitalized themselves before they could be arraigned. Sally impishly kept the incident on the front pages for some days by confiding to reporters that Professor Gottesman was a practitioner of a long-forgotten martial-arts discipline, practiced only in ancient Sumer and Babylonia. "Plain childishness," she said apologetically, after the fuss had died down. "Pure self-indulgence. I'm sorry, Gus."

"Do not be," the Professor replied. "If we were to tell them the truth, I would immediately be placed in an institution." He looked sideways at his friend, who smiled and said, "What, about the rhinoceros rescuing you? I'll never tell, I swear. They could pull out my fingernails."

Professor Gottesman said, "Sally, those boys had been *trampled*, practically stamped flat. One of them had been *gored*, I saw him. Do you really think I could have done all that?"

"Remember, I've seen you in your wrath," Sally answered lightly and untruthfully. What she had in fact seen was one of the ace-of-clubs footprints she remembered in crusted mud on the Professor's front steps long ago. She said, "Gus. How old am I?"

The Professor's response was off by a number of years, as it always was. Sally said, "You've frozen me at a certain age, because you don't want me getting any older. Fine, I happen to be the same way about that rhinoceros of yours. There are one or two things I just don't want to know about that damn rhinoceros, Gus. If that's all right with you."

"Yes, Sally," Professor Gottesman answered. "That is all right."

The rhinoceros itself had very little to say about the whole incident. "I chanced to be awake, watching a lecture about Bulgarian icons on the Learning Channel. I heard the noise outside." Beyond that, it sidestepped all questions, pointedly concerning itself only with the Professor's recuperation from his injuries and shock. In fact, he recovered much faster than might reasonably have been expected from a gentleman of his years. The doctor commented on it.

The occurrence made Professor Gottesman even more of an icon himself on campus; as a direct consequence, he spent even less time there than before, except when the rhinoceros requested a particular book. Nathalie, writing from Zurich, never stopped urging him to take in a housemate, for company and safety, but she would have been utterly dumbfounded if he had accepted her suggestion. "Something looks out for him," she said to her husband. "I always knew that, I couldn't tell you why. Uncle Gustave is *somebody's* dear stuffed Charles."

Sally Lowry did grow old, despite Professor Gottesman's best efforts. The university gave her a retirement ceremony too, but she never showed up for it. "Too damn depressing," she told Professor Gottesman, as he helped her into her coat for their regular Wednesday walk "It's all right for you, Gus, you'll be around forever. Me, I drink, I still smoke, I still eat all kinds of stuff they tell me not to eat—I don't even floss, for God's sake. My circulation works like the post office, and even my cholesterol has arthritis. Only reason I've lasted this long is I had this stupid job teaching beautiful, useless stuff to idiots. Now that's it. Now I'm a goner."

"Nonsense, nonsense, Sally," Professor Gottesman assured her vigorously. "You have always told me you are too mean and spiteful to die. I am holding you to this."

"Pickled in vinegar only lasts just so long," Sally said. "One cheery note, anyway—it'll be the heart that goes. Always is, in my family. That's good, I couldn't hack cancer. I'd be a shameless, screaming disgrace, absolutely no dignity at all. I'm really grateful it'll be the heart."

The Professor was very quiet while they walked all the way down to the little local park, and back again. They had reached the apartment complex where she lived, when he suddenly gripped her by the arms, looked straight into her face, and said loudly, "That is the best heart I ever knew, yours. I will not *let* anything happen to that heart."

"Go home, Gus," Sally told him harshly. "Get out of here, go home. Christ, the only sentimental Switzer in the whole world, and I get him. Wouldn't you just know?"

Professor Gottesman actually awoke just before the telephone call came, as sometimes happens. He had dozed off in his favorite chair during a minor intellectual skirmish with the rhinoceros over Spinoza's ethics. The rhinoceros itself was sprawled in its accustomed spot, snoring authoritatively, and the kitchen clock was still striking three when the phone rang. He picked it up slowly. Sally's barely audible voice whispered, "Gus. The heart. Told you." He heard the receiver fall from her hand.

Professor Gottesman had no memory of stumbling coatless out of the house, let alone finding his car parked on the street—he was just suddenly standing by it, his hands trembling so badly as he tried to unlock the door that he dropped his keys into the gutter. How long his frantic fumbling in the darkness went on, he could never say; but at some point he became aware of a deeper darkness over him, and looked up on hands and knees to see the rhinoceros.

"On my back," it said, and no more. The Professor had barely scrambled up its warty, unyielding flanks and heaved himself precariously over the spine his legs could not straddle when there came a surge like the sea under him as the great beast leaped forward. He cried out in terror.

He would have expected, had he had wit enough at the moment to expect anything, that the rhinoceros would move at a ponderous trot, farting and rumbling, gradually building up a certain clumsy momentum. Instead, he felt himself flying, truly flying, as children know flying, flowing with the night sky, melting into the jeweled wind. If the rhinoceros's huge, flat, three-toed feet touched the ground, he never felt it: nothing existed, or ever had existed, but the sky that he was and the bodiless power that he had become—he himself, the once and foolish old Professor Gustave Gottesman, his eyes full of the light of lost stars. He even forgot Sally Lowry, only for a moment, only for the least little time.

Then he was standing in the courtyard before her house, shouting and banging maniacally on the door, pressing every button under his hand. The rhinoceros was nowhere to be seen. The building door finally buzzed open, and the Professor leaped up the stairs like a young man, calling Sally's name. Her own door was unlocked; she often left it so absentmindedly, no matter how much he scolded her about it. She was in her bedroom, half-wedged between the side of the bed and the night table, with the telephone receiver dangling by her head. Professor Gottesman touched her cheek and felt the fading warmth.

"Ah, Sally," he said. "Sally, my dear." She was very heavy, but somehow it was easy for him to lift her back onto the bed and make a place for her among the books and papers that littered the quilt, as always. He found her harmonica on the floor, and closed her fingers around it. When there was nothing more for him to do, he sat beside her, still holding her hand, until the room began to grow light. At last he said aloud, "No, the sentimental Switzer will not cry, my dear Sally," and picked up the telephone.

The rhinoceros did not return for many days after Sally Lowry's death. Professor Gottesman missed it greatly when he thought about it at all, but it was a strange, confused time. He stayed at home, hardly eating, sleeping on his feet, opening books and closing them. He never answered the telephone, and he never changed his clothes. Sometimes he wandered endlessly upstairs and down through every room in his house; sometimes he stood in one place for an hour or more at a time, staring at nothing. Occasionally the doorbell rang, and worried voices outside called his name. It was late autumn, and then winter, and the house grew cold at night, because he had forgotten to turn on the furnace. Professor Gottesman was perfectly aware of this, and other things, somewhere.

One evening, or perhaps it was early one morning, he heard the sound of water running in the bathtub upstairs. He remembered the sound, and presently he moved to his living room chair to listen to it better. For the first time in some while, he fell asleep, and woke only when he felt the rhinoceros standing over him. In the darkness he saw it only as a huge, still shadow, but it smelled unmistakably like a rhinoceros that has just had a bath. The Professor said quietly, "I wondered where you had gone."

"We unicorns mourn alone," the rhinoceros replied. "I thought it might be the same for you."

"Ah," Professor Gottesman said. "Yes, most considerate. Thank you."

He said nothing further, but sat staring into the shadow until it appeared to fold gently around him. The rhinoceros said, "We were speaking of Spinoza."

Professor Gottesman did not answer. The rhinoceros went on, "I was very interested in the comparison you drew between Spinoza and Thomas Hobbes. I would enjoy continuing our discussion."

"I do not think I can," the Professor said at last. "I do not think I want to talk anymore."

It seemed to him that the rhinoceros's eyes had become larger and brighter in its own shadow, and its horn a trifle less hulking. But its stomach rumbled as majestically as ever as it said, "In that case, perhaps we should be on our way."

"Where are we going?" Professor Gottesman asked. He was feeling oddly peaceful and disinclined to leave his chair. The rhinoceros moved closer, and for the first time that the Professor could remember its huge, hairy muzzle touched his shoulder, light as a butterfly.

"I have lived in your house for a long time," it said. "We have talked together, days and nights on end, about ways of being in this world, ways of considering it, ways of imagining it as a part of some greater imagining. Now has come the time for silence. Now I think you should come and live with me."

They were outside, on the sidewalk, in the night. Professor Gottesman had forgotten to take his coat, but he was not at all cold. He turned to look back at his house, watching it recede, its lights still burning, like a ship leaving him at his destination. He said to the rhinoceros, "What is your house like?"

"Comfortable," the rhinoceros answered. "In honesty, I would not call the hot water as superbly lavish as yours, but there is rather more room to maneuver. Especially on the stairs."

"You are walking a bit too rapidly for me," said the Professor. "May I climb on your back once more?" The rhinoceros halted immediately, saying, "By all means, please do excuse me." Professor Gottesman found it notably easier to mount this time, the massive sides having plainly grown somewhat trimmer and smoother during the rhinoceros's absence, and easier to grip with his legs. It started on briskly when he was properly settled, though not at the rapturous pace that had once married the Professor to the night wind. For some while he could hear the clopping of cloven hooves far below him, but then they seemed to fade away. He leaned forward and said into the rhinoceros's pointed silken ear, "I should tell you that I have long since come to the conclusion that you are not after all an Indian rhinoceros, but a hitherto unknown species, somehow misclassified. I hope this will not make a difference in our relationship."

"No difference, good Professor," came the gently laughing answer all around him. "No difference in the world."

Red Roses

Todd J. McCaffrey

Padraig paused to wipe the sweat from his brow and then leaned back into the dirty job. She deserved better but an unmarked grave was all he could give her. She'd been so small, so fragile, so fair, so beautiful, but she'd lasted no longer than the rose she'd borne.

It was dark, it was raining, the winds causing the drops to sheet in on top of him. Fortunately, he'd managed to get the digger in and had hollowed open the grave with no effort. He hadn't gone the whole depth, fearful that he'd uncover the casket, and he had no idea how he'd explain the digging or the fresh dirt when anyone came to ask.

But it was all she asked for in the end, and he had decided to give it to her, church and police be damned.

He had no box for her, of course. In the end, he'd hacked up some bracken and a bunch of roses. The bracken lined the bottom and the roses he put on top of her. He couldn't bear the thought of piling dirt on her bare beautiful face, so he'd stripped off his shirt, jumped down into the hole, and had gently placed it over her, pausing only to kiss her impossibly white face one more time and say, "There, now you're back on his lap."

More dirt, another shovelful. The first had been the hardest. He'd thrown it on her feet even as he thought, *Maybe she isn't dead. Maybe she's just sleeping or in some weird trance.*

Maybe she was tricking him, he thought as he dropped a heavy load on her chest, hoping to startle some response from her under the bed of roses. He stopped then, thinking that perhaps she had moved but, after staring in the rain until he started shivering, he decided it had just been the dead roses settling.

He'd covered her head last, all the same. Even under his smelly shirt, he wanted to give her one last chance to be alive. He paused and waited, the rain battering him, mixing with his tears, but there was no movement, no single sign of life in the dirt below.

So he continued. And now, he was almost done. He thought back to how it had all started.

☙ ✧ ❧

"Are you Padraig Murray?" the man had called as he trudged over the fields.

Padraig hadn't seen him at first, he'd been too busy with the tractor. As soon as he did, he put the tractor in neutral and turned it off. Petrol—even diesel—was too dear to waste on nothing. Not that his farm or his crop were all that much. Padraig had been fighting a losing battle for the past decade to preserve the small patch of land that had been his family's for countless generations.

"And what if I am?" Padraig had called back, scowling at the man in a neat suit bearing a smart leather briefcase. Back over the fences, Padraig could see a new Jaguar car parked in the drive, slightly dusty from the long way on the back roads, looking just as out of place as the man who shouted.

"I need to talk to you," the man said, hefting his briefcase.

A moment of panic, followed by heated anger, flashed through Padraig. Dammit, he'd paid them the money!

"The loan's paid off!" Padraig shouted. "Get off my land and don't bother me at my work."

"Loan?" the man said, looking confused. "I'm here about your great-uncle."

ര ✧ ൯

In the small house, Padraig served the man tea and what biscuits weren't stale.

"The only great-uncle I ever heard about was named Joseph and he disappeared back in the famine," Padraig said as he slid milk and sugar toward the man.

"That's the one," the man said with a nod. "Joseph Murray."

"Are you a historian, then?"

"No, I'm with the county council," the man replied. He held out his hand. Padraig took it. "Gregory Paxton. I'm here to ask what you want to do about the remains."

"What? You found his body?"

Mr. Paxton looked away. "Well, we think so. In fact, we were hoping that you'd provide us with some DNA so we can verify it."

"Did he fall in a bog or something?" Padraig asked. He'd heard of bodies pulled out of the bog still well-preserved after thousands of years. There were no bogs within a hundred miles of here but perhaps his great-uncle had gone wandering or off to Galway hoping to get on one of the ships bound for America. That's what the family had all thought. He remembered something about it: how everyone had been counting on him, how he'd left a family behind that mostly starved in his absence. In Padraig's family, his memory was associated with traitors and blackguards. Perhaps he'd merely been unlucky.

"Bog?" Paxton repeated. "Near as the coroner can tell, he died of a blow to the head."

"And after nearly two hundred years you've found his bones?"

Mr. Paxton licked his lips and looked away. "Well, we'd like the DNA to be certain."

"And how much will that cost me?" Padraig demanded, thinking he'd found the rat in the whole affair: the council was looking to get money off him to identify the remains of a no-account, long-dead relative.

"Actually, Mr. Murray, we'd pay you," Mr. Paxton said, raising his head and meeting his eyes. "For your time and any light you can shed on this mystery."

"What mystery?"

"Why is it that a man who should be dead over a hundred years ago only died last week?"

☙ ✧ ❧

It was all true. Oh, the council didn't pay all that much but Padraig didn't have to worry about petrol or food for a week and the dead man truly was his long-lost great-uncle Joseph Murray.

He'd been found wearing a shirt and breeches. His head was bashed in but he'd been found on a rock. The police were convinced that he'd hit his head in a fall but were clueless as to how that happened. Inside his pockets there'd been some greens, which the farmer who found him identified as a rhubarb stalk and the top of a beet.

"He had a smile on his lips, like he was happy," the farmer had told Padraig shyly as though trying to ease his pain.

"Anything else?" Padraig had asked. The farmer had flinched and hastily shook his head, saying that he had to go home, glancing at Mr. Paxton for permission.

"So, Mr. Murray, do you have any ideas?" Mr. Paxton had asked.

Padraig shook his head. He'd never met this long-lost relative, how should he know anything?

"It's just that he didn't look a day over seventy," Mr. Paxton said to himself. "Like he'd found a way to drink from the fountain of youth or something."

Padraig said nothing. The city folk were always giving farmers shite about fairies and fairy rings. He would do nothing to add to it.

"We can arrange a plot in town, if you'd like," Mr. Paxton offered, seeming ready to forget the whole issue.

"No," Padraig said. "No, I'll take Gran home. I'll bury him near the church."

Outside the police station, Padraig stalked across to the nearest pub. It wasn't that he really wanted a drink—contrary to all opinion, Padraig wasn't much of a drinker—but he was certain he'd meet the farmer inside.

"Mr. Murray!" Sure enough, he was waved over to a table. The farmer had a beer in front of him and the empty glass of another pint on the side. "Tom Mahony."

"I'm grateful for all that you did for my kin," Padraig said as the farmer rose and shook his hand.

"Will you be having any?" Mr. Mahony asked, waving toward the drink.

"No, thanks, I've a fair drive and things to set in order," Padraig told him. "But I'll sit with you for a bit, if you don't mind."

The farmer waved him to the seat opposite and Padraig took it. They chatted about the weather, what crops they had in and how the markets looked and then lapsed into a companionable, if charged, silence.

Finally, the farmer spoke. "There was lightning just before."

Padraig raised his head, meeting the other's eyes.

"Lightning and then a flash of rain, just a mist and a rainbow," Tom continued. His voice dropped as he added, "You know what they say about rainbows."

Padraig smiled and nodded. There wasn't a lad in all of Ireland nor Scotland nor Wales nor even England that hadn't once gone trying to follow the rainbow—just in case there was a pot of gold at the end. "Did you find any?"

"No," the farmer allowed sullenly. "But just at the last, I saw your man—great-uncle, isn't it?—I saw him out of the corner of my eye."

Padraig waited silently.

"It must have been a trick of the light or something," the farmer said, taking a deep draught of his beer, "but it looked like he was on a horse."

"What color?"

"Purple," the farmer said. He drained his glass and rose abruptly, heading toward the door. "My sympathies to you and yours."

ꕤ ✧ ꕤ

And so Joseph Murray had been laid in the family plot in the local church. Father Connelly had decided to mark the date of his death as the day he'd disappeared from the family's reckoning and so, even though the grave was brand-new, the last year on the stone was 1848.

Padraig had visited from time to time just as he'd once managed to be near Tom Mahony's farm and dropped in "just to thank him" as he'd said. But sure enough, neither was fooled, and they spent several hours going over the site where Tom had first spotted Great-uncle Joseph. Neither said anything but both were uncomfortable.

Back at Tom's house, over a cup of tea, Padraig got up the courage to ask, "Are there many fairy rings near?"

"A few," Tom allowed, crossing himself. "They're pretty things and don't seem any harm."

"We've no less than six on my farm," Padraig said musingly. After a moment, he added, "I always wondered about them."

"There was one no less than a hundred yards from where I found your kin," Tom allowed.

They finished their tea in silence. Padraig drove home in silence and that had been that.

☙ ✧ ❧

The days had passed into weeks and the weeks into months. Padraig had taken to visiting the grave once a week. It wasn't a great burden as the great-uncle was laid in the family plot so Padraig would take time from talking with his mother and father, his brother lost in far-off wars, and his wee sister who never had her third birthday, to talk with the great-uncle no one had ever known.

And when it wasn't Sunday, Padraig would work the farm, fighting to keep crops and kill weeds, keep the damned tractor running—even though it was nearly as old as his lost kin—and never wonder beyond how he would cope with tomorrow.

When the rains came, they were vicious. And there was lightning, not all that common in that part of the country.

Padraig found himself starting out one morning in brilliant sunlight and trudging back in the afternoon in the dark of clouds and spitting deluge. The weather was always like that, changing from one moment to the next. But this day was different, almost malevolent in its ferocity.

Lightning cracked right behind him, and Padraig jumped, turning back in fear that the barn had been hit.

Out of the corner of his eye he saw a flash and movement. He turned to look at it fully and then jumped to one side as a fierce beast clattered past him. He tried to get up but was thrown back to the ground by the weight of a bundle, seemingly thrown from the horse now long gone.

"Where is he?" a voice demanded from inside the bundle. Before Padraig could realize that the bundle was a cloak and the voice was a girl's, a pair of hands grabbed his throat and clenched tight with more strength than he imagined. "Where is he?"

Padraig scrambled with one hand to push the girl off even as he said, "Who?"

Either he was lucky with his hand or the question caused the girl confusion but he suddenly found himself able to scramble away far enough to be out of her grasp and able to look at her in the dim light that was left of the day.

His jaw dropped and he gasped. She was beautiful. A beauty like a storm, skin like snow clouds, eyes like lightning, lips like roses, dark hair like clouds on the horizon. She was tiny. She pulled the hood of her cloak back to swipe hair out of her eyes and … were her ears pointed?

Padraig made the sign of the cross. "Mother Mary and Joseph!"

"You know of Joseph?" she demanded, suddenly lunging toward him again.

Padraig scuttled to his feet and discovered that he had the reach on her. Grabbing her by the elbow, he turned toward the house, dragging her behind him. "We've got to get you out of the weather and let your mama know where to find you!"

The small woman dug in her heels and batted at him with her free hand. "Are you in the pay of the Queen?" Her voice rose to a shriek, desperate, angry, tearful, "Let me go! Let me go!"

Padraig did not.

Inside, as he turned on the lights, the girl started. "Those are not torches," she said, eyeing the bulbs suspiciously. She turned back accusingly to him. "Have you captured Pixies to do your bidding?"

She seemed to rise in height but as she'd no more than four feet to start with, it was not enough to deter him.

"Where do you live, then?" Padraig said, moving to bar the door and pulling off his soaked jacket. "I'll give your mam a call. In the meantime, I'll get you some tea." He nodded toward her cloak. "You should get out of that or you'll catch your death."

"My death?" the little girl laughed bitterly. "My death is tied to the rose."

"What?" Padraig said, turning back to her. "What are you on about, girl?"

"The rose," the girl said, reaching into her cloak and pulling it out, "when it withers, I die. My brother, the prince, made it so." Her haughty expression faded, and she seemed to collapse on herself. "I must find him, he was the only one that ever loved me."

"Who?"

"Gran," the little one said. She saw the confused look on his face and added, "In your world he would have been Joseph."

"Joseph Murray?"

Her eyes lit and her face beamed. "You know him? Oh, take me to him, I beg you!"

"Who are you?"

Her eyes narrowed. "If you hope to ensnare me by my true name, it will win you little."

"I just want to get you home," Padraig said, now certain the girl was touched.

"I will not go home, nor can I," the girl replied. She looked up at him, drew a breath, and became a thing of indescribable beauty, of regal bearing, something unreal, unearthly, and beyond mortal ken. "I am Eilin, princess of the most royal house in the Elvenworld, and I have pledged my blood on this quest."

Perhaps, Padraig thought hopelessly, she was one of those—what did they call them? LARP people?—the city yahoos who played all sorts of games dressed in costume and pretending to be elves and whatnot.

"Joseph Murray was born over a hundred years ago," Padraig said.

"Aye, and he was pucked away to Faerie not long after to become my Gran," Eilin said. "He had the raising of me from a baby, and I knew him as his ginger hair turned to white." She faltered then, like a candle in a stiff breeze. When she continued, her eyes were pained and tears dripped down them. "This is what it is like to be mortal?" she said, her hand going to her heart. "The beats, they skip and start."

And then she collapsed. Padraig was on her in an instant, scooping her up and racing up the stairs with her in his arms. She weighed nothing. As he elbowed on the bedroom light, he caught sight of one of her ears. It was pointed. And it wasn't makeup or, if it was, it was better than any he'd ever seen.

He placed her on the bed and leaned over her, listening for breath. There was none. He'd been trained, he was a farmer, he knew that doctors were distant, so he quickly put her on the floor and began breathing for her in a desperate kiss that was more air than passion.

Four breaths, pause, listen, check for pulse. None. He gave her a quick chest compression, worried that he'd crush her tininess, then back to her lips for another breath.

He was near the end of his endurance when she gasped and her eyes fluttered open.

"Think you to take liberties!" she hissed.

"Your heart had stopped, you weren't breathing," he told her. "I gave you the kiss of life."

Her fingers went to her lips and her eyes were wide with amazement. "You kissed me and I did not feel it?"

Padraig's expression must have been answer enough.

"Kiss me again," she demanded.

"I'm sorry," Padraig said, "but you're just a little girl."

"Kiss me," she responded in a voice that could not be denied.

He leaned down and pecked her lips, thinking to humor her.

When he tried to draw back, she hissed at him, "I am no child, kiss me proper."

And from that moment on, Padraig was in thrall. Oh, as a young man he had had his share of kisses—and more—but there had never been a lasting spark, a love strong enough to marry a farmer tied to a doomed land. This girl—this elf—this was his life.

"Oh, I am so sorry," Eilin said when they finally broke for air. "I am so, so sorry. I never knew."

"Knew what?"

"I never knew how beautiful it would be to take a mortal's kiss, how much you would lose in it," she told him. She pursed her lips inwards for a moment, then said, "But please, oh please, kiss me again!"

"I will kiss you forever," Padraig promised when again they finally broke.

"No," Eilin said, "we have only until the rose withers."

The rose withered in ten days. Eilin smiled at him on the dawn of that last day, and they kissed again—a kiss that seemed to last forever but, at the end of it, Padraig realized that she would kiss him no more.

And so now, the last of the dirt.

There. It was done. She was with her Gran again. The man who'd raised her from infancy, in whose lap she'd slept so peacefully, never realizing the depth of their love.

Above the earth there was only Padraig and the rain.

But not for long. He'd bought rhubarb and beets—she'd told him all about them—and he'd made a promise in the deep quiet parts of his heart. He would never love a mortal again.

He would chase the rainbows. Rhubarb and beets would bring him to the land of his love.

About the Authors

Todd J. McCaffrey

Todd J. McCaffrey is an Irish-American author of science fiction best known for continuing the bestselling Dragonriders of Pern series in collaboration with his mother, Anne McCaffrey.

Jody Lynn Nye

Jody Lynn Nye lists her main career activity as "spoiling cats." She lives near Chicago with her current cat, Jeremy, and her husband, Bill. She has published more than 40 books, including *The Ship Who Won* with Anne McCaffrey, and more than 115 short stories. Her latest books are *Fortunes of the Imperium* (Baen Books) and *Dragons Run* (Ace Books).

Mary Pletsch

Mary Pletsch attended Superstars Writing Seminars in 2010 and has since published multiple short stories in a variety of genres, including science fiction, fantasy, and horror. As a collector of vintage My Little

Pony and FashionStar Fillies, she takes her unicorns (purple and otherwise) seriously! Mary is also a glider pilot, Transformers enthusiast, and graduate of the Royal Military College of Canada. She lives in New Brunswick with Dylan Blacquiere and their four cats. Visit her online at www.fictorians.com.

John D. Payne

John D. Payne is a Houston-based writer of fantasy, sci-fi, and literary fiction. His debut novel is *The Crown and the Dragon*, now a major motion picture from Arrowstorm Entertainment.

Jeanette Gonzalez

Jeanette Gonzalez lives on the California coast with a slew of imaginary people who run her life when she's not eating or sleeping. She writes short fiction as well as novels, and she is currently working on an urban fantasy series set in the San Francisco Bay Area.

Sharon Dodge

Sharon Dodge has been a teacher, editor, and captioner, and is currently working on five different novels when not supervising or toddler juggling.

Quincy J. Allen

Quincy J. Allen, is a self-proclaimed cross-genre author. He has been published in multiple anthologies, magazines, and one omnibus. He's written for the Internet show RadioSteam, and has three novels releasing in 2014: a finalist in the RMFW Colorado Gold Contest, *Chemical Burn*, *Jake Lasater: Blood Curse*, and a military sci-fi novel. *Out*

Through the Attic, his first short story collection, is available now. He works part-time as a tech-writer by day, does book design and eBook conversions for WordFire Press by night, and he lives in a lovely house that he considers his very own sanctuary.

Megan Grey

Megan Grey lives in Utah with her husband, two kids, and two dogs (who bark at nothing often enough that she assumes they're talking to their own faerie friends). Her fiction has appeared in *Fireside* magazine and *Sybil's Scriptorium*, and she has a story in an upcoming anthology for the *Animism: The Gods' Lake* animated TV series. Visit Megan at www.megangrey.com.

Kristin Luna

Kristin Luna has been making up stories and getting in trouble for them since elementary school. This is her first publication, and she's working hard on a number of additional stories. Kristin currently lives in San Diego, California, with her husband and three adorable, manipulative pets.

Colette Black

When Colette Black isn't caring for her family, dogs, and a mischievous cat, she spends her time writing. She also loves to travel. Born and raised in the United States, she has also lived in the Philippines and Switzerland. Currently, she resides in the far outskirts of Phoenix, Arizona, where she loves the warm weather and the cotton fields. Her novel, *Noble Ark,* released April 2014, to rave reviews. The sequel, *Desolation,* will be released in October 2014. You can find other short stories in *The Black Side*. Find out more at www.coletteblack.net.

Gama Ray Martinez

Gama Martinez lives near Dallas, Texas, and collects weapons in case he ever needs to supply a medieval battalion. He greatly resents when work and real life gets in the way of writing. Aside from writing, he does normal things like run from bulls and attempt to leave the Earth to be a Martian colonist.

Nathan Barra

Though Nathan Barra is an engineer by profession, training, and temperament, he is a storyteller by nature and at heart. He is drawn to urban fantasy and soft science fiction in both his reading and writing. He is an active blogger, not only on his own site, NathanBarra.com, but also with a group blog, The Fictorians (www.Fictorians.com). Nathan is always up for a good conversation, so please drop him a line through his contact page, or write on his Facebook wall www.facebook.com/WriterNathanBarra.

Robert J. McCarter

Robert J. McCarter lives in the mountains of Arizona with his beautiful wife and his ridiculously adorable dog, pounding away at the keyboard producing software (to make a living) and stories (to fill his soul). He has written several ghost-oriented novels: *Shuffled Off*, *Drawing the Dead*, and *To Be a Fool.* His short stories have appeared in *Andromeda Spaceways Inflight Magazine*, *Every Day Fiction*, *New Sun Rising: Stories for Japan,* and others. Visit him at RobertJMcCarter.com.

Mark Ryan

Mark Ryan grew up in the great plains of the Midwest where he developed his love for music, literature—especially science fiction and fantasy—theater, cinema, games, and basically any form of storytelling. He now works in web design, programming, and game design, while still dabbling in the culinary arts. Mark hopes to one day own a game design company himself.

Nathan Dodge

Nathan Dodge was born in Abilene, Texas, but grew up in Dallas. He received a PhDEE degree from the University of Texas in 1969. He has worked at General Dynamics and Texas Instruments. He taught for sixteen years at the University of Texas at Dallas, where he continues to teach part-time after his retirement in May 2014. Nathan has always wanted to be a writer, and he plans on having a bestseller before his eightieth birthday!

Ezekiel James Boston

Ezekiel James Boston hails from Las Vegas, Nevada, and currently resides in southern Florida. Favoring fantasy, science fiction, and paranormal occult, he's authored more than a hundred short stories, a score of short novels, and half a dozen full-length novels. More of Ezekiel's works can be found at ezekieljamesboston.com.

Lou J Berger

Lou J Berger lives in Denver, Colorado, with three kids, three Sheltie dogs, and a kink-tailed cat with nefarious intent. He's an active member of the Science Fiction and Fantasy Writers of America, has been professionally published in short form, and is writing his first novel, a YA book set in 1978 North Carolina. Visit his website at www.LouJBerger.com.

Scott Eder

Since he was a kid, Scott Eder wanted to be an author. After twenty years mired in the corporate machine, he broke free to bring stories of nobility and strife, honor and chaos, to life. His debut novel, *Knight of Flame,* is available now. When he's not dragging his knights through fire and darkness, look for him on the bowling lanes.

Scott lives with his wife and two children on the west coast of Florida.

Peter S. Beagle

Peter S. Beagle is the legendary author of the classic fantasy *The Last Unicorn,* as well as *A Fine and Private Place, Tamsin, The Innkeeper's Song,* and *The Folk of the Air.* He is also a songwriter and a screenwriter. His works have won him numerous industry awards, widespread acclaim, and the respect of his peers.

Additional Copyright Info

Other WordFire Titles

Our list of other WordFire Press authors and titles is always growing. To find out more and to see our selection of titles, visit us at:

wordfirepress.com